D0770213

M W
& R

God's Spies

God's Spies

■

STORIES IN
DEFIANCE OF
OPPRESSION

EDITED BY

Alberto Manguel

Macfarlane Walter & Ross
Toronto

MACFARLANE WALTER & ROSS
37A Hazelton Avenue
Toronto, Canada M5R 2E3

Canadian Cataloguing in Publication Data

Main entry under title:
    God's spies : stories in defiance of oppression

ISBN 1-55199-040-7

1. Short stories.   2. Political persecution – Fiction.
I. Manguel, Alberto, 1948–   .

PN6120.95.P57G62 1999   808.83'8108   C99-932013-0

THE CANADA COUNCIL | LE CONSEIL DES ARTS
FOR THE ARTS | DU CANADA
SINCE 1957 | DEPUIS 1957

Canada

Macfarlane Walter & Ross gratefully acknowledges support for its publishing program from the Canada Council for the Arts, the Ontario Arts Council, and the Government of Canada through the Book Publishing Industry Development Program.

Printed and bound in Canada

For my daughter Alice,
because of her deeply felt sense of justice,
with much love.

Contents

■

Acknowledgments   xi

Alberto Manguel
Introduction   1

Vladimir Nabokov (Russia/United States)
Tyrants Destroyed   17

Anna Seghers (Germany)
The Dead Girls' Outing   51

Natalia Ginzburg (Italy)
Winter in the Abruzzi   87

Isaac Babel (Russia)
And Then There Were None   95

Vercors (France)
The Silence of the Sea   101

Bessie Head (South Africa)
The Prisoner Who Wore Glasses   135

Edmundo Valadés (Mexico)
Permission for Death Is Granted   145

Seán O'Faoláin (Ireland)
The Death of Stevey Long   153

Paulé Bartón (Haiti)
  Emilie Plead Choose One Egg   181

Wang Meng (China)
  The Stubborn Porridge   185

Nedim Gürsel (Turkey)
  The Graveyard of Unwritten Books   219

Reza Baraheni (Iran)
  The Dismemberment   231

Howard Fast (United States)
  The Large Ant   279

E.B. Dongala (Congo)
  The Man   293

Antonio Skármeta (Chile)
  The Composition   301

Ken Saro-Wiwa (Nigeria)
  Verdict   313

Reinaldo Arenas (Cuba)
  Traitor   331

Rachid Mimouni (Algeria)
  The Escapee   341

Guillermo Martínez (Argentina)
  Vast Hell   357

Gabriel García Márquez (Colombia)
  Bon Voyage, Mr. President   369

Notes on Contributors   399

Sources   405

■

ACKNOWLEDGMENTS

The confidence of my publishers, Macfarlane Walter & Ross, made this anthology possible: my gratitude goes to them. And also to Marie-Catherine Vacher who, with determination beyond the call of friendship, tracked down and bagged an elusive copyright-holder. And, of course, many thanks to Westwood Creative Artists.

In 1996, the magazine *Index on Censorship* asked Craig Stephenson and me to edit an issue on banned fiction from around the world. I came up with a few suggestions, but it was Craig's relentless concern for accuracy, thoroughness, and fair play that allowed us to compile what I believe was an important showcase for literature under threat. Several of those stories rescued by Craig Stephenson have found new life in *God's Spies*; others, which he found but which we could not use then, are now part of this volume. For his help, persistence, keen reading, and care, once again, and as always, my loving thanks.

God's Spies

■

INTRODUCTION

There is a remedy in human nature against tyranny,
that will keep us safe under every form of government

— *Samuel Johnson*

Come, let's away to prison . . .
And take upon's the mystery of things,
As if we were God's spies: and we'll wear out,
In a wall'd prison, packs and sects of great ones
That ebb and flow by the moon.

— *King Lear, act 5, scene 2*

OUR HISTORY is the story of a long night of injustice: Hitler's Germany, Stalin's Russia, the South Africa of apartheid, Ceausescu's Romania, the China of Tiananmen Square, McCarthy's America, Castro's Cuba, Pinochet's Chile, Stroessner's Paraguay, and endless others form the map of our time. We seem to live either within or just on this side of despotic societies. We are never secure, even in our small democracies. When we think of how little it took for upright French citizens to jeer at convoys of Jewish children being herded into trucks, or for educated Canadians to throw stones at women and old men in Oka, we have no right to feel safe.

The trappings with which we rig our society so that it will remain a society must be solid, but they must also be flexible. That which we exclude and outlaw or condemn must also remain visible, must always be in front of our eyes so that we can live by making the daily choice of not breaking these social bonds. The horrors of dictatorship are not inhumane horrors: they are profoundly human – and therein lies their power. Any system of government based on arbitrary laws, extortion, torture, slavery lies at a mere hand's grasp from our own democratic system.

Chile has a curious motto: "By Reason or By Force." It can be read in at least two ways: as a bully's threat, with an accent on the second part of the equation, or as an honest recognition of the precariousness of any social system, adrift (as the Mexican poet Amado Nervo said) "between the clashing seas of force and reason."[1] We, in most Western societies, believe we have chosen reason over force, and for the time being we can depend on that conviction. But we are never entirely free from the temptation of power; we never will be. At best, our society will survive by upholding a few common notions of humanity and justice, dangerously sailing, as my own Canadian motto has it, "A mari usque ad mare," between those two symbolic seas.

Auden famously said that "poetry makes nothing happen."[2] I don't believe that to be true. Not every book is an

---

1. Amado Nervo, *Plenitud* (Buenos Aires, 1918).
2. W.H. Auden, "In Memory of W.B.Yeats," in *Collected Shorter Poems* (London, 1976).

epiphany, but many times we have sailed guided by a luminous page or by a beacon of verse. What role poets and storytellers have on our precarious journeys may not be immediately clear, but perhaps some form of an answer emerged in the aftermath of one particular dictatorship, one which I followed closely over the bloody decade of its rule.

Her name, I remember, was María Angélica Sabelli, and she was one grade below mine at the Colegio Nacional de Buenos Aires. I met her in my second year of high school, during one of the excursions our zealous supervisors liked to organize for us, where we discovered the art of rigging up tents, a taste for reading Rulfo and Hemingway around the campfire, and the mystery of politics. What exactly these politics were we never quite found out, except that at the time they echoed, somewhat bombastically, our vague notions of freedom and equality. In time, we read (or tried to read) arid books on economy and sociology and history, but for most of us politics remained a serviceable word that named our need for comradeship and our contempt for authority. The latter included the school's conservative headmaster; the remote landowners of vast areas of Patagonia where, at the foot of the Andes, we went camping and where, in caves dug into the mountainside, we saw peasant families living out their distant and for us inconceivable lives; and the military whose tanks, on June 28, 1966, we saw lumber through the streets of Buenos Aires, the first of many such processions towards the presidential palace on Plaza de Mayo. María Angélica was sixteen that year; in 1968 I left Buenos Aires, and I never saw María Angélica again. She was small, I remember, with very black and curly hair which she had cut very short. Her voice was unemphatic, very soft and clear, and I could always recognize her on the phone after just one syllable. She painted but without much conviction. She was good at math. In 1982, shortly before the Malvinas War and towards the end of the military dictatorship, I returned to Buenos Aires for a brief visit. Asking for news of old friends, so many dead and disappeared in those terrible years, I was told that among the missing was María Angélica. She had been kidnapped leaving the university, where she had sat on the student council. Officially, there was no record of her detention, but someone had apparently seen her at El Campito, one of the military concentration camps, in a brief moment when her hood had been removed for a medical inspection. The military usually kept their prisoners hooded so that they would not be able to recognize their torturers.

On April 24, 1995, Victor Armando Ibañez, an Argentinian sergeant who had served as a guard at El Campito, gave an interview to the Buenos Aires newspaper *La Prensa*. According to Ibañez, between 2,000 and 2,300 of the men and women, old people and adolescents such as María Angélica, were "executed" by the army at El Campito during the two years of his service, from 1976 to 1978. When the prisoners' time came, Ibañez told the newspaper, "they were injected with a strong drug called pananoval, which made a real mess of them in a few seconds. It produced something like a heart attack. [The injections would leave the prisoners alive but unconscious.] Then they were thrown into the sea. We flew at a very low altitude. They were phantom flights, without registration. Sometimes I could see very large fish, like sharks, following the plane. The pilots said that they were fattened by human flesh. I leave the rest to your imagination," Ibañez said. "Imagine the worst."[3]

---

3. Reprinted in *Harper's*, July 1995, tr. Alex Frankel.

Ibañez's was the second "official" confession. A month earlier, a retired navy lieutenant commander, Adolfo Francisco Scilingo, had confessed to the same method of "disposing of the prisoners." In response to his confession, Argentinian president Carlos Menem called Scilingo a "criminal," reminded the press that the commander had been involved in a shady automobile deal, and asked how the word of a thief could be counted as true. He also ordered the navy to strip Scilingo of his rank.

Since his election in 1989, Menem had been trying to shelve the whole question of military culpability during the so-called "dirty war" that had ravaged Argentina from 1973 to 1982, and during which over 30,000 people were killed.[4] Not content with the deadline for filing charges against the military (which his predecessor, Raúl Alfonsín, had set as February 22, 1988), on October 6, 1989, Menem had offered most of the military involved in human rights abuses a general pardon. A year later, three days after Christmas, Menem issued a general amnesty to all involved in the events that had bled the country for nine long years. Accordingly, he released from prison Lieutenant General Jorge Videla and General Roberto Viola, who had been appointed to the presidency by the military junta, Videla from 1976 to 1981 and Viola for ten months in 1981. In legal terms, a pardon implies not an abolishment of guilt but a relief from punishment. On the other hand, an amnesty (such as the military had granted itself *in extremis* in 1982 and which was repealed by Alfonsín) is, to all intents and purposes, a recognition of innocence that wipes away any

---

4. This figure is the estimate of the National Commission on Disappeared People, quoted in *Nunca Más (Never Again): A Report by Argentina's National Commission on Disappeared People*, ed. and tr. Nick Caistor (London, 1986).

imputation of crime. After the declarations of Scilingo and Ibañez, President Menem briefly threatened the military with a retraction of the 1990 amnesty.

Until the confessions of 1995, the Argentinian military had recognized no wrongdoing in their so-called anti-terrorist activities. The extraordinary nature of guerrilla war demanded, the military said, extraordinary measures. In this declaration they were well advised. In 1977, following a joint report from Amnesty International and the American State Department's Human Rights Bureau accusing the Argentinian security forces of being responsible for hundreds of disappearances, the military hired an American public relations company, Burson-Marsteller, to plan its response. The thirty-five-page memorandum presented by Burson-Marsteller recommended that the military "use the best professional communications skills to transmit those aspects of Argentine events showing that the terrorist problem is being handled in a firm and just manner, with equal justice for all."[5] A tall order, but not impossible in the age of communication. As if moved by the hackneyed motto "The pen is mightier than the sword," Burson-Marsteller suggested that the military appeal to "the generation of positive editorial comment" and to writers "of conservative or moderate persuasions." As a result of their campaign, the former governor of California, Ronald Reagan, declared in the *Miami News* of October 20, 1978, that the State Department's Human Rights Office was "making a mess of our relations with the planet's seventh largest country, Argentina, a nation with which we should be close friends."

Over the years, others rose to the advertisers' challenge. In 1995, shortly after Ibañez's and Scilingo's revelations, an arti-

---

5. R. Scott Greathead, "Truth in Argentina," *New York Times* (May 11, 1995).

cle appeared in the Spanish newspaper *El País*, signed by the prestigious Peruvian novelist Mario Vargas Llosa. Under the title "Playing with Fire," Vargas Llosa argued that, horrible though the revelations might be, they were not news to anyone, merely confirmations of a truth "atrocious and nauseating for any half-moral conscience." "It would certainly be wonderful," he wrote, "if all those responsible for these unbelievable cruelties were taken to court and punished. But this, however, is impossible, because the responsibility far exceeds the military sphere and implicates a vast spectrum of Argentinian society, including a fair number of those who today cry out, condemning retrospectively a violence which they too, in one way or another, contributed to fan."[6]

"It would certainly be wonderful": this is the rhetorical trope of false regret, denoting a change from shared indignation at the "atrocious and nauseating" facts to the more sober realization of what they "really" mean, the impossibility of attaining the "wonderful" goal of impartial justice. Vargas Llosa's is an ancient argument, harking back to notions of original sin: no one soul can truly be held responsible, because every soul is responsible "in one way or another" for the crimes of a nation, whether committed by the people themselves or by their leaders. More than a hundred years ago, Nikolai Gogol expressed the same absurdity in more elegant terms: "Seek out the judge, seek out the criminal, and then condemn both."

Using the case of his own country as a history lesson, Vargas Llosa concluded his *cri de coeur*: "The example of what has happened in Peru with a democracy which the Peruvian people have distorted – because of the violence of extremist groups

---

6. Mario Vargas Llosa, "Jouer avec le feu," *Le Monde* (May 18, 1995).

and also because of the blindness and demagogy of certain political forces – and which they let fall like a ripe fruit in the arms of military and personal power should open the eyes of those imprudent justice-seekers who, in Argentina, take advantage of a debate on the repression in the seventies to seek revenge, to avenge old grievances or continue by other means the demented war they started and then lost."

Burson-Marsteller could not have come up with a more efficient publicizer for their cause. What would an ordinary reader, confident in Vargas Llosa's intellectual authority, read in this impassioned conclusion? After hesitating perhaps at the comparison between Argentina and Peru (where the novelist-turned-politician thunderingly lost the presidential elections), which seems to protest too much, too obviously, the reader is led into a far more subtle argument: these "justice-seekers" – the seekers of that justice which, according to Vargas Llosa, is desirable but utopian – are they not in fact hypocrites who not only must share the guilt for the atrocities but are also to blame for starting a war which they then lost? Suddenly the scales of responsibility are tipped ominously on the victims' side. Not a need for justice, not an urge to officially acknowledge wrongs, but an itch for revenge or, even worse, sheer spite, apparently drives these so-called justice-seekers. The 30,000 disappeared are not to be lamented; they were trouble-makers who started it all. And those who survived – the Mothers of Plaza de Mayo, the thousands forced into exile, the hundreds of tortured men and women who crowd the pages of *Nunca Más* with their sober accounts of utterly indescribable sufferings – should not seek redress lest they be called to judgment themselves. And furthermore, the seventies are now so far away... Would it not be better to forget?

Fortunately, there were readers who were not so confident. Mario Vargas Llosa's article was reprinted in *Le Monde* on May 18, 1995. A week later, the Argentinian writer Juan José Saer published in the same newspaper a response.[7] After correcting a number of important factual errors – Vargas Llosa had called Isabel Perón's presidency a "democratic government" and had ignored the fact that from 1955 until 1983 Argentina had enjoyed barely six years of freely elected leadership – Saer notes that Vargas Llosa's arguments coincide, point by point, with those of the military leaders themselves, who argued that the official tactics of murder and torture were the fault not of those who had put them in practice but of those who had provoked them and forced them into use. Saer also points out that Vargas Llosa's notion of "collective responsibility" might place Vargas Llosa himself in a delicate position since, at a time when Argentinian intellectuals were being tortured or forced into exile, the Peruvian novelist continued to publish willingly in Argentina's official press.

Saer responded to Vargas Llosa's role, accusing him of being a spokesman for the military; he dismissed or ignored his arguments, which were somewhat obviously based on a number of false assumptions. And yet, since these arguments must stand, thanks to Vargas Llosa's craft, as the most eloquent of those penned by the defenders of a military amnesty, they deserve, perhaps, a closer examination.

The notion that guilt must be shared between the military government – come to power by force and using torture and murder to fight its opposers – and the victims – guerrilla

---

7. Juan José Saer, "Mario Vargas Llosa au-delà de l'erreur," *Le Monde* (May 26, 1995).

fighters, political objectors, ordinary civilians with no political associations – is fallacious. While an argument might be found to draw a parallel, on equal terms, between the army of insurrectionists and the official Argentinian army (though, even here, the numbers appear to be in the order of 1 to 1,000), no argument can find a balance of power between the organized military forces and the intellectuals, artists, union leaders, students, members of the clergy who expressed disagreement with them. The civilian who voices an objection to the actions of the government is not guilty of any crime; on the contrary, vigilance is an essential civic duty in any democratic society. But the repression overflowed even the realm of civilian opposition. The National Commission on Disappeared People, led by the novelist Ernesto Sábato, concluded its report: "We can state categorically – contrary to what the executors of this sinister plan maintain – that they did not pursue only the members of political organizations who carried out acts of terrorism. Among the victims are thousands who never had any links with such activity but were nevertheless subjected to horrific torture because they opposed the military dictatorship, took part in union or student activities, were well-known intellectuals who questioned state terrorism, or simply because they were relatives, friends, or names included in the address book of someone considered subversive."[8]

Any government that uses torture and murder as ways of enforcing the law invalidates both its right to govern and the law it enforces, since one of the few basic tenets of any soci-

---

8. *Nunca Más (Never Again): A Report by Argentina's National Commission on Disappeared People*, ed. and tr. Nick Caistor (London, 1986).

ety in which its citizens are granted equal rights is the sacred-
ness of human life. "Clearly," wrote Chesterton, "there could
be no safety for a society in which the remark by the Chief
Justice that murder was wrong was regarded as an original
and dazzling epigram."[9] Any government that does not recognize this truism and does not hold accountable those who
torture and murder can make no claims for its own justice.
No government can rightly mirror the methods of its criminals, responding in kind to what it might deem an act against
the nation's laws. It cannot be guided by an individual sense
of justice, or revenge, or greed, or even morality. It must
encompass them all, these individual deeds of its citizens,
within the parameters established by the country's constitution. It must enforce the law with the law, and within the letter of the law. Beyond the law, a government is no longer
a government but a usurped power, and as such it must be
judged.

It is the trust in this ultimate power of the law that sus-
tained many of the military dictatorship's victims during those
terrible years. In spite of the pain and the bewilderment
caused by the officialized abuses, the belief remained that in
a not too distant future these acts would be brought to light
and judged according to the law. The wish to torture the torturer and to kill the murderer might have been overwhelming, but stronger was the sense that such acts of revenge would
become indistinguishable from the acts that had caused them
and would become, in some abominable way, a victory for
the abusers. Instead, the victims and their families continued

---

9. G.K. Chesterton, "A Defense of Penny Dreadfuls," in *The Defendant*
(London, 1901).

to believe in some form of ultimate earthly judgment, of bringing the guilty ones to trial in front of the society that had been wronged and according to the laws of that society. Only on the basis of such justice being done did they believe that their society might have another chance. Menem's amnesty denied them that long-awaited possibility.

This "absence of justice" was reflected with ghoulish symmetry in the "disappearing" tactics employed by the military, by which their victims – kidnapped, tortured, thrown from airplanes, dropped into unmarked graves – became not officially dead but merely "absent," leaving the anguished families with no bodies to mourn. Another writer, Julio Cortázar, speaking in 1981, described in these words the dictatorship's method: "On the one hand, a virtual or real antagonist is suppressed; on the other, conditions are created so that the family and friends of the victims are often forced to remain silent as the only possibility of preserving the life of those whom their hearts won't allow to presume dead."[10] And he added: "If every human death entails an irrevocable absence, what can we say of this other absence that continues as a sort of abstract presence, like the obstinate denial of the absence we know to be final?" In that sense, Menem's amnesty doesn't cleanse the past – it merely prolongs that sickness of the past into the present.

Menem's revisionist attempt is not original. One of the earliest instances of perfecting the present by erasing the tensions of the past took place in the year 213 BC, when the Chinese emperor Shih Huang-ti ordered that every book in his realm should be thrown to the fire so as to destroy all traces (legend

---

10. Julio Cortázar, "Negación del olvido," in *Obra Crítica*, vol. 3, ed. Saúl Sasnowski (Madrid, 1983).

has it) of his mother's adultery. But no deed, however monstrous or trivial, can ever be abolished once committed – not even by a Chinese emperor, even less by an Argentinian president. This is the adamantine law of our life. The immutability of the past does not depend on the whims of government, nor on cravings for revenge or for diplomacy. No deed can be undone. It can be pardoned, but the pardon must come from the offended person and from no one else, if it is to have any emotional validity. Nothing changes in the deed itself after a pardon: not the circumstances, not the gravity, not the guilt, not the wound. Nothing except the relationship between the torturer and the victims, when the victims reaffirm their sovereignty, "not by weighing our merits," as the Book of Common Prayer has it, "but by pardoning our offences." Pardon is the victim's prerogative, not the torturer's right – and this Menem's government and his supporters, such as Vargas Llosa, have apparently forgotten.

The pardon granted by a victim – the dripping quality of mercy – has no bearing on the mechanics of justice. Pardon doesn't change or even qualify the act, which will cast its shadow forward, throughout eternity, into every new present. Pardon doesn't grant oblivion. But a trial, according to the laws of the society, can at least lend the criminal act a context; the law can contain it, so to speak, in the past so that it no longer contaminates the future, standing at a distance as a reminder and a warning. In a mysterious way, the application of a society's laws is akin to a literary act: it fixes the criminal deed onto a page, defines it in words, gives it a context which is not that of the sheer horror of the moment but of its recollection. The power of memory is no longer in the hands of the criminal; now it is society itself that holds that power, writing the chronicle of its own wicked past, able at last to rebuild itself not over the emptiness of oblivion but over the solid, recorded facts of the atrocities committed. This is a long, dreary, fearful, agonizing process, and the only possible one. This sort of healing always leaves scars.

Menem's amnesty, bowing to the demands of acknowledged murderers and torturers, has postponed the healing for what appears to be a very long time. As it stands today, Argentina is a country bereft of rights: its right to social justice ignored, its right to moral education invalidated, its right to moral authority forfeit. The need to "carry on," the need to "reconcile differences," the need to "allow the economy to flourish once again" have all been invoked by Menem as good reasons for forgiving and forgetting. Supported by literate voices such as that of Vargas Llosa, Menem apparently believes that history can be paid off, that the memory of thousands of individuals like my María Angélica Sabelli can be left to yellow on forgotten shelves in dim bureaucratic offices, that the past can be recovered without expenditure of effort, without making official amends, without redemption. One wishes that Vargas Llosa would read more carefully the furious epilogue of his own 1963 novel, *La Ciudad y los perros* (translated by Lysander Kemp as *The Time of the Hero*), which lays out the consequences of a military system – a military academy – adopting brutally sadistic methods to "educate" its charges. The novel's warning wasn't lost on Peru's military leaders, who after its publication had it burned in a public square in Lima.

While waiting for the act of justice now denied, the victims of Argentina's military dictatorship can, however, still hope for another, older form of justice – less evident but, in the end, longer lasting. The maze of a politician's mind has seldom held the promise of redemption, but that of a writer (especially that of a writer of Vargas Llosa's talents and poetic wisdom, when he isn't writing advertising copy) is almost exclusively built on such a promise, and, in spite of Auden's dictum, it allows no forgetting.

Thanks to his books (and in spite of their author) both the torturers and their victims may know that they were not alone, unseen, unassailable. Justice, beyond the requirements of literary conventions that demand a happy end, is in some essential way our common human bond, something against which we can all measure ourselves. And, as the old English law has it, justice must not only be done but be seen to be done.

Auden's lack of confidence in the writer's ability to change the world is apparently a modern perception. Robert Graves noted that the Irish and Welsh distinguished carefully between poets and satirists: the poet's task was creative or curative, that of the satirist was destructive or noxious, and both changed the course of worldly events.[11] Even nature was supposed to bow to Orpheus's words, and Shakespeare recalled the power of the Irish bards in "rhyming rats to death"; in the seventh century, the great Seanchan Torpest, having discovered that rats had eaten his dinner, slaughtered ten on the spot by uttering a verse that began:

Rats have sharp snouts
Yet are poor fighters.

---

11. Graves, Robert, *The White Goddess*, amended and enlarged edition (New York, 1996).

Against rats or dictators, I believe that writers bring about a wild form of justice in their role as God's spies. "Many brave men lived before Agamemnon's time," wrote Horace in the first century BC, "but they are all, unmourned and unknown, covered by the long night, because they lacked a poet."[12] As Horace implied, we are luckier. Poems and stories that will redeem us (or in which we will find redemption of a kind) are being written, or will be written, or have been written and are awaiting their readers and, throughout time, again and again, assume this: that the human mind is always wiser than its most atrocious deeds, since it can give them a name; that in the very description of the most loathsome acts something in good writing shows them as loathsome and therefore not unconquerable; that in spite of the feebleness and randomness of language, an inspired writer can tell the unspeakable and lend a shape to the unthinkable, so that evil loses some of its numinous quality and stands reduced to a few memorable words.

Alberto Manguel

---

12. Horace, *Odes*, IV.IX.25.

Vladimir Nabokov

∎

TYRANTS

DESTROYED

Sometime in the fourth century BC, *Plato enumerated the possible forms of government and argued that among them all, tyranny was the worst. The government of a ruler who seizes power unconstitutionally and rules by obeying nothing except his will seemed to Plato not only the most noxious but the most inefficient of all political systems, whether in the hands of one man or of several. John Adams clarified the definition: "Despotism, or unlimited sovereignty, or absolute power," he wrote, "is the same in a majority of a popular assembly, an aristocratical council, an oligarchical junto, and a single emperor." From the ancient Greeks to the tyrants of today, to the obscene figures of Stalin, Hitler, Papa Doc, Pinochet, and Khomeini, such autocrats stand for everything a society most dreads, curtailing freedom, compounding crime, punishing protest, censoring displeasure, limiting curiosity, denying creation, promoting stupidity. And yet, as Daniel Defoe suspected, "Nature has left this tincture in the blood, / That all men would be tyrants if they could."*

■

I

T HE GROWTH of his power and fame was matched, in my imagination, by the degree of the punishment I would have liked to inflict on him. Thus, at first, I would have been content with an electoral defeat, a cooling of public enthusiasm. Later I already required his imprisonment; still later, his exile to some distant, flat island with a single palm tree, which, like a black asterisk, refers one to the bottom of an eternal hell made of solitude, disgrace, and helplessness. Now, at last, nothing but his death could satisfy me.

As in the graphs that visually demonstrate his ascension, indicating the number of his adherents by the gradual increase in size of a little figure that becomes biggish and then enormous, my hatred of him, its arms folded like those of his image, ominously swelled in the center of the space that was my soul, until it had nearly filled it, leaving me only a narrow rim of curved light (resembling more the corona of madness than the halo of martyrdom), though I foresee an utter eclipse still to come.

His first portraits, in the papers and shop windows and on the posters – which also kept growing in our abundantly irrigated, crying, and bleeding country – looked rather blurred: this was when I still had doubts about the deadly outcome of my hatred. Something human, certain possibilities of his failing, his cracking, his falling ill, heaven knows what, came feebly shivering through some of his photographs in the random variety of not yet standardized poses and in a vacillating gaze which had not yet found its historical expression. Little by little, though, his countenance consolidated: his cheeks and cheekbones, in the official portrait photographs, became overlaid with a godly gloss, the olive oil of public affection, the varnish of a completed masterpiece; it became impossible to imagine that nose being blown, or that finger poking on the inside of that lip to extricate a food particle lodged behind a rotten incisor. Experimental variety was followed by a canonized uniformity that established the now familiar, stony, and lusterless look of his neither intelligent nor cruel, but somehow unbearably eerie eyes. Established, too, was the solid fleshiness of his chin, the bronze of his jowls, and a feature that had already become the common property of all the cartoonists in the world and almost automatically brought off the trick of resemblance – a thick wrinkle across his whole forehead – the fatty sediment of thought, of course, rather than thought's scar. I am forced to believe that his face has been rubbed with all sorts of patent balsams, else I cannot comprehend its metallic good quality, for I once knew it when it was sickly, bloated, and ill-shaven, so that one heard the scrape of bristles against his dirty starch collar when he turned his head. And the glasses – what became of the glasses that he wore as a youth?

2

Not only have I never been fascinated by politics, but I have hardly ever read a single editorial or even a short report on a party congress. Sociological problems have never intrigued me, and to this day I cannot picture myself taking part in a conspiracy or simply sitting in a smoke-filled room among politically excited, tensely serious people, discussing methods of struggle in the light of recent developments. I don't give a hoot for the welfare of mankind, and not only do I not believe in any majority being automatically right, but I tend to reexamine the question whether it is proper to strive for a state of affairs where literally everyone is half-fed and half-schooled. I further know that my fatherland, enslaved by him at the present time, is destined, in the distant future, to undergo many other upheavals, independent of any acts on *this* tyrant's part. Nevertheless, he must be killed.

3

When the gods used to assume earthly form and, clad in violet-tinted raiment, demurely but powerfully stepping with muscular feet in still dustless sandals, appeared to field laborers or mountain shepherds, their divinity was not in the least diminished for it; on the contrary, the charm of humanness enwafting them was a most eloquent reconfirmation of their celestial essence. But when a limited, coarse, little-educated man – at first glance a third-rate fanatic and in reality a pigheaded, brutal, and gloomy vulgarian full of morbid ambition – when such a man dresses up in godly garb, one feels like apologizing to the gods. It would be useless to try and convince me that actually he has nothing to do with it, that what elevated him to an iron-and-concrete throne, and now keeps him there, is the implacable evolution of dark, zoological, Zoorlandic ideas that have caught my fatherland's fancy. An

idea selects only the helve; man is free to complete the axe –
and use it.

Then again, let me repeat that I am no good at distinguishing what is good or bad for a state, and why it is that
blood runs off it like water off a goose. Amid everybody and
everything it is only one individual that interests me. That is
my ailment, my obsession, and at the same time a thing that
somehow belongs to me and that is entrusted to me alone for
judgment. Since my early years – and I am no longer young –
evil in people has struck me as particularly loathsome,
unbearable to the point of suffocation and calling for immediate derision and destruction, while on the other hand I
hardly noticed good in people, so much did it always seem to
me the normal, indispensable condition, something granted
and inalienable as, for example, the capacity to breathe is
implied by the fact of being alive. With passing years I devel-
oped an extremely fine flair for evil, but my attitude toward
good underwent a slight change, as I came to understand that
its commonness, which had conditioned my indifference,
was indeed so *uncommon* that I could not be sure at all of
always finding it close to hand should the need arise. This is
why I have led a hard, lonely life, always indigent, in shabby
lodgings; yet I invariably had the obscure sensation of my real
home being just around the corner, waiting for me, so that I
could enter it as soon as I had finished with a thousand imaginary matters that cluttered my existence. Good God how I
detested dull rectangular minds, how unfair I could be to a
kindly person in whom I had happened to notice something
comic, such as stinginess or respect for the well-to-do! And
now I have before me not merely a weak solution of evil,
such as can be obtained from any man, but a most highly

concentrated, undiluted evil, in a huge vessel filled to the neck and sealed.

4

He transformed my wildflowery country into a vast kitchen garden, where special care is lavished on turnips, cabbages, and beets; thus all the nation's passions were reduced to the passion for the fat vegetable in the good earth. A kitchen garden next to a factory with the inevitable accompaniment of a locomotive maneuvering somewhere in the background; the hopeless, drab sky of city outskirts, and everything the imagination associates with the scene: a fence, a rusted can among thistles, broken glass, excrements, a black, buzzing burst of flies under one's feet – this is the present-day image of my country. An image of the utmost dejection, but then dejection is in favor here, and a slogan *he* once tossed off (into the trash pit of stupidity) – "one half of our land must be cultivated, and the other asphalted" – is repeated by imbeciles as if it were a supreme expression of human happiness. There would be some excuse if he fed us the shoddy maxims he had once gleaned from reading sophists of the most banal kind, but he feeds us the chaff of those truths, and the manner of thinking required of us is based not simply on false wisdom, but on its rubble and stumblings. For me, however, the crux of the matter is not here either, for it stands to reason that even if the idea of which we are slaves were supremely inspired, exquisite, refreshingly moist, and sunny through and through, slavery would still be slavery inasmuch as the idea was inflicted on us. No, the point is that, as his power grew, I began to notice that the obligations of citizens, admonitions, restrictions, decrees, and all the other forms of pressure put on us were coming to resemble the man himself more and more closely, displaying an unmistakable relation to certain traits of his character and details of his past, so that on the basis of those admonitions and decrees one could reconstruct his personality like an octopus by its tentacles – that personality of his that I was one of the few to know well. In other words, everything around him began taking on his appearance. Legislation began to show a ludicrous likeness to his gait and gestures. Greengrocers began stocking a remarkable abundance of cucumbers, which he had so greedily consumed in his youth. The schools' curriculum now includes Gypsy wrestling, which, in rare moments of cold playfulness, he used to practice on the floor with my brother twenty-five years ago. Newspaper articles and the novels of sycophantic writers have taken on that abruptness of style, that supposedly lapidary quality (basically senseless, for every minted phrase repeats in a different key one and the same official truism), that force of language cum weakness of thinking, and all those other stylistic affectations that are characteristic of him. I soon had the feeling that he, he as I remembered him, was penetrating everywhere, infecting with his presence the way of thinking and the everyday life of every person, so that his mediocrity, his tediousness, his grey habitude, were becoming the very life of my country. And finally the law he established – the implacable power of the majority, the incessant sacrifice to the idol of the majority – lost all sociological meaning, for *he* is the majority.

5

He was a comrade of my brother Gregory, who had a feverish, poetic passion for extreme forms of organized society (forms that had long been alarming the meek constitution we then had) in the final years of his short life: he drowned at twenty-three, bathing one summer evening in a wide, very wide river, so that when I now recall my brother the first thing that comes to my mind is a shiny spread of water, an islet overgrown with alder (that he never reached but toward which he always swims through the trembling haze of my memory), and a long, black cloud crossing another, opulently fluffed-up and orange-colored one, all that is left of a Saturday-morning thunderstorm in the clear, turquoise Sunday's-eve sky, where a star will shine through in a moment, where there will never be any star. At any time I was much too engrossed in the history of painting and in my dissertation on its cave origins to frequent watchfully the group of young people that had inveigled my brother; for that matter, as I recall, there was no definite group, but simply several youths who had drifted together, different in many respects but, for the time being, loosely bound by a common attraction to rebellious adventure. The present, however, always exercises such a perverse influence on reminiscence that now I involuntarily single *him* out against the indistinct background, awarding him (neither the closest nor the most vociferous of Gregory's companions) the kind of somber, concentrated will deeply conscious of its sullen self, which in the end molds a giftless person into a triumphant monster.

I remember him waiting for my brother in the gloomy dining room of our humble provincial house; perching on the first chair he saw, he immediately began to read a rumpled newspaper extracted from a pocket of his black jacket, and his face, half-hidden by the armature of smoke-colored glasses, assumed a disgusted and weepy expression, as if he had hit upon some scurrilous stuff. I remember that his sloppily laced town boots were always dirty, as if he had just walked many miles along a cart road between unnoticed meadows. His cropped hair ended in a bristly wedge on his forehead (nothing foretold yet his present Caesar-like baldness). The nails of his large, humid hands were so closely bitten that it was painful to see the tight little cushions at the tips of his hideous fingers. He gave off a goatish smell. He was hard up, and indiscriminate as to sleeping quarters.

When my brother arrived (and in my recollection Gregory is always tardy, always comes in out of breath, as if hastening terribly to live but arriving late all the same – and thus it was that life finally left him behind), he greeted Gregory without smiling, getting up abruptly and giving his hand with an odd jerk, a kind of preliminary retraction of the elbow; it seemed that if one did not snatch his hand in time it would bounce back, with a springy click, into its detachable cuff. If some member of our family entered, he limited himself to a surly nod; per contra, he would demonstratively shake hands with the cook, who, taken by surprise and not having time to wipe her palm before the clasp, wiped it afterwards, in a retake of the scene, as it were. My mother died not long before his first visits, while my father's attitude toward him was as absentminded as it was toward everyone and everything – toward us, toward life's adversities, toward the presence of grubby dogs to whom Gregory offered shelter, and even, it seems, toward his patients. On the other hand, two elderly aunts of mine were openly wary of the "eccentric" (if anyone ever was the opposite of eccentric it was he) as, for that matter, they were of Gregory's other pals.

Now, twenty-five years later, I often have occasion to hear his voice, his bestial roar, diffused by the thunders of radio; back then, however, I recall he always spoke softly, even with a certain huskiness, a certain susurrous lisp. Only that famous vile bit of breathlessness of his, at the end of a sentence, was already there, yes, already there. When he stood, head and arms lowered, before my brother, who was greeting him with affectionate exclamations, still trying to catch at least an elbow of his, or his bony shoulder, he seemed curiously short-legged, owing, probably, to the length of his jacket, which came down to midhip; and one could not determine whether the mournfulness of his posture was caused by glum shyness or by a straining of the faculties before uttering some tragic message. Later it seemed to me that he had at last uttered it and done with it, when, on that dreadful summer evening, he came from the river carrying what looked like a heap of clothes but was only Gregory's shirt and canvas pants; now, however, I think that the message he seemed to be always pregnant with was not that one after all, but the muffled news of his own monstrous future.

Sometimes, through a half-open door, I could hear his abnormally halting speech in a talk with my brother; or he would be sitting at the tea table, breaking a pretzel, his nightbird eyes turned away from the light of the kerosene lamp. He had a strange and unpleasant way of rinsing his mouth with his milk before he swallowed it, and when he bit into the pretzel he cautiously twisted his mouth; his teeth were bad, and to deceive the fiery pain of a bared nerve by a brief whiff of coolness, he would repeatedly suck in the air, with a sidewise whistle. Once, I remember, my father soaked a bit of cotton wool for him with some brown drops containing opium and, chuckling aimlessly, recommended that he see a dentist. "The whole is stronger than its parts," he answered with awkward gruffness, "ergo I will vanquish my tooth." I am no longer certain, though, whether I heard those wooden words personally, or whether they were subsequently repeated to me as a pronouncement by the "eccentric"; only, as I have already said, he was nothing of the sort, for how can an animal faith in one's blear guiding star be regarded as something peculiar and rare? But, believe it or not, he impressed people with his mediocrity as others do with their talent.

6

Sometimes his innate mournfulness was broken by spasms of nasty, jagged joviality, and then I would hear his laughter, as jarring and unexpected as the yowl of a cat, to whose velvet silence you grow so accustomed that its nocturnal voice seems a demented, demonic thing. Shrieking thus, he would be drawn by his companions into games and tussles; it turned out then that he had the arms of a weakling, but legs strong as steel. On one occasion a particularly prankish boy put a toad in his pocket, whereupon he, being afraid to go after it with his fingers, started tearing off the weighted jacket and in that state, his face darkly flushed, disheveled, with nothing but a dickey over his torn undershirt, he fell prey to a heartless hunch-backed girl, whose massive braid and ink-blue eyes were so attractive to many that she was willingly forgiven a resemblance to a black chess knight.

I know about his amorous tendencies and system of courtship from that very girl, now, unfortunately, deceased, like the majority of those who knew him well in his youth (as if death were an ally of his, removing from his path dangerous witnesses to his past). To this vivacious hunchback he would write either in a didactic tone, with excursions – of a popular-educational type – into history (which he knew from political pamphlets), or else complain in obscure and soggy terms about another woman (also with a physical defect of some kind, I believe), who remained unknown to me, and with whom at one time he had shared bed and board in the most dismal part of the city. Today I would give a lot to search out and interrogate that anonymous person, but she, too, no doubt, is safely dead. A curious feature of his missives was their noisome wordiness: he hinted at the machinations of mysterious enemies; polemicized at length with some poetaster, whose verselets he had read in a calendar – oh, if it were possible to resurrect those precious exercise-book pages, filled with his minuscule, myopic handwriting! Alas, I do not recall a single phrase from them (at the time I was not very interested, even if I did listen and chuckle), and only very indistinctly do I see, in the depths of memory, the bow on that braid, the thin clavicle, and the quick, dusky hand in the garnet bracelet crumpling his letters; and I also catch the cooing note of perfidious feminine laughter.

7

The difference between dreaming of a reordered world and dreaming of reordering it oneself as one sees fit is a profound and fatal one; yet none of his friends, including my brother, apparently made any distinction between their abstract rebellion and *his* merciless lust for power. A month after my brother's death he vanished, transferring his activity to the northern provinces (my brother's group withered and fell apart and, as far as I know, none of its other participants went into politics), and soon there were rumors that the work being done there, both in its aims and methods, had grown diametrically opposed to all that had been said, thought, and hoped in that initial young circle. When I recall his aspect in those days, I find it amazing that no one noticed the long, angular shadow of treason that he dragged behind him wherever he went, tucking its fringe under the furniture when he sat down, and letting it interfere strangely with the banister's own shadow on the wall of the staircase, down which he was seen to the door by the light of a portable kerosene lamp. Or is it our dark present time that was cast forward there?

I do not know if they liked him, but in any case my brother and the others mistook his moroseness for the intensity of spiritual force. The cruelty of his ideas seemed a natural consequence of enigmatic calamities he had suffered; and his whole unprepossessive shell presupposed, as it were, a clean, bright kernel. I may as well confess that I myself once had the fleeting impression that he was capable of mercy; only subsequently did I determine its true shade. Those who are fond of cheap paradoxes took note long ago of the sentimentality of executioners; and indeed, the sidewalk in front of butcher shops is always dampish.

8

The first days after the tragedy he kept turning up, and several times spent the night in our place. That death did not evoke any visible signs of grief in him. He behaved as always, which did not shock us in the least, since his usual state was already mournful: and as usual he would sit in some corner, reading something uninteresting and behaving, in short, as, in a house where a great misfortune has occurred, people do who are neither close intimates nor complete strangers. Now, moreover, his constant presence and sullen silence could pass for grim commiseration – the commiseration, you see, of a strong reticent man, inconspicuous but ever-present – a very pillar of sympathy – about whom you later learn that he himself was seriously ill at the time he spent those sleepless nights on a chair among tear-blinded members of the household. In his case, however, this was all a dreadful misconception: if he did feel drawn to our house at the time, it was solely because nowhere did he breathe so naturally as in the sphere of gloom and despair, when uncleared dishes litter the table and non-smokers ask for cigarettes.

I vividly remember setting out with him to perform one of the minor formalities, one of the excruciatingly dim bits of business with which death (having, as it always has, an element of red tape about it) tries to entangle survivors for as long as possible. Probably someone said to me, "There, *he* will go with you," and he came, discreetly clearing his throat. It was on that occasion (we were walking along a houseless street, fluffy with dust, past fences and piles of lumber) that I did something the memory of which traverses me from top to toe like an electrical jolt of insufferable shame: driven by God knows what feeling – perhaps not so much by gratitude as by condolence for another's condolence – in a surge of nervousness and ill-timed emotion, I clasped and squeezed his hand (which caused us both to stumble slightly). It all lasted an instant, and yet, if I had then embraced him and pressed my lips to his horrible golden bristles, I could not have felt any greater torment now. Now, after twenty-five years, I wonder: the two of us were walking alone through a deserted neighborhood, and in my pocket I had Gregory's loaded revolver, which, for some reason or other, I kept meaning to hide; I could perfectly well have dispatched him with a shot at point-blank range, and then there would have been nothing of what there is today – no rain-drenched holidays, no gigantic festivities with millions of my fellow citizens marching by with shovels, hoes, and rakes on their slavish shoulders; no loudspeakers, deafeningly multiplying the same inescapable voice; no secret mourning in every other family, no assortment of tortures, no torpor of the mind, no colossal portraits – nothing. Oh if it were possible to claw into the past, drag a missed opportunity by its hair back into the present, resurrect that dusty street, the vacant lots, the weight in my hip pocket, the youth walking at my side!

9

I am dull and fat, like Prince Hamlet. What can I do? Between me, a humble teacher of drawing in a provincial high school, and him, sitting behind a multitude of steel and oaken doors in an unknown chamber of the capital's main jail, transformed for him into a castle (for this tyrant calls himself "prisoner of the will of the people that elected him"), there is an unimaginable distance. Someone was telling me, after having locked himself in the basement with me, about an old widow, a distant relative of his, who succeeded in growing an eighty-pound turnip, thus meriting an audience with the exalted one. She was conducted through one marble corridor after another, and an endless succession of doors was unlocked in front of her and locked behind her, until she found herself in a white, starkly lit hall, whose entire furnishings consisted of two gilt chairs. Here she was told to stand and wait. In due time she heard numerous footfalls from behind the door, and, with respectful bows, deferring to each other, half a dozen of his bodyguards came in. With frightened eyes she searched for *him* among them; their eyes were directed not at her but somewhere beyond her head; then, turning, she saw that behind her, through another, unnoticed door, he himself had noiselessly entered and, having stopped and placed a hand on the back of one of the two chairs, was scrutinizing the guest of the State with a habitual air of encouragement. Then he seated himself and suggested that she describe in her own words her glorious achievement (here an attendant brought in and placed on the second chair a clay replica of her vegetable), and, for ten unforgettable minutes, she narrated how she had planted the turnip; how she had tugged and tugged without being able to get it out of the ground, even though she thought she saw her deceased husband tugging with her; how she had had to call first her son, then her nephew and even a couple of firemen who were resting in the hayloft; and how, finally, backing in tandem arrangement, they had extracted the monster. Evidently he was overwhelmed by her vivid narrative; "Now that's genuine poetry," he said, addressing his retinue. "Here's somebody the poet fellows ought to learn from." And, crossly ordering that the likeness be cast in bronze, he left. I, however, do not grow turnips, so I cannot find a way to him; and, even if I did, how would I carry my treasured weapon to his lair?

On occasion he appears before the people, and, even though no one is allowed near him, and everyone has to hold up the heavy staff of an issued banner so that hands are kept busy, and everyone is watched by a guard of incalculable proportions (to say nothing of the secret agents and the secret agents watching the secret agents), someone very adroit and resolute might have the good fortune to find a loophole, one transparent instant, some tiny chink of fate through which to rush forward. I mentally considered, one by one, all kinds of destructive means, from the classic dagger to plebeian dynamite, but it was all in vain, and it is with good reason that I frequently dream I am repeatedly squeezing the trigger of a weapon that is disintegrating in my hand, whilst the bullets trickle out of the barrel, or bounce like harmless peas off the chest of my grinning foe while he begins unhurriedly to crush my rib cage.

10

Yesterday I invited several people, unacquainted among themselves but united by one and the same sacred task, which had so transfigured them that one could notice among them an inexpressible resemblance, such as occurs, for instance, among elderly Freemasons. They were people of various professions – a tailor, a masseur, a physician, a barber, a baker – but

all exhibited the same dignified deportment, the same economy of gestures. And no wonder! One made his clothes, and
that meant measuring his lean, yet broad-hipped body, with
its odd, womanish pelvis and round back, and respectfully
reaching into his armpits, and, together with him, looking
into a mirror garlanded with gilt ivy; the second and third
had penetrated even further: they had seen him naked, had
kneaded his muscles and listened to his heart, by whose beat,
it is said, our clocks will soon be set, so that his pulse, in the
most literal sense, will become a basic unit of time; the fourth
shaved him, with crepitating strokes, down on the cheeks
and on the neck, using a blade that to me is enticingly sharp-
looking; the fifth, and last, baked his bread, putting, the idiot,
through sheer force of habit raisins instead of arsenic into his
favorite loaf. I wanted to palpate these people, so as to partake
at least in that way of their mysterious rites, of their diabolical
manipulations; it seemed to me that their hands were imbued
with his smell, that through those people he, too, was present.
It was all very nice, very prim at that party. We talked about
things that did not concern him, and I knew that if I mentioned his name there would flash in the eyes of each of them
the same sacerdotal alarm. And when I suddenly found myself
wearing a suit cut by my neighbor on the right, and eating my
vis-à-vis' pastry, which I washed down with a special kind of
mineral water prescribed by my neighbor on the left, I was
overcome by a dreadful, dream-significant feeling, which
immediately awakened me – in my poor-man's room, with a
poor-man's moon in the curtainless window.

I am grateful to the night for even such a dream: of late I
have been racked by insomnia. It is as if his agents were accus-
toming me beforehand to the most popular of the tortures

inflicted on present-day criminals. I write "present-day" because, since he came to power, there has appeared a completely new breed, as it were, of political criminals (the other, penal, kind actually no longer exists, as the pettiest theft swells into embezzlement which, in turn, is considered an attempt to undermine the regime), exquisitely frail creatures, with a most diaphanous skin and protruding eyes emitting bright rays. This is a rare and highly valued breed, like a young okapi or the smallest species of lemur; they are hunted passionately, self-obliviously, and every captured specimen is hailed by public applause, even though the hunt actually involves no particular difficulty or danger, for they are quite tame, those strange, transparent beasts.

Timorous rumor has it that he himself is not loath to pay an occasional visit to the torture chamber, but there is probably no truth in this: the postmaster general does not distribute the mail himself, nor is the secretary of the navy necessarily a crack swimmer. I am in general repelled by the homey, gossipy tone with which meek ill-wishers speak of him, getting sidetracked into a special kind of primitive joke, as, in olden times, the common people would make up stories about the Devil, dressing up their superstitious fear in buffoonish humor. Vulgar, hastily adapted anecdotes (dating back, say, to Celtic prototypes), or secret information "from a usually reliable source" (as to who, for instance, is in favor and who is not) always smack of the servants' quarters. There are even worse examples, though: when my friend N., whose parents were executed only three years ago (to say nothing of the disgraceful persecution N. himself underwent), remarks, upon his return from an official festivity where he has heard and seen him, "You know, though, in spite of everything, there is a certain strength about that man," I feel like punching N. in the mug.

II

In the published letters of his "Sunset Years" a universally acclaimed foreign writer mentions that everything now leaves him cold, disenchanted, indifferent, everything with one exception: the vital, romantic thrill that he experiences to this day at the thought of how squalid his youthful years were compared with the sumptuous fulfillment of his later life, and of the snowy gleam of its summit, which he has now reached. That initial insignificance, that penumbra of poetry and pain, in which the young artist is on a par with a million such insignificant fellow beings, now lures him and fills him with excitement and gratitude – to his destiny, to his craft – and to his own creative will. Visits to places where he had once lived in want, and reunions with his coevals, elderly men of no note whatsoever, hold for him such a complex wealth of enchantment that the detailed study of these sensations will last him for his soul's future leisure in the hereafter.

Thus, when I try to imagine what our lugubrious ruler feels upon contact with *his* past, I clearly understand, first, that the real human being is a poet and, second, that he, our ruler, is the incarnate negation of a poet. And yet the foreign papers, especially those whose names have vesperal connotations and which know how easily "tales" can be transformed into "sales," are fond of stressing the legendary quality of his destiny, guiding their crowd of readers into the enormous black house where he was born, and where supposedly to this day live similar paupers, endlessly hanging out the wash (paupers do a great deal of washing); and they also print a photo, obtained God knows how, of his progenitress (father unknown), a thickset broad-nosed woman with a fringe who worked in an alehouse at the city gate. So few eyewitnesses of his boyhood and youth remain, and those who are still around respond with such circumspection (alas, no one has questioned *me*) that a journalist needs a great gift for invention to portray today's ruler excelling at warlike games as a boy or, as a youth, reading books till cockcrow. His demagogic luck is construed to be the elemental force of destiny, and, naturally, a great deal of attention is devoted to that overcast winter day when, upon his election to parliament, he and his gang arrested the parliament (after which the army, bleating meekly, went over at once to his side).

Not much of a myth, but still a myth (in this nuance the journalist was not mistaken), a myth that is a closed circle and a discrete whole, ready to begin living its own, insular life, and it is *already* impossible to replace it with the real truth, even though its hero is still alive: impossible, since he, the only one who could know the truth, is useless as a witness, and this not because he is prejudiced or dishonest, but because, like a runaway slave, he "doesn't remember"! Oh, he remembers his old enemies, of course, and two or three books he has read, and how the man thrashed him for falling off a woodpile and crushing to death a couple of chicks: that is, a certain crude mechanism of memory does function in him, but, if the gods were to propose that he synthesize himself out of his memories, with the condition that the synthesized image be rewarded with immortality, the result would be a dim embryo, an infant born prematurely, a blind and deaf dwarf, in no sense capable of immortality.

Should he visit the house where he lived when he was poor, no thrill would ripple his skin — not even a thrill of malevolent vanity. But I did visit his former abode! Not the multiplex edifice where he is supposed to have been born, and where there is now a museum dedicated to him (old posters, a flag grimy with gutter mud, in the place of honor, under a bell jar, a button: all that it was possible to preserve of his niggardly youth), but those vile furnished rooms where he spent several months during the period he and my brother were close. The former proprietor had long since died, roomers had never been registered, so that no trace was left of his erstwhile sojourn. And the thought that I alone in the world (for he has forgotten those lodgings of his — there have been so many) *knew* about this filled me with a special satisfaction, as if, by touching that dead furniture and looking at the neighboring roof through the window, I felt my hand closing on the key to his life.

12

I have just had yet another visitor: a very seedy old man, who was evidently in a state of extreme agitation: his tight-skinned, glossy-backed hands were trembling, a stale senile tear dampened the pink lining of his eyelids, and a pallid sequence of involuntary expressions, from a foolish smile to a crooked crease of pain, passed across his face. With the pen I lent him he traced on a scrap of paper the digits of a crucial year, day, and month: the date — nearly half a century past — of the ruler's birth. He rested his gaze on me, pen raised, as if not daring to continue, or simply using a semblance of hesitation to emphasize the little trick he was about to play. I answered with a nod of encouragement and impatience, whereupon he wrote another date, preceding the first by nine months, underlined it twice, parted his lips as if for a burst of triumphant laughter, but, instead, suddenly covered his face with his hands. "Come on, get to the point," I said, giving this indifferent actor's shoulder a shake. Quickly regaining his composure, he rummaged in his pocket and handed me a thick, stiff photograph, which, over the years, had acquired an opaque milky tint. It showed a husky young man in a soldier's uniform; his peaked cap lay on a chair, on whose back, with wooden ease, he rested his hand, while behind him you could make out the balustrade and the urn of a conventional backdrop. With the help of two or three connective glances I ascertained that between my guest's features and the shadowless, flat face of the soldier (adorned with a thin mustache, and topped by a brush cut, which made the forehead look smaller) there was little resemblance, but that nevertheless the soldier and he were the same person. In the snapshot he was about twenty, the snapshot itself was some fifty years old, and it was easy to fill this interval with the trite account of one of those third-rate lives, the imprint of which one reads (with an agonizing sense of superiority, sometimes unjustified) on the faces of old ragmen, public-garden attendants, and embittered invalids in the uniforms of old wars. I was about to pump him as to how it felt to live with such a secret, how he could carry the weight of that monstrous paternity, and incessantly see and hear his offspring's public presence – but then I noticed that the mazy and issueless design of the wallpaper was showing through his body; I stretched out my hand to detain my guest, but the dodderer dissolved, shivering from the chill of vanishment.

And yet he exists, this father (or existed until quite recently), and if only fate did not bestow on him a salutary ignorance as to the identity of his momentary bedmate, God knows what torment is at large among us, not daring to speak out, and perhaps made even more acute by the fact that the hapless fellow is not fully certain of his paternity, for the wench was a loose one, and in consequence there might be several like him in the world, indefatigably calculating dates, blundering in the hell of too many figures and too meager memories, ignobly dreaming of extracting profit from the shadows of the past, fearing instant punishment (for some error, or blasphemy, for the too odious truth), feeling rather proud in their heart of hearts (after all, he is the Ruler!), losing their mind between supputation and supposition – horrible, horrible!

13

Time passes, and meanwhile I get bogged down in wild, oppressive fancies. In fact, it astonishes me, for I know of a good number of resolute and even daring actions that I have to my credit, nor am I in the least afraid of the perilous consequences that an assassination attempt would have for me; on the contrary, while I have no clear idea at all of how the act itself will occur, I can make out distinctly the tussle that will immediately follow – the human tornado seizing me, the puppet-like jerkiness of my motions amid avid hands, the crack of clothes being ripped, the blinding red of the blows, and finally (should I emerge from this tussle alive) the iron grip of jailers, imprisonment, a swift trial, the torture chamber, the scaffold, all this to the thundering accompaniment of my mighty happiness. I do not expect that my fellow citizens will immediately perceive their own liberation; I can even allow that the regime might get harsher out of sheer inertia. There is nothing about me of the civic hero who dies for his people. I die only for myself, for the sake of my own world of good and truth – the good and the true, which are now distorted and violated within me and outside me, and if they are as precious to someone else as they are to me, all the better; if not, if my fatherland needs men of a different stamp than I, I willingly accept my uselessness, but will still perform my task.

My life is too much engrossed and submerged by my hatred to be in the least pleasant, and I do not fear the black nausea and agony of death, especially since I anticipate a degree of bliss, a level of supernatural being undreamt of either by barbarians or by modern followers of old religions. Thus, my mind is lucid and my hand free – and yet I don't know, I don't know how to go about killing him.

I sometimes think that perhaps it is so because murder, the intent to kill, is after all insufferably trite, and the imagination, reviewing methods of homicide and types of weapons, performs a degrading task, the sham of which is the more keenly felt, the more righteous the force that impels one. Or else, maybe I could not kill him out of squeamishness, as some people, while they feel a fierce aversion to anything that crawls, are unable so much as to crush a garden worm underfoot because for them it would be like stamping on the dust-begrimed extremities of their own innards. But whatever explanations I conjure up for my irresoluteness, it would be foolish to hide from myself the fact that I must destroy him. O Hamlet, O moony oaf!

14

He has just given a speech at the groundbreaking ceremony for a new, multistoried greenhouse, and, while he was at it, he touched on the equality of men and the equality of wheat ears in the field, using Latin or dog-Latin, for the sake of poetry, *arista, aristifer,* and even "aristize" (meaning "to ear") – I do not know what corny schoolman counseled him to adopt this questionable method, but, in recompense, I now understand why, of late, magazine verse contains such archaisms as:

How sapient the veterinarian
Who physics the lactific kine.

For two hours the enormous voice thundered throughout our city, erupting with varying degrees of force from this or that window, so that, if you walk along a street (which, by the way, is deemed a dangerous discourtesy: sit and listen), you have the impression that he accompanies you, crashing down from the rooftops, squirming on all fours between your legs, and sweeping up again to peck at your head, cackling, caw-ing, and quacking in a caricature of human speech, and you have no place to hide from the Voice, and the same thing is going on in every city and village of my successfully stunned country. Apparently no one except me has noticed an inter-esting feature of his frenzied oratory, namely the pause he makes after a particularly effective sentence, rather like a drunk who stands in the middle of the street, in the independ-ent but unsatisfied solitude characteristic of drunks, and while declaiming fragments of an abusive monologue, most emphatic in its wrath, passion, and conviction, but obscure as to meaning and aim, stops frequently to collect his strength, ponder the next passage, let what he has said sink in; then, having waited out the pause, he repeats verbatim what he has just disgorged, but in a tone of voice suggesting that he has thought of a new argument, another absolutely new and irrefutable idea.

When the Ruler at last ran dry, and the faceless, cheekless trumpets played our agrarian anthem, I not only did not feel relieved, but, on the contrary, had a sense of anguish and loss: while he was speaking I could at least keep watch over him, could know where he was and what he was doing; now he has again dissolved into the air, which I breathe but which has no tangible point of focus.

I can understand the smooth-haired women of our mountain tribes when, abandoned by a lover, every morning, with a persistent pressure of their brown fingers on the turquoise head of a pin, they prick the navel of a clay figurine representing the fugitive. Many times, of late, I have summoned all the force of my mind to imagine at a given moment the flow of his cares and thoughts, in order to duplicate the rhythm of his existence, making it yield and come crashing down, like a suspension bridge whose own oscillations have coincided with the cadenced step of a detachment of soldiers crossing it. The soldiers will also perish – so shall I, losing my reason the instant that I catch the rhythm, while he falls dead in his distant castle; however, no matter what the method of tyrannicide, I would not survive. When I wake up in the morning, at half past eight or so, I strain to conjure up his awakening: he gets up neither early nor late, at an average hour, just as he calls himself – even officially, I think – an "average man." At nine both he and I breakfast frugally on a glass of milk and a bun, and, if on a given day I am not busy at the school, I continue my pursuit of his thoughts. He reads through several newspapers, and I read them with him, searching for something that might catch his attention, even though I know he was aware the evening before of the general content of my morning paper, of its leading articles, its summaries and national news, so that this perusal can give him no particular cause for administrative meditation. After which his assistants come with reports and queries. Together with him, I learn how rail communications are feeling today, how heavy industry is sweating along, and how many centners per hectare the winter wheat crop yielded this year. After looking through several petitions for clemency and tracing on them his invariable refusal – a penciled X – the symbol of his heart's illiteracy – he takes his usual walk before lunch: as in the case of many not over-bright people devoid of imagination, walking is his favorite exercise; he walks in his walled garden, formerly a large prison yard. I am also familiar with the menu of his unpretentious lunch, after which I share my siesta with him and ponder plans for making his power flourish further, or new measures for suppressing sedition. In the afternoon we inspect a new building, a fortress, a forum, and other forms of governmental prosperity, and I approve with him an inventor's new kind of ventilator. I skip dinner, usually a gala affair with various functionaries in attendance, but, on the other hand, by nightfall my thoughts have redoubled their force and I issue orders to newspaper editors, listen to accounts of evening meetings, and, alone in my darkening room, whisper, gesticulate, and ever more insanely hope that at least one of my thoughts may fall in step with a thought of his – and then, I know, the bridge will snap, like a violin string. But the ill luck familiar to overly eager gamblers haunts me, the right card never comes, even though I must have achieved a certain secret liaison with him, for around eleven o'clock, when he goes to bed, my entire being senses a collapse, a void, a weakening, and a melancholy relief. Presently he sleeps, he sleeps, and, since, on his convict's cot, not a single praedormitory thought troubles him, I too am left at liberty, and only occasionally, without the least hope of success, try to compose his dreams, combining fragments of his past with impressions of the present; probably, though, he does not dream and I work in vain, and never, never, will the night be rent by a royal death rattle, leading history to comment: "The dictator died in his sleep."

15

How can I get rid of him? I cannot stand it any longer. Everything is full of him, everything I love has been besmirched, everything has become his likeness, his mirror image, and, in the features of passersby and in the eyes of my wretched schoolchildren, his countenance shows ever clearer and more hopelessly. Not only the posters that I am obliged to have them copy in color do nothing but interpret the pattern of his personality, but even the simple white cube I give the younger classes to draw seems to me his portrait – perhaps his best portrait. O cubic monster, how can I eradicate you?

16

And suddenly I realized I had a way! It was on a frosty, motionless morning, with a pale pink sky and lumps of ice lodged in the drainpipes' jaws; there was a doomful stillness everywhere: in an hour the town would awake, and how it would awake! That day his fiftieth birthday was to be celebrated, and already people, looking against the snow like black quarter notes, were creeping out into the streets, so as to gather on schedule at the points where they would be marshaled into different marching groups determined by their trades. At the risk of losing my meager pay, I was not making ready to join any festive procession; I had something else, a little more important, on my mind. Standing by the window, I could hear the first distant fanfares and the radio barker's inducements at the crossroads, and I found comfort in the thought that I, and I alone, could interrupt all this. Yes, the solution had been found: the assassination of the tyrant now turned out to be something so simple and quick that I could accomplish it without leaving my room. The only weapons available for the purpose were either an old but very well preserved revolver, or a hook over the window that must have served at one time to support a drapery rod. This last was even better, as I had my doubts about the performance of the twenty-five-year-old cartridge.

By killing myself I would kill him, as he was totally inside me, fattened on the intensity of my hatred. Along with him I would kill the world he had created, all the stupidity, cowardice, and cruelty of that world, which, together with him, had grown huge within me, ousting, to the last sun-bathed landscape, to the last memory of childhood, all the treasures I had collected. Conscious now of my power, I reveled in it, unhurriedly preparing for self-destruction, going through my belongings, correcting this chronicle of mine. And then, abruptly, the incredible intensification of all the senses that had overwhelmed me underwent a strange, almost alchemic metamorphosis. The festivities were spreading outside my window, the sun transformed the blue snowdrifts into sparkling down, and one could see playing over distant roofs, a new kind of fireworks (invented recently by a peasant genius) whose colors blazed even in broad daylight. The general jubilation; the Ruler's gem-bright likeness flashing pyrotechnically in the heavens; the gay hues of the procession winding across the river's snowy cover; the delightful pasteboard symbols of the fatherland's welfare; the slogans, designed with variety and elegance, that bobbed above the marchers' shoulders; the jaunty primitive music; the orgy of banners; the contented faces of the young yokels and the national costumes of the hefty wenches – all of it caused a crimson wave of tenderness to surge within me, and I understood my sin against our great and merciful Master. Is it not he who manured our fields, who directed the poor to be shod, he whom we must thank for every second of our civic being? Tears of repentance, hot, good tears, gushed from my eyes onto the windowsill when I thought how I had been repudiating the kindness of the Master, how blindly I had reneged the beauty of what he had created, the social order, the way of life, the splendid walnut-finished new fences, and how I plotted to lay hands on myself, daring, thus, to endanger the life of one of his subjects! The festivities, as I have said, were spreading; I stood at the window, my whole being drenched with tears and convulsed with laughter, listening to the verses of our foremost poet, declaimed on the radio by an actor's juicy voice, replete with baritone modulations:

Now then, citizens,
You remember how long

Our land wilted without a Father?
Thus, without hops, no matter how strong
One's thirst, it is rather
Difficult, isn't it,
To make both the beer and the drinking song!
Just imagine, we lacked potatoes,
No turnips, no beets could we get:
Thus the poem, now blooming, wasted
In the bulbs of the alphabet!
A well-trodden road we had taken,
Bitter toadstools we ate,
Until by great thumps was shaken
History's gate!
Until in his trim white tunic
Which upon us its radiance cast,
With his wonderful smile the Ruler
Came before his subjects at last!

Yes, "radiance," yes, "toadstools," yes, "wonderful," that's right. I, a little man, I, the blind beggar who today has gained his sight, fall on my knees and repent before you. Execute me – no, even better, pardon me, for the block is your pardon, and your pardon the block, illuminating with an aching benignant light the whole of my iniquity. You are our pride, our glory, our banner! O magnificent, gentle giant, who intently and lovingly watches over us, I swear to serve you from this day on, I swear to be like all your other nurslings, I swear to be yours indivisibly, and so forth, and so forth, and so forth.

17

Laughter, actually, saved me. Having experienced all the degrees of hatred and despair, I achieved those heights from which one obtains a bird's-eye view of the ludicrous. A roar of hearty mirth cured me, as it did, in a children's storybook, the gentleman "in whose throat an abscess burst at the sight of a poodle's hilarious tricks." Rereading my chronicle, I see that, in my efforts to make him terrifying, I have only made him ridiculous, thereby destroying him – an old, proven method. Modest as I am in evaluating my muddled composition, something nevertheless tells me that it is not the work of an ordinary pen. Far from having literary aspirations, and yet full of words forged over the years in my enraged silence, I have made my point with sincerity and fullness of feeling where another would have made it with artistry and inventiveness. This is an incantation, an exorcism, so that henceforth any man can exorcise bondage. I believe in miracles. I believe that in some way, unknown to me, this chronicle will reach other men, neither tomorrow nor the next day, but at a distant time when the world has a day or so of leisure for archaeological diggings, on the eve of new annoyances, no less amusing than the present ones. And, who knows – I may be right not to rule out the thought that my chance labor may prove immortal, and may accompany the ages, now persecuted, now exalted, often dangerous, and always useful. While I, a "boneless shadow," *un fantôme sans os*, will be content if the fruit of my forgotten insomnious nights serves for a long time as a kind of secret remedy against future tyrants, tigroid monsters, half-witted torturers of man.

1938

Anna Seghers

∎

THE DEAD
GIRLS' OUTING

George Steiner once argued convincingly that what Hitler
had done was establish on earth a concrete version of imagined Hell: that the ancient idea of a colossal place of suffering was taken from the shadow side of our imagination and
built out of bricks and mortar in a real place and a real
time. Nazi Germany became vaster than its frontiers and
stands forever as a memory of how deep we can descend.
Hitler's extended, methodical plan of destruction was like
no other the world had ever experienced, and, in a curious
way, the Nazi cult of death embraced even its own annihi-
lation. Like everything else infected or perverted through
Nazi usage, language too was changed, and there were
many, such as Günter Grass and Primo Levi, who asked
whether it was still possible to write after Auschwitz.
Among the thousands of writers who escaped death in
concentration camps and were instead forced into exile was
Anna Seghers, who lived for a time in a small village in
Mexico. There she wrote "The Dead Girls' Outing," a
story the German novelist Christa Wolf called "one of the

most truthful and powerful accounts ever to have emerged from the horror."

■

"NO, from much farther away. From Europe." The man looked at me with a smile, as if I had answered "From the moon." He was the owner of the tavern on the outskirts of the village. He pushed himself away from the table and, leaning against the wall, motionless, looked me over as if he were searching me for traces of that uncertain place from which I'd come. Suddenly, the fact that the ordeal had propelled me from Europe to Mexico seemed to me as unreal as it must have seemed to him. The village, like a fortress, was surrounded by a fence of giant cacti. Through an opening, I could see the brownish-grey mountain slopes, naked and wild like those of lunar cliffs. Their mere sight was enough to dismiss any thought that they had once been touched by even a flicker of life. A couple of pepper plants reddened on the edge of a desert ravine. Even these plants seemed on fire rather than in bloom.

The innkeeper had crouched down on the floor, under the enormous shade of his hat. He had stopped watching me; neither the village nor the mountains attracted him. Motionless, he kept his eyes fixed on the only thing that offered him infinite and insoluble riddles: absolute nothingness.

I leaned against the wall in the slim shadows. The haven I had found in this country was too uncertain and too precarious to make me believe that I was out of danger. I had barely emerged from the illness that had succeeded in overtaking me here, and which had lasted several months – while the dangers of war, in all shapes and sizes, had not managed to grab hold of me. My eyes were burning with exhaustion and heat, and yet I was quite able to follow the section of the road that led from the village into the desert. The road was so white that it stayed branded behind my eyelids as soon as I shut my eyes. At the edge of the ravine I could see the corner of the whitewashed wall I had been able to make out from the roof of my hotel, in the larger village up on the hill, from where I had just come. I had asked immediately about the wall and the shack – or rather about that thing, whatever it was, shining on its own, under the evening sky; but no one could tell me. I had set off on foot. In spite of my weakness and the exhaustion that forced me already to catch my breath here, I felt it was imperative for me to discover, all on my own, what that building was. A vague and uneasy curiosity was all that remained of the pleasure travelling once gave me – something that propelled me to leave the daily constraints in which I found myself. As soon as I had satisfied my curiosity, I would climb back to the lodgings that had been chosen for me. The bench on which I was sitting was, up to then, the end of my journey – the westernmost point I'd ever reached on this earth. For a long time now I'd had my fill, even to the point of nausea, of new or outlandish adventures. There was only one adventure left to keep me going: the return home.

Like the mountains themselves, the shack stood in the midst of a shimmering haze which came either from the sun-blazed dust or from my own fatigue – a fatigue that wrapped everything in fog – so that my immediate surroundings faded and the countryside in the distance became as clear as a mirage. I stood up, because my exhaustion felt so disheartening, and the haze before my eyes dissipated itself a little, like smoke.

I walked through the opening in the cactus fence, side-stepped a dog that, covered in dust and motionless as a corpse, was sleeping with outstretched legs in the middle of the road. The rainy season was approaching. The visible roots of the bare and sinuous trees clung to the slope that had begun to turn to stone. The white wall drew suddenly closer. After a momentary clearing, the cloud of dust, or of fatigue perhaps, thickened, taking on, in the folds of the hillside, not the usual dark shade of clouds but a flickering luminosity. I might have thought I was feverish if a slight gust of hot wind had not dispersed the cloud into strips of fog, blowing it towards other mountain slopes.

A green light shone behind the long white wall. No doubt far back there was a pond or a stream diverted from its course, bringing water to the ranch and further on to the village. And yet, there seemed to be no one living in the low building standing there alone, windowless, on the edge of the road. The clear light of the previous evening – assuming it had not been an illusion – had probably come from the man looking after the place. The fence, long since useless and worm-eaten, had detached itself from the entrance gate. But there was an archway over the gate, and on it I could make out the remains of a coat of arms washed smooth by countless rainy seasons. It seemed to me there was something familiar in the ruined coat of arms, and in the two stone shells on either side of it. I stepped towards the open gateway. To my surprise, I heard inside a soft, rhythmical creaking. I took one step further. Now I could smell the scent of the garden's vegetation. The deeper I looked, the fresher and more luxuriant it became. The creaking became more distinct and, somewhere in the bushes that were growing thicker and fuller with sap, I noticed a pendular movement as regular as that of a swing or a seesaw. My curiosity was roused. I went through the gate and ran towards the seesaw. At that same moment someone cried out, "Netty!"

No one, since high school, had ever called me by that name. I had learned to answer to all sorts of names, good names and bad, by which my friends and my enemies were in the habit of calling me – names given to me, throughout those many years, in the street, in gatherings, at parties, in hotel rooms at night, at police interrogations, on the covers of books, in newspaper articles, in court proceedings and on passports. During my illness, when I lay dead to the world, I had sometimes hoped to hear that dear old name of my early years; but it was gone – that name which my fantasies urged me to believe would give me back my health, my youth, my happiness, all those things that might allow me to go back once again to my old life with my old friends, a life so irretrievably lost. Hearing it echo, the emotion made me grab my braids with both hands. I was surprised to be able to grab hold of those two thick braids; so they hadn't been cut off in the hospital.

The tree stump to which the seesaw had been nailed seemed at first also wrapped in a thick cloud; but the cloud thinned and quickly drifted away, leaving nothing but wild rose bushes. Soon, several buttercups began to glitter in the mist that rose from the ground through the thick high grass; then the mist faded, and the dandelions and geraniums stopped mingling into one another before my eyes. Among the flowers were also clusters of lilies of the valley that trembled if one so much as looked at them.

Astride each end of the seesaw was a young girl: my two best friends from school. Leni was vigorously pushing up the seesaw by hitting the ground with her big feet in heavy buttoned-up boots. I suddenly remembered that she always inherited her older brother's shoes, and that her brother had been killed in World War I, in the fall of 1914. At the same time, I was also surprised to notice that Leni's face bore no signs of the terrible events that had upset her life. Her face was as silky and shiny as a fresh apple, with none of the marks or scars from the blows of the Gestapo after her arrest, when she refused to give them information about her husband. When she swung up or down, her heavy Mozart-style ponytail would fly away from her neck. Thick dark eyebrows gave her round face the expression of strength and resolution that had been hers ever since childhood, whenever she was engaged in a difficult task. I knew well that frown on her face, usually as smooth as a mirror and as round as an apple, having seen it on a thousand occasions, during the struggles of a ball game, during a swimming competition or the writing of an essay in class, and later in the heat of political gatherings and during the distribution of tracts. The last time I'd noticed that frown was in my hometown, under Hitler, when, shortly before my final escape, I saw my friends for one final meeting. She also wore it the day her husband didn't arrive on time at the agreed place, so that we knew he'd been arrested at the underground press by the Nazis. No doubt she had also frowned and pursed her lips when, soon afterwards, she too was arrested. That frown, which used to appear only on exceptional occasions, later became a constant feature, once she was left to starve, slowly but surely, in a concentration camp for women, during the second winter of the war. I was surprised that sometimes

I'd been able to forget her face, over which the large ribbon of her Mozart-style ponytail now cast its shadow. I was sure that, even in death, she had kept that face as round as an apple, its forehead marked with the gash-like frown.

On the other end of the seesaw sat Marianne, the prettiest girl in the class, her long thin legs straddling the board. Her ash-blond braids were curled in buns over her ears. On her face, as nobly and as perfectly chiselled as the faces of the medieval stone images of young girls on the walls of Marbourg cathedral, all was grace and gaiety. As in a flower, it was impossible to find in her even a trace of hard-heartedness, of guilt or insensitivity. Even I, forgetting everything I knew about her, lost myself in the joy of seeing her. A tremor crossed her long straight body every time that, seemingly without touching the ground, she pushed the seesaw upwards again. She gave the impression of being capable of flying away quite effortlessly, with her carnation of a mouth and her small hard breasts under the green blouse of faded cloth.

I recognized the voice of old Fräulein Mees, our teacher, coming from behind the low wall that separated the café terrace from the courtyard with the seesaw. She was looking for us. "Leni! Marianne! Netty!" I wasn't surprised and I didn't grab hold of my braids: what other name could my teacher have used, calling out to me and my friends? Marianne lifted her weight off the seesaw, and as soon as the plank hit the ground on Leni's side, she steadied her own feet on the ground so as to allow Leni an easy descent. Then she put her arm around Leni's neck and delicately picked out a few blades of grass from her friend's hair. Everything told or written about these two girls seemed now unbelievable to me. Marianne, who with so much care and friendship held the seesaw for Leni, who with so much delicacy picked out the blades of grass from her hair and even put an arm around her neck – how could she, brutally and with icy words, later have refused that same Leni a friend's assistance? How could she have answered that she couldn't care less about the girl who had arrived by chance, one day, in her class, she no longer knew from where or when, and that the smallest coin spent on Leni and her family was money thrown out of the window, an act of treason towards the state? The Gestapo agents who arrested first the father, then the mother, told the neighbours that Leni's child, left unprotected, was to be placed immediately in a National Socialist re-education centre. The neighbours went in search of the child, who was playing somewhere, and kept her in hiding so that she might later be sent to Berlin to her father's family. They hurried to find Marianne to borrow the money for the journey – Marianne whom they had often seen arm in arm with Leni. But Marianne refused, adding that her own husband was a high Nazi official, and that it was only justice if Leni and her husband had been arrested because they had committed a crime by working against Hitler. The women were afraid they too might be denounced to the Gestapo.

A question crossed my mind: did Leni's daughter wear her mother's same frown when they came in the end to take her away to the re-education centre?

Both together, Marianne and Leni – though one was to lose her child through the other one's fault – now left the little garden where the seesaw was, the arm of the one around the neck of the other, temple against temple. I felt a little sad then; I felt – as it so easily happened when we were in school together – as if excluded from the shared games and the warm friendships of the others. Then they stopped once again and took me with them.

Marching behind Fräulein Mees like three ducklings behind their mother, we reached the café terrace. Fräulein Mees limped a little, which, together with her fat behind, made her look even more like a duck. Over her chest, in the low neckline of her bodice, hung a large black cross. I wanted to smile, like Leni and Marianne, but I held back, because the amusement provoked by her comical appearance was dulled by the far more serious respect she inspired in me. Later, she was never to take off the black cross which she wore in the neckline of her bodice. Resolutely replacing the swastika with this same black cross, she would set off in search of the clandestine religious services held in varying secret places by the Confessional Church.

The café terrace, on the banks of the Rhine, was planted with rose bushes. Next to the girls, the bushes seemed as well behaved, as rigid, as well groomed as garden flowers compared with flowers in the wild. The scent rising from the water and the garden mingled with the tempting smells of the café. From the tables decked in red-and-white checkered cloths which had been set up in front of the long, low building of the inn came the sound of young voices buzzing like a swarm of bees. But something drew me first to the banks of the river, to take in the endless view of sun-drenched countryside. I dragged my two friends, Leni and Marianne, to the garden gate, where our eyes dove into the river whose glittering blue-grey waves rippled not far from the inn. On the opposite bank, the villages and hills with their fields and their woods were reflected in the interlacing discs of sun. The more I glanced around me, the more freely I felt I could breathe, and the more I felt happiness flood my heart. And the oppressing sadness I had felt earlier weighing on my chest was vanishing almost unnoticed. The mere sight of this gently undulating countryside was enough to ripen in my veins, instead of melancholy, a feeling of joy and delight in living, as wheat ripens in familiar earth and air.

A Dutch tugboat pulling behind it a convoy of eight barges crossed the hills reflected in the water. The barges were carrying lumber. The captain's wife was sweeping the deck. Around her, a little dog danced. We, the girls, waited until the wake left by the train of lumber-laden barges disappeared into the Rhine, and nothing could be seen in the water except the reflection of the opposite side meeting the reflection of the garden on ours. We turned and walked back towards the tables, preceded by our unsteady Fräulein Mees, who no longer seemed funny, wearing on her chest the equally unsteady cross that had suddenly become for me meaningful and irrefutable, and as solemn as an emblem.

It is possible that among the students there were girls who were unkempt and sulky: in their brightly coloured summer dresses, with their swinging braids and cheerful curls, they all looked fresh and festive. Since most places were taken, Marianne and Leni shared a single seat and a single cup of coffee. A snub-nosed girl called Nora, in a small checkered dress, with a thin little voice and a crown of braids woven round her head, poured out the coffee with assurance and distributed the sugar as if she were the hostess. Marianne, who ordinarily forgot all about her fellow students, still remembered this outing quite clearly on the day when Nora, who had become president of the National Socialist Women's Association, welcomed her there both as an Aryan woman and as an old schoolmate.

The blue cloud of mist rising from the Rhine, or perhaps from my tired eyes, turned into fog over the girls' tables, so that I could no longer distinguish clearly the faces of Nora, Leni, Marianne, and the others whose names I've forgotten, just as no one single bloom detaches itself from a wreath of wild flowers. For a moment I heard an argument about what might be the best seating arrangement for Fräulein Sichel, the younger of the two teachers, who at that moment was coming out of the inn. The misty cloud melted in front of my eyes and I distinctly recognized Fräulein Sichel, walking towards us in a dress that was light and cool like that of her students.

She sat down right next to me. Nora, with her habitual readiness, served her coffee; she was her favourite teacher. Obliging and willing, she had surrounded Fräulein Sichel's place with a couple of jasmine sprigs.

Had her memory not been as weak as her voice, Nora would certainly have regretted this gesture later, when she had become the president of our town's National Socialist Women's Association. Now she looked on proudly, almost lovingly, as Fräulein Sichel pinned one of the jasmine sprigs to the buttonhole of her coat. During World War I she must have been overjoyed to share the same schedule as Fräulein Sichel in the Women's Service Detachment, where soldiers in transit were given food and drink. And yet, later, she'd force that same teacher, who even in those early days used to quaver like an old woman, to leave her seat on the banks of the Rhine because she, Nora, wanted to sit on a bench clear of Jews. As I was sitting next to her, I suddenly realized that my own memory had failed me, and I felt guilty, as if I had the sacred duty to carve in it forever even the slightest details. Fräulein Sichel's hair hadn't always been white, as I recalled; at the time of our outing, it had been a gossamer brown, except for a few strands next to the temples. Her white hairs were so few that one could count them; and yet they overwhelmed me as if, on that very day, at that very place, I had come across, for the first time, these signs of old age. At our table, all the other girls rejoiced with Nora at being next to the young teacher, never suspecting that later they would spit on Fräulein Sichel, calling her a Jewish sow.

The eldest among us, Lore – she wore a skirt and a blouse, her red hair in waves, and had long been through real love affairs – had in the meantime gone from table to table distributing pastries which she had baked herself. She possessed all kinds of wonderful domestic gifts, in the arts both of loving and of cooking. Lore was constantly obliging, merry, and always ready to indulge in pranks and practical jokes. This carefree attitude, which she had adopted with uncommon precocity, and which the teachers severely reprimanded, was not conducive to marriage, not even to a serious attachment; so that by the time most of the girls had become respectable housewives and mothers, she still kept the looks she had today, a student among other students, in her short skirt and large, scarlet, avid mouth. How could she have come to such a miserable end? She committed suicide by taking a whole tube of sleeping pills. One of her lovers, a Nazi, had threatened her with deportation to a camp for soiling her race by cuckolding him with a Jew. He had spied on her for a long time before discovering her in the arms of this forbidden friend. In spite of his jealousy and his thirst for revenge, he hadn't succeeded in catching her in the act until, shortly before the war, during a civil defence routine, the air raid warden had forced all the residents to leave their beds and their rooms, and to go down into the cellar – including Lore and her forbidden lover.

Now, surreptitiously (but we were all aware of it), she was giving the last of the small cinnamon cakes to Ida, who was also clever and remarkably beautiful, and coiffed with innumerable natural curls. She was her only friend at school, because Lore, given the nature of her interests, was regarded with a certain disapproval by the others. We gossiped thoroughly about Ida and Lore's merry meetings, and also about the fact that they used to visit swimming pools together, where they would meet athletic companions and organize swimming parties. What I don't know is why Ida, now secretly biting into her cake, was never excluded from our circle by the more bourgeois mothers and daughters; perhaps because her father was a teacher, while Lore's was merely a barber. Ida stopped her dissolute lifestyle in time, but she too remained unmarried, because her fiancé was killed at Verdun. Her sorrow led her to nursing, so as to make herself useful at least to the wounded. Unwilling to abandon her chosen profession after the armistice of 1918, she entered the Episcopalian Church as a deaconess. By the time she became a matron in the National Socialist Nurses' Organization, her charms had faded somewhat and her curls were tinged with grey as if sprinkled with ashes, and even though she couldn't boast a fiancé among the soldiers of the new war, her thirst for revenge and her animosity were still ardently alive. She taught the younger nurses the official rules, advising them that, while caring for prisoners of war, they were to avoid small talk and ordinary acts of kindness inspired by a misplaced pity. But the order she gave to use fresh gauze for their countrymen exclusively had no effect. Because the site where she performed her new functions, the hospital so far from the front lines, was hit by a bomb that buried both friends and enemies, including of course Ida's curly head, which, at this very moment, Lore was caressing with impeccably manicured fingers such as she alone in the whole class possessed.

Just then Fräulein Mees tapped her coffee cup with a spoon and ordered us to place our contributions for the coffee in the flowered dish which she sent around the tables, carried by her favourite pupil. With equal diligence and resolution she was later to organize collections for the Confessional Church banned by the Nazis. Accustomed to tasks of this sort, she became the treasurer in the end. A position not without danger, and yet Fräulein Mees continued to collect alms with the same vivacity and good nature. Today, Gerda, her favourite pupil, allowed the coins to tinkle as they fell in the plate, carrying it back to the innkeeper. Without being beautiful, Gerda's movements had charm and ease. She possessed a horse-like head, thick bushy hair, large teeth, and pretty brown equine eyes, faithful and slightly hooded. She left the innkeeper and ran back – also like a small horse, always galloping – to ask permission to stay behind and take the following boat back. She had heard that the innkeeper's child was very sick and, as there was no one else to look after the child, Gerda wanted to stay and be the nurse. Fräulein Mees silenced the objections raised by Fräulein Sichel, and Gerda left in a gallop to look after the child as if she were off to a party. She had been born to nurse the sick and to practise charity, to be a teacher in a sense almost unknown in the world today, as if her vocation had been to search everywhere for children to whom she would become indispensable. Of course, everywhere she went she always found people in need of help.

True, her life ended absurdly, without anyone attending her. But nothing of what she had accomplished throughout her life was lost, not even the smallest of her charitable deeds. In the end, her life itself was easier to destroy than the traces she had left in the memories of so many people whom by chance, some day, she had assisted. And yet, there was no one to help her the day when her own husband, in spite of her opposition and her threats, hung a flag with a swastika outside their window on May 1, as ordered by the New State, so as not to be fired from his job. There was no one to calm her when, running back home from the market, she saw the window of her own house draped in the sinister flag. Filled with shame and despair, she raced up the stairs and opened the gas. There was no one to save her. At the last moment she was left desperately alone, in spite of the multitudes she had assisted.

The siren of a steamer was heard coming down the Rhine. On its white hull was written, in gold letters, *Remagen*. Even though it was far away, I could easily make out the name with my poor eyes. I could see the clouds of steam like fleece above the chimney, and the cabin portholes, and I followed the wake that faded and resurfaced endlessly. In the meantime, my eyes had grown accustomed to this familiar and friendly world. After the passing of the Dutch tugboat I could see everything with even more precision. That small steamer, the *Remagen*, on the broad quiet river brushing past villages, rows of hills, and processions of clouds, was touched with a clarity that nothing in the world could tarnish. And already I could distinguish, with my own eyes, on the steamer's deck and behind the portholes, the well-known faces of those whose names the young girls were now calling: "Herr Schenk! Herr Reiss! Otto Helmholz! Eugen Lütgens! Fritz Müller!"

The young girls cried out in chorus: "It's the high school outing! It's the upper grade!" They were, like us, on their outing: would they disembark here, at the steamer's next stop? After briefly consulting with each other, Fräulein Sichel and Fräulein Mees ordered us to line up in groups of four, because they wanted to avoid at all costs a meeting between the two classes. Marianne, whose braids had come undone from playing on the seesaw, began to arrange them once again over her ears, since her friend Leni, whose chair she had shared after their game, and who had keener eyes, had just seen that Otto Fresenius, Marianne's beau and her favourite dancing partner, was also on board. Leni whispered to her: "They're getting off. He's signalling with his hand."

Fresenius, a gangling seventeen-year-old with chestnut hair, had been stubbornly signalling for a long while and seemed on the point of jumping into the water to join his girlfriend. Marianne had her arm around Leni's neck. Her friend, whom she would later refuse to acknowledge when asked for help, was like a sister to her, a faithful support in the joys and pains of love, scrupulously carrying letters and setting up secret rendezvous. Her friend's mere presence was enough to turn Marianne, always beautiful and lively, into a miracle of such sweetness and grace that she stood out like a child in a fairy tale among the other girls in her class. Otto Fresenius had confided his feelings to his mother, with whom he shared many secrets. Since the mother too was delighted with his choice, she imagined that later on, if they waited as was deemed proper, nothing would stand in the way of marriage. Indeed, the engagement took place, but not the wedding, since the beau was killed in 1914, in a student battalion, on the Argonne.

The steamer *Remagen* turned to dock at the landing. Our two teachers, who had to wait for the steamer coming in the opposite direction to take the girls back, started to count us at once. Leni and Marianne watched the docking with enraptured attention. Leni had turned her head with such intense curiosity that one might have thought her able to foresee how her own future, the unfolding of her own destiny, depended on the meeting or the parting of these two lovers. If only Leni – and not the mobilization decreed by Kaiser Wilhelm and the precision of the French sharpshooters – had been able to decide, then these two would certainly have become man and wife. She felt deeply how well the two young people suited each other in body and soul. Had things happened this way, Marianne would never have refused, later on, to watch over Leni's child. Otto Fresenius might have found in time a way of helping Leni to escape. Over the years, he would doubtlessly have drawn on the beautiful face of Marianne, his wife, such profound marks of loyalty, of a dignity which both would have deeply respected, that it would have prevented Marianne from turning her back on her schoolmate.

Now, spurred by his love, Otto Fresenius, whose stomach would be ripped open by a bullet during World War I, was the first to cross the gangplank in the direction of the inn's garden. Marianne, one hand never leaving Leni's shoulder, gave the other one to Fresenius and left it in his. Not only to Leni and to me, but to all of us who were still children, it was obvious that these two were lovers. For the first time, they made us realize with utter clarity what a couple really was – not a couple as it appears in dreams, poems, stories, or classical dramas, but a true, authentic couple, just as nature herself would have chosen to bring together.

One finger still linked to one of her friend's fingers, Marianne carried on her face an expression of complete abandonment that became in time an expression of eternal fidelity towards the lanky chestnut-haired boy for whom she'd go into a widow's mourning when the military post returned her letter with the stamp "Dead in the Course of Duty." In those difficult days when Marianne despaired of life, any life – Marianne, whom I once used to see delighting in life with all its small and its great joys, the joy of love or the amusement of a swing – her friend Leni, around whom she now had her arm, met a soldier on leave, Fritz, son of railway workers from our town. While Marianne remained for a long time wrapped in a black cloud, beautiful and deathly sad, Leni became an appetizing ripe and fresh fruit. For a while, the two friends found themselves distanced from each other, following human custom which decrees that happiness and unhappiness must turn away from each other. At the end of her mourning, and after several rendezvous in cafés by the Rhine, her fingers knotted together as she had them now, and carrying the same expression of eternal fidelity on her tender oval face, Marianne would choose a new friend, one Gustav Liebig, who had survived World War I safe and sound and who later on would become Sturmbannführer of the S.S. in our town. This was something Otto Fresenius would never have become, even if had returned unharmed from the war – neither Sturmbannführer of the S.S. nor the Gauleiter's right-hand man. The unmistakable marks of integrity and loyalty noticeable even now in his young features would have rendered him inadequate for a calling and a task of that sort. Leni felt truly reassured when she heard that her schoolmate, for whom she then still felt a sisterly love, had settled to her new destiny, promising

new joys. Just as she was now, she was far too foolish to sus-
pect that the fate of young men and young men is the fate of
the country, the fate of the nation, and that is why, sooner or
later, the unhappiness or the joy of her schoolmate would cast
a shadow over her or fill her with sunlight.

Marianne's face, slightly and almost fortuitously leaning
against her friend's arm, seemed then, as Leni and I both
clearly noticed, full of silent and indelible promise, the token
of an indestructible union. Leni breathed deeply, as if bearing
witness to such love were for her a particularly special kind of
happiness.

Later she was to be arrested by the Gestapo, like her husband. But Marianne would disown her long before then:
Liebig, her brand-new husband to whom she'd swear eternal
fidelity in turn, would tell her so many horrible things about
her schoolmate's husband that she would not be able to
remain friends with such a despicable girl. Leni's husband had
refused time and again to enter either the S.A. or the S.S.
Marianne's husband felt proud of both the lower and the
upper ranks and would have been his superior officer in the
S.S. When he realized that the other man despised such glorious memberships, he drew the town's authorities' attention
to his negligent fellow citizen.

The entire boys' class, accompanied by their teachers, had
gradually disembarked. Herr Neeb, a young teacher with a
small blond moustache, after bowing his head towards his two
female colleagues, inspected our group of girls with a piercing
eye. He noticed that Gerda, whom he was unconsciously
seeking, wasn't there: she was still at the inn, busy with nursing and washing the innkeeper's child, knowing nothing
of the mob of boys in the garden, nor that Herr Neeb, the

teacher, was sorry for her absence. He had noticed her on other occasions because of her large brown eyes and her sense of devotion. It wasn't until 1918, after the end of World War I, when Gerda was herself teaching and both found themselves supporters of the school reforms put forward by the Weimar Republic, that they met again and for all time, at the Association of School Reform Supporters. But Gerda was to remain more faithful than Herr Neeb to their old aspirations and goals. After marrying the young girl whom he had chosen because of her ideas, it wasn't long before he cast them aside for the sake of a peaceful and comfortable life for both. That was why he too hung the flag with the swastika from their dining room window: if he refused, the law threatened to take away his job and thereby his family's bread.

I wasn't the only one to feel the disappointment of Herr Neeb when he saw that Gerda wasn't among us – Gerda, whom he would later unerringly find and make his to the point of becoming at least partly responsible for her death. Else was, I think, the youngest of us all; she was a plump girl with thick braids and a round red mouth like a cherry. She casually remarked, affecting indifference, that one of us, Gerda, had stayed back at the inn to nurse a sick child. Else – who being small and featureless we all forgot very quickly, just as one quickly forgets having seen a certain fat bud on a bush – had not yet had a love affair, but she enjoyed unearthing the love affairs of others and burrowing into them. Right then, the sudden glint in Herr Neeb's eyes told her that she had guessed correctly. She added casually: "The sickroom is just behind the kitchen." In spite of her evident cunning (her child's eyes full of sparkle allowed her to guess Neeb's thoughts far better than she'd be able to later, with adult eyes clouded by experience), Else was destined to wait a long time for a love of her own. Because the man who would one day become her husband, Ebi the carpenter, had still to live through the coming war. He had a goatee and a pot belly, and he was much older than she was. When, after the war, the carpenter married Else, still plump and with her snub nose, the fact that she had studied accountancy at the School of Commerce became a considerable asset in their business. The carpentry shop and their three children meant everything to them. Later, the carpenter was to say that in his line of business, it was all the same to him whether in Darmstadt, the province's capital, the ministerial councillors belonged to a grand duke or to the Social Democratic Party. Furthermore, he saw in Hitler's ascent to power and the outburst of a new war a sort of natural catastrophe, comparable to a tempest or a snowstorm. By then he was quite old. And Else's hair too showed a fair number of white strands. He certainly had no time to change his mind when in less than five minutes, during the English air raid on Mainz, his wife, Else, the carpenter himself, their three children, and the workers were all killed, blown to shreds and turned to dust together with the house and the shop.

While Else, round and hard like a small ball that nothing can crumble except a bomb, bouncingly took her place among the girls, Marianne placed herself at the far corner of the last line where Otto could stand next to her, hand in hand. Beyond the gate, they watched the water where their shadows mingled with the reflection of the hills, the clouds, and the white wall of the inn. They didn't say a word; they were certain that nothing could keep them apart, neither the lines grouped in fours, nor the departure of a steamer, not even, later, death itself, which they would reach together in peaceful old age, they thought, among their numerous children.

The oldest of the teachers in the boys' class (he walked shuffling his feet, he always coughed, and the boys called him Greybeard) crossed the dock and entered the garden, surrounded by his pupils. They sat down quickly and hungrily at the table that we, the girls, had left, and the innkeeper, pleased that Gerda was still looking after her sick child, brought out her flowered china freshly washed. Reiss, head teacher in the boys' class, began to sip his coffee. He made so much noise that one would have thought a bearded giant was drinking.

Contrary to what usually happens, the teacher saw all his young students die, one after the other, during the war that followed and during this last one, whether in black-white-red regiments or in regiments carrying the swastika. And yet he lived through all these events unscathed. Because gradually he became not only too old to fight but also too old to utter opinions that might have led him to prison or to a concentration camp.

While the boys congregated around Greybeard – a few well behaved, others behaving like rascals, all like gnomes in a fairy tale – the flock of girls, farther away in the garden, chirped and fluttered elfishly. After we were counted, it was discovered that a few were missing. Lore was sitting among the boys, because on that day, and throughout her life (before a Nazi's jealousy put an end to her choices), she preferred to remain as long as possible in male company. Next to her, a girl named Elli chuckled loudly, having noticed among the boys her partner from the dance class, a small chubby-cheeked boy called Walter. That day his trousers, which to his great regret he still wore short, fitted somewhat too tightly over his round buttocks. Later, a smart S.S. member in spite of his rather advanced age, he would lead a convoy of deportees in which Leni's husband would be taken away forever. Leni was still standing at an angle so that Marianne might continue to exchange a few more words with her lover; she was far from guessing how many future enemies surrounded her there in that garden. Ida, the future deaconess, was walking down towards us, whistling and performing funny dance steps. The boys' round eyes and the contented sideways glare of the old coffee drinker followed with pleasure the curly head tied with a velvet ribbon. One day, during the winter of 1943 in Russia, when her hospital was suddenly caught under the bombing, she would recall, as clearly as I do now, that velvet ribbon in her hair, and the white and sunny inn, the garden on the banks of the Rhine, the boys arriving and the departing girls.

Marianne had let go of Otto Fresenius's hand and her arm was no longer on Leni's shoulder. She stood alone in the girls' line, alone and abandoned in her dreams of love. In spite of her earthy nature, Marianne now stood out among her classmates in her almost uncanny beauty. Otto Fresenius returned to the boys' table, next to Neeb, the young teacher. Neeb, like a good friend, refrained from joking or asking questions, for he too was in search of a girl in that same class and respected the love affairs of others, even of the very young. Death would tear Otto away from the girl he loved long before his older teacher. He nevertheless had the joy of knowing eternal fidelity during his short life and was to ignore all the evil, all the temptations, all the pettiness and the shame to which the other, his elder, was to sacrifice his life in order to hold for himself and for Gerda his official post.

Fräulein Mees, with her enormous indestructible cross hanging over her bosom, watched over us scrupulously, so that none of the girls would run away before the arrival of the steamer and join her dance partner. Fräulein Sichel had gone off in search of a girl called Sophie Meier and found her at last on the seesaw with a boy, Herbert Becker, who like Sophie was thin and wore glasses, so that they looked more like sister and brother than like a couple of lovers. Herbert Becker ran away when he saw the Fräulein approaching. Later, I saw him many times run through the streets of our town, the face contorted in a rictus, grimacing. Under his glasses he still wore his sly boyish face when, several years ago, I came across him in France, where he had returned from the war in Spain. Fräulein Sichel sharply scolded Sophie for lagging behind, and the girl had to wipe her glasses, wet with tears. In time, not only the teacher's hair – where once again I was astonished to notice the presence of grey strands – but also that of her pupil Sophie, now still black as ebony like that of Snow White, were to turn completely white when, placed together in a sealed car, they would be deported to Poland by the Nazis. Surprisingly, Sophie became all wizened and old when she died in the arms of Fräulein Sichel, as if the two had been twin sisters.

We consoled Sophie and wiped her glasses dry. Fräulein Mees, clapping her hands, gave the signal to leave for the steamer dock. We felt full of shame, because the boys' class was watching as we were forced to parade in line, amused at the sight of the limping and unsteady waddle of our teacher. I was the only one for whom the amusement was overshadowed by the respect inspired by her constancy and strength of will, which neither her summons to appear in front of the so-called People's Tribunal set up by Hitler nor the threat of prison was able to shake. All together on the dock, we waited for the steamer to moor. A sailor caught the rope, wrapped it around the post, and set down the gangplank with such extraordinary agility that it seemed to me like the welcome to a new-found world, the seal that guaranteed the uniqueness of our crossing, next to which all other journeys would pale – journeys beyond infinite sea, mere adventures escaped from a childhood dream. Such journeys were far from holding the exhilarating power, the truth I found here in the scent of wood and water, in the slight sway of the gangplank, in the creaking of the cables, as we set off on the Rhine on a twenty-minute crossing that would carry me back to my hometown.

I jumped on deck and sat next to the helm. The steamer's small bell rang out, the ropes were hauled aboard, the steamer turned. The white curve of glittering foam cut into the river. All of a sudden I thought of the foamy white wakes that all manner of ships, under all manner of latitudes, cut into the seas. Never again would a journey impress me as strongly with its evanescent and final character, never again would water seem to me so unfathomable and yet so near. Abruptly, Fräulein Sichel came and stood next to me. She seemed wonderfully young in the sunlight, in her dotted dress and with her small firm breasts. With sparkling grey eyes, she told me that, since I loved to travel and write stories, I was to prepare for our next German lesson an account of our class's outing.

The girls who preferred the deck to the cabins came and sat all around me on the benches. In the garden beyond, the boys whistled and waved. Lore answered back with a shrill whistle, but Fräulein Mees scolded her severely; on shore the whistles continued as loudly as before. Marianne leaned over the railings and wouldn't take her eyes off her Otto, as if this separation were to be as eternal as the later one of 1914. Once she was no longer able to make out the young man's features, she put an arm around my neck and another around that of Leni. At the same time as I felt the softness of her delicate naked arm, I sensed on my neck the scorching of the evening sun. I too looked back at Otto Fresenius, who continued to stare after his Marianne, as if, while she leaned her head against Leni, he might be able to capture her with his eyes and keep forever this memory of an indestructible friendship.

In tight embrace, the three of us looked upstream. Over the vineyard-covered hills, the slanting afternoon sun swelled the fruit trees covered in pink and white bloom. In the fire of the evening sun, a few windows sparkled. The villages seemed to grow as we drew near, then to shrink again after we had barely gone by them. We already felt the traveller's nostalgia, which can never be appeased since everything he sees is only just touched in passing. We crossed under the Rhine bridge over which, not long afterwards, would pass the military convoys of World War I, with all those boys who were now sipping coffee in the garden, and with the boys of all the other schools. When that war was over, the Allied soldiers would cross that bridge, and later still Hitler and his army of adolescents come to take back the Rhineland. The new military convoys headed for the new world war would roll across it, leading the sons of this nation to death. Our steamer passed close to Petersaue Island, on which stood one of the bridge's pillars. All of us saluted the three little white houses that had been familiar to us since our childhood as if they had sprung up from those picture books that tell stories about witches. The little houses and an angler were reflected in the water, as well as the village on the far side. With its fields of wheat and turnip, overlooking a fringe of pink apple trees, the village spread out in a gothic triangle its swarm of gabled houses pressed one against the other, up to the delicate tip of the steeple high on the side of the hill.

The evening sun now sent its rays into the cup of a valley crossed by a railway line, or towards a faraway chapel, and the reflection of it all mirrored itself once again on the surface of the Rhine before disappearing into darkness.

We all fell silent in the peacefulness of the fading light, listening to the croaking of a few crows and to the howling of the sirens of the Amöneburg factories. Even Lore was now completely silent. Marianne, Leni, and I had linked arms in a gesture of solidarity which reflected the great solidarity of all things under the sun. Marianne still kept her head pressed against Leni's. How was it possible that, later on, a lie, a delusion seeped into her thoughts, making her believe, she and her husband, that they alone possessed the monopoly of love in their country and that they had the right to despise and denounce the young girl against whom she was now leaning? No one ever reminded us, while there was still time, of that outing. They made us write many essays on our country, and on the history of our country, and on our love for our country, but it was never pointed out to us that the flock of girls tenderly leaning against one another, travelling upstream in the slanted evening light, was an essential and integral part of that same country.

Now a branch of the river split sideways, leading to the port from where the freshly cut wood, retailed and bound, was ready to leave for Holland. The town seemed to me still far away, and I was under the impression that it would never be able to force me to come to a halt and disembark. And yet its lumber docks, its lines of plane trees, and the warehouses along the coast were far more familiar to me than any of the foreign cities in which I would later be forced to halt my journey. Gradually I recognized the streets, the roofs, the familiar-looking steeples, undamaged and welcoming, like those places long since disappeared mentioned in stories and songs. It seemed to me that, on that short day of my class's outing, all kinds of things were torn away from me and then returned.

When the steamer circled to dock, and the idle loafers began to assemble to watch our arrival, we seemed to be returning not from an outing but from a voyage that had kept us away for several years. The familiar town, full of busy corners, buzzing with activity, had not a single tear in it, not a single trace of scorching, and my anxiety settled, and I felt at home again.

Lotte was the first to say goodbye, as soon as we moored. She wanted to attend evening mass at the cathedral whose bells could be heard down by the dock. Later, Lotte would end up in the convent of Nonnenwerth on an island in the Rhine, from where she'd be taken over the Dutch border with a group of nuns; but fate was to pursue them even there. The class said their farewells to the teachers. Fräulein Sichel reminded me once more of the account I was to write, her grey eyes glittering like two small smooth and shiny pebbles. Then we dispersed in groups and walked away in the direction of our various homes.

Leni and Marianne went arm in arm towards the Rhine-strasse. Marianne had a red carnation between her teeth. She had picked one exactly like the carnation Leni wore in the ribbon that held her Mozart braid. For me now, Marianne is always carrying that carnation between her teeth, even when I see her answer angrily to Leni's neighbours, or when

I imagine her lying in the ashes of her parents' house, the half-calcinated body among the smoky shreds of her clothes. Because the firemen arrived too late to save Marianne; the fire caused by the bombing, spilling over from the houses that had been hit directly, reached the Rhinestrasse where her parents lived and where she found herself then, on a visit. Her death was not less horrible than that of Leni, whom she had rejected, and who died of sickness and hunger in a concentration camp. And yet, because of that rejection, Leni's child escaped the bombing, for the Gestapo placed her in a Nazi re-education centre not far from there.

With several schoolmates I walked unhurriedly towards the Christhofstrasse. At first, I felt uneasy. Just as we were coming from the Rhine and turning to enter the town centre, I felt a pressure on my heart, as if something absurd, painful, threatened me, perhaps a terrible piece of news, or a misfortune that the sun-drenched outing had made me forget, hare-brained as I was. Then I realized that it was impossible for the Christhof Church to have been destroyed in a night air raid, because we could hear the angelus tolling. Nothing justified the anguish that had gripped hold of me at the idea of coming home down that road; I simply couldn't tear from my mind the feeling that the entire core of my town had been destroyed by the bombs. I also realized that the newspaper photograph I'd seen, in which all the streets and the squares either had been wiped out or stood in ruins, must have been mistaken. First I thought that, following Goebbels's order, in order to hide the vastness of the attack, they had quickly erected a fake town in which nothing was left of the stone houses of the old one, but which nevertheless gave the impression of being solid and impressive. Were we not all well accustomed to this kind of mirage and deception, and not only after the air raids but also on other occasions more difficult to understand?

And yet the houses, the stairs, the fountain stood upright as usual. Even Braun, the wallpaper store (which, it was said, had burnt down with the entire family during this war, after having had only its windows shattered by a shell during the first), still displayed its counter of flowered or striped wallpaper, so that now Marie Braun, walking by my side, was able to enter her father's shop quickly. The second to leave our group to go home was Katherina; she ran towards her young sister Toni, who was playing under the plane trees on a stone slab by the fountain. No doubt the fountain and the plane trees had long since been reduced to dust, but the children lacked nothing for their games; for them too, their last hour was to come in the cellars of the neighbouring houses. Little Toni too would die in the house inherited from her father, together with her granddaughter, as little as Toni herself was on this day, amusing herself by filling her cheeks with water, imitating the fountain. Also Katherina, the big sister who was now catching hold of her by her braids, and the mother and the aunt who welcomed her at the door with kisses – all of them were to die in the cellar of the family house. During that time, Katherina's husband, an upholsterer who had followed in his father's business, was taking part in the occupation of France. With his small moustache, his fat upholstering fingers, he considered himself part of a people stronger than all others – until he received the news that his house and his family had been reduced to rubble. The little sister turned round once again and showered me too with the last mouthful of water she had succeeded in storing in her cheeks.

I walked the rest of the way alone. On the Flachsmarkt-strasse I met Lise Möbius, very pale, also a classmate, whose two-month-old pneumonia had prevented her from joining our outing. The Christhof Church's call to vespers had drawn her into the street. She ran by me, her two long brown braids dangling and a pince-nez on her small face, hurried as if she were going to a game and not to the evening service. Later she would beg her parents for permission to enter the Nonnen-werth convent with Lotte. But only Lotte received permission, and Lise became a teacher in an elementary school in our town. I saw her many other times running to mass with her pale sharp little face and wearing the same pince-nez as today. Her faithfulness to her religion earned her the scorn of the Nazi authorities. But even when she was demoted to a school for disadvantaged children, she didn't allow that to trouble her because her faith had accustomed her to persecutions of all sorts. This caused the most extreme among the Nazi women, the most treacherous and sarcastic of her neighbours, to become sweet as lambs when, during an air raid, they found themselves huddled around Lise in the shelter. The eldest suddenly remembered they had found themselves like this once before, crouching down with that same neighbour, with Lise, in that same cellar, when during World War I the first bombs had exploded. Now they pressed themselves against the small despised teacher, as if it was her faith and her calm demeanour that had once before appeased death. The most insolent and mocking were even ready to receive something of the faith of that small teacher who, in their eyes, had always been shy and fretful but who, once again, on this day, showed herself full of confidence and trust. Lise crouched among the grotesque pale faces, in the artificial light of the shelter, under the bombings

that would practically annihilate the entire town, including Lise
and her neighbours, both the believers and the unbelievers.

The shops had just shut. I walked down the Flachsmarkt-
strasse through a buzzing crowd thick with people on their
way home. They rejoiced in the day that was ending and were
looking forward to a peaceful night. Just as their houses carried no sign of the shelling, neither from the first great ordeal
of 1914–18 nor from the later bombings, in the same way
their serene and familiar faces, lean or full, with moustaches or
beards, smooth or covered in warts, did not yet carry any of
the signs of their children's crimes or of the knowledge of that
crime and their witnessing and tolerating that crime out of
cowardice, for fear of the state's power. And yet it would not
be long before they would have their share of that power,
bloated with pride and insolent despotism. Or perhaps they
had eventually learned to enjoy it – the baker with the curly
moustache and the pot belly at whose bakery at the corner of
the Flachsmarktstrasse we used to shop for streusel cake, the
ticket inspector on the streetcar passing by us at this very
minute, sounding its bell? The peacefulness of this evening, the
quick footsteps of the people on their way home, the pealing
of the bells, the sirens of the distant factories announcing the
weekly break, the humble satisfaction of that day's work just
like every other day and which I sipped as if it were a comfort-
ing beverage – all this, did it perhaps fill their children with such
loathing that they would avidly gulp down the war propaganda
fed to their parents, and dream of casting off their work clothes,
covered in flour or dust, and pull on a military uniform?

Once again, I felt a touch of anguish as I entered my street, as
if I knew it had been wiped away. But the presentiment quickly
faded. Because walking down the last section of the Bauhof-

strasse, I was able to follow again my favourite route, the one I always took going home and which led me past two large ash trees that, left and right, displayed their crowns like a triumphal arch over the street, joining each other, whole and indestructible. And I could see already in the middle of the lawn the clusters of white, red, and blue geraniums and begonias, blocking the pavement. As I drew near, the evening breeze, stronger than those I had ever felt on my temples, detached from the wild rose bush a cloud of leaves that seemed to me at first to reflect the reddening of the sun but that actually possessed that natural colouring. As always after a day's outing, I rediscovered, like a long-forgotten sound, the whistling of the wind rising from the Rhine and trapped in my street. I felt very tired, and was happy to find myself at last in front of my own door. But climbing the stairs seemed unbearably difficult. I lifted my eyes towards the second storey, where we lived. My mother was out on the small glassed-in balcony, bedecked with geranium pots and overlooking the street. How young she looked, my mother, so much younger than me! How black her straight hair was, compared to mine! Because mine was turning grey already, and not a single grey strand could be seen in hers. There she was, blissful, made for a busy family life with the joys and sorrows of every day, and not for a cruel, atrocious end, in a faraway village to which she was banished by Hitler. She recognized me and waved as if I were returning from a long voyage. She would laugh and wave in the same way every time I returned from an outing. I ran as fast as I could towards the stairs.

I stopped brusquely on the first landing. I suddenly felt far too tired to climb as quickly as I had wanted to, only a moment earlier. The blue-grey fog of exhaustion enveloped everything. And yet around me was a burning clarity, and not the usual gloom of a stairwell. I made an effort to climb and reach my mother. The stairs, which the fog prevented me from seeing, seemed to rise to unattainable heights – steep stairs, impossible to climb, as if set against a mountain wall. Maybe my mother was out in the hall, waiting on the landing. But my legs seemed to give way under me. As a small girl, the last time I had felt this anguish was at the thought that something terrible might prevent me from seeing my mother again. I imagined her waiting for me in vain, separated from me by only a few steps. Then I calmed myself, thinking suddenly that if I collapsed here from exhaustion, my father would immediately find me. He hadn't died, he would soon be home because it was Saturday. He liked staying out, strolling, a little longer than my mother would have wished, chatting at the street corner with the neighbours.

Then the sound of clashing dishes announced the evening meal. Behind every door, I could hear the clapping of hands preparing the dough with a familiar rhythm. I was surprised by this way of preparing flatbreads: instead of rolling out the tenacious dough, she patted it out between the palms of the hands. At the same time, I could hear in the courtyard the forlorn cry of turkeys, and I asked myself with astonishment why they were now raising turkeys in the courtyard. I wanted to turn around, but I was dazzled by the very strong light coming from the courtyard windows. The steps seemed lost in fog, the stairwell seemed to grow on every side, deep and fathomless as an abyss. The recesses of the windows quickly filled with gathering clouds. I found the strength to think: "What a shame! I so wish that my mother had kissed me. If I'm too tired to climb upstairs, how will I be able to get back to the village, high above, where I'm expected for the night?"

The sun's heat was as strong as ever; its light burned as sharp as ever, falling obliquely. As always, I found it strange that there was no twilight here, only a brutal passage from day to night. I gathered my strength and started climbing with a quick step, even though the staircase lost itself in an unbridgeable chasm. The banister, twisting and turning, became a huge fence-like enclosure of giant cacti. I found the way to the tavern where I had stopped after leaving the village. The dog was gone. A couple of turkeys that had not been there before were pecking for food on the road. The owner was still crouched by the door, and next to him, crouched as well, a friend or relative, very like him, lost in thought or nothingness. At their feet the shadows of their hats collected like puddles. The owner made no movement as I drew near; I wasn't worth it, I had been filed away among his usual perceptions. I was far too tired to take another step; I sat down at the table where I had found myself earlier. My intention was to return to the hills once I had caught my breath. I wondered what I would do with my time, today and tomorrow, here and there, because I felt as if time were an infinite river flowing, as impossible to grasp as the air. Have we not been brought up from our earliest childhood to hold sway over time by any possible means, rather than to surrender humbly to it? Suddenly, I thought again of the homework my teacher had given me: to write an account of our outing. I decided that tomorrow morning, or perhaps even this very evening, once I no longer felt so tired, I would sit down to my appointed task.

1943–44
Translated by Alberto Manguel

Natalia Ginzburg

■

WINTER
IN THE
ABRUZZI

*The tenets of Mussolini's Fascism were simple: a belief
in the supremacy of his chosen people over all other races,
and a devotion to "Il Duce." All instruments of democracy
and all sources of opposition were abolished, and the
progress of the nation took precedence over any particular
social needs. During Mussolini's dictatorship, all civil
rights were subject to Il Duce's will and, as in Nazi
Germany, Communists and Jews were relentlessly
persecuted. For three years, from 1940 to 1943, Natalia
Ginzburg, her husband, and their children were sent into
domestic exile to the village of Pizzoli, in the Abruzzi
mountains. In spite of the danger, Leone Ginzburg continued his anti-Fascist activities, and in 1944 he was arrested,
tortured, and killed. Natalia Ginzburg's first novel,* The
Road to the City, *was published by the company she and
her husband help found, Einaudi, but under a pseudonym,
"Alessandra Tornimparte," since, as the work of a Jew, it*

was not allowed to appear in print. She survived the war and for a time joined the Italian Communist Party. As an independent, she was elected twice to the Chamber of Deputies. Natalia Ginzburg died in 1991.

■

God has given us this moment of peace

THERE ARE ONLY two seasons in the Abruzzi: summer and winter. The spring is snowy and windy like the winter, and the autumn is hot and clear like the summer. Summer starts in June and ends in November. The long days of sunshine on the low, parched hills, the yellow dust in the streets and the babies' dysentery come to an end, and winter begins. People stop living in the streets: the barefoot children disappear from the church steps. In the region I am talking about almost all the men disappeared after the last crops were brought in: they went for work to Terni, Sulmona or Rome. Many bricklayers came from that area, and some of the houses were elegantly built; they were like small villas with terraces and little columns, and when you entered them you would be astonished to find large dark kitchens with hams hanging from the ceilings, and vast, dirty, empty rooms. In the kitchen a fire would be burning, and there were various kinds of fire: there were great fires of oak logs, fires of branches and leaves, fires of twigs picked up one by one in the street. It was easier to tell the rich from the poor by looking at the fires they burnt than by looking at the houses or at the people themselves, or at their clothes and shoes which were all more or less the same.

When I first arrived in that countryside all the faces looked the same to me, all the women – rich and poor, young and old – resembled one another. Almost all of them had toothless mouths: exhaustion and a wretched diet, the unremitting over-work of childbirth and breast feeding, mean that women lose their teeth there when they are thirty. But then, gradually, I began to distinguish Vincenzina from Secondina, Annunziata from Addolerata, and I began to go into their houses and warm myself at their various fires.

When the first snows began to fall a quiet sadness took hold of us. We were in exile: our city was a long way off, and so were books, friends, the various desultory events of a real existence. We lit our green stove with its long chimney that went through the ceiling: we gathered together in the room with the stove – there we cooked and ate, my husband wrote at the big oval table, the children covered the floor with toys. There was an eagle painted on the ceiling of the room, and I used to look at the eagle and think that was exile. Exile was the eagle, the murmur of the green stove, the vast, silent countryside and the motionless snow. At five o'clock the bell of the church of Santa Maria would ring and the women with their black shawls and red faces went to Benediction. Every evening my husband and I went for a walk: every evening we walked arm in arm, sinking our feet into the snow. The houses that ran alongside the street were lived in by people we knew and liked, and they all used to come to the door to greet us. Sometimes one would ask, "When will you go back to your own house?" My husband answered, "When the war is over". "And when will this war be over? You know everything and you're a professor, when will it be over?" They called my husband "the professor" because they could not pronounce his name, and they came from a long way off to ask his advice on the most diverse things – the best season for having teeth out, the subsidies which the town-hall gave, and the different taxes and duties.

In winter when an old person died of pneumonia the bell of Santa Maria sounded the death knell and Domenico Orecchia, the joiner, made the coffin. A woman went mad and they took her to the lunatic asylum at Collemaggio, and this was the talk of the countryside for a while. She was a young, clean woman, the cleanest in the whole district; they said it was excessive cleanliness that had done it to her. Girl twins were born to Gigetto di Calcedonio who already had boy twins, and there was a row at the town-hall because the authorities did not want to give the family any help as they had quite a bit of land and an immense kitchen-garden. A neighbour spat in the eye of Rosa, the school caretaker, and she went about with her eye bandaged because she intended to pay back the insult. "The eye is a delicate thing, and spit is salty," she explained. And this was talked about for a while, until there was nothing else to say about it.

Every day homesickness grew in us. Sometimes it was even pleasant, like being in gentle slightly intoxicating company. Letters used to arrive from our city with news of marriages and deaths from which we were excluded. Sometimes our homesickness was sharp and bitter, and turned into hatred; then we hated Domenico Orecchia, Gigetto di Calcedonio, Annunziatina, the bells of Santa Maria. But it was a hatred which we kept hidden because we knew it was unjust; and our house was always full of people who came to ask for favours and to offer them. Sometimes the dressmaker made a special kind of dumpling for us. She would wrap a cloth round her waist and beat the eggs, and send Crocetta around the countryside to see if she could borrow a really big saucepan. Her red face was absorbed in her work and her eyes shone with a proud determination. She would have burnt the house down to make her dumplings come out a success. Her clothes and hair became white with flour and then she would place the dumplings with great care on the oval table where my husband wrote.

Crocetta was our serving woman. In fact she was not a woman because she was only fourteen years old. It was the dressmaker who had found her. The dressmaker divided the world into two groups – those who comb their hair and those who do not comb their hair. It was necessary to be on the lookout against those who do not comb their hair because, naturally, they have lice. Crocetta combed her hair; and so she came to work for us and tell our children long stories about death and cemeteries. Once upon a time there was a little boy whose mother died. His father chose another wife and this stepmother didn't love the little boy. So she killed him when his father was out in the fields, and she boiled him in a stew. His father came home for supper, but, after he had finished eating, the bones that were left on the plate started to sing

Mummy with an angry frown
Popped me in the cooking pot,
When I was done and piping hot
Greedy daddy gulped me down.

Then the father killed his wife with a scythe and he hung her from a nail in front of the door. Sometimes I find myself murmuring the words of the song in the story, and then the whole country is in front of me again, together with the particular atmosphere of its seasons, its yellow gusting wind and the sound of its bells.

Every morning I went out with my children and there was a general amazed disapproval that I should expose them to the cold and the snow. "What sin have the poor creatures committed?" people said. "This isn't the time for walking, dear. Go back home." I went for long walks in the white deserted countryside, and the few people I met looked at the children with pity. "What sin have they committed?" they said to me. There, if a baby is born in winter they do not take it out of the room until the summer comes. At midday my husband used to catch me up with the post and we went back to the house together.

I talked to the children about our city. They had been very small when we left, and had no memories of it at all. I told them that there the houses had many storeys, that there were so many houses and so many streets, and so many fine big shops. "But here there is Giro's," the children said.

Giro's shop was exactly opposite our house. Giro used to stand in the doorway like an old owl, gazing at the street with his round, indifferent eyes. He sold a bit of everything; groceries and candles, postcards, shoes and oranges. When the stock arrived and Giro unloaded the crates, boys ran to eat the rotten oranges that he threw away. At Christmas nougat, liqueurs and sweets also arrived. But he never gave the slightest discount on his prices. "How mean you are, Giro," the women said to him, and he answered "People who aren't mean get eaten by dogs". At Christmas the men returned from Terni, Sulmona and Rome, stayed for a few days, and set off again after they had slaughtered the pigs. For a few days people ate nothing but *sfrizzoli*, incredible sausages that made you drink the whole time; and then the squeal of the new piglets would fill the street.

In February the air was soft and damp. Grey, swollen clouds travelled across the sky. One year during the thaw the gutters broke. Then water began to pour into the house and the rooms became a veritable quagmire. But it was like this throughout the whole area; not one house remained dry. The women emptied buckets out of their windows and swept the water out of their front doors. There were people who went to bed with an open umbrella. Domenico Orecchia said that it was a punishment for some sin. This lasted for a week; then, at last, every trace of snow disappeared from the roofs, and Aristide mended the gutters.

A restlessness awoke in us as winter drew to its end. Perhaps someone would come to find us: perhaps something would finally happen. Our exile had to have an end too. The roads which separated us from the world seemed shorter; the post arrived more often. All our chilblains gradually got better.

There is a kind of uniform monotony in the fate of man. Our lives unfold according to ancient, unchangeable laws, according to an invariable and ancient rhythm. Our dreams are never realized and as soon as we see them betrayed we realize that the intensest joys of our life have nothing to do with reality. No sooner do we see them betrayed than we are consumed with regret for the time when they glowed within us. And in this succession of hopes and regrets our life slips by.

My husband died in Rome, in the prison of Regina Coeli, a few months after we left the Abruzzi. Faced with the horror of his solitary death, and faced with the anguish which preceded his death, I ask myself if this happened to us – to us, who bought oranges at Giro's and went for walks in the snow. At that time I believed in a simple and happy future, rich with hopes that were fulfilled, with experiences and plans that were shared. But that was the best time of my life, and only now that it has gone from me forever – only now do I realize it.

1944
Translated by Dick Davis

Isaac Babel

■

AND THEN THERE
WERE NONE

After Lenin's death in 1924, Josef Stalin, general secretary of the Communist Party Central Committee, began to assemble the disparate parts of the Soviet Union under his tyrannical wing. He isolated and disgraced his political allies. During Stalin's regime, from 1928 to 1953, 1,500 men and women writers were executed or died in the gulag among millions of their compatriots, and their manuscripts were locked up in the secret vaults of the KGB. Isaac Babel, who had become famous almost overnight with the publication of his first stories in 1924, became a target for Stalin, both for being a liberal and for being a Jew. Babel refused to write according to the directives of the party. According to his daughter, he "retreated into silence despite the large rewards promised him on condition that he publish again." His answer to Stalin's briberies was: "Creativity does not dwell in palaces." Finally, in the dawn of May 16, 1939, he was arrested and wasn't heard of again until fifteen years later, when the date of his death appeared on an official document: March 17, 1941. Falsely accused of being a

*member of a terrorist conspiracy, he had been condemned to
death by firing squad.*

■

T
HE PRISONERS are dead, all nine of them. I
feel it in my bones.

Yesterday, when Corporal Golov, a worker
from Sormovo, killed the lanky Pole, I said to our staff officer
that the corporal was setting a bad example for the men and
that we ought to make up a list of the prisoners and send
them back for questioning. The staff officer agreed. I got a
pencil and paper out of my knapsack and called Golov. He
gave me a look of hatred and said, "You look at the world
through those spectacles of yours."

"Yes, I do," I replied. "And what do you look at the world
through, Golov?"

"I look at it through the dog's life of us workers," he said
and, carrying in his hands a Polish uniform with dangling
sleeves, he walked back toward one of the prisoners. He had
tried it on, and it did not fit him – the sleeves scarcely reached
down to his elbows.

Now Golov fingered the prisoner's smart-looking under-
pants. "You're an officer," Golov said, shielding his face from
the sun with one hand.

"No," came the Pole's curt answer.

"The likes of us don't wear that sort of stuff," Golov muttered and fell silent. He said nothing, quivering as he looked
at the prisoner, his eyes blank and wide.

"My mother knitted them," the prisoner said in a firm voice.

I turned around and looked at him. He was a slim-waisted youth with curly sideburns on his sallow cheeks. "My mother knitted them," he said again and looked down.

"She knits like a machine, that mother of yours," Andrushka Burak butted in. Burak is the pink-faced Cossack with silky hair who had pulled the trousers off the lanky Pole as he lay dying. These trousers were now thrown over his saddle. Laughing, Andrushka rode up to Golov, carefully took the uniform out of his hands, threw it over the saddle on top of the trousers, and, with a slight flick of his whip, rode away from us again. At this moment the sun poured out from behind the dark clouds. It cast a dazzling light on Andrushka's horse as it cantered off perkily with carefree movements of its docked tail. Golov looked after the departing Cossack with a bemused expression. He turned around and saw me writing out the list of prisoners. Then he saw the young Pole with his curly sideburns, who glanced at him with the calm disdain of youth and smiled at his confusion. Next, Golov cupped his hands to his mouth and shouted, "This is still a republic, Andrushka! You'll get your share later. Let's have that stuff back."

Andrushka turned a deaf ear. He rode on at a gallop, and his horse swung its tail friskily, just as though it was brushing us off.

"Traitor," Golov said, pronouncing the word very clearly. He looked sulky and his face went stiff. He knelt down on one knee, took aim with his rifle, and fired, but he missed.

Andrushka immediately turned his horse around and charged right up to the corporal. His fresh, pink-cheeked face was angry. "Listen, brother!" he shouted loud and clear and was suddenly pleased by the sound of his own strong voice. "Want to get hurt, you bastard? Why the fuss about finishing off ten Poles? We've killed them off by the hundreds before now without asking your help. Call yourself a worker? Make a job of it, then." And looking at us in triumph, Andrushka galloped off.

Golov did not look up at him. He put his hand to his forehead. Blood was pouring off it like rain off a hayrick. He lay down on his stomach, crawled over to a ditch, and for a long time held his battered, bleeding head in the shallow trickle of water.

The prisoners are dead. I feel it in my bones.

Sitting on my horse, I made a list of them in neat columns. In the first column I numbered them in order, in the second column I gave their names, and in the third the units to which they belonged. It worked out to nine altogether. The fourth was Adolf Shulmeister, a Jewish clerk from Lodz. He kept pressing up to my horse and stroked and caressed my boot with trembling fingers. His leg had been broken with a rifle butt. It left a thin trail of blood like that of a wounded dog, and sweat, glistening in the sun, bubbled on his cracked, yellowish bald pate.

"You are a *Jude*, sir!" he whispered, frantically fondling my stirrup. "You are –" he squealed, the spittle dribbling from his mouth, and his whole body convulsed with joy.

"Get back into line, Shulmeister!" I shouted at the Jew, and suddenly, overcome by a deathly feeling of faintness, I began to slip from the saddle and, choking, I said, "How did you know?"

"You have that nice Jewish look about you," he said in a shrill voice, hopping on one leg and leaving the thin dog's trail behind him. "That nice Jewish look, sir."

His fussing had a sense of death about it, and I had quite a job of fending him off. It took me some time to come to, as though I had had a concussion. The staff officer ordered me to see to the machine guns and rode off. The machine guns were being dragged up a hill, like calves on halters. They moved side by side, like one herd, and clanked reassuringly. The sun played on their dusty barrels, and I saw a rainbow on the metal.

The young Pole with the curly sideburns looked at them with peasant curiosity. He leaned right forward, thus giving me a view of Golov as he crawled out of the ditch, weary and pale, with his battered head, and his rifle raised. I stretched out my hand toward him and shouted, but the sound stuck in my throat, to choke and swell there. Golov quickly shot the prisoner in the back of the head and jumped to his feet. The startled Pole swung around to him, turning on his heels as though obeying an order on parade. With the slow movement of a woman giving herself to a man, he raised both hands to the back of his neck, slumped to the ground, and died instantly.

A smile of relief and satisfaction now came over Golov's face. His cheeks quickly regained their color. "*Our* mothers don't knit pants like that for us," he said to me slyly. "Scratch one and give me that list for the other eight."

I gave him the list and said despairingly, "You'll answer for all this, Golov."

"I'll answer for it, all right!" he shouted with indescribable glee. "Not to you, spectacles, but to my own kind, to the people back in Sormovo! They know what's what."

The prisoners are dead. I feel it in my bones.

This morning I decided I must do something in memory of them. Nobody else but me would do this in the Red Cavalry. Our unit has camped in a devastated Polish country estate. I took my diary and went into the flower garden, which was untouched. Hyacinths and blue roses were growing there.

I began to make notes about the corporal and the nine dead men. But I was immediately interrupted by a noise – an all-too-familiar noise. Cherkashin, the staff toady, was plundering the beehives. Mitya, who had pink cheeks and came from Orel, was following him with a smoking torch in his hands. They had wrapped greatcoats around their heads. The slits of their eyes were ablaze. Myriads of bees were trying to fight off their conquerors and were dying by their hives. And I put aside my pen. I was horrified at the great number of memorials still to be written.

1923
Translated by Max Hayward

Vercors

■

THE SILENCE
OF THE SEA

*When the Germans abandoned Paris in August 1944,
after four years of military occupation, they left behind a
population divided into betrayers and betrayed, into those
who had sided with the enemy and those who had resisted
it. Among those who had collaborated with the Nazis were
Henry de Montherlant and Lucien Rebatet, Louis-Ferdi-
nand Céline, and Pierre Drieu La Rochelle, all of whom
now occupy certain and yet uneasy places in the French literary pantheon. Among the many more who resisted was
Jean Bruller, who took on the name of Vercors, a Maquis
stronghold between Grenoble and the Drôme. Under that
name, he directed the clandestine Éditions de Minuit, a
publishing company he founded for loyal French writers,
since Vercors believed that any legalized publication
amounted to compromise. Not all writers agreed: Sartre
and Aragon, although they were both resistants, continued
to publish openly, as did Valéry and Giono. Paul Éluard
summed up the literary resistance in a line of verse: "We
shall make justice out of evil."*

■

I

THERE WAS A GREAT DISPLAY of military preparations before he arrived. First came two troopers, both very fair; one thin and gangling, the other squarely built with the hands of a quarryman. They looked at my house without going in. Later an N.C.O. arrived, and the gangling trooper went with him. They spoke to me in what they thought was French, but I didn't understand a word. However, I showed them the unoccupied rooms and they seemed satisfied.

Next morning an enormous grey army touring-car drove into my garden. The driver and a slim, fair-haired, smiling young soldier extricated two packing-cases from it, plus a large bundle wrapped up in grey cloth. They took the whole lot up to the largest room. The car went away, and a few hours later I heard hoofbeats. Three horsemen appeared. One dismounted and went off to have a look at the old stone building. When he came back all, men and horses alike, went into the barn which I use as my workroom. I saw later that they had driven the clamp from my carpenters' bench between two stones, in a hole in the wall, fastened a rope to the clamp and tied the horses to the rope.

For two days nothing more happened. I never saw a soul. The troopers went out early with their horses; in the evening they brought them back; and then they went to bed in the straw with which they had stuffed the attic.

Then, on the morning of the third day, the big touring-car returned. The smiling young man heaved a large officer's suitcase on his shoulder and carried it up to the room. Then he took his kitbag which he put in the room next door. He came downstairs and, speaking in good French to my niece, asked her for some sheets.

It was my niece who went to open the door when there was a knock. She had just brought me my coffee, as she did every evening (coffee helps me to sleep), and I was sitting in the back of the room in comparative darkness. The door opens straight on to the garden, and all round the house runs a red-tiled path which is very useful when it is wet. We heard footsteps and the sound of heels on the tiles. My niece looked at me and put down her cup. I kept mine in my hands.

It was night, but not very cold; all that November it was never very cold. I could see a massive figure, a flat cap, a mackintosh thrown round the shoulders like a cape.

My niece had opened the door and was waiting in silence. She had pulled the door right back to the wall and was standing up against the wall not looking at anything. For my part, I was drinking my coffee in little sips.

"If you please," said the officer in the doorway. He gave a little nod of greeting and seemed to be gauging the depth of the silence. Then he came in.

He slid the cape onto his arm, gave a military salute, and took off his cap; then he turned to my niece and, with a quiet smile, made her a very slight bow. Then he faced me and made me a deeper bow. "My name," he said, "is Werner von Ebrennac." I had time for the thought to cross my mind quickly: That's not a German name; perhaps he is descended from a Protestant émigré. Then he added, "I am extremely sorry."

The last word, which he drawled slightly, fell into the silence. My niece had closed the door and was still leaning against the wall looking straight in front of her. I hadn't got up. Slowly I put down my empty cup on the harmonium, then crossed my hands and waited.

The officer went on. "It had to be done, of course. I would have avoided it if I could. I am sure my orderly will do his best not to disturb you." He was standing in the middle of the room, huge and very thin; he could easily touch the beams by raising his arm. His head was hanging forward a little as if his neck didn't grow out from his shoulders, but from the top of his chest. He wasn't round-shouldered, but it looked as if he were. His narrow shoulders and hips were most striking, and his face was handsome; it was very masculine, and there were two big hollows in his cheeks. I couldn't see his eyes, which were hidden in the shadow of his brow, but they seemed light-coloured; his hair was fair and smooth, brushed straight back and giving out a silky glitter under the chandelier.

The silence was unbroken, it grew closer and closer like the morning mist; it was thick and motionless. The immobility of my niece, and for that matter my own, made it even heavier, turned it to lead. The officer himself, taken aback, stood without moving till at last I saw the beginning of a smile on his lips. His smile was serious and without a trace of irony. With his hand he made a vague gesture whose meaning I did not grasp, and fixed his eyes on my niece, still standing there stiffly, so that I had leisure to examine his strong profile, his thin and prominent nose. I saw a gold tooth shining between his half-closed lips. He turned his eyes away at last, stared at the fire on the hearth, and said, "I feel a very deep respect for people who love their country." Then he raised his head abruptly and looked at the carved angel over the window. "I could go up to my room now," he said, "but I don't know the way." My niece opened the door which gives on to the back staircase and began to climb the steps, without looking at the officer, just as if she had been alone. The officer followed her, and it was then I noticed that he was lame in one leg. I heard them cross the anteroom; the German's steps, a strong one, then a weak one, echoed down the corridor. A door opened and closed again; then my niece came back. She picked up her cup and went on drinking her coffee. I lit my pipe, and for a few minutes neither of us spoke; then I said, "Thank the Lord he looks fairly decent." My niece shrugged her shoulders. She took my velvet jacket on her lap and finished the piece of invisible mending which she had begun.

Next morning the officer came down while we were having breakfast in the kitchen. Another staircase leads to it, and I don't know if the German heard us or if he came that way by accident. He stopped in the doorway and said, "I have had a very good night. I should hope yours was as good as mine." He looked round the huge room with a smile. As we had very little wood and less coal, I had repainted it, we had brought in some furniture, some copper pans and old plates, so as to shut ourselves in there for the winter. All that, he took in, and we caught the gleam of the edge of his very white teeth. I saw that his eyes were not blue, as I had thought, but a golden brown. At last he crossed the room and opened the door on to the garden. He took a couple of steps and turned back to inspect our long low house with its ancient brown tiles and its covering of creepers. His smile broadened. "Your old mayor had told me I was to stay at the Château," he said, pointing with a backward flick of his hand at the pretentious building which could be seen a little higher up the hill, through the bare trees. "I shall congratulate my men on their mistake. Here it is a much more beautiful château." Then he closed the door, saluted us through the window pane, and disappeared.

That evening he came back at the same time as before. We were having our coffee. He knocked but didn't wait for my niece to open the door; he opened it himself. "I am afraid I am disturbing you," he said. "If you would rather, I will come in through the kitchen; then you can keep this door locked." He crossed the room and stopped a moment with his hand on the doorknob, looking into the various corners of the smoking-room. Then he made a slight bow. "I wish you a very good night," he said, and went out.

We never locked the door. I am not sure that our motives for this omission were very clear or unmixed. By a silent agreement, my niece and I had decided to make no changes in our life, not even in the smallest detail – as if the officer didn't exist, as if he had been a ghost. But it's possible that there was another sentiment mixed with this wish in my heart: I can't hurt anyone's feelings, even my enemy's, without suffering myself.

For a long time, for more than a month in fact, the same scene took place every day. The officer knocked and came in. He spoke a few words about the weather, the temperature, or some other subject equally unimportant: all that these remarks had in common was that they did not call for an answer. He always lingered a moment on the threshold of the little door, and looked around him. A ghost of a smile would betray the pleasure which he seemed to get from this examination – the same examination every day, and the same pleasure. His eyes would rest on the bowed profile of my niece, invariably severe and impassive, and when at last he took his eyes off her I was sure I could read in them a kind of smiling approval. Then he would say with a bow as he left, "I wish you a very good night."

One evening everything changed abruptly. Outside, a fine snow mixed with rain was falling, terribly cold and damping. On the hearth I was burning the heavy logs which I kept especially for nights like this. In spite of myself I kept imagining the officer outside and how powdered he would be with snow when he came in. But he never came. It was much beyond his usual time, and it annoyed me to realise how my thoughts were taken up with him. My niece was knitting slowly, with a concentrated air.

At least we heard steps, but they came from inside the house. I recognised the unequal tread of the officer, and I realised that he had come in by the other door and was now on his way from his room. No doubt he hadn't wanted to appear before us unimpressive in a wet uniform, and so he had changed first.

The steps, a strong one, then a weak one, came down the staircase. The door opened, and there was the officer. He was in mufti, and was wearing a pair of thick grey flannel trousers and a steel-blue tweed coat with a warm brown check. It was large and loose-fitting and hung with easy carelessness. Beneath his coat a cream woollen pull-over fitted tightly over his spare and muscular body.

"Excuse me," he said. "I'm feeling cold. I got wet through, and my room is very chilly. I will warm myself at your fire for a few minutes." With some difficulty he crouched down by the hearth, put out his hands, and kept on turning them round. "That's fine," he said, and moved round to warm his back at the fire, still squatting and clasping one knee in his hands.

"Here it's nothing," he said. "Winter in France is a mild season. Where I come from, it's very hard. Very. The trees are all firs, close-packed forests with the snow heavy on them. Here the trees are delicate, and the snow on them is like lace. My home reminds me of a powerful thickset bull which needs all its strength to keep alive. Here everything is intelligence, and subtle poetic thought."

His voice was rather colourless, with very little resonance, and his accent was fairly slight, only noticeable on the harsher consonants. The general effect was of a kind of musical buzzing. He got up and rested his arm on the top of the high chimney-piece, leaning his forehead on the back of his hand. He was so tall that he had to stoop a little, whereas I shouldn't even have caught the top of my head there. He remained for a long time without moving or saying anything. My niece was knitting with machinelike energy, nor did she once look up at him. I was smoking, half stretched out in my big soft armchair. I imagined that nothing could disturb the weight of our silence, that the man would bid us good-night and go. But the muffled and musical buzzing began again; one couldn't say that it broke the silence, for it seemed to be born out of it.

"I have always loved France," said the officer without moving. "Always. I was only a child in the last war, and what I thought then doesn't count. But ever since I have always loved it – only it was from a distance, like the Princesse Lointaine." He paused before saying solemnly, "Because of my father."

He turned round with his hands in his coat-pockets and leant against the side of the chimneypiece; he kept bumping his head a little against the shelf. From time to time he slowly rubbed the back of his head against it with a natural movement, like a stag's. An armchair was there for him just at hand, but he didn't sit down. Right up to the last day he never sat down. We never gave, nor did he ever take, anything remotely like an opening for familiarity.

"Because of my father," he repeated. "He was intensely patriotic. The defeat was a great blow to him. And yet he loved France. He liked Briand, he believed in the Weimar Republic and in Briand, and he was very enthusiastic. He used to say, 'He is going to unite us like husband and wife.' He thought the sun was going to rise over Europe at last."

While he was talking he was watching my niece. He did not look at her as a man looks at a woman, but as he looks at a statue. And a statue was exactly what she was – a living one, but a statue all the same.

"But Briand was defeated. My father saw that France was still led by your heartless *grands bourgeois* – by people like your De Wendels, your Henry Bordeaux, and your old Marshal. He said to me, 'You must never go to France till you can do it in field-boots and a helmet.' I had to promise him that, for he was nearly dying, and when war broke out I knew the whole of Europe except France."

He smiled, and said, as if that had been a reason:

"I am a musician, you see."

A log fell in, and some embers rolled out from the hearth. The German leant over and picked up the embers with the tongs; then he went on:

"I am not a performer. I am a composer. That is my whole life, and so it's comical for me to see myself as a man of war. And yet I don't regret this war. No. I think that great things will come of it."

He straightened himself, took his hands out of his pockets and half raised them.

"Forgive me: I may have said something to hurt you. But I was saying what I think and with sincere good feeling. I feel it because of my love of France. Great things will come of it for Germany and for France. I think, as my father did, that the sun is going to shine over Europe."

He took a couple of steps and bowed slightly. As on every evening he said, "I wish you a very good night." Then he went away.

I finished my pipe in silence, then I coughed slightly and said, "It's perhaps too unkind to refuse him even a farthing's worth of answer." My niece lifted her head. She raised her eyebrows very high, her eyes were shining with indignation.

Almost I felt myself blushing.

From that day his visits took on a new shape. Very rarely indeed did we see him in uniform; he used to change first and then knock on our door. Was it to spare us the sight of the uniform of the enemy? Or to make us forget it, to get us used to his personality? No doubt a bit of both. He used to knock, and then he would come in without waiting for the answer which he knew we would not give. He did it in the simplest and most natural way, and would warm himself at the fire, which was the excuse he always gave for his arrival – an excuse by which none of us was taken in, and whose useful conventionality he made no attempt to disguise.

He did not come every evening without fail; but I do not remember a single one in which he did not talk to us before he left. He used to lean over the fire, and while he was warming some part or other of himself at the blaze his droning voice would quietly make itself heard and, for the rest of the evening, there was an interminable monologue on the subjects – his country, music, France – which were obsessing his mind; for not once did he try to get an answer from us, or a sign of agreement or even a glance. He used not to speak for long – never for much longer than on the first evening. He would pronounce a few sentences, sometimes broken by silences, and sometimes linking them up with the monotonous continuity of a prayer; sometimes he leant against the chimneypiece without moving, like a caryatid; sometimes, without interrupting himself, he would go up to an object or a drawing on the wall. Then he would be silent, bow to us, and wish us a good night.

One day he said (it was in the early stages of his visits): "What is the difference between the fire in my home and this one here? Certainly the wood, the flame, and the fireplace are exactly alike. But not the light. That depends on the things on which it shines – the people in this smoking-room, the furniture, the walls, and the books on their shelves . . .

"Why am I so fond of this room?" he went on thoughtfully. "It's not particularly beautiful – Oh, excuse me!" he laughed. "I mean to say it's not a museum piece . . . Take your furniture: it does not make one say, 'What lovely things!' No. And yet this room has a soul. All this house has a soul!"

He was standing in front of the shelves of the bookcase, and with a light touch his fingers were fondling the bindings.

"Balzac, Barrès, Baudelaire, Beaumarchais, Boileau, Buffon . . . Chateaubriand, Corneille, Descartes, Fénelon, Flaubert . . . La Fontaine, France, Gautier, Hugo . . . What a roll-call!" he said, shaking his head with a little laugh, "and I've only got as far as the letter 'H'! Not to Molière, nor Rabelais, nor Racine, nor Pascal, nor Stendhal, nor Voltaire, nor Montaigne, nor any of the others!" He went on slowly moving along the bookshelves, and from time to time he muttered an exclamation, I suppose when he came to a name which he had not expected. "With the English," he went on, "one immediately thinks of Shakespeare; with the Italians, it is Dante. Spain: Cervantes. And with us at once: Goethe. After that one has to stop and consider. But if someone says, 'And France?' then who comes to the tip of one's tongue? Molière? Racine? Hugo? Voltaire? Rabelais? Or which of the others? They jostle each other like the crowd at the entrance to a theatre till you don't know which to let in first."

He turned round, adding in all solemnity, "But when it comes to music, then it's our turn: Bach, Händel, Beethoven, Wagner, Mozart . . . Which name comes first?

"And now we are at war with each other," he said slowly, shaking his head. He had come back to the fireplace, and he let his eyes rest smiling on my niece's profile. "But this is the last time! We won't fight each other any more. We'll get married!" His eyelids crinkled, the hollows under his cheekbones went into two long furrows and he showed his white teeth. "Yes, yes," he said gaily, and a little toss of the head repeated this affirmation. "When we entered Saintes," he went on after a silence, "I was happy that the population received us well. I was very happy. I thought: This is going to be easy. And then I saw that it was not that at all, that it was cowardice." He became serious again. "I despised those people, and for France's sake I was afraid. I thought: Has she *really* got like that?" He shook his head. "No, no, I have seen her since, and now I am happy at her stern expression."

His gaze fell on mine. I looked away. It hesitated for a little at various points in the room and then turned again on the unrelentingly expressionless face which it had left.

"I am happy to have found here an elderly man with some dignity, and a young lady who knows how to be silent. We have got to conquer this silence. We have got to conquer the silence of all France. I am glad of that."

Silently, and with a grave insistence which still carried the hint of a smile, he was looking at my niece, at her closed, obstinate, delicate profile. My niece felt it, and I saw her blush slightly, and a little frown form gradually between her eyebrows. Her fingers plucked the needle perhaps rather too quickly and tartly, at the risk of breaking the thread.

"Yes," went on his slow, droning voice. "It's better that way. Much better. That makes for a solid union – for unions where both sides gain in greatness . . . There is a very lovely children's story which I have read, which you have read, which everybody has read. I don't know if it has the same title in both countries. With us it's called 'Das Tier und die Schöne' – 'Beauty and the Beast.' Poor Beauty! The Beast holds her at his pleasure, captive and powerless – at every hour of the day he forces his oppressive and relentless presence on her . . . Beauty is all pride and dignity – she has hardened her heart . . . But the Beast is something better than he seems. Oh, he's not very polished, he's clumsy and brutal, he seems very uncouth beside his exquisite Beauty! But he has a heart. Yes, he has a heart which hopes to raise itself up . . . If Beauty only *would*! But it is a long time before Beauty will. However, little by little she discovers the light at the back of the eyes of her hated jailer – the light which reveals his supplication and his love. She is less conscious of his heavy hand and of the chains of her prison . . . She ceases to hate him. His constancy moves her, she gives him her hand . . . At once the Beast is transformed, the spell which has kept him in that brutish hide is broken: and now behold a handsome and chivalrous knight, sensitive and cultivated, whom every kiss

from his Beauty adorns with more and more shining qualities! Their union gives them the most perfect happiness.
Their children, who combine and mingle the gifts of their
parents, are the loveliest the earth has borne . . .

"Weren't you fond of this story? For my part, I always
loved it. I have reread it over and over again. It used to make
me cry. I loved the Beast above all because I understood his
misery. Even today I am moved when I speak of it."

He was silent, then he took a deep breath and bowed.

"I wish you a very good night!"

One evening when I had gone up into my room to look for
my tobacco I heard someone playing the harmonium: playing
the "Eighth Prelude and Fugue," which my niece had been
practising before the catastrophe. The score had remained
open at that page, but up to the evening in question my niece
had not been able to bring herself to go on with it. That she
had begun again caused me both pleasure and astonishment:
what deep inward need could have made her change her
mind so suddenly? But it was not my niece – for she had not
left her armchair or her work. Her eyes met mine and sent me
a message which I could not decipher. I looked at the long
back bowed over the instrument, the bent neck, the long,
delicate, nervous hands whose fingers changed places over the
keys as rapidly as if they had each a life of their own.

He only played the Prelude, then he got up and came
back to the fire.

"There is nothing greater than that," he said in his low
voice, which was hardly more than a whisper. "Great – that's
not quite the word. Outside man – outside human flesh. That
makes us understand, no, not understand but guess . . . No:

have a presentiment . . . have a presentiment of what nature is . . . of what – stripped bare – is the divine and unknowable nature of the human soul. Yes, it's inhuman music."

He seemed to be following out his own train of thought in a dreaming silence; he was slowly biting his lip.

"Bach . . . he could only be a German. Our country has that character; that inhuman character. I mean – by 'inhuman' – that which is on a different scale to man."

Then, after a pause:

"That kind of music – I love it, I admire it, it overwhelms me; it's like the presence of God in me . . . but it's not my own.

"For my part, I would like to compose music which is on the scale of man; that also is a road by which one can reach the truth. That's *my* road. I don't want to follow any other, and besides I couldn't. That, I know now; I know it to the full. Since when? Since I have lived here."

He turned his back on us and leant his hands on the mantelpiece. He gripped it with his fingers and held his face towards the fire through his forearms, as if through the bars of a grating. His voice became lower and even more droning.

"Now I really need France. But I ask a great deal; I ask a welcome from her. To be here as a stranger, as a traveller or a conqueror, that's nothing. France gives nothing then, for there is nothing one can take from her. Her riches, her true riches, one can't conquer; one can only drink them in at her breast. She has to offer you her breast, like a mother, in a movement of maternal feeling . . . I know that that depends on us . . . but it depends on her too. She must consent to understand our thirst, she must consent to quench it, and she must consent to unite herself with us."

He stood up, his back still turned to us, his fingers still gripping the stone. "As for me," he said a little more loudly, "I must live here for a long time. In a house like this one. As a child of a village like this village . . . I must . . ."

He was silent. He turned towards us. He smiled with his mouth, but not with his eyes, which were looking at my niece.

"We will overcome all obstacles," he said. "Sincerity is bound to overcome all obstacles.

"I wish you a very good night!"

I can't remember today everything that was said during the course of more than a hundred winter evenings, but the theme hardly ever varied; it was the long rhapsody of his discovery of France: how he had loved her from afar before he came to know her, and how his love had grown every day since he had had the luck to live there. And believe me, I admired him for it. Yes, because nothing seemed to discourage him, and because he never tried to shake off our inexorable silence by any violent expression . . . On the contrary, when he sometimes let the silence invade the whole room and, like a heavy unbreathable gas, saturate every corner of it, of the three of us it was he who used to seem most at ease. Then he would look at my niece with that expression of approval which was both solemn and smiling at the same time, and which he had kept ever since his first day, and I would feel the spirit of my niece being troubled in that prison which she had herself built for it. I would notice it by several signs, of which the least was a faint fluttering of her fingers, and so when at last Werner von Ebrennac set the silence draining away gently and smoothly with his droning voice, he seemed to make it possible for me to breathe more freely.

He would often talk about himself: "My house is in the forest; I was born there; I used to go to the village school on the other side; I never left home until I went to Munich for my examinations, and to Salzburg for the music. I've lived there ever since. I don't like big cities. I know London, Vienna, Rome, Warsaw, and, of course, the German towns, but I would not like to live in any of them. The only place I really liked was Prague – no other city has such a soul. And above all Nuremberg. For a German it is the city which makes his heart swell because there he finds the ghosts which are dear to his soul. Every stone is a reminder of those who made the glory of the old Germany. I think the French must feel the same thing before the Cathedral of Chartres. There they too must feel the presence of their ancestors beside them, the beauty of their spirit, the greatness of their faith, and all their graciousness. Fate led me to Chartres. Oh, truly, when it appears over the ripe corn, blue in the distance, transparent, ethereal, it stirs one's heart! I imagined the feelings of those who used to go there on foot, on horseback or by wagon in the olden time. I shared their feelings, and I loved those people. How I wish I could be their brother!"

His face grew stern: "No doubt it's hard to believe that of somebody who arrived at Chartres in a huge armoured car; but all the same it's the truth. So many things are going on at the same time in the heart of a German, even the best German! Things of which he would so gladly be cured." He smiled again, a faint smile which slowly lit up all his face; then he said:

"In the country house nearest my home there lives a young girl. She is very beautiful and very sweet. My father at any rate would have been very glad if I had married her.

When he died we were practically engaged, and they used to let us go out for long walks alone together."

My niece had just snapped her thread, and before going on he waited until she had threaded her needle again. She did it with great concentration, but the eye of the needle was very small and it was no easy matter. Finally she succeeded.

"One day," he went on, "we were in the forest. Rabbits and squirrels scampered before us. All kinds of flowers were there, narcissus, wild hyacinth, and amaryllis. The young girl cried out in her joy. She said, 'I'm so happy, Werner. I love, oh, how I love these gifts from God!' I too was happy. We lay down on the moss in the midst of the bracken. We did not say a word. Above our heads we saw the tops of the fir trees swaying and the birds flying from branch to branch. The young girl gave a little cry: 'Oh, he's stung me on the chin! Dirty little beast, nasty little mosquito!' Then I saw her make a quick grab with her hand. 'I have caught one, Werner! Oh, look, I'm going to punish him: I'm – pulling – his – legs – off – one – after – the – other . . .' And she did so . . .

"Luckily," he went on, "she had plenty of other suitors. I did not feel any remorse, but at the same time I was scared away for ever where German girls were concerned."

He looked thoughtfully at the inside of his hands and said:

"And that's what our politicians are like too. That's why I never wanted to associate with them in spite of my friends who wrote to me: 'Come and join us.' No: I preferred to stay at home always. It wasn't a good thing for the success of my music, but no matter: success is a very little thing compared to a quiet conscience. And indeed I know very well that my friends and our Führer have the grandest and the noblest conceptions, but I know equally well that they would pull mosquitoes' legs off, one after the other. That's what always happens with Germans when they are very lonely: it always comes up to the top. And who are more lonely than men of the same Party when they are in power?

"Happily they are now alone no longer: they are in France. France will cure them, and I'm going to tell you the truth: they know it. They know that France will teach them how to be really great and pure in heart."

He went towards the door and said, swallowing his words as if talking to himself:

"But for that we must have love."

He held the door open for a moment and, looking over his shoulder, he gazed at my niece's neck as she leant over her work, at the pale, fragile nape of her neck whence the hair went up in coils of dark mahogany, and then he added in a tone of quiet determination:

"A love which is returned."

Then he turned his head, and the door closed on him as he rapidly uttered his evening formula:

"I wish you a very good night."

The long spring days came at last, and now the officer came down with the last rays of the setting sun. He still wore his grey flannel trousers, but he had on his shoulders a lighter woollen jacket, the colour of rough homespun, over a linen shirt with an open neck. One evening he came down holding a book with his forefinger closed in it. His face brightened with that half-withheld smile which foreshadows the pleasure we are confident of giving others. He said:

"I brought this down for you. It's a page of *Macbeth*. Ye gods, what greatness!"

He opened the book:

"It's at the end. Macbeth's power is slipping through his fingers, and with it the loyalty of those who have grasped at last the blackness of his ambition. The noble lords who are defending the honour of Scotland are awaiting his imminent overthrow. One of them describes the dramatic portents of this collapse . . ."

And he read slowly, with a pathetic heaviness:

"Now does he feel
His secret murders sticking on his hands;
Now minutely revolts upbraid his faith-breach;
Those he commands move only in command,
Nothing in love: now does he feel his title
Hang loose about him, like a giant's robe
Upon a dwarfish thief."

He raised his head and laughed. I wondered with stupe-faction if he was thinking of the same tyrant as I was, but he said:

"Isn't that just what must be keeping your Admiral awake at night? I really pity that man in spite of the contempt which he inspires in me as much as in you.

"Those he commands move only in command,
Nothing in love . . .

"A leader who has not his people's love is a very miserable little puppet. Only . . . only, could one expect anything else? Who in fact except some dreary climber of that kind could have taken on such a part? And yet it had to be. Yes, there had to be someone who would agree to sell his country, because today – today and for a long time to come – France cannot fall willingly into our open arms without losing her dignity in her own eyes. Often the most sordid go-between is thus at the bottom of the happiest union. The go-between is none the less contemptible for that, nor is the union less happy."

He closed the book with a snap and stuffed it in his coat pocket, mechanically giving the pocket a couple of slaps with the palm of his hand. Then he said with a cheerful expression lighting up his long face:

"I have to inform my hosts that I shall be away for a couple of weeks. I am overjoyed to be going to Paris. It's now my turn for leave, and I shall spend it in Paris for the first time. This is a great day for me. It's my greatest day until the coming of another one, for which I hope with all my heart, and which will be an even greater day. I shall know how to wait for years if necessary. My heart knows how to be patient.

"I expect I shall see my friends in Paris, where many of them have come for the negotiations which we are conducting with your politicians to prepare for the wonderful union of our two countries. So I shall be in a way a witness to the marriage . . . I want to tell you that I am happy for the sake of France, whose wounds will thus be so quickly healed, but I am even happier for Germany and for myself. No one will ever have gained so much from a good deed as will Germany by giving back to France her greatness and her liberty!

"I wish you a very good night."

2

We did not set eyes on him when he came back.

We knew he was there (there are many signs which betray the presence of a guest in the house, even when he remains invisible). But for a number of days – much more than a week – we never saw him.

Shall I admit it? His absence did not leave my mind at peace. I thought of him, I don't know how far it wasn't with regret or anxiety. Neither I nor my niece spoke of him. But in the evening when we sometimes heard the dull echo of his uneven step upstairs I could clearly see from her sudden obstinate busying with her work, from the faint lines that gave her face an expression which was both set and expectant, that she was not immune from thoughts like mine.

One day I had to go to the Kommandantur for some business about declaring tires. While I was filling in the form they had given me, Werner von Ebrennac came out of his office. At first he did not see me. He spoke to the sergeant who was sitting at a little table before a long mirror on the wall. I heard the sing-song inflection of his low voice, and, although I had nothing more to do, I waited there without knowing why, yet curiously moved, and expecting I know not what climax. I saw his face in the mirror, it seemed pale and drawn. He raised his eyes until they caught my own. For two seconds we stared at each other, then he suddenly turned on his heel and faced me. His lips parted, and slowly he raised his hand a little, then almost immediately let it fall again. He shook his head almost imperceptibly with a kind of pathetic irresolution, as if he had said "No" to himself, yet never taking his eyes off me. Then he made a very slight bow, as he let his glance fall to the ground, hobbled back into his office, and shut himself in.

I said nothing of this to my niece, but women have a cat-like power of divination; for the whole evening she never stopped lifting her eyes from her work every minute to look at me; to try to read something in my face, which I forced myself to keep expressionless by pulling assiduously at my pipe. In the end she let her hands drop as if tired and, folding up her material, asked if I minded her having an early night. She passed two fingers slowly over her forehead, as if to drive away a headache. She kissed me good-night, and I thought I could read a reproach and a somewhat oppressive sadness in her beautiful grey eyes. After she had gone a ridiculous anger took possession of me: a rage at being ridiculous, and at having a niece who was ridiculous. What was the point of all this nonsense? But I could give no answer to myself. If it was nonsense its roots all the same went very deep.

It was three days later that, just as we were finishing our coffee, we heard the irregular beat of his familiar steps grow clear; and this time they were obviously bent in our direc-tion. I suddenly remembered that winter evening six months ago when we first heard those steps. I thought, And it's rain-ing today too – for it had been raining hard all the morning. A long-drawn obstinate downpour which drowned every-thing outside and was even bathing the inside of the house in a cold and clammy atmosphere. My niece had covered her shoulders with a printed silk scarf where ten disturbing hands drawn by Jean Cocteau were limply pointing at each other; as for me, I was warming my hands on the bowl of my pipe – and to think we were in July!

The steps crossed the anteroom and began to make the stairs creak. The man was coming down gradually with a slowness which seemed to increase, not as if a prey to hesitation, but like somebody whose will-power was being strained to the utmost. My niece had raised her head and was looking at me; during all this time she fixed on me the transparent, inhuman stare of a horned owl. And when the last stair creaked, and a long silence followed, her fixed expression vanished, I saw her eyelids grow heavy, her head bend and all her body fall back wearily into the armchair.

I don't believe that the silence lasted more than a few seconds, yet they seemed very long. I felt I could see the man behind the door, with his forefinger raised to knock and yet putting back, putting back the moment when by the mere gesture of knocking he would have to face the future . . . At last he knocked. And it was neither the gentle knock of someone hesitating nor the sharp knock of nervousness overcome; they were three full, slow knocks, the calm sure knocks that mean a decision from which there is no going back. I expected to see the door open at once as on other occasions, but it remained closed; and then an uncontrollable agitation took possession of me, a medley of questioning and of wavering between conflicting impulses, which every one of the seconds that went by with what seemed to me the increasing velocity of a cataract only made more confused and inextricable. Ought we to answer? Why this sudden change? Why should he expect us this evening to break the silence whose healthy obstinacy had had his full approval, as his behaviour up to now had shown? This evening – this very evening – what was it that our dignity demanded of us?

I looked at my niece to try to catch from her eyes some prompting, some sign, but I met only her side face. She was watching the handle of the door. She was watching it with that inhuman, owl-like stare which I had noticed already; she was very pale, and I saw her upper lip draw itself tight with pain over the delicate white line of her teeth. For my part, before this inward drama so suddenly revealed to me, something that went so far beyond the mild twinges of my own irresolution, I lost all resistance. At that moment two new knocks came, two only, two quick and gentle knocks, and my niece said, "He is going to leave," in a voice so low and so utterly disheartened that I did not wait any longer and said loudly: "Come in, sir."

Why did I add "sir"? To show that I was asking him in as a man and not as an enemy officer? Or, on the contrary, to show that I knew very well *who* had knocked, and that the words were addressed to him? I don't know, and it doesn't matter. The fact remains that I said "Come in, sir" and that he entered.

I had expected to see him appear in civilian clothes, but he was in uniform. Rather would I say that he was more in uniform than ever, if that will convey that it was quite clear to me that he had donned this attire with the deliberate intention of thrusting it on us. He had pushed the door back to the wall, and he was standing straight up in the doorway, so erect and so stiff that I almost began to doubt if it was the same man in front of me and, for the first time, I noticed how surprisingly he resembled Louis Jouvet, the actor. He stood like that for a few seconds, stiff, straight, and silent, his feet a little apart and his arms hanging inert beside his body, his face so cold and so completely impassive that it did not seem as if the slightest emotion could ever dwell there.

But seated as I was deep in my armchair and with my face on a level with his left hand, I noticed that hand; my eyes were caught by that hand, and they stayed there as if chained to it, because of the pathetic spectacle it offered me, and which touchingly belied the man's whole attitude . . .

I learnt that day that, to anyone who knows how to observe them, the hands can betray emotions as clearly as the face – as well as the face, and better – for they are not so subject to the control of the will. And the fingers of that hand were stretching and bending, were squeezing and clutching, were abandoning themselves to the most violent mimicry, while his face and his whole body remained controlled and motionless.

Then his eyes seemed to come back to life. They rested on me for a moment; I felt as if I had been marked down by a falcon. They were eyes shining between stiff wide-open eyelids, the eyelids, stiff and crumpled at the same time, of a victim of insomnia. Then they rested on my niece – and never left her.

At last his hand grew still, all the fingers bent and clenched in the palm. His mouth opened and the lips as they separated made a little noise like the uncorking of an empty bottle, then the officer said in a voice that was more toneless than ever:

"I have something very serious to say to you."

My niece sat facing him, but she lowered her head. She twisted round her fingers the wool from her ball, which came unwound as it rolled onto the carpet; this ridiculous task being doubtless the only one that would lend itself to being performed without her giving it a thought – and spare her any shame.

The officer went on – with such a visible effort that it seemed it might be costing him his life:

"Everything that I have said in these six months, every-thing that the walls of this room have heard . . ." He took a deep breath as laboriously as an asthmatic and kept his lungs full for a moment. "You must . . ." He breathed out again: "You must forget it all."

The girl slowly let her hands fall into the hollow of her skirt where they remained lying helplessly on their sides like boats stranded on the sand; and slowly she raised her head, and then, for the first time – for the very first time – she gave the officer the full gaze of her pale eyes.

He said, so that I scarcely heard him, in less than a whis-per, "Oh, welch' ein Licht!" And, as if his eyes were really unable to endure that light, he hid them behind his wrist. Two seconds went by; then he let his hand fall, but he had lowered his eyelids and now it was his turn to keep his gaze fixed on the ground . . .

His lips made the same little noise, and then he said in a voice that went down, down, down:

"I have seen those men – the victors." Then, after several seconds, in a still lower voice:

"I have spoken to them." And at last in a whisper, slowly and bitterly:

"They laughed at me."

He raised his eyes to me and gravely nodded his head three times, almost imperceptibly. He closed his eyes, then said:

"They said to me: 'Haven't you grasped that we're having them on?' That's what they said. Those very words. 'Wir prellen sie.' They said to me: 'You don't suppose that we're going to be such fools as to let France rise up again on our frontiers? Do you?' They gave a loud laugh and slapped me merrily on the back as they looked at my face: '*We* aren't musicians!'"

As he spoke these last words his voice betrayed an obscure contempt which might have been the reflection of his own feelings towards the others or simply the echo of the very tone in which they had spoken.

"Then I made a long speech – and a spirited one too. They went: 'Tst! Tst!' They answered me: 'Politics aren't a poet's dream. What do you think we went to war for? For the sake of their old Marshal?' They laughed again. 'We're neither madmen nor simpletons: we have the chance to destroy France, and destroy her we will. Not only her material power: her soul as well. Particularly her soul. Her soul is the greatest danger. That's our job at this moment – make no mistake about it, my dear fellow! We'll turn it rotten with our smiles and our consideration. We'll make a grovelling bitch of her.'"

He was silent. He seemed out of breath. He clenched his jaw with such force that I saw his cheekbones stand out and a vein, thick and winding as a worm, beat under his temple. Suddenly all the skin of his face moved in a sort of underground shiver – as a puff of wind moves a lake; as with the first bubbles the film of cream thickens on the surface of the milk one is boiling. His eyes met the pale, wide-open eyes of my niece, and he said in a low voice, level, intense, and constrained, almost too overburdened to move:

"There is no hope." And in a voice which was even lower, more slow and more toneless, as if to torture himself with the intolerable but established fact: "No hope. No hope." Then suddenly in a voice which was unexpectedly loud and strong and, to my surprise, clear and ringing as a trumpet call, as a cry: "No hope!"

After that, silence.

I thought I heard him laugh. His forehead, racked with anguish, was as wrinkled as a hawser. His lips trembled – the pale yet fevered lips of a sick man.

"They reproached me, they were rather angry with me: 'There you are, you see! You see how infatuated you are with her. There's the real danger! But we'll rid Europe of this pest! We'll purge it of this poison!' They've explained everything to me. Oh, they've not left me in the dark about anything. They are flattering your writers, but at the same time in Belgium, in Holland, in all the countries occupied by our troops, they've already put the bars up. No French book can go through any more except technical publications, manuals on Refraction or formulas for Cementation . . . But works of general culture, not one. None whatever!"

His glance passed above my head, flitting about and coming up against the corners of the room like a lost night-bird. At last it seemed to find sanctuary in the darkest shelves – those where Racine, Ronsard, Rousseau were aligned. His eyes stayed fixed there, and his voice went on with a groaning violence:

"Nothing, nothing, nobody!" And as if we hadn't yet understood or weighed the full measure of the threat: "Not only your modern writers! Not only your Péguy, your Proust, your Bergson . . . But all the others! All those up there! The whole lot! Every one."

His glance once more swept over the bindings which glittered softly in the twilight, with a kind of desperate caress. "They will put out the light altogether," he cried. "Never again will Europe be lit up by that flame." And his grave hollow voice made my breast echo with an unexpected and startling cry, a cry whose last syllable seemed drawn out into a wail.

"Nevermore!"

Once more the silence fell. Once more, but this time how much more tense and thick! Underneath our silences of the past I had indeed felt the submarine life of hidden emotions, conflicting and contradictory desires and thoughts swarming away like the warring creatures of the sea under the calm surface of the water. But beneath this silence, alas! There was nothing but a terrible sense of oppression. At last his voice broke the silence. It was gentle and distressed:

"I had a friend. He was like a brother. We had been to school together. We shared the same room at Stuttgart. We had spent three months together in Nuremberg. We never did anything without each other: I played my music to him; he read me his poems. He was sensitive and romantic. But he left me. He went to read his poems at Munich, to some of his new friends. It was he who used always to be writing to me to come and join them. It was he that I saw in Paris with his friends. I have seen what they have made of him!"

He slowly shook his head as if he had to return a sorrowful refusal to some request.

"He was the most violent of them all. He mingled anger with mockery. One moment he would look at me with passion and cry: 'It's a poison! We've got to empty the creature of its poison!' The next moment he would give me little prods in the stomach with the end of his finger. 'They're scared stiff now, ha-ha! They're afraid for their pockets and for their stomach – for their trade and industry! That's all they think of! And as for the few others, we'll flatter them and put them to sleep, ha-ha! It will be easy!' He laughed at me till he went pink in the face. 'We'll buy their soul for a mess of pottage!'"

Werner paused for breath.

"I said to him: 'Have you grasped what you are doing? Have you really *grasped* what it means?' He said, 'Do you think that is going to frighten us? Not with our kind of clear-headedness!' I said: 'Then you mean to seal up the tomb – and for ever?' He replied, 'It's a matter of life or death. Force is all you need to conquer with, but it's not enough to keep you masters. We know very well that an army counts for nothing in keeping you masters.' 'But at the price of the Spirit!' I cried. 'Not at that price!' 'The Spirit never dies,' he said. 'It has known it all before. It is born again from its ashes. We've got to build for a thousand years hence: first we must destroy.' I looked at him. I looked right down into his pale eyes. He was quite sincere. That's the most terrible thing of all."

His eyes opened very wide, as if at the spectacle of some appalling murder: "They'll do what they say!" he cried, as if we wouldn't have believed him. "They'll do it systematically and doggedly. I know how those devils stop at nothing."

He shook his head like a dog with a bad ear. A murmur came from between his clenched teeth, the plaintive, passion-ate moan of the betrayed lover.

He hadn't moved. He was still standing rigidly and stiffly in the opening of the door, with his arms stretched out as if they had to carry hands of lead, and he was pale – not like wax, but like the plaster of certain decaying walls: grey, with whiter stains of saltpetre.

I saw him stoop slowly. He raised his hand and held it for-ward, palm down, towards my niece and myself, with the fin-gers a little bent. He clenched it and moved it up and down a little, while the expression on his face tightened with a kind of fierce energy. His lips parted, and I don't know what kind

of appeal I thought he was going to make to us: I thought –
yes, I thought that he was going to exhort us to rebel. But not
a word crossed his lips. His mouth closed, and once again his
eyes closed too. He stood up straight. His hands rose up the
length of his body and, when they reached the level of his
face, performed some unintelligible movements, something
like certain figures in a Javanese religious dance. Then he
seized his forehead and his temples, pressing down his eyelids
with his stretched-out little fingers.

"They said to me: 'It's our right and our duty.' Our duty!
. . . Happy is the man who discovers the path of his duty as
easily as that."

He let his hands fall.

"At the crossroads you are told: 'Take that road there.'"
He shook his head. "Well, that road doesn't lead up to the
shining heights of the mountain-crest. One sees it going
down to a gloomy valley and losing itself in the foul darkness
of a dismal forest! . . . O God! Show me where *my* duty lies!"

He said – he almost shouted: "It is the Fight – it's the
Great Battle of the Temporal with the Spiritual."

With pitiful insistency he fixed his eyes on the wooden
angel carved above the window. The ecstatic, smiling angel,
radiant with celestial calm.

Suddenly his expression seemed to relax, his body lost
its stiffness, his face dropped a little towards the ground, he
raised it.

"I stood on my rights," he said more naturally. "I applied
to be reposted to a fighting unit, and at last they've granted
me the favour. I am authorised to set off tomorrow."

I thought I saw the ghost of a smile on his lips when he
amplified this with:

"Off to Hell."

He raised his arm towards the east – towards those vast plains where the wheat of the future will be fed on corpses.

"So he surrenders. That's all they can manage to do – surrender. They all do. Even this man does."*

My niece's face gave me a shock: it was as pale as the moon. Her lips, like the rim of an opaline vase, were wide open, almost in the grimace of the Greek tragic masks, and, at the line where the hair rose from the forehead, I saw beads of sweat – not slowly gather, but gush out – yes, gush out.

I don't know if Werner von Ebrennac noticed. The pupils of his eyes and those of the girl seemed moored to each other, as a boat in a current is tied to a ring on the bank, and moored moreover by a line so tightly stretched that one would not have dared to pass a finger between the pairs of eyes. Ebrennac with one hand had taken hold of the door-handle; with his other he held the side of the doorway. Without moving his gaze a hair's-breadth, he slowly drew the door towards him. He said – in a voice that was strangely devoid of expression: "I wish you a very good night."

I thought that he was going to close the door and go; but not at all. He was looking at my niece. He looked at her, and said, or rather whispered, "Adieu."

He did not move; he remained quite motionless, and in his strained and motionless face his eyes were the most strained and motionless things of all, for they were bound to other eyes – too wide open, too pale – the eyes of my niece. That lasted and lasted – how long? – lasted right up to the

---

* This paragraph was added to the original by Vercors in 1950 and translated by his widow, Rita Vercors, for this anthology. – *Ed.*

moment when at length the girl moved her lips. Werner's eyes glittered. I heard:

"Adieu."

One could not have heard the word if one had not been waiting for it, but at last I did hear it. Von Ebrennac heard it too, and he drew himself up, and his face and his whole body seemed to relax as if they had taken a soothing bath.

He smiled, and in such a way that the last picture I had of him was a smiling one; then the door closed and his steps died away in the depths of the house.

The next day, when I came down to have my morning glass of milk, he was gone. My niece had got breakfast ready as she always did. She helped me to it in silence, and in silence we drank. Outside, a pale sun was shining through the mist. It struck me as being very cold.

October 1941
Translated by Cyril Connolly

Bessie Head

■

THE PRISONER
WHO WORE
GLASSES

*Bessie Head was born in a mental hospital in South
Africa, where her white mother was committed because the
father of her child was a black stablehand, and was handed
over to black parents who looked after her until she was
thirteen. In 1964 she accepted a teaching post abroad; when
she left, the South African authorities cancelled her exit
visa, thereby depriving her of citizenship until, fifteen years
later, she was granted a new nationality in Botswana.
During her years in South Africa, Head lived under the
apartheid regime, the repressive policy of racial separation,
and from exile she denounced its intrinsic injustice. Under
apartheid, the Publications Act, which controlled all
published matter, established more than ninety clauses
under which a writer's books could be banned; if a writer
was banned for political activity, the writer could no longer
publish anything at all, whether political or not. According
to Nadine Gordimer, many of whose books were banned,*

*black writers in particular were the target of police raids:
manuscripts were taken away and either destroyed or
buried in police files, and typewriters were confiscated.
No manuscript was ever returned.*

■

S CARCELY A BREATH of wind disturbed the stillness of the day and the long rows of cabbages
were bright green in the sunlight. Large white
clouds drifted slowly across the deep blue sky. Now and then
they obscured the sun and caused a chill on the backs of the
prisoners who had to work all day long in the cabbage field.
This trick the clouds were playing on the sun eventually
caused one of the prisoners who wore glasses to stop work,
straighten up and peer short-sightedly at them. He was a thin
little fellow with a hollowed-out chest and comic knobbly
knees. He also had a lot of fanciful ideas because he smiled at
the clouds.

"Perhaps they want me to send a message to the children,"
he thought, tenderly, noting that the clouds were drifting in
the direction of his home some hundred miles away. But
before he could frame the message, the warder in charge of
his work span shouted: "Hey, what you tink you're doing,
Brille?"

The prisoner swung round, blinking rapidly, yet at the
same time sizing up the enemy. He was a new warder, named
Jacobus Stephanus Hannetjie. His eyes were the colour of the
sky but they were frightening. A simple, primitive, brutal
soul gazed out of them. The prisoner bent down quickly and

a message was quietly passed down the line: "We're in for trouble this time, comrades."

"Why?" rippled back up the line.

"Because he's not human," the reply rippled down and yet only the crunching of the spades as they turned over the earth disturbed the stillness.

This particular work span was known as Span One. It was composed of ten men and they were all political prisoners. They were grouped together for convenience as it was one of the prison regulations that no black warder should be in charge of a political prisoner lest his prisoner convert him to the views. It never seemed to occur to the authorities that this very reasoning was the strength of Span One and a clue to the strange terror they aroused in the warders. As political prisoners they were unlike the other prisoners in the sense that they felt no guilt nor were they outcasts of society. All guilty men instinctively cower, which was why it was the kind of prison where men got knocked out cold with a blow at the back of the head from an iron bar. Up until the arrival of Warder Hannetjie, no warder had dared beat any member of Span One and no warder had lasted more than a week with them. The battle was entirely psychological. Span One was assertive and it was beyond the scope of white warders to handle assertive black men. Thus, Span One had got out of control. They were the best thieves and liars in the camp. They lived all day on raw cabbages. They chatted and smoked tobacco. And since they moved, thought and acted as one, they had perfected every technique of group concealment.

Trouble began that very day between Span One and Warder Hannetjie. It was because of the shortsightedness of Brille. That was the nickname he was given in prison and is the Afrikaans word for someone who wears glasses. Brille could never judge the approach of the prison gates and on several previous occasions he had munched on cabbages and dropped them almost at the feet of the warder and all previous warders had overlooked this. Not so Warder Hannetjie.

"Who dropped that cabbage?" he thundered.

Brille stepped out of line.

"I did," he said meekly.

"All right," said Hannetjie. "The whole Span goes three meals off."

"But I told you I did it," Brille protested.

The blood rushed to Warder Hannetjie's face.

"Look 'ere," he said. "I don't take orders from a kaffir. I don't know what kind of kaffir you tink you are. Why don't you say Baas. I'm your Baas. Why don't you say Baas, hey?"

Brille blinked his eyes rapidly but by contrast his voice was strangely calm.

"I'm twenty years older than you," he said. It was the first thing that came to mind but the comrades seemed to think it a huge joke. A titter swept up the line. The next thing Warder Hannetjie whipped out a knobkerrie and gave Brille several blows about the head. What surprised his comrades was the speed with which Brille had removed his glasses or else they would have been smashed to pieces on the ground.

That evening in the cell Brille was very apologetic.

"I'm sorry, comrades," he said. "I've put you into a hell of a mess."

"Never mind, brother," they said. "What happens to one of us, happens to all."

"I'll try to make up for it, comrades," he said. "I'll steal something so that you don't go hungry."

Privately, Brille was very philosophical about his head wounds. It was the first time an act of violence had been perpetrated against him but he had long been a witness of extreme, almost unbelievable human brutality. He had twelve children and his mind travelled back that evening through the sixteen years of bedlam in which he had lived. It had all happened in a small drab little three-bedroomed house in a small drab little street in the Eastern Cape and the children kept coming year after year because neither he nor Martha ever managed the contraceptives the right way and a teacher's salary never allowed moving to a bigger house and he was always taking exams to improve his salary only to have it all eaten up by hungry mouths. Everything was pretty horrible, especially the way the children fought. They'd get hold of each other's heads and give them a good bashing against the wall. Martha gave up something along the line so they worked out a thing between them. The bashings, biting, and blood were to operate in full swing until he came home. He was to be the bogey-man and when it worked he never failed to have a sense of godhead at the way in which his presence could change savages into fairly reasonable human beings.

Yet somehow it was this chaos and mismanagement at the centre of his life that drove him into politics. It was really an ordered beautiful world with just a few basic slogans to learn along with the rights of mankind. At one stage, before things became very bad, there were conferences to attend, all very far away from home.

"Let's face it," he thought ruefully. "I'm only learning right now what it means to be a politician. All this while I've been running away from Martha and the kids."

And the pain in his head brought a hard lump to his throat. That was what the children did to each other daily and Martha wasn't managing and if Warder Hannetjie had not interrupted him that morning he would have sent the following message: "Be good comrades, my children. Cooperate, then life will run smoothly."

The next day Warder Hannetjie caught this old man of twelve children stealing grapes from the farm shed. They were an enormous quantity of grapes in a ten-gallon tin and for this misdeed the old man spent a week in the isolation cell. In fact, Span One as a whole was in constant trouble. Warder Hannetjie seemed to have eyes at the back of his head. He uncovered the trick about the cabbages, how they were split in two with the spade and immediately covered with earth and then unearthed again and eaten with split-second timing. He found out how tobacco smoke was beaten into the ground and he found out how conversations were whispered down the wind.

For about two weeks Span One lived in acute misery. The cabbages, tobacco, and conversations had been the pivot of jail life to them. Then one evening they noticed that their good old comrade who wore the glasses was looking rather pleased with himself. He pulled out a four-ounce packet of tobacco by way of explanation and the comrades fell upon it with great greed. Brille merely smiled. After all, he was the father of many children. But when the last shred had disappeared, it occurred to the comrades that they ought to be puzzled. Someone said: "I say, brother. We're watched like hawks these days. Where did you get the tobacco?"

"Hannetjie gave it to me," said Brille.

There was a long silence. Into it dropped a quiet bombshell.

"I saw Hannetjie in the shed today," and the failing eye-sight blinked rapidly. "I caught him in the act of stealing five bags of fertilizer and he bribed me to keep my mouth shut."

There was another long silence.

"Prison is an evil life," Brille continued, apparently discussing some irrelevant matter. "It makes a man contemplate all kinds of evil deeds."

He held out his hand and closed it.

"You know, comrades," he said. "I've got Hannetjie. I'll betray him tomorrow."

Everyone began talking at once.

"Forget it, brother. You'll get shot."

Brille laughed.

"I won't," he said. "That is what I mean about evil. I am a father of children and I saw today that Hannetjie is just a child and stupidly truthful. I'm going to punish him severely because we need a good warder."

The following day, with Brille as witness, Hannetjie confessed to the theft of the fertilizer and was fined a large sum of money. From then on Span One did very much as they pleased while Warder Hannetjie stood by and said nothing. But it was Brille who carried this to extremes. One day, at the close of work Warder Hannetjie said: "Brille, pick up my jacket and carry it back to the camp."

"But nothing in the regulations says I'm your servant, Hannetjie," Brille replied coolly.

"I've told you not to call me Hannetjie. You must say Baas," but Warder Hannetjie's voice lacked conviction. In turn, Brille squinted up at him.

"I'll tell you something about this Baas business, Hannetjie," he said. "One of these days we are going to run the

country. You are going to clean my car. Now, I have a fif-
teen-year-old son and I'd die of shame if you had to tell him
that I ever called you Baas."

Warder Hannetjie went red in the face and picked up his
coat.

On other occasion Brille was seen to be walking about the
prison yard, openly smoking tobacco. On being taken before
the prison commander he claimed to have received the
tobacco from Warder Hannetjie. All throughout the tirade
from his chief, Warder Hannetjie failed to defend himself but
his nerve broke completely. He called Brille to one side.

"Brille," he said. "This thing between you and me must
end. You may not know it but I have a wife and children and
you're driving me to suicide."

"Why don't you like your own medicine, Hannetjie?"
Brille asked quietly.

"I can give you anything you want," Warder Hannetjie
said in desperation.

"It's not only me but the whole of Span One," said Brille,
cunningly. "The whole of Span One wants something from
you."

Warder Hannetjie brightened with relief.

"I think I can manage if it's tobacco you want," he said.

Brille looked at him, for the first time struck with pity,
and guilt.

He wondered if he had carried the whole business too far.
The man was really a child.

"It's not tobacco we want, but you," he said. "We want
you on our side. We want a good warder because without a
good warder we won't be able to manage the long stretch
ahead."

Warder Hannetjie interpreted this request in his own fashion and his interpretation of what was good and human often left the prisoners of Span One speechless with surprise. He had a way of slipping off his revolver and picking up a spade and digging alongside Span One. He had a way of producing unheard-of luxuries like boiled eggs from his farm nearby and things like cigarettes, and Span One responded nobly and got the reputation of being the best work span in the camp. And it wasn't only take from their side. They were awfully good at stealing certain commodities like fertilizer which were needed on the farm of Warder Hannetjie.

1973

Edmundo Valadés

■

PERMISSION FOR DEATH IS GRANTED

In 1810 Father Miguel Hidalgo y Costilla, a parish priest in the Mexican village of Dolores, tried to rouse the Indian peasants against their tyrannical Spanish masters and led them in the first outbreak of what would be known as the Mexican Revolution when it crystallized a full century later. In 1917, after a bloody civil war, a constitution was drawn up, granting ownership of lands and water to the Republic, which in turn had the right to bestow it on private persons. The terms of the constitution also excluded the Church from any involvement with public education, made marriage a civil contract, and limited the activities of the clergy. The ruling aristocracy, however, paid little attention to the constitution. The land which the government occasionally turned over to the peasants was often unworkable; the aristocracy continued to rule and the Indians continued to be destitute.

■

O N THE PLATFORM the engineers are talking, laughing. They slap each other on the backs and tell clever jokes, a few dirty stories with hard punchlines. Little by little their attention is drawn towards the crowd in the hall. They stop discussing their latest party, giving the details about the new girl in the whorehouse. Their talk now turns to the men below, the collective farmers attending the assembly, down there, in front of them.

"Of course they must be saved. Assimilate them into our own civilization, cleanse their skin, corrupt their souls."

"You're sceptical, sir. And you doubt our efforts, and the efforts of the Mexican Revolution."

"You know it's useless. Those monkeys are hopeless. They're rotten with liquor, with ignorance. Look what came from giving them the land."

"You only see the obvious: you're a defeatist, my friend. We are the ones to blame. We gave them the land, and then? We sat back, terribly pleased with ourselves. But what about the mortgage payments, the fertilizers, the new techniques, the machinery? Will they invent all that on their own?"

The chairman, playing with his moustache, looks down at the hall through his glasses, unconcerned with the comings and goings of the engineers. When the strong, earthy animal smell of the men settling down on the benches reaches his nostrils, he takes out a coloured handkerchief and blows into it noisily. He also was once a peasant, but that was long ago. Now, thanks to the city and his official position, all that is left from those days are his handkerchief and the calluses on his hands.

The men in the hall take their seats solemnly, with the wariness peasants always show when entering a closed room, an assembly hall or a church. They say only a few words; they talk about harvests, rain, farm animals, mortgages. Many carry net lunchbags hanging from their shoulders, ready in case they get hungry. A few are smoking calmly, in no hurry, as if the cigarettes were growing out of their very hands. Others stand, leaning against the side walls, their arms crossed over their chests, mounting a peaceful guard.

The chairman shakes his bell and the sound makes the voices fade away. The engineers begin. They speak of technical problems, of the need of increasing production, of improving the crops. They promise to help the farmers, they urge them to voice their needs.

"We want to help, you can trust us."

Now it's the turn of the men in the hall. The chairman invites them to speak out. One hand rises slowly, timidly. Others follow. The farmers mention a few of their problems: the water, the elders, the mortgage, the school. Some are precise, to the point; others get entangled in their words, don't manage to make themselves clear. They scratch their heads and turn around to try and find what they were going to say, as if the idea had gone and hidden itself somewhere else, in the eyes of a fellow worker, or high above their heads where the lamp is hanging.

There, in one corner, a few of the men are whispering. They are all from the same village. Something serious seems to be worrying them. They consult with one another, discussing who is to speak for all of them.

"I think it should be Jilipe. He knows a lot."

"You, Juan, you spoke the other time."

They can't make up their minds. The men whose names have been mentioned wait to be pushed forward. An old farmer, perhaps one of the elders, decides for them:

"Let it be Sacramento."

Sacramento waits.

"Go on, lift your hand."

The hand goes up but the chairman doesn't see it. Others are more visible and are called first. Sacramento looks at the old man. One of the younger farmers, almost a boy, lifts his hand as high as it will go. Over the forest of hairy heads five dark fingers appear, dirty with earth. The chairman sees the hand. The group has the floor.

"Now stand up."

The hand goes down as Sacramento rises to his feet. He tries to find a place for his hat. The hat becomes a vast nuisance, it grows, it doesn't seem to fit anywhere. Sacramento holds it in his hands. The men at the table become impatient. The chairman's voice springs up, full of authority, of command:

"You! You asked to speak. We're waiting."

Sacramento fixes his eyes on the engineer at the far end of the table. It seems as if he will speak only to him, as if the others had all disappeared and only the two of them had remained in the room.

"I want to speak for all of us at San Juan de las Manzanas. We bring a complaint against the municipal president because he's always fighting us and we can't take it no more. First he took some land away from Felipe Perez and Juan Hernandez because it was next to his own. We sent a telegram to Mexico City and they didn't even bother to answer. We got together and talked, and thought that it would be a good idea to go to the Agricultural Committee to get the lands back. Well, it was of no use, neither going there nor showing the papers. The municipal president kept the lands."

Sacramento speaks without changing the expression on his face, as if he were mumbling some kind of old prayer of which he knows both the beginning and the end by heart.

"So then, when he saw us all angry, he accused us of being troublemakers. You would have thought it was us who had taken the lands. And then he came back with his accounts – mortgage papers, sir. He said we were behind in the payments. And the agent agreed. He said we had to pay all sorts of interests. Crescencio, who lives over the hill, near the water, and who understands about numbers, added them up and saw that it wasn't true: he just wanted to make us pay more. So the municipal president brought some gentlemen from Mexico City, with all kinds of documents, and they said that if we didn't pay they'd take all our lands away. You see, so to speak, he made us pay for what we didn't owe him . . ."

Sacramento tells his story with no emphasis, with no deliberate pauses. It's as if he were plowing the land. His words fall like seeds, sowing.

"Then afterwards the thing about my son, sir. The boy's hot-blooded, sir. I didn't want him to do it. I tried to stop him. He had drunk a bit and the wine had gone to his head. There was nothing I could do. He went out to find the municipal president, to talk to him, face to face . . . They killed the boy, just like that, saying that he was stealing one of the municipal president's cows. They sent him back dead, his face blown to shreds . . ."

Sacramento's throat trembles. Only that. He's still standing, like a tree that has taken root. Nothing else. His eyes are still fixed on the engineer, the same one at the far end of the table.

"Then there was the water. Because there was very little, because of the bad rains, the Municipal President had closed the canal. And the cornfields were drying up, and the people were fearing a bad year . . . so we went to see him, to ask him to give us just a little water, sir, just enough for our crops. And he greeted us with angry words, and wouldn't listen. He didn't even get off his mule, to spite us."

A hand tugs at Sacramento's sleeve. One of his fellow farmers whispers something to him. Sacramento's voice is the only sound in the hall.

"If this were not enough – because, thanks to the Holy Virgin, there were more rains and we saved about half the crops – there was what happened on Saturday. The Municipal President went out with his men, bad men they are, and stole two of our girls: Lupita, who was going to marry Herminio, and Crescencio's daughter. They took us all by surprise, because we were out in the fields, and so we couldn't stop them. They dragged them struggling to the hills and then left them there. When the girls managed to get back they were in very bad shape, beaten up and everything. We didn't have to ask to know what had happened. And now the people were really furious, fed up of having to be at the mercy of such a master."

For the first time Sacramento's voice shook, with menace, anger, determination.

"And as no one will listen to us, because we've been to all the authorities and we don't know where justice is to be found, we want to make arrangements here. You," and Sacramento's eyes now swept the engineers until they reached the head of the table, "you, who promised us help, we ask your permission to punish the municipal president of San Juan de las Manzanas. We ask you to allow us to take justice in our hands . . ."

All eyes are now fixed on the men on the platform. The chairman and the engineers look at each other in silence. Then they talk.

"This is absurd. We can't allow this unthinkable request."

"No, my friend. It's not absurd. Absurd would be to leave the matter in the hands of those who have done nothing, of those who haven't even listened. It would be cowardly to wait until our justice made justice. These men would never believe in us again. I'd rather stand on these men's side, with their primitive justice, yes, but justice of some kind, and assume whatever responsibility is to be assumed. As far as I'm concerned we simply have to grant them what they ask."

"But we're civilized, we've got institutions; we can't just set them aside."

"It would be justifying outlaws, savages."

"What worse outlaw than the man they accuse? If he had offended us as he has offended them, if he had caused us the grievances he has caused them, we would certainly have killed him. We would certainly have ignored a system of justice that doesn't work. I say that we should vote on their proposal."

"I agree."

"But these people are all liars; we should at least try to find out the truth. And anyway, we have no authority to grant a request like that."

Now the chairman intervenes. The peasant inside him rises to speak. His voice admits no argument.

"The assembly will decide. I'll take the responsibility."

He turns towards the hall. His voice is a peasant's voice, the same voice that he must have used in the hills, mixed with the earth, speaking to his people.

"We are voting on the proposal of the farmers of San Juan de las Manzanas. Those who agree they should be given permission to execute the Municipal President, please raise your hands . . ."

All hands rise. Even those of the engineers. There is not a single man who has not lifted his hand, showing his approval. Each finger points to an immediate, unavoidable death.

"The assembly grants permission to the farmers of San Juan de las Manzanas for their request."

Sacramento, who has remained standing, calmly finishes his speech. There is neither joy nor pain in what he is about to say. His expression is serene, clear-cut.

"Thank you for the permission, sir, because, as no one would listen to us, since yesterday morning the municipal president of San Juan de las Manzanas is dead."

1955
Translated by Alberto Manguel

Seán O'Faoláin

■

THE
DEATH OF
STEVEY LONG

*After the Great Potato Famine of the 1840s, which halved
the population of Ireland, and three Home Rule Bills
(though the last never came into effect), Ireland was left
divided, its northern half still under the authority of Great
Britain and in a constant state of bloody civil unrest. In the
North, the ancestral hatred between Catholics and Protes-
tants imbued every person and every event and seeped into
the background of every Irish writer. In the South, in the
Irish Republic, the tension was compounded by the
overwhelming presence of the Catholic Church, which exer-
cised its censorship relentlessly. Seán O'Faoláin, who had
fought in his youth for an independent Ireland and had
found himself banned after his first book was published,
considered the future of his country in 1946, in his own
middle age: "A parochial Ireland, bounded by its shores,
has no part in our vision of the ideal nation that will yet
come out of this present dull period."*

■

MACROOM CASTLE was built somewhere in the sixteenth century by the MacCarthys, a building of great height raised on a solitary outcrop of rock and with a moat and a demesne reaching down to the river-edge. As Macroom is the last town on the western road through the mountainy divide of Cork and Kerry the castle has always become a barracks in troubled times, the last outpost for the wild, disaffected country beyond. It has a long history: it suffered at least one siege, and passed through several hands. The O'Sullivans lost it in 1606 to the Earl of Cork and in 1675 the crown confiscated it and put troops in it to overawe the rebels to the West, that broken land impenetrable to everyone but tories and raparees. It had its dungeons and its secret passages, and in fact when the Tans took it over as a barracks, in their time, they thought it best to close up several doors that, it seemed to them, led nowhere. But it was not a suitable place to imprison anyone; the river bred too many rats and moles and beavers, and when the mountains sent their rain-water churning down the rocky valleys the floods rose so high that they overflowed into the basement, and from the later-built cells a little higher up a prisoner could see the trees and the hedges growing out of the water almost on a level with his eye.

In one of these cells, his elbows resting easily on the window-sill, stood Stevey Long gazing westward to where the faint blue of the mountains was barely discernible against a white sky. Beside him was a little man whose finger-tips barely clutched the stone edge on which Stevey leaned, and as he strained up to peep at the mountains Stevey looked down at him with amusement.

"They'll shoot you tonight, Fahy," said Stevey suddenly.

"Ah, shtop that talk now, Long," said the little man with an imploring upward glance.

"Oh, but I hear them saying it," said Stevey. "'Bring out that fat murderer of a teacher,' they'll say. Or they'll say, 'Bring up that assassin of a teacher, and we'll teach him'."

"Oh, suffering Heart!" wailed the teacher. "Me nerves is all upsot. Shtop it now, Long. It's not fair."

As Stevey gazed off contemptuously at the mountains the teacher defended himself.

"Anyway," he said, "I never let on to be a fightin' man. And it's all very well for you. You haven't a wife and seven children."

"Seven children?" asked Stevey. "Is that all you have, teacher? You ought to be ashamed of yourself."

"Isn't it enough? You're mocking again, Long. Saying your prayers would befit you better. That dirty tongue of yours will bring the wrath of God on us."

"My tongue," said Stevey vehemently, "is our only hope."

"Then why," said the teacher peevishly, "don't you get round that bastard of a jailer for us?"

"Oh! Oh! Bastard? Naughty word, teacher. Naughty word!"

"Go to hell," said the little man in an agony of anger and fear, and he retired to a corner of the cell, by now almost in tears.

Stevey went to the iron door of the cell and listened for any sound in the passage-way. Then in one of his sudden rages he stooped over his companion.

"Haven't I told him enough lies to drown a cathedral? Said I was at Festubert? Said I had an English wife? Said I knew Camden Town and Highgate like the palm of me hand? Told him every dirty story I ever read or heard? And what have you done but sit there and cry?" – and he raised his hand as one might to a child – "you long-faced lubber!"

Stevey returned to the window.

"And after all that," he continued, "all he says is, 'Aow! How interesting!' God, how I despise the English!"

"It's no use, Stevey," said the teacher. "We can't get round him."

The teacher would have been secretly pleased if Stevey would believe it. For two weeks he had had to sit in that unsanitary cell listening at all hours of the day and night to Stevey and the Tan who had been on cell-fatigue since they came, exchanging indecent stories. Stevey poured them out without an effort of memory: stories he had heard in the pubs and garages and lavatories of Cork, stories he had read in the *Decameron*, the *Heptameron*, French joke-books, Maupassant, the Bible – at first to the amazement, and gradually to the horror of the little teacher. He had read nothing since he left his Training College ten years before, and he still talked of Dickens on the strength of the one novel he was obliged to read there. What horrified him most of all was to find himself gradually inveigled into listening to these stories, and (with a start) he would find himself grinning with delight before he realized that the sewer-stream had been let loose once again. Stevey was a plumber by trade – he was always saying how proud his father was of "the profession" – and he would begin to talk of red-lead or three-inch pipes, and proceed slowly via lavatory-traps, the sewers of Paris, chronic constipation,

tablets for anaemia, or cures for impotency, to the brothels of
the world or the famous courtesans of history – all with great
seriousness and a show of modest indignation – and he would
illustrate with a vast amount of inaccurate, and even for his
subject, defamatory detail at which the teacher's eyes would
swell and his fat head would shake with wonder and sudden
enlightenment. Or he would spend a whole night hinting at
his affairs with the loose girls of the city, returning quickly to
the cess-pools or chloride-of-lime if the teacher showed disapproval, or to Margaret of Navarre or Boccaccio as if his
life, too, were one long legend and romance. But he could
pollute even the sweetest women of literature, and the teacher
would find himself trapped again when Stevey would fling
Madame Bovary or Boule de Suif or Tess into the same bawdy-
box as Mata Hari or some creature out of the *Rat Bleu et Jaune*
or some local beshawled laneway light-o'-love just previously
removed to the city madhouse. To the Tan he was as the
Shahrazade to her Persian king. The Englishman heard such
stories from him as he had never heard in tap-room or bar-
rack-square – even an old story would become fresh and vivid
in Stevey's mouth, and weak with laughter he would scarcely
have enough strength to turn the key in the door as he stag-
gered off roaring with delight to retail what he had heard
to his comrades upstairs. Then Stevey would, as now, return
to the window muttering contemptuous curses under his
breath and appeal to Fahy for something to add to his stock
of bawdry. When Fahy would reply with an apologetic wail
that, "I was always on the althar, Stevey," or, "I was a great
Confraternity man, Stevey," the gunman would lose himself
in gazing at the pale, far-off horizons, wave after wave of land,
paling into the all-but-invisible peaks of the real hinterland

fifty miles away. Since the days of the Earls of Cork a hundred rebelly Irishmen must have gazed just as longingly at those changeless mountain-tops, thinking first of the misfortune of their capture, then of wives or friends, then of the fate in store for them, but soon reduced, as they looked out on the unattainable freedom of the hills, to thinking of nothing at all, waiting only for the dusk and the dark and the forgetfulness of sleep. None can have spent his hours, as Stevey did, thinking to coax his English jailer with bawdry, but few, if any, can have been as cruel, and as cunning, and (it must be admitted) as fearless, as Stevey Long.

Suddenly steps clanked down the passage-way and the cell began to taint of gas – the jailer had turned on the tap outside the door, and the little blue flame leaped up on the shelf above the lintel, and the circle cut in the centre of the door was filled by an eye.

"Hey!" whispered the Tan.

"Yes," said Stevey, at the door in a flash.

"You two blokes are to be moved."

"Where?" asked Stevey while the little teacher crowded up against him to listen.

"Cork Male Prison," said the Tan.

Stevey groaned. There was an end to his hopes of escape from the castle, and he knew Cork Jail well enough not to like it. The eye disappeared and was replaced by a pair of lips.

"But you ain't goin'!" they whispered cautiously.

"Why not?" asked Stevey, excited with hope.

"Cos' I 'ave other plans for you," said the Tan, blinking a wink at them. "I won't 'ave it. 'Ere's the order," he said curtaining the circle for a moment with a buff paper. "There's two deserters here from the Wiltshires, higher up than you, right upstairs, and I'm jolly well going to run them out on this order. They came in an hour ago and they're blind and blotto with Irish moonshine."

"Oh," said Stevey, "but you can't . . ."

"See if I don't," said the Tan, and he opened the door and entered the cell. He cornered Stevey by the window and prodded his chest with his finger as it were a revolver or a knife.

"Hark at me!" he said.

"Yes?" said Stevey and the little teacher put in his fat face to listen.

"Go away, you," growled the Tan, and Fahy retired like a kicked dog. "Go and stand by the door and hear if anybody's coming."

He turned to Stevey.

"You know about my wife?"

Stevey did indeed know about the wife. She had been, he always knew it, his main hope. She was London-Irish and a Catholic, and it was she who made Stevey declare his wife was London-Irish and a Catholic too, by Heaven.

"Yes," said Stevey.

"She keeps on nagging at me in her letters," complained the Tan. "She's delicate, and she has nerves, and she's a Catholic." (This last seemed to be a great grievance with him.) "I was proud of all that when I married her. It's so romantic, I thinks to myself, to have a delicate wife that's a Catholic into the bargain. But now! She says I'm earning blood-money. I told her about you, and she writes and says she weeps to think of you. But that's all right. She weeps to think of anything, she does. I don't mind that. But now she says such things about leaving the kids and going to live with her married sister that I don't trust her."

"I wouldn't trust her," says Stevey.

"How I 'ate married sisters," said the Tan; and then, "Why wouldn't you trust her?"

"She's all alone in London," said Stevey in a gloomy voice.

"She's got her kids. She's got her married sister."

"Ah," said Stevey in a hollow voice, "but where's her husband? From what we know of women," he continued seriously, "and especially married women," he added with an air of sad wisdom, "you can't trust a woman that's separated from a man that she thinks isn't fond of her."

"Nor I don't trust her," said the Tan. "And I'm goin' home. That's where you come in."

"Yes," said Stevey like a shot. "I could get you out of this country within ten hours, without anybody knowing it – if I were free."

"You've said so. Dozens of men – deserting, if you like to put it that way."

"It's my job," said Stevey. "City of Cork Steam Packet to Liverpool. Think you were travelling first-class. Easy as that."

"I'll chance it," said the Tan. "Back to London I must get. To tell you the truth I'm sick of this bloody place."

From inside his uniform he pulled a hacksaw and a length of stout rope. Stevey took them in a grab.

"After dark," said the Tan. "I'll bring supper as usual. Now get to work and quietly. If that blade cracks I can't get you another one."

As he opened the door to go Stevey's mind flamed; as fast as a bullet it flew to the old coach road south-west of the castle where they would probably begin their trek west or east.

"Sst," he called.

The Tan turned.

"Take a message for me to the village," said Stevey.

"No," said the Tan.

"You must," said Stevey. With a stub of pencil he wrote on a sheet of paper from the Tan's pocket-book, and gave it to him. The Tan read it and winked back at Stevey.

"It's the little bicycle-shop just across the bridge," said Stevey.

"You're a clever fellow," said the Tan. "Of course we must have bikes."

When he was gone Stevey wound the rope round the belly of the teacher and put him with his back to the door so as to cover the spyhole and listen for approaching feet. Then he began, stealthily at first, to saw at the first of the three bars in the window.

"This scratching," he said, "will be heard all over the town of Macroom."

"If we only had a bit of grease for it," said the teacher like a fool.

"I once read about Casanova," said Stevey, and then he stopped talking and hacked away.

"By God," cried the teacher, "I once heard a story about that fellow . . ."

"Eat it," said Stevey, working like a madman.

The evening was now falling, and as Stevey worked the interior of the cell grew dark. Away to the south-west the sun was sinking over the distant mountains and as she sank they grew first a rich, deep brown, and then purple, "their very peaks became transparent," and lastly they paled into an unreal mist. The last level rays threw Stevey's shadows on the iron door and the limed wall, and the little teacher's face was warmed to a ruddy glow. As the air grew cold and rarefied they heard all the sounds of the village life, the children that cried out in their play and the cart that lumbered over the cobbles of the bridge.

About half-past six o'clock the teacher, weary and stiff for so long standing in a fixed position, was almost glad to announce the approach of footsteps. By that time Stevey had cut to within a feather's breadth the top and bottom of two of the bars, filling with clay from the floor the shining track of the saw through the steel. The clanking steps came to the door – it was their friend the Tan. He laid their supper on the bench and bent his head to whisper.

"I'm going with you," he said to Stevey. "Mind you promise to get me out of it safe and sound."

"I swear to Christ," said Stevey like a shot.

The little teacher was like a kettle on the hob with excitement.

"Naow!" said the Tan. "No swearing. Parole. Give me your parole, word of honour."

"Word of honour," said Stevey, without a thought.

"Oh, God, yes, word of honour," said the teacher heatedly.

"Shut up, you," said the Tan angrily, and the little fellow piped down miserably, fearing to be left behind if he angered either of them.

"The Tommies are gone to Cork," said the Tan with a grin. "There'll be hell to pay when they get in with the Shinners in Cork Jail. When will we go?"

"When is sundown?" asked Stevey. "Is there a moon?"

The Tan consulted his diary.

"Six forty-six, sun sets. Full moon, eight-ten."

"It'll be dark at eight," said Stevey. "We'll go then."

"Is he coming?" said the Tan, pointing to the teacher.

"We'll bring him," said Stevey.

The Tan looked at the teacher and then he went away without a word. They ate but little that night and Stevey kept going and coming in a corner of the cell.

"God," he said nervously, "I'm like a cistern tonight."

"Will we go wesht?" asked the teacher, stuttering with terror.

"You'll go wesht if you're not careful," said Stevey. "Remember that bastard has a gun in his hind-pocket. And we have none."

They kept watching for the faint moon but the reflected glow of the village and the fluttering light of the gas-jet confused them. All the country to the west was now wrapped in night and the mountains could no longer be seen. With the fall of darkness their ears became sharper and they could hear now the last cries of the children quite plainly and the murmur of the river far below. A mist spread itself over the land before their window, and a faint mooing of cattle occasionally came out of the darkness. As he peered into it Stevey made up his mind that he would not go west – he was sick of that wild, broken country where, as he used to say, "they ploughed the land with their teeth," sick of the poor food, the dry bread and jam, the boiled tea and salted bacon, sick of the rough country girls. He was pining for the lights and gaiety of the city and he decided he would do a little "deserting" of his own. When the Englishman came down, sharp at eight, he had donned a civilian's coat over his green-black policeman's trousers and a wide-brimmed bowler hat that pressed his two ears out like railway signals.

"Ready?" he whispered.

Stevey nodded. From outside he extinguished the jet and plunged the cell in darkness. Stevey unwound the rope from the belly of the teacher, and the Tan pressed with all his might on the cut bars. They would not give. Stevey dropped the rope and threw his weight on them and still they held. The Tan swore, the teacher entangled himself in the rope, and Stevey searched in the dark for the saw. At last he found it and with a few sharp rasps the blade broke through the steel. It was easy then to bend the bars up on a level with the higher coping, and when the rope had been tied to the uncut bar and flung out into the dark they were ready.

"I'll go first," said Stevey, "and signal with one pull on the rope if everything is clear below. Send him after" – pointing to the teacher. "And come last yourself."

"Oh," moaned the teacher, as he looked at the aperture, "I'm too fat to get through that." But they paid no heed to him.

Stevey wriggled out first, his feet scraping the wall as he was pushed behind by the other two.

"I'll never get through them bars," wailed the teacher in a deep whisper to nobody in particular.

Stevey vanished downward, swaying as he went, hand over hand. He landed in a great bed of stinging nettles and resisting an impulse to turn and run for it he listened for a second. The little river gurgled noisily below him; he could distinctly hear the quiet munching of cattle just beyond the mound where he stood. He pulled the rope once and stood looking up. A faint white radiance was beginning to appear where the moon was rising on his left. Stevey saw the teacher's fat legs waving in the air and his fat bottom squirming skyward. But there he remained, not advancing an inch, and after a long pause he was pulled in again, and Stevey saw the bare shins of the Tan, then his black trousers dragged up to the knees, then his body following after. In a second he too was among the nettles.

"Where's Fahy?" asked Stevey in a whisper.

"Come on," said the Tan fiercely.

The fat pale face of the teacher appeared at the window.

"I can't get out," he wailed in a loud whisper.

"Use the saw," said Stevey. "We can't wait." And he clambered down the mound, grinding his teeth as a pile of loose stones rumbled after him down the slope.

"Ssh!" said the Tan. "The sentries will hear us."

"Lie still," said Stevey, and they dropped on the dew-wet grass. They heard a sentry's voice call to his mate, and the mate's reply. They heard the grounding of arms, and then the noisy river, and the wind in the willows above them shivering and whispering incessantly by the river's edge. After a while they rose and in a stooping posture they half-walked, half-ran along by the edge of the river through the grass, feeling the ground (when they left the river) rise steeper and steeper, and when they fell panting again on the ground, there below them was the black pile of the castle and the hundred eyes of the town.

"That bloody teacher nearly ruined us," said the Tan.

"He'll never get out," said Stevey.

But he soon forgot him, and he did not in fact live to know what happened to him in the end. They were now standing on the soft dust of the old coach road, below them the next valley, and, as if it were standing on the tip of the distant ridge beyond, the great ruby moon. To Stevey it was all familiar and congenial, but to the Englishman it was cold and desolate.

"We're out of it," said Stevey gaily, and he slapped the Englishman on the back.

"I'm in it," said the Tan gloomily. "Well, where are the bikes?"

At that Stevey squared his shoulders and clenched his fists. He looked up and down the narrow, shaded road, and then at the Tan. He looked down at the far-off lights of the town and at the Tan again. Then he jerked his head onward.

"This way," he said. "They should be here."

He went on ahead, peering right and left, whispering in a low voice as he went "Jimmy? Jimmy?" When he passed a blasted oak a bicycle fell clattering on the road at his feet. He peered up and there was a gaitered leg and the tail of the inevitable trench-coat. Everything was happening just as he expected it.

"Here's one," he shouted. "Try is the other there," and he pointed backwards to the opposite side of the lane. As the Tan groped in the far ditch Stevey whispered madly to the hidden figure.

"Have ye the skits?"

"Yes."

"Get 'em ready."

"How many are there?" said the voice.

"One."

Then Stevey shouted back to the Tan.

"Have you got it?"

"No."

"Here," called Stevey. "Hold this one."

The unsuspecting man came forward to hold the bicycle, and as he took it Stevey passed behind his back. The bicycle crashed as Stevey leaped like a tiger at his neck, roaring at the

same time to "Jimmy" to give a hand. Two trench-coated figures leaped from the hedges at the cry and fell on the struggling shouting soldier, and in two minutes he was bound with
Stevey's trouser belt and his kicking legs held and tied with
a bit of cord. Finally his yelling mouth was stoppered by
Stevey's handkerchief and then, except for their panting and
an occasional squirm from the helpless man at their feet
everything was deadly quiet again.

"Gimme his skit," said Stevey.

The captive looked up with the light of terror glaring in
his eyes. Stevey stood over him for a second with his finger
wavering on the trigger.

"Here," he said then to one of the two. "You do it. I gave
him my word I wouldn't."

He made for the bike, dusting himself as he went, and
threw his leg over the saddle. A horrible double sound of a
revolver being discharged tore through the night.

"Gimme that," said Stevey.

The revolver was handed to him, and he thrust it in his
pocket.

"Are you sure he's finished?" he asked.

"Sure," said the other.

"Good-bye boys," said Stevey, and he pedalled swiftly
along the dark lane.

Presently he freewheeled on to the lower road and came
to a dimly-lighted pub. An old cart and a sleepy horse were
tethered outside the door. This was the pub known as The
Half-way House, and Stevey decided that he needed a free
whisky. First peering through the glass door he entered.
There was nobody inside but the bar-girl and an old farmer
leaning in the corner of the counter and the wall; the girl said

nothing, and the old farmer merely nodded. Those were tough times, and they had heard the double shot.

"Any Tans about?" said Stevey when he had ordered his drink.

The girl only shook her head silently and poured the drink, watching him as he swallowed it. The farmer lowered his eyes to sip his porter whenever Stevey looked at him, raising them slowly whenever he felt he was not being watched, nodding and smiling foolishly whenever Stevey's eyes caught him. A tiny clock among the whisky bottles ticked so loudly in the silence that Stevey looked up at it startled. It was nearly nine o'clock.

"By God, it's late," he said.

The girl nodded and said nothing, and when Stevey looked at the farmer he was turning his glass round and round in its own wet circle, his eyes shooting side-glances towards Stevey all the while.

"Christ," swore Stevey, "you are a talkative pair!" And putting down his empty glass he strode out between the swinging doors and walked to his bicycle. Then it occurred to him to return on tip-toe and listen at the glass-doors. The old farmer was speaking:

"Aye," he was saying, "a bit o' money is a great thing."

"Yes," said the girl listlessly.

"Sons how are ye!" said the farmer.

"Aye," responded the girl. There was a pause, and then:

"Money is betther than sons any day," said the farmer.

"Yes sure," said the girl with a sigh.

With a superior grin Stevey mounted and rode away.

Had Stevey kept his word with the Englishman he might be alive today. He would certainly have avoided Cork that night. But now, knowing nothing of what awaited him and with nobody to warn him, he covered, in less than four hours, the forty odd miles that separate Macroom from Cork. He had cycled along the winding roads among the bogs where the mountains come down to the plains, and when the mountains vanished from sight he pedalled over a bare, high plateau where he measured the distance not by prominent hills or valleys but by a tree here and a tree there, or a cross-road, a familiar house, or a school. At last he came to the valley of the city river and for miles he cycled above it, straight as a crow's flight to the edge of the city. It was about one o'clock when he stood looking down over all its sleeping roofs as over a vale of quietness, a slight drizzle of rain beginning to fall, a gentle wind blowing it in his eyes as he peered across to the uttermost farthest light that marked the remote side of the city to the north where his father lived. He might have made a long detour to reach Fair Hill, but why should he? Had he known the city was under curfew he would never have dared to do anything else, but his two weeks in Macroom Castle were two weeks cut off from the world, and now, flinging his bike into the ditch, he dropped downhill into the danger of the streets.

After his three long months in the mountains it was sweet to feel the ring of the pavements instead of the pad-pad of the mud roads, to see the walls and the gas-lamps all about him, so sheltering after the open darkness of the country nights. But as he went on the streets were so strangely empty, even for one o'clock in the morning – there was not even a wandering dog abroad – that Stevey became worried and ill at ease. As he approached the open business section of the city especially he began to realize what a grave risk he was taking in coming back into the city at all where he was well known for a gunman; but to come late at night, with no crowds to mingle with, and the police on the alert for late wanderers was doubly dangerous. Still, as the mist thickened, became heavier, finally changed into a wind-blown downpour, it did not occur to him that any reason other than bad weather was required to explain the strange emptiness of the streets, until suddenly, not more than a few blocks away, a dozen rifle-shots broke through the hiss of the falling rain, loud above the river purling in its narrow bed. Stevey halted in his stride. Then as there was no repetition of the sound he went on, down to the quays that shone under the arclights webbed with moisture.

The rain hissed into the river, cold and spearlike, and his calves were now wet, and his face and shoulders and he could feel his coat was sodden through. Then, in and out of the glow of the lamps on the pathway in front of him he saw a girl racing in his direction, calling as she ran to another girl to hurry, the other calling to her to wait. It was a relief to Stevey to meet somebody, but when the first girl, who ran against the rain with lowered head, rushed into his arms and then screamed and cowered away from him into the wall – he stood angry and astonished.

"Oh! Sir, sir!" she wailed. "I'm goin' home."

"Hello, hello!" said Stevey. "What's up with you?"

"I'm goin' home, sir," she said again, trying to cower past him. "I am, honest."

"Well, go home!" cried Stevey exasperated, and passed on. The other girl, he found, had turned and fled from him as from the devil.

Stevey now observed that the houses towering about him were almost pitchy black. All the erect oblongs of light had long since moved up nearer the roofs, wavered there for a while, and then vanished suddenly; the sitting-rooms had become bedrooms and then been blotted out, and now only red eyes of light showed bedroom walls where one could no longer see bedroom windows. Once a moving candle-flare showed the turn of a stairs, a landing, a high window. Bare boards, thought Stevey, under bare feet unheeding the silver of hammered nails in the white wood, long white neck-frilled night-dresses bending over the balustrade to call to a tiled hallway for surety of locked doors. A blind sank down, squares walking up its yellow ground. A pair of gold parallelograms disappeared, and then began to reappear and vanish, faint or defined, but never steady for a moment, and to Stevey's thought a woman curved over the flames, her fingers slipping her shoes from her feet, silken stockings falling after. All the while the rain lashed the shining pavement – a real mixture of March wind and April shower – and the spouts poured their overflow across the cement flags. Everyone was asleep in bed but he. He possessed the whole city, as if it had been made for him alone.

Again the rifle-shots rang out and this time they were followed by a rattle of machine-gun fire and a few isolated explosions. Again Stevey halted, drawing into a door and peering along the quays. He felt that after his fortnight in prison and his three months in the hills he was become a stranger to this city-world in which he had once moved so easily and safely, and he wished he had made a call in some friendly house before entering the city – it almost seemed to him as if something strange and unusual were occurring around him. He left the quays at this thought, and began to dodge among the side-lanes and the back-streets, but to cross the river he finally had to come into the open. As he crossed the railway bridge he saw on the opposite quay, spread across the street, a squad of

soldiers whose accoutrements and arms glinted in the rain and
the arclights, and seeing their weapons at the ready he drew
back behind a girder and waited. They were approaching
gradually and he knew that he would certainly be discovered
if he remained there. He moved in quick bird-like leaps across
the bridge, from the shelter of one girder to the shelter of
another, peeping all the time at his enemy. Then he had to
leave the bridge and cross the street. His heart beat faster; he
breathed quickly. He heard a cry of "Halt" and he took to his
heels. Over his head, by his very ears it seemed to him, whistled the bullets. At once he took to the side-lanes, up and
down and in and out until he had lost his pursuers and himself
thoroughly, and exhausted he fell back into a doorway to
think. It did not take him long to realize this time that it was
Curfew, long threatened even while he was in the mountains,
suddenly clapped on the city while he was in jail, and he had
walked like a fool into the net. His hand stole to the revolver
in his pocket. If he had been caught with that it would have
meant anything. Now completely unnerved he left the door,
halting at the slightest noise, looking around every lane-
corner and down every passage-way before he dared pass
them by. Gradually he began to recognize where he was – in
the network of lanes between the river and the fish-markets,
an isolated quarter to leave which would bring him into the
open streets once more. A lecherous pair of cats made him
leap for an arched alley-way. He laughed at himself the next
minute but he realized that he could never hope to reach Fair
Hill in this way, across the other bridge and along another set
of naked quays. Over his head Shandon boomed out two
o'clock – there would be at least three hours more of Curfew.
He wiped the sweat of fear from his forehead and peeped cau-

tiously out of his alley-way, thanking his good-fortune that he did so, for the next instant the heavens seemed to open with light and every cranny and crevice of the lane was flooded by a powerful searchlight. At the same moment he heard the soft whirring of a car and low voices. He was taut and trembling like a string that has been made vibrate by a blow. He thought he heard steps approaching and he slunk backwards down the alley, halting in doors and watching the flooded light of the lane, beyond the tunnel of the arch. He came to the alley-end and his feet crunched on the head of a dead fish, the guts oozing under his heels. He glanced about the great pitch-dark square – he was in the markets. In the limelight of the arch far down the alley he saw two khaki figures who turned towards him and entered the arch and faced the wall. It was enough for Stevey – he turned and crouched his way along the markets, slipping on the rotting vegetables and the slime of fishgut, resting in door after door with something of the feeling that he had walked into the wrong region, that here were troops of men, that in any other part of the city it would have been far different if not entirely safe. But he felt his last turn taken when a whirring lorry roared suddenly around the corner and its floodlight poured into the street, lighting the very pavement at his feet, where he stood with his back to a door; and as if to give him no possible chance he saw, and cursed as he saw, that the jambs and lintel and panels were pure white. With the instinct of the trapped man he crushed back against it and the nearer the car came the more he crushed. Slowly, as he pressed against it, the door swung open behind him. He passed in and closed it behind him and listened, not even breathing, while the car passed slowly by. Then he began to breathe tremblingly, and panting, and with his hand to his heart, he laughed quietly to himself. Trust Stevey, said he to himself, to get out of any corner.

The hallway was blackness unbroken, and with his two hands out, one grasping his revolver, a crucified gunman, he groped his way in. His feet struck the first knee of the stairs, and he began to climb. A window-sill and an empty pot – he passed it by. A lead-lined sink and a dripping tap – he moved on upwards. A door. Was this a man or a family, or a lone woman? Damn dangerous business this, thought Stevey to himself; but not half so dangerous as the streets. What should he do? Sleep in the hall? Clear out? Neither. Was it Stevey Long not to get himself a good doss for the night? As his father would say, he must think of "the profession." He moved up higher and came to a landing window. Through it he could see Shandon dark against the glowing sky of the city. Across in another house he could see a back-window all lit up, and framed in it two men, both in pants and shirts. He could hear their quarrel, see the bigger of the two crash his fist into the face of the other, see a ragged-haired lane-woman drag them apart. Then the light vanished as she moved away upstairs with the candle, and the small man wiping the blood from his cheeks stumbled downstairs out of sight. Looking up diagonally Stevey saw a landing; looking down, the dark well of the stairs; through the window a tin roof on which the chutes above dripped and dripped. He went up to the landing and here he noticed a streak of yellow light at the base of the door. He tapped softly, hardly knowing what he was doing. He knocked again and still there was no reply. He peeped through the keyhole and there before a warm fire he saw an old woman sitting bolt upright in her chair.

Even to Stevey the old woman was a touching sight, her corrugated hands clasping her crucifix, her mouth all wrinkled and folded, her eyes lost in the firelight. He was moved by the peace of this room high above the markets and the river, warm after the rain. How cosy she looked! – no, not cosy, but how calm, and yes, how holy! How holy! Stevey smiled and shook his head at her. He looked at her more closely. Then he entered, closing the door softly behind him. He laid his hand on her shoulder – on her face – on her left breast. She was dead.

He looked around him slowly, and slowly he removed his wet coat, hanging it on a chair before the glowing fire. Then he sat quietly warming his hands to the flames, stretching his long legs, and drying his face. He chuckled quietly to himself. Here was joy!

He awoke before dawn and thinking he felt a little cold he threw fresh coals on the fire. Feeling thirsty he drank half the milk in the glass beside him. Then he fell asleep again until a church bell tolling faintly in the distance gradually percolated through to his senses. For a full two minutes he stared sleepily and in wonder at the corpse seated beside him, and then, as the cries of the market-girls came to his ears his mind reverted to the city. He realized at once that he was back among his own people, as safe as a house.

He rose stretching his stiff shoulders and began to move through the house. As for the old lady, he did not trouble himself about her – heart disease no doubt or a sudden stroke, and he remembered the warm fire and the fresh glass of milk. One room was full of strange lumber, and as he peeped at the markets through the drawn blinds his hand fell idly on an old album. When he opened it and it began to ping-pong out its little tune he shut it with a fright and hoped nobody heard. The back-room was an ordinary sitting-room. He saw a chess-board and wondered cunningly who played chess in that seemingly empty house. Surely there must be a man somewhere he thought, and he felt certain of it when his eye fell on a great brass-horned gramophone, every inch of its dark maw pasted over with foreign postage stamps. He felt it best to get out of the house as soon as possible and hearing Shandon bells strike eight he decided that now was the best time – it was Monday morning and he could mingle with the crowds going to work; they would be too preoccupied to notice his wet, wrinkled clothes, his dirty boots, his unshaven face. First, however, he returned to the dead room to look for food. He found bread, and a pot of jam, and milk that was only just a little sour. He was raising the milk to his lips when his eye caught a black-japanned tin box by the window and the glint of silver in it. He strode across and looked down at the wad of notes and the loose pile of florins and shillings and half-crowns and little worn sixpenny pieces. The lock, he noticed, had been broken at some time previously. Without a thought he put his hand on the thick roll of notes and filled a fistful of silver into his pocket. Then, abandoning the food he had prepared for himself he turned and tramped down the stairs, opened the hall door and walked right into the arms of a raiding patrol as it alighted from a lorry. He looked right and left and made one step as if to attempt an escape, but in a second a dozen rifles were pointed at his heart. In another second he was seated high on the car with a crowd of market-people gathered wonderingly about him.

In a dream he found himself smoking one of a bundle of cigarettes handed him on all sides from the sympathetic fish-women. All they knew was that he was a "Shinner" and they cheered him repeatedly for it. As he sat there in a daze one woman actually put a little tricolour rebel flag into his hand, and he waved it feebly from time to time, and the fish-wives and the onion-girls cheered him wildly as he was driven away. As they turned the corner of the markets one of the guards smiled grimly and said "Good-bye-ee," and Stevey smiled weakly in return and stuffed the flag into his pocket.

It was the last smile Stevey Long smiled on this earth. The search of the house discovered, hidden under the stairs, a conglomeration of explosives, bombs and grenades and incendiaries, finished and unfinished. It took the military an hour to remove them all, and to crown the amazement of the market-folk, they then brought up a coffin, carrying it in lightly, carrying it on four bending shoulders. At his court martial, which they held an hour later at drumhead – martial law was in force – question after question was fired at Stevey and he dodged and twisted like a hare, but he was a hare in a net. By degrees they wearied him, and finally cowed him.

"Where did he get that revolver?"

"I found it," said Stevey.

"Where?"

"In the fields."

"There were two bullets discharged?"

"Were there?" said Stevey innocently.

"When did you find it?"

"Last night."

"Where did you come from last night?"

At that Stevey paused, feeling that these questions were leading back to Macroom Castle, realizing that he could not substantiate any statement he might make as to his where-abouts the evening before. The President repeated the question testily.

"Where did you come from?"

"East Cork."

"Where in East Cork?"

"Midleton."

"What were you doing in that house?"

To this Stevey replied truthfully, and though it was the only true thing he said that day, they did not believe him.

"Do you mean to say," asked the president, "that the people of Midleton didn't know a curfew order was in force in Cork?"

A few such questions drove Stevey to the wall, but it was when they told him that the woman was shot by a point four-five bullet, of the same calibre as the gun found on him, and charged him with the murder of the old lady that he paled and grew thoroughly confused and realized the danger in which he stood. His advocate did his best for him but it was no use, and when in the end Stevey was asked if he had anything to say he grew excited and began to talk foolishly, leaning forward and waving his hands, swearing that he would tell the whole truth this time, and contradicting almost everything he had previously said. His advocate tried again to save him but the president intervened; he had caught his man and now he would have a little sport with him.

"Let the prisoner speak," he said, and leaned back in his chair and glanced at his colleagues. They, in turn, glanced back at him and drew their fingers over their mouths and looked down at the table – the old man, they thought, was in a good mood today.

The truth was, said Stevey, that he was coming from East Cork and he was ambushed by Sinn Feiners. He fired two shots at them . . .

"At your own people?" asked the colonel.

"Well they fired at me," cried Stevey with an oath.

"Go on," said the colonel politely.

"The bastards fired at me," said Stevey in a towering rage at his imagined enemies.

"One moment," said the president. "Where did you really get this revolver? Do you admit possessing it?"

"Ain't I telling you?" said Stevey. "It was a Tan that gave it to me."

"Indeed?" said the colonel politely. "Go on."

"I fired at them, once, twice. And then, I'm sorry to say, I ran."

"To Cork?" asked the colonel sarcastically.

"I got a bike," said Stevey sullenly.

"Where?" asked the president, leaning forward. "Can we substantiate that?"

"Well, to tell the truth," said Stevey, "I – I stole it."

"Like this money we found on you? You admit you stole that, too?"

"Yes, I stole it, I took it," admitted Stevey.

"Can we even confirm that you stole the bike?" asked the president. "Where did you steal it? Where is it now?"

Stevey told six more lies in his efforts to avoid admitting the bicycle was in a ditch on the wrong side of the city. The old colonel lost his patience here.

"Where did you steal the bike?" he roared.

"It was in the dark I stole it," muttered Stevey and the court rocked with laughter.

"It's true," wailed Stevey.

"Remove the prisoner," said the old colonel in disgust.

In order to disgrace him as well as punish him he was sentenced for murder and robbery under arms.

1932

Paulé Bartón

■

EMILIE PLEAD
CHOOSE
ONE EGG

From 1957 to 1986, the Duvalier family held absolute
power over Haiti. François Duvalier, "Papa Doc,"
supported by a private military gang, the Tonton
Macoutes, had himself elected president for life and, while
leading the country into ever-increasing poverty, ruled the
country as a dictator until his death in 1971. He thought
of himself as a writer and in 1966 published what he called
his Essential Works, *which he believed embodied the true*
essence of Haitian literature. "It is the destiny of the people
of Haiti to suffer," President Jean-Claude Duvalier, who
had inherited the post from his despotic father, said in 1980.
The atrocities committed during the Duvalier regime were
countless and the people of Haiti lived in a state of near
slavery. Health conditions were poor, illiteracy high, and
the media subjected to strict government censorship. Most
writers and artists lived in exile, in Montreal, Paris, New
York, and Dakar. Paulé Bartón, by profession a goatherd,

was thrown into prison for satirizing Duvalier in a story. After his release, he left Haiti and lived in several countries in the Caribbean, composing folk tales. He died in Costa Rica in 1974.

■

E MILIE was talking with Bélem while looking at the gathered loud of nesting birds. "Which bird going to hatch today's woe, guess that?" Emilie said, she said, "I'll carry that egg to the man who took my donkey for my debt, I'll give him that a breakfast gift!"

"The tax man?" Bélem said.

Emilie said, "That's it, you guessing good today," she said. "Now guess which egg woe is in."

Bélem said, "How can I guess? Look how many eggs there look!"

"Got to make choices in this life," Emilie said, "Each morning a riddle to untie the knot of it, and then use that rope to tie up bad luck thinking to any tree here."

Bélem sang, "*Tie up bad luck thinking to a tree here, Fry that woe egg up for the debt man dear,*" then he said, "That makes a good song!" he laughed then.

Emilie she said, "I'll sing it on the way over to his hut, I'll sing it to my donkey too. But now guess which egg!"

But Bélem said, "I sigh. There's too many eggs out there! I tell you my eyes worrying over each one, they look the same all," he said more.

Emilie then, "Got to make a choice hurry! That debt man yawning toward his breakfast table hurry!" Emilie said.

"You asking me something hard here I tell you. You ask a very tight riddle knot, you talking a mystery under just one bird!" Bélem said.

"Got to make a choice! The debt man now sitting at the table now," Emilie said.

Bélem said, "It's like asking does water from the same well taste more better after carried in buckets to your thirsty mouth by a donkey or an ox, which one? It's like asking which of two sticks the same size to knock a lemon down with, which one?" he said.

Emilie said, "Make a choice my friend. You get to taste the drinking water in your throat whoever brings it anyway. You get to squeeze the lemon on your tongue whatever stick knocks it down anyway. That debt man choose my donkey instead my table and chair to take, yes he make that choice one over the other, you know this?"

Bélem said, "O.K. I say all the eggs got woe today's woe in them, how's that if I say that, there I say that!" he said.

Emilie said, "That's no choice, oh my that's no choice! Now the donkey and ox both spilling water, empty gone, now the lemons shriveling up to yellow lizard eyes on the trees, now the debt man thinking greedy want of my table and chair. Which egg will stop all this, friend?" Emilie plead him to choose one egg quick.

But Bélem could not choose, so Emilie hid her table and chair then. Emilie says, "All right Bélem friend, it's all right," she soothes that way.

Bélem he had a wound he felt then somewhere on him, but he couldn't find it. He said, "Emilie, I hurt on me somewhere, can you see the wound?"

Emilie said, "No," she covers the table and chairs with fronds.

Bélem he says, "The salt sea will find this wound on me, it always does when I swim in it, always clean my wound." But Emilie knew the wound of confusion and no-choice was too deep inside for the salt sea to sting it clean for Bélem right now.

Translated by Howard Norman

Wang Meng

■

THE STUBBORN PORRIDGE

*The fluctuations of modern China's reforms and counter-
reforms created fearful confusion for many Chinese
politicians and intellectuals. Those in favour one year
found themselves in prison the next, and others whose
ideas had been criticized were suddenly hailed as heroes.
Wang Meng, one of the most influential writers after the
Revolution, was condemned to twenty years of forced
labour in "internal exile" for a short story he had written
in his early twenties. Living with peasants in the remote
Xinjiang autonomous region, he learned the local language
through the forced recitation of Mao's quotations, and later
he wrote about his experience among the Uighur people in
a number of short stories. After Mao's death and during
Deng Xiaoping's "Era of Reformation," Wang was
rehabilitated and awarded the status of professional writer;
in 1986 he was appointed minister of culture. But following
the massacre in Tiananmen Square on June 4, 1989,
Wang resigned his post and soon after was attacked in the
official press. In an anonymous letter published in the*

186 | WANG MENG

*Writers' Union Magazine, Wang's story "The
Stubborn Porridge" was declared to be a criticism of
Deng's reforms and "a veiled satire of the Chinese
Communist system." In an unprecedented action in a
country of stringent censorship, Wang sued both the
anonymous writer and the magazine's editor (who many
intellectuals believed were one and the same person),
but the Intermediary Court in Beijing refused to accept
the case.*

■

T HE OFFICIAL MEMBERS of our family are:
Grandfather, Grandmother, Father, Mother,
Uncle, Aunt, I, my Wife, my First Cousin on
my Father's side, my First Cousin's Husband and my lovely,
lanky Son. Our ages are respectively eighty-eight, eighty-
four, sixty-three, sixty-four, sixty-one, fifty-seven, forty,
forty and sixteen. An ideal ladder-like structure. And then we
have an unofficial member, unofficial but indispensable – our
housekeeper, Elder Sister Xu, age fifty-nine. She has been
with us for forty years, and we all call her Elder Sister Xu. A
clear case of all men born equal with natural rights.

We lived together peaceably, united as one. On all issues
big and small, such as whether this summer is hotter than usual,
whether to drink Dragon's Well tea at eight yuan an ounce or
green tea at forty fen an ounce, or which brand of soap to use –
the gentle Violet or the intimidating Golden Armor – Grandfather had the last word. Strifes and contentions, overflowing
rhetoric and behind-doors plotting were absolutely unheard

of. We even shared the same hairstyle, distinguishing between male and female, of course.

For the last several decades, we all got up at ten past six in the morning. At 6:35 Elder Sister Xu would have our breakfast ready: toasted slices of steamed bread, thin rice porridge, pickled turnip heads. At ten past seven we would all set out, respectively to work or to school. Grandfather had already retired, but still showed up every morning at the Neighborhood Committee as officer on duty. We all came back at twelve. By then Elder Sister Xu would have lunch waiting for us, bean-curd paste noodles. After a short nap, we would all get up at one thirty and start off again, respectively to work or to school. Grandfather, however, slept until half-past three. Then he would get up, wash his face and clean his teeth for the second time and sit on the sofa to read the newspapers. At around five, Grandfather and Grandmother and Elder Sister Xu would have a consultation about the menu for supper. This was a daily routine, which never lost its interest for the three participants although the results never changed from one day to the next. Let's say rice for supper tonight. As to dishes, let's make it one meat, one half-meat half-vegetable and two vegetables. As to soup, let's skip it today. Or let's have soup today. After this discussion, Elder Sister Xu would go into the kitchen and get down to work, chopping away. Thirty minutes later she was bound to pop out: "To think that I could have forgotten! I had not asked about the pork in the half-meat half-vegetable. Should it be sliced or shredded?" Well, there is no denying the importance of the issue. Grandfather and Grandmother looked at each other significantly, and one of them would say: "Might as well be sliced." Or they might say: "Let's make it shredded." And their decision would be faithfully implemented.

Everybody was satisfied with this life, Grandfather first and foremost. Grandfather had suffered in his youth and would often admonish us: "A full stomach, unpatched clothes, good health, a well-furnished home and all the generations living together – why, this is even beyond the dreams of landlords in the old days. Now you people, don't let it go to your heads. What do you know of the pangs of hunger?" But Father and Mother and Uncle and Aunt would protest that they knew full well the pangs of hunger. When you are hungry, they said, your chest and stomach go into constrictions, your head dangles, your legs wobble. They added that extreme hunger felt the same as overeating, you want to throw up. Our whole family, headed by Grandfather and Grandmother, were followers of the maxim that happiness lies in contentedness and were faithful upholders of the existing system of things.

But lately, things have been changing. We were constantly assailed by new fads and fashions. Just within the last few years, a color TV, a refrigerator and a washing machine had made their way into our home. Besides, my Son's speeches were often interspersed with English. Grandfather was most liberal and open-minded, garnering a stock of new terms from the papers after his daily nap or from radio and TV programs after supper. He would often take a poll of public opinion. "Now is there anything to be reformed or improved in our family life?" he would ask.

Everybody would hasten to say no, especially Elder Sister Xu. She prayed that this kind of life would go unchanged from day to day, year to year, generation to generation without end. My Son came up with a proposal. He blinked hard as if there was a worm inside his eyes. He proposed that we buy a cassette recorder. Grandfather agreed, acting on the principle that heeding advice led to the attainment of perfection. So there was an addition to our family belongings in the shape of a Red Lamp brand cassette recorder. At the beginning we were all thrilled. One would say a few words, another sing snatches of Peking opera, this one would imitate a cat's meowing while another would read a passage from the papers, and we would tape it and play it back. How we enjoyed it all! And to think that Grandfather's father and grandfather had never known the existence of such a thing as a cassette recorder. But after the first few days, the thing began to pall. The songs on cassette, which we played on the machine did not sound as nice as those on radio or TV. The cassette recorder was put aside to collect dust. Everybody realized that these new gadgets had their limitations after all. They were not as durable as the old "song box." Nothing could take the place of tradition, nothing could compare with order and harmony within the family.

That same year, the uneventful pace of our family life was ruffled by an order canceling the long noon break for napping, to be replaced by a short forty to sixty minute break. The compensation was that each work unit must provide free lunch. A mixed blessing for us, however. We were glad for the free lunch but nevertheless distressed by the change; we just could not adjust. After two days of free lunch, we were all affected with constipation and other symptoms of the Heat Syndrome. Then it was announced that free lunch would be canceled, and we were left wondering what was going on anyway. What were we to do? Grandfather admonished us always to take the lead in keeping on the path shown to us by the government. So there was a big hassle over buying lunch boxes, preparing lunch and taking them along to the office.

Elder Sister Xu suffered from insomnia, toothache, eye infection and accelerated heartbeat. It wasn't long before some work units prolonged the noon break. Others did not officially revert to the long noon break but surreptitiously put off the start of the afternoon work-hour without staying later to make up for it. Our family reverted to our lunch of bean-curd paste noodles. Elder Sister Xu was immediately cured of all her complaints, no more eye infections, no more toothache; her sleep was on schedule, and her heartbeat under perfect control at seventy to eighty beats a minute.

But the surging waves of reform rolled onwards, and the rousing winds of change swept all before it. All creatures under heaven were in motion, all affairs on earth in transition. Just as our fellow creatures right and left, uplifted by self-examination and restrained in sorrow, were putting the past behind them and mapping out new dreams of reform and regeneration, friends and relatives who used to praise us as a model family and an exemplary household now started urging us to move with the times. It seemed that new models of family life had cropped up in Guangdong, or Hong Kong it may be, or even the United States.

Grandfather took the lead in proposing that we change from a Monarchy to a Cabinet system. The members of the Cabinet would be nominated by Grandfather himself, to be approved by the Plenary Session of the Family Congress, including Elder Sister Xu, a nonvoting member, and the reins of government would be rotated among the official members of the Cabinet. Except for Elder Sister Xu, Grandfather's proposition was unanimously approved. Father was designated to take over the reins of government and entrusted with the reform and modernization of our Menu.

The fact was, Father had always had his food ready for him and his work cut out for him. Which meant that he ate what was put in front of him and did whatever part of the household duties that was assigned to him. Now saddled with the momentous task of overseeing the Menu for the whole family, he was embarrassed and overwhelmed. When challenged by such major issues as what kind of tea leaves to buy, or the choice between sliced or shredded pork, he would invariably turn to Grandfather. He would never say anything without quoting Grandfather: "The Patriarch said to buy Chrysanthemum brand mosquito incense." "The Patriarch said not to make soup tonight." "The Patriarch said not to use detergent for dishwashing. Might be poisonous, these chemicals. Hot water and baking soda, much cleaner, and thriftier too."

Trouble followed immediately. Elder Sister would ask Father whenever she had a question, and Father would ask Grandfather coming back to Elder Sister Xu with, "The Patriarch said so and so." So far as Elder Sister Xu was concerned, she might as well go directly to Grandfather. But that might hurt Father's feelings, and she was also afraid to bother Grandfather. Grandfather did not want to be bothered with trifles and had repeatedly ordered Father: "Make your own decisions! Don't always come to me!" So Father would go back to Elder Sister Xu with: "The Patriarch has said that I am to decide. The Patriarch has said that he doesn't want to be bothered."

Soon there were murmurs from Uncle and Aunt. Murmurs against what? Nobody knew for sure. Probably impatience with Father's ineptness. Perhaps a suspicion that Father was using Grandfather's name in vain, "fabricating the edict of the Emperor," as the saying goes. Possibly also disaffection with Grandfather for not completely giving up the reins of government, or annoyance at Elder Sister Xu's nagging. And finally resentment at everybody else for okaying the Cabinet system and confirming someone like Father as member of the Cabinet.

Grandfather became aware of the murmurs and formally invested Father with authority, admonishing him at the same time to accept the delegation of power to lower levels, as was in keeping with the times. Father, cornered, promised not to invoke Grandfather's name in future dealings. Having gotten his Mandate, he went ahead and delegated power to Elder Sister Xu to decide between soup or no soup, and shredded or sliced pork.

Sister Xu would not be Empowered. How can I decide, she sniveled between tears. She was so overwhelmed by the burden of responsibility that she missed a meal. The family encouraged her: "You have worked so long in our family. Power should go with office. You just take over, we are all behind you. Go ahead, buy whatever you like, cook whatever you like, and we'll eat whatever you put before us. We have faith in you."

Elder Sister Xu smiled through her tears and thanked everyone for showering her with such honors. So, for a while, things went on as before. But soon murmurings began to be audible, as it was plain that Elder Sister Xu did not have the true Mandate. Imperceptible signs of disrespect gradually evolved into outright complaints. It began with my Son, got taken up by my First Cousin and her Husband, and soon even I and my Wife were infected. At first, it was just sarcastic comments: "Our menu has been lying there unchanged for four decades. Must have antique value by now." "Such single-minded adherence to convention! Such rigidity! Rejection of all change!" "Our family's lifestyle is a fine example of living in a time capsule!" "Elder Sister Xu's perspectives are so restricted! Lack of culture, of course. She's all right as a person, but hopelessly backward. To think that now, in the eighties, our living standards must adapt to *her* level!"

Elder Sister Xu had no inkling of what was simmering around her. On the contrary, she began to enjoy her new status and went ahead with her own version of Reform. In the first place, the two platefuls of pickled turnip heads for breakfast were reduced in quantity to one, only served up in two plates. The sprinkling of sesame oil over the pickles was abolished. The bean-curd paste for lunch, which used to be stir-fried with a bowl of pork cubes, was now changed to plain bean-curd paste cooked in water. The soup, which used to be served on alternate days, now only turned up once a week. And when it did appear, it had changed from egg drop soup to plain water with a dash of soy sauce, sprinkled with chopped spring onions. With the money thus saved, she went and bought royal jelly as a gift offering to Grandfather. So! She was squeezing us to curry favor with Grandfather! And we could only stand by helplessly and fume! More infuriating, according to my Son's report, was the fact that after making the plain soup, she would scoop out a bowl with the thickest sprinkling of chopped spring onions for herself, before the family was served. On another occasion, she was seen cracking melon seeds as she chopped the vegetables. She must have embezzled the family's public funds! "Power corrupts. Absolute power corrupts absolutely!" My Son had found his newly acquired theory fully validated.

From Father downwards, nobody intervened or put a stop to the murmurs. Taking silence as acquiescence, my Son fired the first shot, choosing the moment when Elder Sister Xu was enjoying her clandestine soup. "Enough is enough! I'm sick of your substandard meals. And saving the pick of the chopped spring onions for yourself! That's the limit! Starting tomorrow, I want everybody to enjoy a modern life."

Elder Sister Xu cried and made a scene, but nobody did anything to stop the rush of events. We felt that my Son should have a chance. He was young, fired with ideas and full of energy. It seemed the time was ripe for the likes of him to take over. Talent must be fostered, after all. Of course I and members of the family tried to console Elder Sister Xu. "You have cooked in our family for the last forty years, your achievements outweigh everything else. Nobody can take that away!"

My Son broke out into an orgy of rhetoric: "Our family's way of eating had persisted unchanged for forty years. The problem does not stop here. What is worse, we have been served too many carbohydrates and too little protein. Lack of protein affects our growth, reduces the generation of anti-bodies in the white blood cells. The result is the weakening of the constitution of the population as a whole. People in the West take in seven times more protein than we do. In terms of animal fat their intake is fourteen times greater than ours. We are not as tall, nor as strong, nor as energetic as they are, not to mention body shape. They sleep once a day, six hours at the most, yet see how they carry on nonstop from morning to night. Look at us, even with our daily nap, we are still lumps of inertia. You might say how can we compare with devel-oped countries. All right then, let's take our own national minorities. Now let me tell you something: the food structure of us Hans cannot compare with that of the minorities – you can't say that they are economically more developed than we are, can you? Our intake of protein is far lower than those of the Mongols, the Uighurs, the Hassacks, the Koreans of the North or the Tibetans of the Southwest. Now how can you expect to survive without a change in our food structure? Take breakfast for instance – the everlasting slices of steamed bread and thin porridge with pickles on the side! Heavens! Is this the kind of breakfast fit for middle-income urban residents of China in the eighties of the twentieth century? How shockingly primitive! Porridge and pickles – perfect symbols of the sickman of Asia. This is an insidious form of genocide! A disgrace to our ancestors! This is the root of the decline of Chinese civilizations! Emblematic of the backward culture of the Yellow River! If we had eaten bread and butter instead of porridge and pickles, would we have lost the Opium War to the British in 1840? Would it have been necessary for the Empress Dowager to flee to Chengde during the invasion of the Eight Allied Armies in 1900? Would the Japanese army have dared to incite the September 18 incident in 1931? Would not their regiments have collapsed in fright if they had seen our lips smeared with butter and our chins dripping with cream? If in 1949 our leadership had outlawed all porridge and pickles and ordered the nation to shift to bread and butter and ham and sausage and eggs and yogurt and cheese and honey and jam and chocolate thrown in, wouldn't we have achieved a leading place in the world community long long ago in terms of national growth rate, science and technology, art, sports, housing, education and number of cars per capita? Getting down to basics, porridge with pickles is the root of our national disasters, the fundamental reason for the super-stability of our unchanging feudal system! Down with por-ridge and pickles! So long as porridge and pickles are not wiped out, there is no hope for China!"

The speaker was fired and the audience moved. I was seized with threefold sentiments of surprise, joy and fear. Sur-prise and joy that without my realizing it, my Son had actually outgrown his slit pants and no longer asked me to wipe his bottom for him. He had enriched his mind so massively, accu-mulated so much new learning, raised such searching ques-tions and seized on such a crucial issue! I felt deeply that heaven and earth should give way to my Son. It could truly be said that, nourished on porridge and pickles, he harbored visions of butter and ham. It is no exaggeration to say that he has poured forth the sweeping winds of modernization, enveloping everything within the four dimensions. Truly may it be said, the young are to be feared, the world is theirs.

But I was also alarmed. I feared the way he had seized on all current abuses with his wit and annihilated everything with a sentence. I feared that this kind of exaggerated rhetoric was just so much air and would end in nothing. According to my half century of experience, whenever a complex problem was neatly dissected and laid out in black and white, whenever the solution to overwhelming odds was easy and ready-made, as soon as the first ecstasy of analysis and prescription was over, the agent would be reduced to impotence. With this one and only twig to carry on the family tree, Heaven forbid that he should be so afflicted!

Just as I had anticipated, my First Cousin snorted and mumbled under her breath: "All very nice indeed! If we had had that much bread and butter, we would have achieved modernization long ago!" "What!" my Son, still on the crest of his zeal, shot back at his aunt. "Khruschev had proposed his 'stewed beef and potatoes' brand of socialism in the sixties, and now you are proposing a 'bread and butter' version of modernization! What a coincidence! Modernization, let me tell you, is the automatization of industry, the collectivization of agriculture, the ultra-modernization of science, the conversion of defense to multiple civil uses, the whimsicality of thought, the impenetrability of terms, the distortion of art, the limitless multiplication of controversy, the paring down of academe, the mystification of concepts and the transformation of man into a set of paranormal functions. The sea of '-ization' is boundlessly shifting, butter gives it shape. The garden of delights is inaccessible, but bread builds a bridge. Of course bread and butter will not be showered down from the skies like bombs from an imaginary enemy, don't you think I know that much? What do you take me for, an idiot? But we must raise the question, we must set up a goal. A nation without a goal is like a man without a head, never knowing its own potential . . ."

"Well said, well said," Grandfather interjected, "the two of you are moving in the same direction. No need to argue." And so the controversy died down.

My Son believed in action. Right away the next morning, bread and butter, eggs, milk and coffee were on the table. Grandfather and Elder Sister Xu simply could not take coffee and milk. Uncle thought of a solution: chopped spring onions fried in a wok, add pepper corn, cassia bark, fennel, ginger skin, pepper, seaweed and dried hot pepper; when the mixture is cooked, add a dash of Cantonese soy sauce, then pour into coffee and milk. It's bound to drown out the barbarian stink. I tried a mouthful, it worked; the taste of coffee and milk was not discernible anymore. I also wanted to add this potion into my own cup of coffee, but seeing my Son's glare, I sacrificed my palate for his sake and gulped down the stinking mess. Alas, these little emperors of the four-two-one syndrome – four grandparents and two parents revolving around the single child – what are they leading our country into!

In three days, the whole family was in an uproar. Sister Xu was in the hospital with acute diarrhea. The doctors suspected colon cancer. Grandmother was afflicted with nervous hardening of the liver. Grandfather was hopelessly constipated. Father and Uncle, like the filial sons that they were, tried to ease his bowel movement by breaking up the constipated mass with bamboo chopsticks stuck up his rectum, but to little effect. Our First Cousin had to be operated on, while her Husband's gums were all infected and swollen. My wife would throw up after every meal, and having got rid of her western breakfast, would sneak away to her parents' home for thin porridge and pickles, keeping it a secret from our Son, of course. A greater cause for alarm was the fact that my Son had run through our monthly budget in three days. He announced that without extra funds, he would not even be able to provide thin porridge for the rest of the month. Affairs having come to this, I had no choice but to stick my neck out and join with Father and Uncle to depose my Son and restore the family life to normal.

Father and Uncle had no option other than to look to Grandfather, and Grandfather had no option other than to turn to Elder Sister Xu. But Elder Sister Xu was in the hospital and had announced that even after she was released from hospital she would not cook. If anybody thought her a burden, she declared, they could send her packing. Grandfather deluged her with a thousand protestations, reasserting his own philosophy of putting personal loyalty and obligations above all else. He assured Elder Sister Xu that she was preeminent on both counts, closer than Grandfather's own kin, valued above his own flesh and blood, deserving both loyalty and obligations from the family. Grandfather vowed that Elder Sister Xu was part and parcel of the family to her last breath. That if we were down to our last piece of steamed bread, Elder Sister Xu would have a bite. That if we were down to our last glass of water, Elder Sister Xu would have three sips. That if we made a fortune, Elder Sister Xu would have her share. That if our luck went down, Elder Sister Xu would still be taken care of. That such a thing as using people first and then kicking them out was beyond contempt. Grandfather threw himself into protestations, words rolling, tears streaming. Elder Sister Xu took in every word, heart and liver warming, eyes overflowing, nose dripping. Things came to such a pass that the medical staff on duty decided that this communication was detrimental to the patient's condition, and Grandfather, still teary, had to leave.

Back home, Grandfather called a plenary meeting. At the meeting, he announced that though he was getting on in years, he did not hold rigid ideas about what to eat and such like matters, even less would he harbor vaulting ambitions toward autocratic rule. "But," he pointed out, "since you had insisted that I do something about the situation, I had no choice but to speak to Elder Sister Xu. I found her heart broken by your complaints and her stomach wrecked by my Great-Grandson's western breakfast. So I give up. Eat what you like. As for me," he added, "it is just as well that I starve to death."

At this, we looked at each other and all rushed in to assure Grandfather that he had done a good job: for a good fifty years now, old and young each had their place, four generations coexisting under one roof. My First Cousin declared that she would cook for Grandfather, that is to say, she herself, her Husband, Grandfather, Grandmother and Elder Sister Xu would be one Eating Unit. Father hastened to declare that he would make up a second Unit with Mother, but that he would have to exclude me and my Wife, on account of our New-Wave Son who would not fit in with their eating habits. I also declared that I was with my Wife, while Uncle and Aunt banded together. My Son was a single-member Unit. My First Cousin's Husband seemed pleased and remarked: "Might as well eat separately, more like a modern lifestyle; four generations eating together is so old-fashioned, like something out of *The Dream of the Red Chamber*. And anyway, so many people eating together around one table makes such a crush, not to mention the danger of catching hepatitis." My First Cousin retorted: "But where can you find such a big family in the U.S.? Can you imagine them overcoming the generation gap and sitting together to a meal?" An expression of resignation seemed to flicker across Grandfather's face.

Barely two days passed before the arrangement to eat in separate Units was up against the wall. At around eleven, my First Cousin's Unit would take over the kitchen. Armed as she was with the authority and prestige of Grandfather, we could only stand by and look on longingly. After Grandfather came Father's turn, and after Father came Uncle. When my turn came round, it was already two o'clock in the afternoon. I had to rush to work without lunch. At supper, the cycle was repeated. Something must be done. We talked about the possibility of each Unit setting up its own stove. Coal gas tanks were out of the question. To acquire the one we now have for the whole family, we had made fourteen personal visits, hosted seven dinners, given two scrolls of painting, five cartons of cigarettes and eight bottles of wine as gift offerings, and the whole process had taken thirteen months and thirteen days. You could say that we had put as much energy in it as firstborn infants in sucking, or old men in shitting. Buying stoves was also an arduous process. Besides, even if you do get a stove, you need a certificate to buy coal briquettes. No certificate, no briquettes. And even if you do get hold of the certificate and buy the briquettes, there was nowhere to store them. If we decided to set up four separate stoves according to the modern consciousness, we would need to expand the kitchen by thirty square meters. Or better, to install four extra kitchens. Or even better, to set up five individual apartments. Man's appetite for consumption is like a galloping fire. The current alarm at overconsumerism in the press is just a waste of breath, the more you talk, the hotter it gets. Suddenly it occurred to me like an epiphany that all this twaddle about modern consciousness and renovating your concepts and the right to privacy was just so much hot air if you do not build more houses.

Discussion on the soft science of separate stoves got us nowhere. Meanwhile, a whole tank of coal gas was exhausted in nine days. Starting this year, the Petroleum and Gas Company had introduced the new method of issuing certificates for gas supply. We were limited to fourteen tickets per year, so every tank must last at least twenty-six days to ensure cooking and hot water for the entire family all the year round. If we ran through one tank in nine days, our whole quota of certificates would not last more than four months, and what were we to do for the other eight months of the year? This was not only destroying the order of our own lives, but subverting the national planning!

We were completely dismayed: sighs, complaints, gossip and rumor filled the air. Some said we could live on uncooked mixed dough. Some said each Unit's cooking should be limited to seventeen minutes. Some said this separation into eating Units was a clear case of the relations of production outrunning the level of development of the forces of production. Some said the more you reform the worse it gets, that we were much better off when Grandfather's word was law and Elder Sister Xu ran the show. Others cursed the U.S., saying the Americans were like a pack of wild animals with no family and not a shred of filial piety. We have our own excellent tradition of familial virtues, why should we learn from the Americans? Why indeed? But what were we to do? After the last episode, we were ashamed to bother Grandfather again with questions and requests, so we went up to my First Cousin's Husband.

My First Cousin's Husband was the only member of the family who had had a taste of things foreign. During the last few years, he had ordered two suits, bought three ties and had been in the U.S. for six months for "further studies," in Japan for a ten-day visit and in the Federal Republic of Germany for a tour of seven cities. Well-informed, carrying himself with an air, capable of saying "Thank you" and "Excuse me" in nine different languages, he was considered the true scholar in the family. But coming from outside the clan, he was aware of his inferior status and always behaved with discretion and modesty, thus winning our deep respect.

On this occasion we were at our wit's end, hopelessly mired in the strange circle of dilemmas. Seeing the urgency of the case and the sincerity of our supplication, he returned trust for trust and delivered the goods.

"As I see it," my First Cousin's Husband began, "the basic issue is the system. Whether we eat sliced steamed bread or not is of no account. The basic issue is not what we eat, but who makes the decision and by what process this decision is arrived at. Through the feudal patriarchal order? By seniority of age and rank? By leaving things to anarchism? By relying on whims and caprices of the moment? According to published menus? Is accepting the inevitable a form of predestination? Let me tell you, the key is Democracy. Without Democracy, you won't know the taste of what you're eating no matter how good it is. Without Democracy, nobody will make a stand for reform no matter how vile the food is. Without Democracy, one can only eat in an unenlightened way, not knowing the sweetness of sugar nor the bitterness of bitter melon. How can one tell the difference, when neither the sweetness nor the bitterness has anything to do with one's own choice! Without Democracy, one would be passive and dumb. The Subject would lose consciousness of the act of eating, and the Eating Subject would be alienated from its nature and reduced to a manure manufactory. On the other hand, the Eating Subject may be lost in confusion, now capricious, now indiscreet, grasping at palpable gains and seeking only short-term effects, exuding hostility to its neighbors, and ultimately turn into a stomach-flaunting headless monster. In a word, without Democracy there is no choice, and without choice the Conscious Subject is alienated from its own identity."

We listened in awe, nodding in agreement. It was as if an enlightening fluid had been injected into our brains.

Uplifted by our reception, my First Cousin's Husband continued: "The seniority system is all right for a stagnant agricultural society. One might even go so far to say that it brings order, the sort of order suited to illiterates and idiots. I suppose people born with lower IQs will accept this kind of order – dull, sluggish, moribund. But it kills competition, it stifles man's initiative, creativity and changeability. We all know that without change there would have been no mankind, we would still be apes. Moreover, the system of seniority represses the young. A man's energy is at its most vital, his mind at its most active, his aspirations at their most ardent before the age of forty. Yet in reality, at this age they are all languishing at the bottom . . ."

My Son interpolated: "How true!" A few tears trickled down his cheeks.

I signaled him to stay out of this. The fact is, ever since the fiasco of his western breakfast program, his image had been somewhat damaged. People tended to associate him with risky adventures, empty theories and even a hint of the Red Guard rebel spirit – more hindrance than help in any undertaking. The other members of the family, including my First Cousin and her Husband, did not take kindly to my Son. His endorsement would only discredit my First Cousin's Husband's proposal.

"All this is fine, but what are we to do?" I asked.

"Make a stand for Democracy!" he cried, "Hold elections! Democratic Elections, this is the key, the acupuncture point, this is the nostril of the ox where you insert the ring, this is the central link of the chain! Everybody run for elections! Let everyone make an election speech, like bidding for a contract: how much you charge, the kind of food you will supply, the obligations of the members of the family who join your program, how much you expect to get paid. Everything must be Open, Transparent, Codified, Documented, Legalized, Programed and Systemized. Let the Ballot decide! Let the People cast their vote! Let the majority rule! The minority must give in to the majority. This principle in itself is an indication of a new concept, new spirit, new order, offsetting Rigidity on the one hand, and Anarchism on the other!"

Father thought this over very carefully, the lines of his forehead creasing even deeper as his thoughts were profound. Finally he said: "Yes, I am all for it. But there are two obstacles to overcome. One is the Patriarch, he might object. The other is Elder Sister Xu . . ."

My First Cousin's Husband answered: "No problem as far as the Patriarch is concerned. He rides with the times. And anyway, he is sick and tired of overseeing the food. The real problem is Elder Sister . . ."

Here my Son lost patience: "What is Elder Sister Xu to us, and what are we to Elder Sister Xu? She is not a member of our family, she has no right to vote, anyway."

My mother remonstrated: "My Grandson, did you say that Elder Sister Xu has no right to vote? You don't know what you are talking about. Elder Sister Xu might not share our family name, might not be one of the clan. But let me tell you, you won't get anything done unless you have her on your side. I have been in this family my whole life, I should know! What do you know?"

The camp of my First Cousin and her Husband was split over this issue. My First Cousin's Husband held that making a special case for Elder Sister Xu would be betraying the principle of Democracy. Democracy and special considerations were mutually incompatible. My First Cousin retorted that it was very well to talk, but what was the use of highfalutin talk if it was out of touch with reality? Belittling Elder Sister Xu was as good as belittling Tradition, belittling Tradition would cost you your footing in reality and, without a firm footing in reality, any project for reform was just daydreaming, and a daydream reform was just hot air. My First Cousin did not stand on ceremony with her Husband. She said outright: "Don't think you are somebody just because you have been over the seas and can say a few foreign words! Actually in our family, you are not worth Elder Sister Xu's little finger!"

At these words, My First Cousin's Husband paled, smiled aloofly and walked out of the room.

A few days later, Uncle tried to patch things up and find a solution. He pointed out that the so-called two obstacles were but one, that Elder Sister Xu may be a die-hard Conservative, but she always listens to Grandfather. If Grandfather gives the nod, so will she. There was no basis for the conflict between the democratic process and Elder Sister Xu's special case, even less reason to bring such an imaginary conflict to a crisis.

Uncle's words dispelled the clouds. Everything seemed so clear. All our worries were much ado about nothing. All this hassle over conflicting views and such, it was really in the eye of the beholder: now it's there, and then it's gone, now it's looming, and then it's shrinking. The real test is how to find a common ground for different opinions so as to create a relaxed, friendly and trustful atmosphere. We were all much elated and full of confidence. Even my First Cousin's Husband and my Son couldn't help smiling with relief.

We unanimously entrusted Uncle and Father with the task of winning over Elder Sister Xu. Just as Uncle had predicted, it was smooth sailing all the way. True, Elder Sister was stoutly opposed to elections. "A lot of fuss and bother over nothing!" she snorted. But she also announced that having gotten safely out of this last illness she had retreated from all worldly contention. She supported nothing, opposed nothing. "If you want to lunch on flies, I'll eat flies. If you want to dine on mosquitoes, I'll eat mosquitoes. Just don't ask me about anything." She didn't even care whether or not she had the right to vote. She declared that she had nothing to say on any issue and would not join in on the family discussions. For all intents and purposes, Elder Sister Xu had faded from the historical stage.

We all elected the Husband of my First Cousin to be in charge of the election. What with a general housecleaning, and wiping of windowpanes, and hanging up of calligraphy scrolls, and setting out vases of the latest design of plastic flowers, the approaching date for the election actually brought a festive atmosphere. Democracy brings change, there's no denying. The day finally arrived. My First Cousin's Husband directed the operation. He wore his overseas gray suit and black tie and requested that we each make a campaign speech on "My Program to Run the Household."

Nobody spoke. One could hear the flies buzzing. My First Cousin's Husband asked: "What! No one running? I thought you were all full of ideas!"

I said: "Cousin, why don't you begin and set an example? You see, we are not used to Democracy. Quite embarrassing, really."

His Wife, my First Cousin, butted in: "Certainly not. What has it to do with him?"

My First Cousin's Husband explained in a quiet gentlemanly manner: "I am not running for election. It was not for my personal interest that I brought up the idea of Democracy. Now if you had elected me, that would discredit the idea of Democracy! And anyway, I am applying for studies abroad. I am in touch with several institutions in North America and Australia. Once I have bought enough foreign currency on the black market, I will leave. If anyone in present company volunteers to help me out a little, I'd be grateful. I'm borrowing in RMB and repaying in foreign currency . . ."

We looked at each other, completely flabbergasted. It occurred to us in a flash that this Election gadget was just asking for trouble! Wasn't it a trap, too, this speechifying, making promises right and left? Such lack of respect for one's ancestors. So inconsiderate to one's neighbors. And anyway, how can you please everybody if you were elected to run the household? There must be a screw loose somewhere, not leaving well enough alone, but playing with Elections! It occurred to us then and there that we had eaten our porridge and pickles and bean-curd paste noodles for the last several decades without Democratic Elections, and we had done just fine. Without Democratic Elections, we had neither starved nor burst with food, we had neither gnawed at bricks nor drank dog's piss by mistake, nor had we sipped our noodles into our nostrils or up our arses. But now we have to meddle in this wretched Democracy, ending up with diarrhea on the one hand and starvation on the other! This is the Chinese for you. We are not satisfied until we have got everybody bloated with edema.

But then it occurred to us that since we had already made a commitment to Democracy, we might as well enjoy a taste of it. Since the stage was already set for Elections, we might as well have a go at it. Since we were all gathered together, especially since the Patriarch had put in an appearance, the show should go on. And anyway, why should we write off Democratic Elections without giving it a chance? Supposing it works? Supposing Democratic Elections resulted in good food, tasty and healthy, comprising all the requirements of smell, taste and color, nurturing the yin and energizing the yang, reviving the blood and instilling vital energy, strengthening the constitution while keeping the body in shape; supposing it could save grocery bills and conserve energy, meet sanitary requirements without bureaucracy, reduce smoke and muffle noise; supposing everybody could have a say without having to rack their brains, and someone were in charge but without having the last word; supposing nobody had to eat leftovers yet all waste avoided, and oysters could be had without hepatitis and fish without the tang of the sea; supposing Democratic Elections could bring these benefits, it would be foolish not to have a go at it.

So the election took place: filling the ballot, putting it into the ballot box, supervising the opening of the box, counting the ballot. Eleven ballot forms were handed out, eleven retrieved. Thus the Election was declared valid. Of the ballot forms retrieved, four were blank, that is to say, no candidate's name was written in. One came up with "anybody will do," which was as good as void. Of the rest, there were two votes for Elder Sister Xu, three votes for Grandfather and one vote for my Son.

Grandfather had the most votes, but not the required majority. It was not half, not even one third of the votes. What was to be done? Was he elected? We had not thought of that beforehand. We sought out my First Cousin's Husband for enlightenment. My First Cousin's Husband said there were two kinds of "laws" in the world, one documented, the other undocumented. Strictly speaking, undocumented laws were not binding. For instance, he explained, the limit on the number of presidential terms was not written in the U.S. Constitution and was not law in the strict sense of the word. It was just a convention. The basic concept of Democracy, according to him, was majority rule. But what was a majority? Wasn't majority relative? What is a simple majority? Anything more than half? What is an absolute majority? Anything over two-thirds? It all depends on tradition and working concepts. As to our Election, he said, since it was our first try, and since we were all flesh-and-blood family members, it was up to us to decide.

Here my First Cousin barged in and announced that since Grandfather had the most votes he was elected. She assured us that this was not a case of Feudal Authoritarianism, but the workings of a Modern Democracy. She added further that there was no danger of Patriarchal Authoritarianism in our family anyway, much less that it would constitute the Main Contradiction and the Main Danger. According to her, on the contrary, we should be wary of Anarchism under the guise of so-called Anti-feudalism, and steer clear of Liberalism, Self-centeredness, Subjectivism, Overconsumerism, Epicureanism and the Blind Worship of Things Foreign, like the fallacy that the moon over the U.S. is rounder than it is over China and other such foreign dogmas.

Here my Son suddenly got all worked up and announced in no uncertain terms that he had not cast the vote for himself. As he said it, all eyes were turned on me, as if I had cast the vote for him, as if I were guilty of the dishonorable practice of voting for my own flesh and blood. I blushed in spite of myself. Then I asked myself, who would think so, and why should they think so? Did it occur to them that even if I had voted for my son it would not comprise any offense, because not voting for my Son, I could only have chosen between My Father, My Mother, My Wife, My First Cousin etc. And anyway, according to the currently fashionable Freudian theories, would my First Cousin necessarily be more removed from me than my own Son? After all, my Son might be suffering from the Oedipus complex and harboring plans to kill me and marry my Wife. Had they thought of that? Why should they point the accusing finger at me the minute my Son makes a move?

By now, my Son was shouting at the top of his voice. He said the fact that he had one vote meant that the voice of humanity was not completely stifled, that the torch was still alight and would one day burst into a prairie fire. He said that he had concerned himself with the Reform of the family Menu purely in a spirit of giving, out of respect for the humanist tradition and an all-encompassing Love. Coming to the word *Love*, tears as big as soybeans dropped from his eyes. He said there was order in the family but no Love, and order without Love, like marriage without Love, was immoral. He said that he could have detached himself from our familial eating system long ago and gone his own way and dined on snails and cheese and asparagus and tuna fish and shrimps and veal and Kentucky Fried Chicken and sandwiches and McDonald's hamburgers and apple pie and vanilla ice cream. He also added that he loved his Aunt, meaning my First Cousin, but that he found Aunt's views unacceptable, no matter how enticing they might sound to the ears.

At this point Uncle put in a word. Note he did not interrupt; that would have been rude. But to put in a word denotes intimacy and wisdom and a spirit of Democracy, in a word it was conferring an honor on the speaker. Uncle began by saying that my First Cousin's wording of the Main Contradiction and the Main Danger was not in keeping with the official wording of the issue. He himself felt that it was advisable never to emphasize any one aspect of a problem as the Main Danger. According to his own lifetime experience as a practicing physician, he said, the minute you pinpointed constipation as the Main Danger, it was bound to end in universal diarrhea, leading to a sellout of all pills for diarrhea and distrust of doctors in general. On the other hand, if you pointed to diarrhea as the Main Danger, it was bound to end in universal constipation leading to hernia, with the additional problem of pent-up energies building into a Heat Syndrome and leading to fistfights. The pent-up energies are fanned by fire, and the fire must be quelled by water. Only when the five elements are balanced can one maintain good health. Thus, concluded Uncle, one must be on guard against diarrhea on the one hand, and constipation on the other. Deal with the one or the other as they come. It is best, of course, to be neither constipated nor suffering from diarrhea. As Uncle finished, I thought I heard the sound of clapping.

After the clapping, we discovered that our problem was still there. Moreover, our metabolism seemed to have been hastened by all this discussion of the five elements. Anyway, we were hungry. So we decided that as Grandfather had the most votes, he should be in charge.

Grandfather did not agree. He said that cooking was a technical issue. It has nothing to do with politics, ideology, seniority, status, power, privilege or one's place in the hierarchy. He said what we needed to elect was not the best leader but the best cook. Nothing else but skill at stewing and stir-fry were the required qualifications.

My son applauded, and everybody felt this was truly an original line of thinking, a new breakthrough. But some pointed out that time was short, that they were hungry. The fact was, although the search for the right person to oversee our household menu was still in the stage of discussion, yet when the hour came round we all wanted our dinner. The discussion might have results, or the discussion could end in nothing, but we all wanted our dinner. Some agreed with the decision arrived at in the discussion, and some did not, but we all wanted our dinner. With permission we wanted our dinner, without permission we wanted it just the same. And so, we each went our several ways to feed our bellies.

Setting up the cooking competition was quite complicated. The requirements were that we each had to make one batch of steamed bread, one pot of rice, two scrambled eggs, a platter of chopped pickled turnips, one bowl of thin porridge and one stewed rump. To work out this program, we had altogether spent thirty days and thirty nights in discussion. There had been tension, arguments, quarrels, tears and reconciliations. By the end, we were so exhausted that we could hardly make water or walk on our own two legs. The overall result was that we had hurt each other's feelings, but had also exchanged views, that we had exhausted ourselves but also had a lot of fun. When the question of the two scrambled eggs was brought up, we tumbled over each other with laughter as if we shared a secret joke. When the requirement for chopping pickled turnips was brought up, the whole company was downcast, as if we had suddenly aged. To make a long story short, the cooking skill competition took place and the results were released. The grading went very smoothly, nobody raised any objections. The results were thus:

First Class First Grade: Grandfather and Grandmother.

First Class Second Grade: Father, Mother, Uncle, Aunt.

Second Class First Grade: I, my Wife, my First Cousin, my First Cousin's Husband.

Third Class First Grade: my Son.

We were then concerned that my Son, only getting Third Class, might be hurt, so we decided to give him a certificate of Special Honor, the "Star of Hope" certificate. Of course it goes without saying that he was still Third Class in spite of being "Star of Hope." Anyway, theories and terms and methodology may vary, but order was invariable.

Time passed. People were vaguely aware that all things in heaven and earth find their own balance. So after a while, our fever of excitement over the great eating debate fizzled out, and the heat of controversy over theory and terms and methodology and experimentation gradually cooled down. We did not rack our brains over whether it was a technical problem or a cultural issue, a question of institutional struc-ture, or something never dreamt of in our philosophy. We stopped racking our brains over the problem. It seemed that without solving these knotty questions, we still managed to feed our bellies.

Elder Sister Xu passed away peacefully. She lay down for her afternoon nap and never woke up. We all remember her, respect her and venerate her memory. My Son went to work for a joint-venture company. He has probably realized his tar-get of bread and butter daily with mounds of animal fat. On holidays back home, he would say that he has had his fill of rich foods and now only hankers after porridge and pickles, thin soup and bean-curd noodles, adding in a shamefaced sort of way: "Concepts change easily, but the palate is stubborn."

Now, Uncle and Aunt have moved into their own apartment in a new building and do their own cooking. They have a brand new kitchen with pipe gas and an exhaust fan. They have tried stewed rump, and they have tried scrambled eggs, but they still cannot do without sliced steamed bread, thin porridge, pickled turnips, thin soup and bean-curd paste noodles. Our First Cousin's Husband finally made it abroad for "further studies," studying and working at the same time, and his wife joined him later. He writes: "Here, our favorite food is porridge and pickles. Picking up our bowl of porridge with pickles to go, we feel as if we were back in home sweet home, and for the moment we forget that we are wanderers in a strange land. It can't be helped, it seems that porridge and pickles are in our genes."

I stay with Father and Grandfather, and we live happily ever after. We eat much more meat and chicken and fish and milk and sugar and fat than ever before, we have all put on weight. Our table is groaning under dishes of fancy food in an ever-changing round of novelties. We had stir-fried pork, and we had sea slugs, we had fried peanuts, and we had cream pastry, we had cold bean-curd skin, and we had shrimp salad. We even had abalone and scallops on one occasion. The abalone and the sea slugs came and went, the salad was eaten and forgotten. But thin porridge and pickles outlasted them all. Even after a gourmet feast of all the delicacies extracted from seas and mountains, we still have to sit down to a dessert of porridge and pickles. Only with porridge and pickles as a base can our digestive organs – esophagus, stomach, intestines, liver, spleen and gall bladder – operate normally. Without this last touch of thin porridge and pickles, stomachache and gas would immediately attack us, and who knows what else, perhaps even cancer. Thanks to porridge and pickles, we have so far been preserved from stomach or intestinal cancer. I can state that porridge and pickles make up the Headrope in the Net System of our Eating; the gourmet dishes are only subsidiaries, the Meshes of the Net. Only when the Headrope is pulled up can all the Meshes open out.

After Elder Sister Xu's death, Mother shouldered the momentous task of cooking. According to rote, Mother would ask Grandfather and Grandmother: "Soup or no soup? Pork – shredded or sliced?" The Faithful repetition of this ancient query was soothing to the heart, an expression of a moral sentiment, a dedication to the memory of Elder Sister Xu. Her spirit seemed to come alive in the observance of this seemingly empty ritual of question and answer. Grandfather finally announced that so long as there was porridge and pickles, slices of steamed bread and bean-curd paste noodles, all the rest was immaterial and would be left to Mother's discretion. He begged Mother not to challenge him with all sorts of knotty questions. Mother answered submissively and did as she was told, but always felt something missing if she didn't ask first. When the food was on the table, she would peer around apprehensively, carefully studying Grandfather's face for any signs of disaffection. If Grandfather coughed, she would say softly to herself, perhaps there had been a speck of sand in the rice. Perhaps the pickles had been too salty. Or too bland. She would thus murmur to herself, not daring to ask outright. Of course, even if she had asked Grandfather from the beginning, there might still have been specks of sand in the rice.

One of these days, Mother was bound to pick up her courage again and go up to Grandfather asking most submissively, conscious that she was bothering Grandfather against his injunctions: "Pork – sliced or shredded?" And Grandfather's tone as he answered would be benevolent even in firmness. Even if it was only to say, "Do not ask me," it would still be a sort of answer. And then Mother, her mind set at ease, would go back to finish her cooking.

A friend from England came for a visit, a friend of Father's from the forties. He stayed with us for a week. We went out of our way to hire a western-style chef to make steak and pastry for him, but he said: "Frankly, I am not here to eat this nondescript mess that you take to be western food. Please give me something at once traditional and unique. Please!" What could we do? We had no choice but to give him thin porridge and pickles.

"What simplicity! What elegance! How tender! How soothing! Where else but in the mysterious Orient can one meet with this kind of elixir!" I taped his rhapsody of thin porridge in his impeccable Oxford accents and played the cassette to my Son.

1989
Translated by Zhu Hong

Nedim Gürsel

■

THE
GRAVEYARD OF
UNWRITTEN
BOOKS

After ejecting the Greeks from Smyrna, and abolishing both the sultanate and the caliphate that had presided over the civil and religious affairs of the Ottoman Empire, Mustafa Kemal, known as Ataturk, established the Turkish Republic in 1923. While forcefully Westernizing his country – secularizing the state, emancipating women, introducing the Latin alphabet, adopting Western dress and developing industry – he ruled firmly over his people until his death in 1938. Since then, Turkey has seen occasional relinquishment of the government's abusive powers but an increasing influence of religious extremism. In recent years, conservative elements have succeeded in enforcing stricter censorship against journalists, artists, and writers. Certain writers, such as Nedim Gürsel, have seen their work banned; others have been thrown into jail. And not only contemporary authors are persecuted. In 1997, the actor Mahir Günsiray was imprisoned for reading out a passage of Kafka's The Trial *during a defence statement in court. Kafka, the judge said, was in this novel "insulting to the Turkish authorities."*

■

BEFORE MOVING TO PARIS, to Rue du Figuier (Fig Tree Street), I thought of writing as a way of life. I haven't changed my mind but, since I settled on this street lined with old buildings, the writing craft (which implies being in touch with the world and with its people, taking the pulse of the sea, streets, cities, children and trees, earth and birds, day and night, that is to say, nature and human society – that opening towards the Other) has transformed itself, first into complete solitude and then, progressively, into an authoritarian domination. I'm no longer as I used to be, tender and free in my relationship to words. I no longer abandon myself easily to the words circling over my head, like the small moths that are drawn to my lamp at night, through the open window. Instead of savouring their exquisite shapes – the iridescent glitter of their wings, the sounds they make as they fly about – instead of overcoming my longing for my country and my mother tongue by caressing them with my eyes, I take on the role of an implacable and crafty hunter.

I don't believe that there is a direct link between my new address and the obligatory change in my conception of what the writer's craft should be. At least, that was my belief until

the day when, out of curiosity, I began to research the history
of my street and the origin of its name. Earlier on, I had lived
in Paris in similar lodgings, small bed-sitters or single rooms
under the eaves where, bent over white sheets of paper spread
out over my desk, I would constantly stare at the overcast sky,
at the blackened walls, or at the television antennae standing
erect across from me like a field full of scarecrows. I have
more or less the same kind of view from here. But the Hôtel
de Sens, flanked by its turrets that rise up at the level of my
new flat, adds a new dimension to the scene. I can't tear my
eyes away from the courtyard of this astonishing building,
surrounded by high walls. No matter what time I choose to sit
down and write, I see the words scatter away instead of lining
up neatly on the blank space of the page in front of me and
then take wing towards the courtyard of the Hôtel de Sens,
which, with its corner turrets, its loopholes, its gargoyles, its
newly built porch reminiscent of a ruined drawbridge, resem-
bles a fortress more than a sixteenth-century mansion, so
common in this old neighbourhood of Paris. All my efforts
are in vain! I can no longer make the words obey me, nor can
I exercise control over them, as I used to in the past. Even if I
catch a few words in mid-flight to imprison them on paper,
others succeed in escaping. And yet, in earlier times, a robust
understanding existed between us, since my freedom as a
writer depended on their will to serve me. Until now, placed,
displaced, crossed out, lined up according to grammatical
rules, they were always under my yoke – under my command, I should say – when I wrote my books. They never
behaved in such an unruly manner, even when I'd try to
invent new narrative procedures, thereby upsetting their syn-
tax; I still had a good grip on them. Letters too. They didn't

use to make me lose my temper as easily as they do now, splitting off from one word to attach themselves to another and, through various acrobatic acts, dispel the meanings with which I try to infuse the words. Now, however hard I try to write, they proclaim their freedom from my guardianship and their will to do as they please. As the pressure on them increases, they tend ever more forcefully towards revolt and defiance. Our agreement, the interdependence born from the relation between master and slave, has changed into a bizarre game of pursuit. Even though I appear, in the eyes of most readers, to be a respectable writer, I've become a pitiful blindfolded fool in a game of blind man's bluff. I could certainly not have guessed, when writing out the working title of this story, that an *L* would escape from the word it was in, to come and dislodge the *R*. But that is exactly what happened. And the rest followed. Once "The Well of Rocks" changed into "The Well of Locks," the other letters followed the steps of the first mutineers and stopped listening to me once and for all. I was obliged, whether I wanted to or not, to change the text according to their whims. Now the words, whose mastery I've lost since my moving to Rue du Figuier, began to detach themselves from the sentences and then, as I continued to write my story, started to swim up to the surface like air bubbles in water, floating off towards the Hôtel de Sens. At first I imagined that their flight was caused by the peculiar name of the building, Hôtel de Sens, which would translate as "the Mansion of Meaning" in English. They might indeed have been attracted by such an eloquent title. How could I have known that the Hôtel de Sens, rising before me as if out of another world and whose drafts of medieval air, winding their way through the gloomy maze of corridors, made me shiver, owed its name to Tristan de Salazar, Archbishop of Sens, who ordered its construction? Where could I have learned that what was capturing my words – my dear words plucked with a thousand and one difficulties from the uttermost recesses of my memory and from the most sensitive folds of my being, to be offered to my readers – happened to be a disaffected well in the courtyard of the Hôtel de Sens?

That afternoon, I worked until late at the library. Since the sixteenth century, the Hôtel de Sens had been the residence of several old French families; now, for the past three decades, it had been in use as a library. After having concealed so many secrets, passions, dead loves, and terrible crimes, it now housed thousands of printed volumes. In the ancient ballroom where, in times gone by, under the light of flaming torches, the noblemen of the kingdom had danced and made merry with their ladies, a few passionate book lovers such as myself now sat so absorbed in their reading that they failed to notice when, behind the stained glass windows, it was growing dark.

I stayed at the library until late, oblivious that the Parisian night had fallen suddenly on the roofs. A hand touched my shoulder, making me jump. It was the librarian, saying that the closing time was long past, that seeing me read without once lifting my head from the book in which I was immersed, he hadn't wanted to disturb me, but that now I had to leave. If I wished, I could borrow the book I was reading. After thanking him for his understanding, I left carrying the book. As I was walking down the stairs, he shouted after me:

"The doorman has locked the entrance gate. Go across the courtyard; you'll be able to exit through the back door."

As far as I know, the Hôtel de Sens has no entrance other than the portico resembling a drawbridge. To avoid further disturbing the librarian, I didn't ask him exactly where the back door was. I quickly walked down the stairs and found myself in the courtyard. Night had fallen, and it was pitch dark. A ray of yellow light filtering through the windows of the great hall fell on the courtyard. I walked straight towards it, lifted my eyes, and saw the librarian watching my progress. We stared at each other. Then, all of a sudden, just as I was about to ask him, with gestures, what direction to take, the light was switched off and I was left in the dark. The city lights didn't reach the courtyard over the high walls. I decided to climb back upstairs and look for the librarian who had just switched off the lights, and then leave in his company. As I was about to retrace my steps, the librarian appeared behind me. Directing his flashlight towards the darkest corner of the courtyard, he whispered in my ear:

"This way, sir. We'll pass under the gate of the Well of Rocks."

There was no well and no rock in sight. The beam of light, after sweeping over the rough cobbles of the yard, shone upon the cement. He noticed my hesitation.

"Sir, I quite understand your uneasiness," he continued. "Apparently, in spite of your coming here so often, you are not familiar with the history of the building in which our library is lodged."

"True, I knew nothing about it until today. But in that book you lent me I read that Tristan de Salazar, Archbishop of Sens, had ordered its construction towards the end of the fifteenth century."

"I meant the history, sir, the very ancient past of the building. According to your library card, you live at number 4, Rue du Figuier. Let us say that your knowledge of history is

limited to a few centuries. In that case, have you ever wondered about the origin of the name of your street?"

I had no time to chat with the librarian. I wanted to leave
and return home as quickly as possible. But, in order not to
appear discourteous after his earlier kindness, I nevertheless
made an effort to answer his question:

"Had I not been curious about it, I would not have asked
you for the book called *The Streets of Paris*. Unfortunately, I
didn't find the slightest information in it on the history of
Rue du Figuier before the sixteenth century. It was probably
built at the same time as the Hôtel de Sens."

"No. According to irrefutable documents, the street dates
back to the thirteenth century. But let us go back even further
in time. I'm convinced that several centuries before the building of the Hôtel de Sens, even in an age when this whole neighbourhood didn't exist and Paris, called then Lutetia, was a walled
fortress of some twenty thousand inhabitants on the Île de la
Cité, there was a fig tree growing among rocks exactly where
this street now lies. Later, a well was dug among the rocks at
the foot of the tree, so that those who wanted to rest in the
tree's shade could also refresh themselves with a drink from the
well. In fact, the well was used mainly for watering the crops,
since the area was farmed for marshland produce. The well still
exists. The fig tree is long since dead, but the water from that
well served to mix the mortar used in the building of the Hôtel
de Sens. And Queen Margot, after ordering the execution of
her overnight lovers, had them thrown into this same well."

I was starting to itch with impatience. All this talk didn't
interest me in the least.

"Please excuse me," I said. "I have an urgent meeting elsewhere. What if we chatted about this some other day? I'll be

back tomorrow. Right now, let us get out of here."

"I understand your haste, sir, but you should indeed pay attention to my story. Our leaving depends to some degree on the Well of Rocks."

"I don't understand. A while ago you said I would be able to leave by the back door."

"Yes, but in order to reach it, we must climb down into the bottom of the well, since the gate I mentioned isn't here, but in the inner courtyard."

"How is that possible?" I asked anxiously. "Look over there; I live on the top floor of the building opposite. From my window I can see the whole of the Hôtel de Sens. If there were a courtyard other than this one, it would certainly not have escaped my notice."

"I know you spend the night writing to the light of your lamp, and that you often lift your head from your papers to look at the Hôtel de Sens. I've been watching you since you moved here. But you can't learn anything from such a great height. I've been working in this library for the past twenty years and it is only recently that I've discovered this inner courtyard."

"Impossible. In the oldest documents which I've consulted in the archives, on the most detailed plans of the building, there was never any mention of such a courtyard. You must have seen a mirage."

He didn't answer. He simply smiled superciliously. I was on the point of losing my patience.

"If you don't mind, I want to get out of here at once," I insisted.

"It cannot be done."

"Why?"

"We must first climb down into the Well of Rocks."

He asked me to follow him and he started to lead the way. At the end of the courtyard, we stopped by the wall. Pointing the beam of his flashlight towards one of the mossy stones, he said:

"We'll make our way through here."

In the light, I saw the stone move on its base. In front of us a passage opened, big enough for a small child. The librarian climbed through it first; then he lit my way with his flashlight. I found myself inside a narrow and gloomy gallery. Crouching as we walked, we reached the inner courtyard at last. In the very centre of this secret courtyard, which I guessed was surrounded by the inside walls of one of the corner turrets, there was indeed a well. We approached it. The librarian began to climb down the rope ladder that lost itself in its depths. I followed. Curiously, I didn't feel the least anguish. There was no room in me for even the slightest unease. Everything seemed rather natural to me. My earlier absentmindedness while I was reading in the library the documents relating to Rue du Figuier, my conversation with the librarian, my arrival close behind him in this secret courtyard, our descent into a dry well by means of a rope ladder – all seemed quite commonplace, just as if every night I followed this route on my way home to my desk. Nothing disturbed me: neither the librarian's sententious words, nor the insects scuttling away in the beam of his flashlight, not even the spiderwebs clinging to my feet during the descent. At last we reached the bottom of the well. In front of us stretched a gallery with a higher ceiling, and we were able to proceed with ease. We had walked for a long while inside that dark tunnel with dripping walls when suddenly we began to hear the sound of rattling chains. The further we went, the louder the sound grew. We stopped in front of an iron door. The librarian knocked. The door creaked open and, as soon as we stepped inside, I was blinded by the light. We were inside an immense storeroom lit with spotlights. Attendants in official uniforms moved feverishly in all directions. As soon as my eyes grew accustomed to the spotlights, I saw a pile of books in the middle of the room. The attendants were picking them up by the armful and placing them on metal shelves that towered all the way up to the ceiling; once the shelves were full, they prevented access to the books by securing them with chains.

"We are now in the Well of Rocks," said the librarian. "Please hide the book you just borrowed. If the attendants see it, it too will be secured under lock and key."

I slipped the book I was holding into the inside pocket of my jacket, and we followed the line of shelves. No one paid any attention to us. They were all busy stashing away on the shelves the books that were being thrown from above into the middle of the storeroom, and then chaining them in.

"These are the books banned by the authorities," the librarian continued. "Don't pay attention to their number. If you were to count them, you'd realize they are hardly more than a hundred. But when a book is banned, all copies of that book are also pulled out of circulation. They are then brought here to be placed under lock and key. Sometimes I'm called upon to help draw up the lists of banned titles."

So the librarian was in fact an informer! This fake scholar, this hypocrite who earned his living thanks to the books he lent to readers, spent his nights compiling blacklists!

"How can you take part in such shameful activities!" I shouted at him.

"Don't be angry, my dear sir," he answered in a mocking tone, "I have a passion for books, I'm mad about books. I love books and therefore I punish them. They're like my children to me."

"But books don't need to be taught manners!"

"Why not? Like human beings, they are born, they grow up, and they can turn out good or bad. Then, my dear sir, they die. Their pages fall out and they disappear like corpses rotting underground."

"No! Books are immortal! Human beings die, but not books!"

"Some die even before seeing the light of day. Your own, for instance."

"My own?"

"Yes, a few of your books, those placed here in chains, are first among the books that were aborted or stillborn. And you didn't even know it."

The librarian's words turned my blood to ice. The Ministry of Justice had only just lifted the ban on certain books of mine. So what did the librarian mean? Noticing my astonishment, he stopped one of the attendants hurrying past us and asked him to put down his armload of books. The attendant did so, as if obeying the orders of a superior. After having clicked his heels and saluted, he hurried away. The librarian chose a book from the pile and handed it over to me.

"Look, here's your latest book."

I trembled as I saw my name on the cover. It carried the title of one of the stories I had tried in vain to write without ever being able to see its end. It was a beautiful edition, carefully printed. As I leafed through it, I felt terrified. Here were all the stories I had planned to write since my move to Rue du Figuier.

"Before martial law was proclaimed in the country, this was the graveyard of unwritten books," the librarian explained. "Then the banned books were added to them. You have several books in both categories. Gradually, as judges who support freedom of thought authorize the reissuing of your censored volumes, the number of your unwritten books increases. In a sense, it is you yourself who bans them. I only do my duty. Deep down inside, I'm fond of writers. If you wish to continue to write, leave your new lodgings at once. Don't bother with words that rebel against you and that will no longer listen to you. When you have moved far away from the Well of Rocks, drifting once again towards the light of your lamp, they will most certainly return, as if by a miracle, to find you once again."

I felt an irresistible impulse to escape from the cursed graveyard as quickly as possible. The repulsive man who called himself a librarian was obviously the graveyard's caretaker. And, what was worse, he was also a loathsome gravedigger! I didn't allow him to accompany me to the door. I started to run after my words fluttering towards the Hôtel de Sens. I opened the iron door and, after it had creaked shut behind me, made up my mind to write the tale of how my last story, which I had wanted to call "The Well of Rocks," had become "The Well of Locks" and, finally, "The Graveyard of Unwritten Books." As I ran, I felt I was being pursued by the sound of rattling chains. Then the damp walls of the gallery shook, as if the shelves loaded with books were collapsing behind me.

1991
Translated from the French by Alberto Manguel

Reza Baraheni

∎

THE
DISMEMBERMENT

*Until he was deposed in 1979, Mohammad-Reza Shah
Pahlavi reigned as despot over the kingdom that was once
Persia. The United States enthusiastically supported the
Shah's regime. It was estimated that over 30,000 Americans
lived during the seventies in Iran, training the Shah's army
or working for American corporations. During that time,
hundreds of politicians and intellectuals critical of the government were tortured and killed, or were hounded into exile.
Aided by the CIA, the Shah's secret police terrorized
civilians at home and harassed dissidents and students who
had sought refuge abroad. Reza Baraheni, novelist, poet,
and the founder of modern literary criticism in Iran, was
imprisoned and tortured for over a hundred days in 1973,
and forced to leave the country. He went to the U.S. and
worked with international organizations to expose the
violations of human rights in Iran. Baraheni had hoped
that the overthrow of the Shah would bring some form of
democracy to his troubled country. He was mistaken. He
returned to Iran early in 1979, when the Shah had just fled*

*the country and everyone was preparing for the revolution.
Ayatollah Khomeini returned to Iran and proclaimed the
Islamic Republic as the form of the future government. Baraheni worked with the Writers Association of Iran, which he
had helped to found a decade earlier, wrote articles on the
rights of women and oppressed nationalities, and kept
producing his own novels and poetry. He spend a good part
of the fall of 1981 and the winter of 1982 in the prisons of
the new regime. He was released after pressure from world
writers and intellectuals, but was fired from his post as professor of literature at the University of Tehran. Baraheni
formed what he called the "Basement Workshop for Fiction
and Poetry," training the young generation of Iranian writers
in his home. In the 1990s, he was in the forefront of the
writers' struggle for freedom of speech and democracy in Iran.
He is one of the original drafters and signatories of the
"Text of 134 Iranian Writers" and the "Draft Charter of
the Writers Association of Iran," which form the basis of the
recent democratic movement in his country. Escaping two
abduction attempts by the Ministry of Intelligence in 1996,
Baraheni first went to Sweden and later accepted asylum
in Canada.*

■

H E COMMANDED, "Bring the saw up here."
Ascending the ladder, I was in a position
to see the withered, fleshless, dust- and blood-
smeared limbs of that one. I gazed at them, afraid, my mouth
parched and dry, my breath strangled in my throat, the saw,

large and gleaming white, savage saw with teeth, long and sharp, rude and merciless, held in one hand, my other hand grasping the rungs of the ladder, one by one – staring at him, appalled, from behind – that one, who was breathing heavily and mumbling something which I couldn't hear. And as I moved up, rung by rung, my eyes were fixed on neither earth nor sky, but first on his feet, then the calves of his legs, then his burnt-out thighs – that one, the man whose name I am afraid to let pass my lips, although I admire it – and, of course he had a tattered loincloth, there, red and gray, blood-soaked, around his waist, a narrow waist, the hair around his waist sticky with blood as if they had wanted to pluck out each hair with their dagger-like, dreadful, sharp nails, but had instead picked at the flesh underneath, leaving the hair standing in place on a surface of torn and ravaged flesh.

"The saw!" he commanded.

"Bringing it," I said.

"Faster," he said, "bring it faster!"

"Bringing it faster!" I said.

And I moved faster – as if I were able to! – and closed my eyes so as not to see – as if I were able to! – as if it were possible to become blind! – there before my eyes loomed the bloodied spike, whose gleaming point had passed through his body and protruded from his back – his back, him, that one whose name I did so like – point passing through his body and out his back through the timber of the rack to which he was fastened. Now I opened my eyes and looked at the spike with my eyes open and it was the same I had seen with my eyes closed.

"The saw!" he shouted.

And I said, "Bringing it," and took another step upward and raised my right hand and stretched the handle of the saw, the handle on Mahmoud's end, out to Mahmoud, and Mahmoud, from the other side of the man, from the side where his face – and the face of that one whose name made me afraid because I liked it so – could be seen, took the saw by its long, white, vertical handle.

And he said, "Up, come higher up so that we can begin." And I moved another rung higher up, stopping right next to his head; his sweat-soaked, burning, fiery profile seemed . . . in an aura of light? . . . No, but red and vast and even god-like. His thick beard seemed to grow out of his face in my direction.

"Measure the arm!" shouted Mahmoud, his end of the saw in hand, and I changed the handle of my end of the saw to my left hand and raised my right hand and bent forward a bit and placed my little finger on the pulsating wrist of him – that one whom I liked so because I was afraid of him – and spread my comparatively rude fingers up his forearm, the fingers of the right hand along his naked forearm below the elbow, touching his inflamed body, sensing his humid, torrential fever to the capillary depths of me.

Then the cries, I heard the wailing, the rhythmical, howling voices of the assembled host of my countrymen, crying out in chorus, "His right hand first! His right hand first! His right hand first!"

And, these words having been repeated several times, like a ritual tribal chant, Mahmoud shouted, "Begin!" and with a harmonious, rhythmical motion we began, Mahmoud pulling the saw as I released it, I pulling the saw as Mahmoud released it and the saw slipping and slicing through the flesh with the grating sound of a potter's wheel in a Ghaznein or Rey or Baghdad bazaar. What with Mahmoud pulling mightily upon the saw when I released it and myself pulling mightily upon the saw when Mahmoud released it, the arm was soon severed, two hands-breadth lengths from the wrist, just above the elbow, and Mahmoud shouted, "Bring the oil! Oil!" And from the foot of the ladder they handed me the bucket full of boiling, steaming, fiery hot oil, and I handed it to Mahmoud, and he managed with agility to hold it and to twist the severed stump of the arm into the oil and keep it there until the blood coagulated.

And then I heard his loud voice, like a spear – his voice, that one whom I liked because I feared him so – shouting something like *"Annal haq!"*[1] or perhaps that very phrase "Annal haq!" And the people, the calamity-stricken dogs, wailed an answer in chorus: "Now his left hand! Now his left hand! Now his left hand!" And we fell to our work, but cutting through the left arm was harder than cutting through the right arm had been; this one thing I couldn't understand: why should cutting through one arm be more difficult than cutting through the other? Isn't it so, after all, that a man's two arms are equal in strength or in weakness, equally thick and muscular or spindly and stringy and weak? I had descended the ladder. Mahmoud had done the same. The warm-odored blood of the one-armed man had spilled onto my knees and the apron of my winding sheet which had soaked it up drop by drop. I had descended the ladder, and then Mahmoud moved his ladder to the other side and I did the same, moved my ladder to the other side, and although there were still chopped-ground pieces of flesh and bone on the saw, the saw still seeming to vibrate with that awful grating sound, I felt no shame at holding it in my hand – it was our intention, our aim

---

[1]. Literally, "I am the Truth"; metaphorically, "I am God."

to kill any and all shame in ourselves; and we had killed shame in ourselves, because shame for Mahmoud was a worthless commodity – the sweat of shame must never befoul the countenance of man. Saw in hand, after changing the place of my ladder, I felt more at ease and ascended the ladder rung by rung. Mahmoud did the same. I was more nimble this time; I was a better murderer; I was more of a murderer. Mahmoud had once told me, "A man gets used to it." And I had been able to get used to it, this being the first time I had ever dismembered anyone. Mahmoud had said, "A man gets used to it," and then had told me how he himself, at the very beginning, had been ill-at-ease at the prospect of taking up a sword or spear or even a small dagger in his hand but how later he had been able to attack a man who had angered him with a small cheese knife: the man had leveled accusations at Mahmoud's ancestry, and Mahmoud had flung the knife straight at him, and the knife had struck the man directly in the right shoulder, in such a way that it deprived the howling wretch of the use of his arm. After that, it had been mere child's play to attack another man, this one thick-boned, thick-bodied, larger than himself – attacking from behind, of course, and laying him out with a single blow – and Mahmoud's confrères had dragged the corpse to the river and given it a kick and a push with their heavy-booted feet, after allowing the blood to drain out through the gashes, a kick and a push and a toss into the river like a sack full of old bones and bloodless meat; after that Mahmoud had become famous for his courage and his valor by strangling two men with his bare hands – killing another man by a fierce kick to the ribs – killing one of his own brothers by night, they said, and blinding one of his own sons by day. He had also slain many in war, and when they took prisoners and brought the captured commandants, lately converted into eunuchs, before him or when they brought the young soldiers before him, some with nails extracted, tongues sliced out, fingers, ears, or noses sliced off, Mahmoud would stand them all beside the river as target dummies for his sword practice; he had tested his speed at decapitation by sword and was found capable of knocking the heads off twenty castrated captains in the wink of an eye; Mahmoud was capable of noting with complete composure the place between the thighs of those captives whose manliness they had torn out by the roots – Mahmoud had the habit of noting this and suddenly erupting with a laughter so deep and wild and lusty and joyful, so full of relish that the newly castrated victims felt themselves strong and sound as ever – for a moment, of course, only for a moment – because they heard the laughter and the next moment a spasm in their throats, a turbulence in their bowels, eyeballs darting to and fro in alarm, skulls swelling with a brain-rattling raging convulsion that forced the eyeballs to protrude from their sockets looking like rotten, trampled peaches: Mahmoud appeared on the back of his tall, narrow-bodied, immaculately trimmed white horse, and, first bending down to kiss his horse's neck, he took his sword from our elder servant and galloped away, and there was an end to the convulsions and spasms, an end to the turbulence in the bowels and eyeballs protruding from their sockets – the sword swinging horizontally sliced through unresistant soft as cheese necks and sliced and severed and hacked, and Mahmoud flung his sword into the sand with the skill and artistry only he among men could aspire to, the elder servant being responsible for gathering in these swords. And when Mahmoud came back, dismounted, and washed his hands and face, cleansing himself for prayer with fresh spring water, then all men of this land stood in emulation of their leader at prayer.

"What are you wasting time for? Begin!" he said, and I began, but I don't know why cutting through his left arm was harder than cutting through his right – I mean, the left arm was literally more difficult to cut through! Was I not more at ease this time? Nimbler? More of a murderer? Why was his left arm so difficult to cut through? I looked to Mahmoud and saw that it hadn't surprised him at all; in sensing my confusion, he said, "It's always like this – the resistance increases – but the resistance of this stubborn head of a braying ass will lessen!" Starting in again, we cut only through the skin – thin, sickly arm resisting like a bar of iron – Mahmoud, enraged, removed his left hand from the handle of the saw and grabbed him by the beard, growling, "If you resist, I'll cut your head off!" and receiving no answer, as he – that one whom I did so like – had seemed to sink into himself after having once cried out and seemed to have no intention of ever saying anything again, shouted, "You there! Bring me an axe! A Tashkent blade!" Before long they gave him one from below, and he gave it to me and said, "Go a step higher, give the axe a good powerful swing and cut the cursed thing off at the shoulder! No more need for measuring!" And I did what he told me, and never had I done anything that he had not told me: went a step higher, raised the axe above my head and the crowd and Mahmoud, and swung the blade in a wide arc from east to west. "Whap!" It came down and the arm, instead of hanging from the left side of his body, was now hanging from the left side of the rack. Then they gave the oil to Mahmoud from below, and Mahmoud took the oil to the severed stump and plunged the stump, like the head of an animal, into the oil and with this action arose a scream, a strong and loud and mythic cry: "*Annal haq!*" or something like "*Annal haq!*" – and then the people, yelping and howling dogs, crying in chorus: "And now his feet! And now his feet! And now his feet!" And we, upon hearing their cry, we – who had gone so far as to place the responsibility for the affairs of the people in their very own hands and had said, "We will provide the backdrop. You will be encouraged and rewarded for effort. You will be moved to great works. You will but speak and we will act upon your word" – upon hearing the cry "And now his feet!" descended our ladders calmly and obediently, the axe in my hand and the bucket of burning oil in Mahmoud's hand – the hand of my Agha, my master . . . my God. We descended to treat those feet – his feet, the feet of that one whom I did like awfully well because I feared him and did not know why I feared and liked him – to the pummeling they deserved.

As we descended everything was quiet. The people were waiting, after all their clamor – the bearded lambs, weak, mustachioed little lambs to be bought and sold on the bazaar, young and old, ugly and handsome, were waiting, still far from any real comprehension of blood. But I could hear the warm call of blood, the sound of the beating pulse in the severed stump of his arm pounding to my ears, and the smell of blood, that warm odor of blood, first to strike the nose at birth. I again tasted and perceived; it went warmly and pleasantly to work in the fibers of my brain, and I sensed that my eyes had become red, sunset red, that beautiful shade of red, blood red.

Having descended, we found that they had placed two stools on either side of the man bound to the rack, the man from whose stumps blood was still dripping onto the ground. Mahmoud wanted wine. They brought it. I wanted water.

They brought it. We both wet our lips, he with wine, I with water. Mahmoud looked at me, and I bowed my head. He looked at me out of the corners of his eyes. Whenever he grew heated, whenever he drank wine and grew heated, whenever he became amorous, he would look at me out of the corners of his eyes, and the corners of his two eyes would shine like lamps. And now here, right in front of the people standing around us but at some distance from us, Mahmoud laughed with his eyes, looking at me as a lover does, as a man full of lust does. I was ready to kiss his hands, his powerful hands, I was willing, not just from habit, but from love, to kiss his powerful hands. Whenever he glanced at me from the corners of his eyes gleaming like two lamps, I returned his glance only for a moment, a fast fleeting moment, and like the swift motion sound of Mahmoud's sword through the air, a look with the speed of a sword slicing the air, in this fleeting look everything was exchanged with each other – I became subdued and gentle – Mahmoud seemed to swell to a magnificence, the magnificence of an eagle, and I, gentle and subdued as the amorous female dove – he became hot and sharp and large and powerful – I became deep and delicate and soft and felt the scraping of his rough, tumultuous fingers over my body – I sensed that I must kiss the sand of the Oxus shore once again, must wash my mouth with the sand of the shore, fill my mouth with the sand of the shore, must claw at the sand of the shore of the Oxus and stuff the soft, delicate, humid sand into my mouth, a lover of that asphyxiation, that dying, that burial in the sand. Mahmoud looked at me out of the corners of his eyes. He circled the man bound to the rack, the tall man bound to the rack, and the rack itself. The people were more intent upon watching the man with no arms than watching me and Mahmoud. After their chorus of clamor, they were watching the man and enjoying themselves. Mahmoud looked at me. His eyes had become like flames. The wine had already found its way to his eyes. He had already set the bucket of oil down. His hands were still spattered with blood. Like myself, he wore a winding sheet. This custom I do not understand. If I put on a winding sheet, that's one thing, but why Mahmoud? A winding sheet is not fitting for him; a man who gives the orders shouldn't wear a winding sheet. He came over, a full head taller than I. He placed his long, powerful, red, warm, blood-covered hands on my neck. He bent down to me, moving his head closer to mine; he pulled me to him, pressed me to him, turned his head away from me, and I raised my head. How pure I still was, how gentle and kind and womanish and even childish! I raised my head and looked at him, my eyelids half-closed, he pressed his lips to mine, gently at first, then passionately and cruelly, and my knees trembled, then my shoulders, then the space between them, then my knees again and the back muscles of my upper arms – I trembled, trembled, trembled, my fingers growing longer and more delicate, transformed into long, narrow filaments, dark and passionate, and relieved of my inhibitions, I put my arms around his neck and lifted my heels from off the sand, kissing him with my whole mouth, with full lips, as if through this kiss I could attach my chest and belly and crotch to his body and hold them there and die in his mouth . . . And then the cursed howling of the people arose once more: "And now his feet! And now his feet! And now his feet!" Mahmoud pitilessly dropped me at the peak, wrenched his lips from mine, his hands from my body, and just like that, moved away from me, and like a bud blossoming for him suspended in midair, I broke on my branch, withered and fell, the choral clamor of the howl-composing dogs having subsided, to hear his voice, the voice which had just now enclosed me in the fortress of its love, saying, "Begin!" And fallen from the sky unsatisfied, I moved toward the feet of the man bound to the rack. Blood-befouled oil still dripped from his severed left arm. His two arms hung toward the earth, hung from the rack, severed from the trunk, and shiny white bone could be seen protruding from the midst of the torn, worthless heap of flesh, the coagulated blood, the veins, connected and disconnected, of each arm. Already flies and mosquitoes were settling on the carcasses. Of what possible use are arms that have been separated from the body? Arms which will never again be able to perform the orders of their owner? The fingers dead and clutched stiffly together? What possible task can they perform? . . . Mahmoud said, "What is it? What are you looking up there for?" I turned with an unwitting laugh, raising my head to look up there again, and, indeed, such a spectacle was quite something to behold – the sight of that creature up there was quite something to behold. That man hanging up there – was he able to turn his head back and see to his left? If he could turn his head and see his arms now, what would he really think of them? I wasn't immersed in my own thoughts about him – I was immersed in his thoughts, sensed myself swimming about in his mind and turning slowly to his severed arms. Rather, I *was* he and was turning toward my *own* arms – my head not unlike the face of a clock, clock face hanging from the sky, and now the clock-hands of my mind gearing me for the movement toward my arms – swimming deep to the inside of his mind, my mind, looking at my arms, more like two decapitated children than like arms cut off, popping out in blisters. I wanted to, at that moment, pick up something and drive the flies and mosquitoes away from the stumps of my arms, but I had no hands. Then it happened that I raised my own, intact arms and jumped and waved in the direction of my arms which were his arms, and suddenly a swarm of flies and mosquitoes arose from the severed stump, and then, as if nothing had happened, I descended into my own thoughts about my arms: what had I felt when they were cutting them off? Of what particular nature was my agony? Difficult to tell, but when I was able to recall the sound of the grating of the saw or the falling of the axe and to hear it, I raised my right hand, unwittingly, and took firmly ahold of my left arm where it had been cut off by the axe – as if trying to reaffirm the existence of my own hands and arms. Mahmoud said, "Are you all right? What is it with you? Why have you turned so pale?" "Nothing," I said, "the weather's too hot." He sent them to bring water, and when they brought it, he said, "Wash your hands and face." On Mahmoud's order I washed my hands and face as if I were performing some kind of sacred ritual. At Mahmoud's orders I had become handsomer, my hair growing longer and shinier, giving off a subtle perfume, my heart becoming pure and naive. And at Mahmoud's orders I would frequently sense a sacred aura of radiance about my head and often times around my buttocks, such a soft, languorous feeling when this radiance wound itself down into the cleft of my buttocks and the space between my thighs and concentrated there. And I would feel that Mahmoud must be with me; his warm and lustful breath, regular and rhythmical, condensing on the back of my neck, must, in its rising and falling rhythm, invade me and drive me to completion – must rule me and drive me forward – and I must strain and struggle, clawing at the pillow or mat or stones or sand and cram myself full of Mahmoud – always waiting for the dagger at my back – Mahmoud the dagger at my back – if he were to abandon me, I would die, no longer to have those sweet and feverish moments of ecstasy, the hot breath of Mahmoud full of fire and violence, his caressing murmurs.

He said, "It's taking a long time," and I said, "Yes," and he said, "It's getting late," and I said, "Yes," and he said, "When you're feeling a little better, we'll begin," and I said, "I'm better," and he said, "Well, let's begin then," and I said, "Begun!" And we moved toward the small gleaming saws. And surely this part of our work wasn't terribly difficult, because cutting off feet, on the whole, is easy work. It's not unlike beheading a chicken . . . In my own mind I had practiced the action of cutting off a foot scores of times and Mahmoud had cut off scores of feet. We both had the necessary skill and were able to maintain our coolness through an extreme of concentration on the job at hand, although we knew that the man they had hung up there, before being stretched and hung on the rack, had run so much that his legs were streaming with blood. Directly preceding his run they had placed a helmet on his head, one of those helmets which cover the entire head and face and neck, on which nothing can make a dent, and then, with full ceremony, as if they were dressing a young bride in her wedding gown, they had dressed him in flimsy armor of polished tin. During those several moments neither he nor they had spoken a word. And then the man who had dressed him in the armor and the man who had placed the helmet on his head stood aside, and the people, these very dog-wailing people, this howling chorus, standing a stone's throw away from him, had shouted: "Run! Run! Run!" And he had started to run and the whole city of men had begun to pursue him over the sand with rough, hard, small stones which had been gathered from the riverbed over the last three or four days. When they had commenced throwing, he, with all the power left in his body, had run in darkness and terror and infinite loneliness, and the people with all the force in their bodies ran after him, chasing him under the sun, and stoned him, pelted him with stones so relentlessly that the iron hook of his helmet nearly opened, which would have resulted in the helmet falling off his head, leaving him bareheaded to face the stones and to be crushed and maimed by them. Finally, from an excess of fatigue and thirst, an excess of terror and despair, he had fallen, his two eyes staring wildly out of the two small holes in the helmet, looking frantically through these two small holes, moving in terror from side to side, seeing nothing but the sand and sensing the demons, pelting him with stones, and when he had fallen several comparatively large stones had struck his tin armor and helmet and the clang of stone striking his helmet exploding through his brain and buzzing in his ears, deafening them – trapped in an utterly dark world, trapped in his tin armor and the dark enclosure of his helmet. The guards had come and eventually ordered the stoning to stop and the people, who always yielded to the strength and power of the guards and, in truth, were incapable of anything but obedience, had stopped throwing stones at him. Then the sweating guards and their thick-necked hefty son of a bitch squadron leaders had divested him of helmet and armor and carefully, almost respectfully, laid them to the side of the sand, and then one of the guards had emptied two buckets of water over him and he had regained consciousness, and the guards had permitted him to rest a bit, and when he was able to raise his head just a bit off the ground, they had clasped him under the armpits and dragged him slowly to the rack. On two sides of the rack were fastened sheets of cloth on which were written the sentence of the man: to be stoned, to be nailed upon the rack, to be dismembered, the tenor of the words indicating that they had wanted to make the condemned man understand: "Because you have eyes, we will pluck your two eyes out." This was a sacred tribal ritual, although the tribe itself understood nothing of it, but in that limbo state of theirs between animal and human they needed some stimulus, to overthrow the monotony and custom of their ordinary lives and absorb their imaginations in the eternal quest for excitement and stimulation and more excitement and more stimulation like a fireworks display going on forever, colorful and enervating, carrying them soaring to the very zenith of emotion, impelling them to sudden and momentary and collective action. And Mahmoud and I had been able to introduce into their daily routine something harsh and swift, harsh and swift and fraught with vision, that would totally shatter their subjectivity and free them from their looseness and their torpor, preparing at the same time something beautiful and wondrous, a kind of nourishment for their subconscious, trusting that the more violent and intense and emotional it was, the faster it would sink into their imaginations, that any event of a fierce and deeply affecting nature would, regardless of how terrible, how hellish, by forced penetration of all the crevices and orifices of their unconscious, transform them completely to the depths of their being in such a way that they would come to sense the Mahmoudi will – the Mahmoudi will which changes and affects everything in such a way that they would be compelled to accept Mahmoud's way, and, through him, my way – wanting Mahmoud and, through Mahmoud, wanting me as well. And I want it this way, for I believe, and this belief constitutes a sizable portion of my instincts and emotions, that all the crevices and orifices of mankind and history, and contemporary mankind in particular, must come to be crammed full of Mahmoud; for I believe that contemporary mankind has (and this applies to the past as well) no being apart from Mahmoud. If it were otherwise, there would be no reason for me to sit on this side and Mahmoud on that, cutting off the feet of the man bound to the rack. No action is practical for Mahmoud without prior knowledge and calculation; he understands everything well; his genius is in his meticulously precise comprehension of the need for action followed by direct or indirect action. Dismemberment, for example, was a singularly fixed and definite action – Mahmoud had perceived that the action should be performed, the man dismembered, but he had also designated a special procedure for the action, and I well knew that he privately insisted on this order and for this reason it had been so set up that he sever the left foot and I the right. Of course, it really made no difference, right or left – a foot is a foot – what difference if a man severs the left or severs the right? But I always agree with Mahmoud and grant that he has the power to see the truth, and he liked to begin everything from the left side; it is the people's custom, he said, to believe in the superiority of the right side, and in order that they might not think of him as boasting of his superiority, he liked to begin everything from the left side. For this reason, Mahmoud and I had agreed that I would always start from the right and he from the left. Subconsciously he had perceived that to the left, perhaps, will go the victory, so he started from the left and gave the right to others, believing that the illusion of superiority should belong to the others, the essential victory, meaning the victory of pretensions to belonging to the left, should be his. Mahmoud was not a deceiver of the people, but a man who transformed their consciousness, transfigured their souls and looks and actions and words, and even revolutionized their instincts and approaches to life. All his people, even his own guards, disliked something in him, but when he turned his face upon them and stood before them and looked straight into their eyes, they immediately stood alert and attentive, ready at a single glance or gesture of his hands or a simple direction of his tongue to realize his wishes; there was great force in even the movement of Mahmoud's finger. One day Mahmoud, without any cause, except perhaps to intimidate the others, had shouted at one of his officers, a man who had boasted of being braver than himself in the taking of a fortress, "Go off somewhere and die!" and the brave officer had immediately unsheathed his dagger and slit his own jugular vein, falling at Mahmoud's feet. Another time he had ordered a poet, who had wanted me for a night in private conference, to eat a chunk of fresh, steaming cow dung in his presence, and later, in Kashmir, had ordered him to milk the goats and herd the cows. I have never forgotten the delicate hands of that poet, fondling my neck and under my ear lobes. I don't imagine that he will have forgotten my ear lobes after all that, or that Mahmoud will have forgotten his transgression. The day will no doubt come to pass when he will shout: "Hold the head of this cursed poet under hot water until he ceases to breathe!" I alone know this man Mahmoud; now that the two of us have made our ablutions for the performance of this sacred tribal ritual, now more than ever before, I know Mahmoud. He had given himself to the ritual of dismemberment with all the rigor of a Hindu ascetic, and, in truth, the dismemberment bore no little resemblance to a sacred ritual in which a man meditates upon the achievement of an ascetic discipline and absolute resignation. The act itself was a pious prayer-chant rising from the saw teeth points, from the meeting of intractable saw ledge and bone. Mahmoud respected the tribal, national rites. He could cut through the feet of a man in such a way that you would swear he was kneeling in devotion on a prayer rug, that he had been transformed into dust and ashes of the ground. In essence, whatever takes place before one's eyes, one must take delight in the disciplined harmony of an event ruled by a perfect order. Mahmoud had created the harmony and rhythm of this prayer which arose from the gleaming, grating teeth of the saw, and the radiant aura of this harmony settled upon the teeth of the people and stimulated their mouths to water, their hearts to pound, and the meta-morphosed heart, twisted, diverted from its initial direction, lost its original beat and began to beat with another purpose; poor hearts that have given themselves up to be transformed and diverted eternally, accepting everything easily – every-thing, of course, by which Mahmoud, through his own actions or those of his guards, had sought to conquer them. The heart stretched out of shape, expanded, or contracted into a round ball, or took a variety of other forms. They had interfered with the ordered rhythm and harmony of the natural human heart, the heart belonging to the earth, to the earth and the mud and the water, to the uprush and flow of things; they had imposed upon it another order, which brought itself another rhythm, another harmony, designed for the realization of other ends, and had done this in such a way that the heart had been converted into an automatic device, the key to the initial and continued beating of which lay concealed in the seal-ring of

Mahmoud and his guards. The people and their hearts were in need of guidance, a discipline other than nature; if not, would they have surrendered their own natural order of things? They needed some discipline beyond the bestial. Mahmoud had revealed this discipline, this new order of things. It originated from his thoughts, soaring, with magnificent slogans and concise catch-phrases, like eagles' wings spread into the hearts of the people seeking something to replace their hearts' natural order. This new order had changed the hue of things earthly and heavenly, had penetrated and taken root in all the subjective and objective states of the tribe. The heart beat, and with every beat, cried out: "Mahmoud!" Didn't my own heart – didn't my own heart cry out, "Mahmoud! Mahmoud!" Didn't my arms and the sharp, red button ends of my joyous young pectorals, didn't my smooth, ivory flanks, my curved eyelids, and the black curls at my temples, from which the initial sweat of my passion always flowed, rolling deliciously down my cheek between my ear and lip, didn't my whole being shriek, "Mahmoud! Mahmoud!"? Was not the name of Mahmoud written on the satin white joints of my knees, on my ankles, on the roselike knuckles of my hands? Did I not coo the name "Mahmoud . . . Mahmoud . . ." in the agonies of my passion? When I awoke at morning, was it not the name of Mahmoud I heard echoing from every wall and door? Hadn't I seen the manly face of Mahmoud on all the banners which fifty modern, hired painters had depicted with the perfumed odor of their colors? Hadn't a thousand poets described, in words of frankincense and balsam perfumes, soothing, agreeable rhythms woven into their texture, from every syllable of which rang the noblest and loftiest of sentiments, his thick, powerful, taut and muscular arms for me to see, his discerning eagle eyes, his chest covered with kinky capillary flowers of hair, for me to see and arise in worship of Mahmoud? Hadn't these poets placed him, in admiration of his radiance and beneficence, upon the backs of golden horses for me to see? Hadn't all this display been set before my eyes that I might trust in his magnificence and genius and power forever? Had they not conveyed him in and out of the objective and subjective gates of my consciousness, strewing the way with heaps of slaughtered enemies, that I might see this earthly God being transformed into a heavenly one? And, when all is said and done, had not he, this Mahmoud, descended from that godly sky to grace us here below — had he not embraced me and drowned me in himself that I might revere him — I revered him because he had seized me in his embrace — he was mixed in with my very being, his name constantly buzzing in my head like the chant of prayer beads, calling me to his side. And I, his devoted one, took so much ecstasy in the universe of his tumultuous hands that if they had cut off my head in that state, I would have been unaware. And this God who had descended from the sky, who had been with me so often, was now seated, wearing a winding sheet, across from me, who was also wearing a winding sheet, and was allowing me to participate in a holy, religious ritual, a grand, tribal historical ritual. He had descended from the sky to sit across from me, and he said, "Cut, my flower, cut, for it's getting late," and the grating sound of the saw to which ears had become accustomed, the ears of the people as well as our own, arose. Before doing anything, of course, we had felt for and found that little bulge on the foot. And while searching for it, we had looked at each other — we must have been proud of all this — I had lifted my head to look into the eyes of Mahmoud only in order to find the small bulge, and Mahmoud had looked at me amorously as if wanting to reward me by helping me find the bulge immediately, and I, under the burning sun, had felt in his caressing glance of favor and violent delicacy that I was being bathed in cool water, in a fresh spring in the middle of the forest, and his look was so mesmerizing that I could hear the simple, soft and lyrical sound of my own muscles moving in the water and could see myself there, even when the grate of the saw was most deafening, submerged in his loving benevolence.

The grating of the saws, the saws of dismemberment, spread through space, through the silence of space. We had bound the legs of the condemned man so tightly that even the worst of tortures could not have caused them to jerk. The legs were black and blue and blood-covered, and while cutting through, I looked only at the foot, thinking of this small and delicate foot, this worthless portion of mine to be severed from the leg, from cities and fields and villages it must have passed, in what water and on what mornings it must have been washed, in the caressing hands of what woman it must have been fondled – this sort of feeling came easily to me – and the sound of the saw winding through space, calling the foot to witness – the foot like a slender column, old and left over from ancient times, the veins like the faded, illegible characters of an inscription, the inside of the bone exactly like the slightly varicolored circles of a black carrot, only thicker, firmer and more visible. The saw cut through and the foot was becoming severed from the leg, soaked in blood, the blood sinking into the sand, the black blood, and the end of the leg like a dirty pole-end pouring out blood, black blood. I looked at Mahmoud, who had settled to the ground on his firm and powerful knees and was finishing up the work. He was never afraid of blood, and had accustomed us to not being afraid of blood. He was capable of making his ablutions in blood and standing before the people in prayer, capable, following the slaughter of the populace of a small town, of delivering an oration on the greatness of God, capable of freeing twenty of the tribe's thinkers from his prisons only to catch and kill them all later in one place saying that they had been standing under a wall when it fell. But he was a person who, whatever he wanted, others wanted as well: If he wanted blood, the people wanted blood, too; if he wanted water, the people wanted water, too; and if he wanted nothing, the people, too, wanted nothing. Of course it would hardly ever occur that Mahmoud would want nothing for himself. He might possibly at times want nothing for the people, and they accepted this, as well – the totality of this nothing put at their disposal by Mahmoud. But it would hardly ever occur to him to want only nothing for himself. In addition, over his years of inexperience and experience, over the years of this great historical experience, he had realized that the people cannot be kept waiting; the people must be kept busy; they must be engaged in some kind of violent and intense activity. He believed that the people, all of the people, were childish and must have their toys and games in the form of murders, martyrdoms, religious trinkets, celebrations, periods of mourning, wars – not, of course, real, all-out wars – hunger and famine, drought and thirst, depravity, rot, cholera, and plague. And the people must always be patient. They must attend to the great words, words great and sonorous; the men and women who speak these words must learn how to be proud, must learn how to absorb the words of these men and women into their consciousness and take pride in themselves and

Mahmoud throughout history and throughout the world. I pondered on this and contented myself with my worthless portion of the dismemberment. I sawed through to the flesh on the underside. And then we separated the feet from the legs and threw them into a bucket and took the two small buckets of hot oil which they had brought over to the pole-like, severed stumps of his legs and held the ends of the stumps in the oil. Mahmoud arose. But this time no such thunderous voice as before issued from the fellow nailed to the rack by four nails. Rather, I heard him whispering, "My feet, my children. My feet, my children." And in truth, from just whose throat had it come? And why was this pleading voice so familiar? The sound was like the caressing voice of a woman in the ears of the man bound to the rack. Had ever a woman praised her feet in such a way? It seemed then as if a woman had stretched herself out upon his body, caressing the feet, her feet at his head, her head at his feet, moaning, "My feet, my children." And now he, somewhere in his mind, from some corner of his mind, from some corner of his dismembered, metamorphosed memory, could clearly hear that caressing, feminine voice and repeated, "My feet, my children," and we had thrown his feet, like two freshly smothered infants, into a bucket, and Mahmoud, ignoring the whispering man, said, "Tiring work; it would seem that cutting off feet is more difficult than cutting off arms," and I said, "That's true," realizing that I had been mistaken in this, and listened to the agonized whispers of the man bound to the rack, asking myself why this pleading voice was so familiar. And the people? For them it was impossible to see the feet. In addition, when we had severed the arms of the man bound to the rack, the people, each arm having come loose and each stump having been held in oil, had heard the thunderous cry of "*Annal haq!*" and become excited and had shouted, and their shouts in full powered unison and harmony had reached everyone and everything in this world which has ears and mind. The "*Annal haq*" cry of the man had incited them against him, and their howling cries had refreshed and stimulated us. In truth between us and the people a question and answer of a very particular nature had formed. But we had answered first and had let them ask the question, and then we had given another answer and given them permission to ask another question, and they had imagined that in this succession of questions and answers they were asking us first and then we were answering. We knew all too well that the opposite of this was true. We had set the answer before them in the form of an objectively perceived event, a murder, a suicide, a slaughter, a dismemberment, a lunacy. This was a questioning and answering in which they were obliged to participate but never had before. Our answer to their question, the question they had not asked, had provided a backdrop of fact; they were not to question that fact, rather, that fact having been established, go beyond to question on the basis of that fact, and we, at some later stage, answer them, an answer in the form of a violent act, a lunacy, a stripping naked, another brilliant gamble. And they became contented; even in the depths of their unconscious they were unable to perceive that this scale of weights and measures was missing a pan, that there was only one side to this scale, that being the side on which Mahmoud and I were sitting, the two of us, with sobriety and dignity, at the maximum of love and at one in each other's arms. But now we had accustomed them to a routine, the man saying "*Annal haq*" with the severing of each hand, and for this reason, when the man bound to the rack after the severing of his feet, instead of crying *"Annal haq,"* had contented himself with saying and repeating, "My feet, my children," and the people were unable to hear this beautiful, lyrical utterance, in that harmonious epical world of theirs, and find a place for it, and a kind of murmur, an ignorant muttering of anger had arisen. They didn't want to merely watch, but wanted, and to a degree saw themselves condemned, to hear the voice of the victim. Of course, they, like all true born artists who approach the world through intuition and direct sensual relation to it, had become aware of the technical, artistic and subconscious problem of the eyes and ears as the two doors, the two large doors of man's imaginative vision. These two doors admit the basic nourishment and primary materials to the mind; they strike a match, and the imaginative faculty, like a storeroom full of cotton, suddenly bursts into flame, and this conflagration of a hundred flames, large and small, in the form of words, flows onto the tongue and changes into shouting, those wailing shouts speaking of their thirst for imagination and adventure. The one thing the people never counted in all this was the torture endured by their eyes and ears. The imaginative faculty threw them forward in such a way that they acted as if they hadn't perceived that they had been stripped naked under the influence of the movement of the wind or the collision of the air against their bodies; and because this time the storeroom of their stimulation seeking imagination had not burst into flame, instead of changing to a chorus of howlers, they had mumbled and whispered among themselves, and the whispering grew into grumbling and the grumbling into an uproar, indicating that they were not satisfied. This, of course, was the opposite of what Mahmoud had foreseen. He detested these whisper-mumbling grumblings of the people, and perhaps he was right, because he believed that rebellion of the people develops from this very thing. Mahmoud did not wish the people to have differences among themselves; they must be united. If they were dissatisfied, they should have let Mahmoud hear of it. If they were satisfied, they should have let Mahmoud hear of it, as one, and in the official manner. They never opposed Mahmoud. Really, the thought of opposition to Mahmoud never occurred to them. They hovered in space neither hating nor loving Mahmoud, but their hatred was not of the kind which terminates in rebellion. Thus, it was necessary for them to declare that they were satisfied, to ask for more; they wanted something more exciting from Mahmoud, so why didn't they shout and demand it of him? Mahmoud had the power to decide at once and to act at once and thus, when addressing me in a manly but gentle voice he said, "Sweet one, get those feet and bring them here," I understood immediately how he intended to answer the insatiable eagerness for spectacle. I went to the bucket and got the feet; they were warm and slippery and soft, and it seemed that they had become pieces of boneless, lean, red meat. I brought the feet to Mahmoud. He took them and looked at them and gave a laugh, and this in such a way that it seemed as if he were standing there looking at a pair of nice, clean, shiny shoes. He shouted, "Bring me two sport spears!" and they brought them immediately. Holding the feet at the heel, he stuck them, one by one, on the ends of the spears and pressed on them to secure them, and then he said to me, "Go stand on that side," and he crossed over to the left side of the man bound to the rack and stopped opposite me and said, "Hoist the spear aloft, sweet one." And he hoisted his spear, too, and the spears, on their ends the feet of the man bound to the rack, took a position on either side of the head of the man bound to the rack, the right foot in my keeping and the left in Mahmoud's, because of Mahmoud's leftist affectations, and then I heard the weak and beautiful and lyrical voice of the man bound to the rack saying, "My feet, my children," and then the wailing voice of the people, the howling of the dogs in chorus crying, "And now his tongue! And now his tongue! And now his tongue!" And when this had been repeated a number of times in full chorus, we lowered the spears. We took the feet off the ends of the spears and threw them into the bucket, and without keeping them waiting, proceeded to answer the hearty shouts of the people: we requested a long and sharp pair of scissors, and when they brought them we requested a ladder, and when they had brought the ladders, two ladders, one for Mahmoud and one for me, we ascended them to tear out the roots of his speech, of the implement of speech . . .

. . . Mahmoud, who had reached the top of the ladder, called down, "What are you standing there looking so dumbstruck for, on the second rung of the ladder? Up, boy, up, come higher!" So I moved on up, reaching the top of the ladder on the left side of the man's face, and then, working together, we cut out his tongue. With no trembling of our hands, no error in our work; and in cutting out his tongue, what else did we cut out? By cutting out his tongue we forced him to accept strangulation as his fate. We converted the tongue into a memory in his mind and himself into a captive of the tongueless ruins of his memory. We taught him to keep our tyranny imprisoned in his mind; by cutting out his tongue we made him his own prisoner, keeper of his own prison and prisoner of himself. We bound him within silent walls, unknown walls, timeless walls, tongueless walls. We forced him not to think, and if he should think not to speak, because he no longer had a tongue; the tongue that moved freely in his mouth, pushing words out through his lips and teeth, words concrete, sane, emotional and intellectual, had been cut out by the roots, and the slippery, blood-covered tongue, blood fresh and brightly colored, was held in Mahmoud's hand, and Mahmoud tossed it into a tub which had been placed beside the buckets. Words ceased to exist, and he forgot letters and sounds and words and speech: the joyous, lyrical *s*'s, the *sh*'s of shimmering celebration, the *p*'s of steely power, the blazing *b*'s, the pain-diminishing *d*'s he forgot, *p*'s spitting upon the *f*'s foundering in misery, the *ch* of birds chirping the names of swallow and chickadee in flight, the sacred *m*'s of mind and meaning, the fascinating infatuation of the *n*'s, the tall aspen trees of towering *a*'s[2]... he forgot all connections, swallowing them deep into his mind, affixing deaf and dumb locks to them, hiding them away in the tongueless cells of silence. His tongue had been stilled, tossed into a bucket of coagulating blood like the corpse of a headless kitten. The artful workings of the tongue in the limited space of the mouth had ceased, plunged into absolute silence – the tongue which had once begun to form words, imitating sounds and voices one by one: birds, mothers, fathers, the flow of water, the fluttering of the leaves – the tongue which later had overflowed itself with words of affection, had adopted the nimbleness and agility and liveliness of a new-flying bird, had started out in childhood pronouncing the words of book after book, at first slowly, with difficulty and curiosity, then easily, artfully and with agility, every word penetrating the mind like a ray of the

---

2. The Persian aleph (or A) is a long, thin vertical stroke. – *Ed.*

sun and setting it aflame, awakening feelings latent and primitive, original and creative, which built bridges from word to word, the tongue pushing itself forward and side to side articulating the mind, performing mellifluently, had proceeded from lane to lane: had said to a woman, "I love you," – had called a mother "Mother," – had called a father "Father," – had greeted a little boy affectionately with a "Hi there," – had shown a little girl a dove, calling it "Dove," and the little girl had imitated, saying "Dove, dove." The tongue, like a conquering but unconquered spirit, had violated the limits of the mouth, and on the public roads before small assemblages the mouth had opened and the golden tongue had burst forth with the word "Freedom!" and had moved onto the crossroads to proclaim "Freedom!" and had violated, yes violated, the narrow circumference of the crossroads to bellow "Freedom!" in the public squares, and the throat, that wondrously natural loudspeaker, had projected it with a hitherto unequaled magnificence. Yes, he, the man whom we had imprisoned, stoned, and then dismembered, had stood at the crossroads of history and had shouted: "Freedom!" And we, with a simple pair of scissors, had driven him back into the dungeon of his memory. We had thrown open a cleft in his mind and had buried his tongue in the small grave of that cleft. Mahmoud and I had cut out his tongue and had thrown it into the middle of a tub full of his coagulating throat's blood. And now his mouth was full of blood, and Mahmoud shouted, "Swallow it!" and he couldn't because his mouth was full of blood and Mahmoud shouted for the last time, "Swallow it!" And giving me a piece of cloth, he said, "Wipe the blood off his mouth," and he couldn't swallow and the foaming blood flowed from his mouth and I wiped the vomited blood away from around his mouth with my cloth, and while I was doing this, he who was nailed up there opened his eyes suddenly, and I, who was standing there, looked into them. My face was reflected in his eyes, but from behind that reflection of my face, his eyes looked at me; his two eyes like prisoners looking outside through holes in the prison wall, peered at me from their deep-set sockets. He had taken on a sort of bizarre, unaccountable actuality. I couldn't tell whether his look was one of rage or hatred or of surrender – he simply looked at me – I couldn't tell whether supplication or helplessness or rebellion lay con-cealed there – he simply looked – I couldn't tell whether his look was directed at me or at something else, whether he cared anything for me or not, whether he knew anything or not – he simply looked. No movement in his eyes – he simply looked – how real these eyes had become! The eye sockets were like two hollowed-out stones into which had been set two bloodshot emeralds, and the bushy eyebrows seemed to have been woven into the two sides of his forehead out of reddish-brown hair and drops of blood and sweat, but noth-ing could equal the lucid, eternal actuality of his eyes. Mah-moud, who had already descended the ladder, called, "Shut his eyes," and I raised my blood-soaked hands and shut them, and the look of those eyes simply staring at me was no longer upon me. I wiped around his mouth and beard with my cloth, descending the ladder when I finished. Mahmoud said, "I knew the tongue would finish him off," and I said, "Yes." And then Mahmoud called for a spear in the same manner that he always called for everything, and as soon as they had brought one, he took the spear and impaled the tongue which lay in the coagulating blood, and he lifted it on the point of the spear, and he raised it on high, in accordance with national custom, holding it there and shouting, "He is dead! Here is his tongue!" And the people commenced cheering and shouting and in the tumult they pushed aside the guards and rushed forward and surrounded the three of us, Mahmoud and me and the dead man bound to the rack, and looked at me first, laughing, and then at Mahmoud, laughing, and then at the image of the man on the rack, laughing as if to burst their bellies, laughing uncontrollably, as if to burst their bellies and endanger civil health and well-being, and then trumpets sounded from the four corners of the desert, and the initial rites of the festival were performed. And as soon as the rites had begun, the people, astonished, watching the corpse, backed slowly away. Faced with this great historical victory they were capable of only laughter which froze into awe. In the long run it was imperative for them to face this historical moment, and now was set before them something great, something which would settle into the depths of their consciousness and transform them with a nauseating and crippling power, something which, like a sharp spike, would impale and split the fiber of their souls, striking home, obliterating them. At first they had exploded into one extreme, the extreme of collective, full-bodied laughter, and since it was the laughter of intoxication, for one intense moment of excitement their lips and teeth and eyes and bellies had burst into motion; their hearts' blood had come to a boil, streaming into their eyes, their ears, their cheeks, and they, their nostrils dilating with the convulsion of laughter, were frozen in place. And they, as if a large hand had grabbed them, who seemed to be asleep, by the shoulders and shaken them and awakened them, they came to themselves with those same lips and open mouths and red eyes and laughter-convulsed faces, or it is possible, of course, that they had not come to themselves at all, rather that a large hand had swooped down from the sky or shot up out of the earth to wipe the collective laughter off their faces, and they had set foot into the hemisphere of another extreme, the extreme of awe. They had surged forward laughing, and the laughter had expanded and encompassed them all, had violated the limits of their lips and mouths and reduced even the air, the free air to laughter, and suddenly, that invisible hand, be it earthly or heavenly, had, with one swipe, mopped the laughter from their convulsed faces. A hand had swept back the waves of laughter and nothing remained but awe. If the first extreme had exploded its way to the outer world, the second extreme had sobbed its way convulsively and terrifyingly to the inner world – a sobbing that no one would ever hear – a sobbing that even the weeper himself would never hear. In between these two extremes, in a limbo between the hell of laughter and the hell of awe (Paradise never!) they had tried to comprehend something of their destiny, and therefore, with the rhythmical coordination of an army which withdraws cunningly to catch the enemy later in ambush, they had moved back, awe-stricken and conquered, as if trying during their withdrawal to hang onto something, something beyond the meanings of commonplace concepts such as life and death, murder and martyrdom, something beyond these routine individual concepts, in which might be revealed the effect of their universal destiny on the course of history, time and the future, something that might invest their convulsive laughter and their mute awe with a significance, not simple but profound, albeit lucid and illuminating. Had they been able to hang onto something at that moment? Surely they had done their best, surely they had made every effort to escape being transformed in their perplexity and their awe; surely they had tried to deliver themselves . . . from what? . . . they were still in the dark as to what they were trying to deliver themselves from, still in the dark as to what course of action to take should they be delivered. And into the hands of what force were they to deliver themselves as an alternative to this force which impelled them to jump from one totally positive extreme to one totally negative. No matter how hard they tried, they were unable to find anything meaningful in this limbo between two extremes, between two hells; their vain efforts reached a climax, rather an anticlimax in their withdrawal. And when Mahmoud's voice was heard shouting "Bring a charcharkheh!"[3] they awoke, emerged from that sleep state at an extreme of rhythmical awe. They looked around themselves; they looked at each other; they even rubbed their eyes and stretched, and, no longer awed, wondered why and of what they had stood in awe. They looked at each other and tried to speak to each other but were unable. They had only a mutual awareness of their situation in common, an awareness originating from the imperceptible ties that bound them together. They could not tell under the spell of what magic, what opiate they had been, but as they looked at each other, it came back to them where they were, what they had done, what they should do and with whom they should do it. Mahmoud and I came back to them, as well, and especially Mahmoud who again shouted: "Bring a charcharkheh!" And they really snapped to it and withdrew behind the lines that had been designated for them. The guards again returned and took up their posts, facing them, their backs to

3. A four-wheeled chariot. – *Ed.*

us. A smile of self-esteem could be seen on their faces; pride sat upon their chests like the coruscating insect of a medal. They stood behind the designated lines, as if destiny, not Mahmoud, had drawn them, full of pride, indefatigable, contented and as unswerving in their devotion as faithful dogs, dogs, who remain, even after long days of starvation, faithful to their merciless masters. When Mahmoud shouted, "Bring a charcharkheh!" they displayed a mood of expectation, a curiosity as to how this "charcharkheh" would be used: Do the wheels of such a thing move? What person or persons would it carry? And, over what roads would this strange thing, the "charcharkheh," pass? Things excited them more than human beings, and upon hearing the word "charcharkheh" their mouths fell open in amazement, as if they had been stimulated sexually. I could even sense this stimulation swelling up beneath their clothing. Of course, at first they were ashamed, only daring to sneak looks at one another, but then, when Mahmoud shouted again, "Bring a charcharkheh!" and repeated it several times, they got over their shame and laughed a bit and turned to look at the men beside them and behind them. They did this simultaneously, with an artful harmony of action. Then it was that their smiles appeared and they began shifting their weight from one foot to another, and they were plunged into a state of still hesitant lustfulness, and in that state, their hands seemed to hang from the atmosphere, which had absorbed their bodies and arms and shoulders, and a voluptuous lethargy possessed them, under the spell of which they were unable to think what to do with themselves, their hands, the swelling beneath their clothing. A sensation like the burning flame of a lantern had begun to play across their buttocks, and this flame, set in motion, had begun to oscillate from one buttock to the

other, and they were unable to deal with this oscillating sensation which had combined pleasurably, rhythmically, in harmony with the swelling under their clothing. The backs of
their thighs grew taut, and the hairs on their thighs stood on
end like tiny sharp spears pointing toward the body center of
their lust, and they were unable to deal with the sensation of
these hairs standing on end. In this state of expectancy, every
moment of which seemed like a century, they were unable to
think of what to do with their hands, the backs, the fronts, the
sides of their bodies, until Mahmoud shouted once more: "I
said bring a charcharkheh!" And upon once again hearing the
shout, especially the word "charcharkheh," they grew bolder
and raised their hands and seized at the clothing of others, in
front of them and behind them, according to their sexual and
spiritual proclivities. And each of them, having one on the back
or front of another, used his other hand, feverish with excitement, to loosen and throw aside his own garments. The word
"charcharkheh" had driven them to such a frenzy of excitement that they had turned to fire itself and desired consummate
penetration of another or of themselves by another, and, in fact,
the more skilled ones had already been able to bend over for
another or to bend over in front of another, or to kneel before
another or to push another to his knees before them, to facilitate the penetration of themselves or others who wished to be
penetrated. At first they did this in separate columns of two,
naturally in rampant disorder at this stage, but as soon as the two
or three or four in each column were able to get their hands on
each other, bestowing their bounty on the ones before them
and drinking deep of the bounty of those behind, and when
each of the men in each column commenced to puff and pant
in a soft, lustful, sensuous way; driven to and fro with each

breath, when the movement of one column fell into rhythm with the movement of another column and eventually the movements of all the clusters fell into rhythm with the movements of each other, establishing the inevitable harmony of action, if you had watched from afar, you would have seen that all of the people, that is to say, all of the men, were locked to each other, and, panting and thirsting and fever-stricken, were undulating to and fro in perfect harmony with their hearts' beat; if you had looked from afar, you would have seen that the people had understood "the middle road of moderation in all things" and had plunged themselves into the middle of each other's roads, their chins pressed to the spine in the small of each other's backs, pumping forward and backward. And all of them having been absorbed into the pervading harmony of action, these columns of men, these magnificent men of history, these men who could change human destiny, these rugged, gigantic men, started to whisper something, a murmur at first, of course, gradually becoming a distinct voice, the voice of each one blending with the rhythmic movements of legs and thighs and buttocks, into a single melodious, truly resplendent cry – a single, united cry, distinct and lustful and virile arose to the sky devastating the four corners of the world. They shouted, "Charcharkheh! Charcharkheh! Charcharkheh!" And then the heads of the long columns of men locked together moved together and formed the columns into a circle, the man at the fore of each column joining himself to the aft of the next and the circles stretching in length as those with no one before them sought and found and penetrated those with no one behind.

The joining of fore to aft of the columns took little more than a moment, forming, as a result, a long spiraling, snake-twisted column, opening and stretching out to include the other columns, to join itself to the men with no one behind them, like a gigantic loop, a snake-twisted, masculine and impotent column growing longer and longer by the moment. At first there had been two points, one before and one behind, and a straight line had joined these two points, and then another line had formed through the attraction of two other points to each other, then other lines had formed between other points, then a single straight column and beside it other straight columns, and then the columns had twisted and straightened and in this movement had formed curves like small circles and the other columns had penetrated them from behind and then other columns penetrated other columns, and this coiling snake had been formed, and now its loop was opened from the end and moved toward the west, all moving in a single column toward the west, each of them wallowing and steaming intensely in the depths of another, their hands clasped about the bellies of those ahead and sensing the hands of those behind clasped about their own bellies, the chins of those in front pressed to the back of still another, in a single column, wallowing and steaming in the depths of each other. Then this straight line stretched itself from east to west, and the thousand-headed snake opened its coil and extended its whole length from east to west, and Mahmoud shouted once more, "Charcharkheh! Charcharkheh!" and they, gasping and thirsting and fever-stricken, shouted back "Charcharkheh!" and repeated "Charcharkheh! Charcharkheh! Charcharkheh!" The thousand-headed snake had now become a long dragon, striving with its head to bite its own tail. Still shouting "Charcharkheh! Charcharkheh!" moving from side to side and shouting from the head of the column to the tail, wallowing and steaming inside each other, they moved clenched together so tightly, so rhythmically and harmoniously from fore and aft, that the circle about to form in the next few moments was pulled tighter as if they were participating in some kind of religious ritual, a religious ritual in which one must forget himself and take part in a group effort, in this form of course, by means of universal copulation, the depths of one be hacked out and he, by extraordinary effort, hack out the depths of another that the religious ritual might be performed at the peak, at the climax of pleasure, pain and torture. The sweaty odor of bodies, the odor of navels adhering to the flesh of the back, of buttocks held fast to the groin, of hands clasped around waists, the sensual odor of the tight, wet and sticky inner depths, of phalluses thrust into these depths, had arisen, and this religious ritual, the ritual of virile religion, was set in the midst of these funky body perfumes, and the dragon slouched forward and tried to bite its own tail, taking the form of a circle – no – an interwinding cord of flesh, pulling back at the tail end, lurching forward at the head. And finally the head reached the tail, and before the eyes of all the people of this land, that is to say of all the men locked together, the head connected with the tail, and then the shouting of the voices reached its climax, the panting and puffing quickened, the odors thickened and the cry of "Charcharkheh! Charchar-kheh! Charcharkheh!" split the sky . . . Mustachioed men, bearded men, these great historical men, the men of this great sexual resurrection, the men of this gigantic circle of lust, were climaxing and coming inside one another, and this upon simply hearing the word "Charcharkheh," which they were supposed to have brought but had not brought yet. There was also another possibility: perhaps it wasn't the charcharkheh that had excited them. Perhaps it was the execution, the execution which had taken several hours, which had moved them to behave in this manner. Perhaps it was the odor of blood, blood dripping from the severed stumps of arms and legs soaking our winding sheets, that had driven the people, already thirsting for the blood of the man bound to the rack, to this frenzied orgy of universal copulation. Perhaps the sight of that blind and tongueless figure, that armless, legless carcass hanging above all of them in the middle of this circle of desert (who looked disheveled, sweaty, like a man in the midst of copulation with a woman), had moved them to drown themselves in each other.

I think Mahmoud had a lot to do with this. Having finished off the man on the rack, he now wished to bring the mass hysteria of the people to a resounding climax. The people could never have foreseen this; they could not have known that they would suddenly, at the height of their passionate display, be seized unawares and driven their better instincts overcome, to take part in an action of which the imagination of man can hardly conceive. At the climax of this event, Mahmoud had given them a great gift, a gift consisting of only a single word; but this word had a double significance for them. Mahmoud had shouted, "Charcharkheh," and the people had seen in that word the crystallization of all their desires and had been exalted; they had caught this great gift of Mahmoud, this emotion-packed word, and pressed it to their breasts and been driven wild by it. They had been excited by an object, nay, not even the object itself but the sound, the sound of the name of that object, and this had been a major factor in transforming their minds. Although they had ultimately directed their assault upon flesh, arms, legs and orifices of flesh, it had been, after all, this beautiful sound of "Charcharkheh" that had raised them to this fever pitch of excitement; and it had been this object and the very name of this object which had given them the courage to perform. I really wanted, while they were boiling and wallowing in each other and shouting "Charcharkheh," to be there in the middle of them – no – to be in their minds that I might understand what form this "Charcharkheh" had taken in their minds that they had been able to associate "Charcharkheh" with copulation. Of course, I knew that people were excited by luxuries – a pretty pen, a delicate pencil, a crown, a few medals, a hand with fingers covered by expensive varicolored jewels, a henna-dyed beard, a thick mustache excited them. Such luxuries, not even of the body and therefore able to excite anyone, excited these people. I had often seen the people stare in amazement and wonder as Mahmoud mounted his "Charcharkheh" and rode it from street to street all the way to the palace. Of course they were watching Mahmoud, but they had never seen Mahmoud in the street without his "Charcharkheh" and they imagined this "Charcharkheh" to be bound up with some kind of secret and that this secret related Mahmoud and the "Charcharkheh" to each other and invested them with the power to excite and stimulate the people. When the people saw Mahmoud's "Charcharkheh" in the streets, moving swiftly along, their pubic hair began to tingle and a bulge swelled beneath their clothing. At first they were gentle and soft, but they soon became rough and dangerous and laid hands on themselves underneath their clothing. Summer, winter, spring or fall – it made no difference to them. As Mahmoud went by mounted upon the "Charcharkheh" they became excited and beat themselves off, and before they could finish, Mahmoud and his "Charcharkheh" passed from their street on to his palace, one of the many palaces he had in the city itself or on the outskirts of the city, and they retained only a kind of dizzy, lustful torpor, a heavy sleepiness issuing from the blood vessels around the eyelids, a kind of dreamy languor and lethargy, and stumbled off to their huts with the image of a crumpled "Charcharkheh," a "Charcharkheh" deflated and dissolved and deteriorated, an image of the "Charcharkheh" like fat heated on the fire, melting and dripping onto the ground. They found something religious in this ritual, something which drew them inward from the margins and sides of the square, drew them to the center, and changed them into martyrs and heroes, into murderers and victims, even into religious objects like windows of a mosque, coffins of wood, into a ceremonial chant. And this religious ritual burgeoned in their depths, in their bowels, in their groins, from their dirt-crusted knees and filthy ankles and stinking toes, a fiery spark burgeoning within them from the tips of their toes, driving their senses and emotions, their fervor and frenzy upward with the speed of nervous impulse to the heart and from there, with that same speed and pervasiveness of nervous impulse, to the brain, and then these people, standing there in the closely packed crowd with their erect phalluses were transformed into actors in a great religious mystery of hysteria. And when they raised their arms and beat their breasts mercilessly and tore out their hair and pummelled their own heads, and when they lashed roughly at their own backs with chains and the blood streamed from the torn flesh and crushed bones of their backs, and when they jabbed at their own heads with daggers, their right hands clasped in the hands of the men in front of them, and split the flesh open to the skull, and when after the performance of all these pious actions, actions ominous and sensuous and fraught with evil, they began to moan and weep, wallowing in each other, anointing each other with their own blood and sweat, at that moment someone should have been there to perceive and depict and portray the magnificence of this hysteria, in which the national genius was expressed to the full – no – not only a single perception, a single portrait – rather a perception, a portrait of the event from every possible angle – someone who would hold this portrait before the eyes of history, so that history, great and holy and ancient history which had led them to this, would deign to give them a smile of support and patronage, a smile which should resemble the foam appearing on the lips of a mad man, dripping from the lips of an epileptic at the height of a seizure. They had brought the "Charcharkheh – Charcharkheh – Charcharkheh," and Mahmoud was writing this history, this very history. Mahmoud was able to write history. At this very moment he was writing it. The people had never seen the "Charcharkheh" come to a standstill before their eyes. They had always seen the "Charcharkheh" moving, Mahmoud mounted upon it. But they had never seen the "Charcharkheh" come to a standstill before their very eyes. The "Charcharkheh" was strongly built. It had four large iron wheels. Its knotted wood of walnut gleamed. The nails holding it together shone like burning stars. Two tall horses, which were known to be the gift of one of the Arab Emirs to Mahmoud, one white and one black, were harnessed to the "Charcharkheh." A wood pole separated the two horses from each other; the two horses seemed like two statuesque generals, fully ripe and perfect. The word "Charcharkheh" was still sensual to the spectators and now they saw to their utmost astonishment that the "Charcharkheh" had materialized, the abstraction of the word became the actuality of the object itself, for now not the word but the "Charcharkheh" itself stood before them.

The astonished people were mesmerized by the beauty, by the symmetry and latent force of the horses and the "Charcharkheh." Mahmoud looked neither at the horses nor at the "Charcharkheh." He watched the people, and the people watched the horses and the "Charcharkheh." And I stood there watching Mahmoud and the people and the horses and the "Charcharkheh." Mahmoud always gave his permission to the people to look at pretty things, and this "Charcharkheh," this symmetrical beauty, built by Mahmoud's craftsmen, was indeed a pretty thing, and Mahmoud always permitted the people to look at pretty things. According to Mahmoud, one must bedazzle the people, and the people must live bedazzled and open their lips bedazzled and speak bedazzled. Mahmoud somehow always kept them in that state of suspense, that concentrated state of bedazzlement, that state of consternation. Should they become demystified, turn their backs on Mahmoud, evacuate the cities, pick a direction and leave? Mahmoud watched the people, trying to see what actions would ensue, those moments of burgeoning lust, the ceremony of universal copulation having come to an end. Frantic with joy at seeing the "Charcharkheh" and the horses, the people laughed, rubbed their hands together, emitting squeaking sounds, puckering their lips at the horses and making smooching sounds, as if they were all standing at the side of a huge vessel on the seashore waiting for a lovely woman to alight from the ship so that they might, all together from up close, witness the advent of her beauty. And it so happened that the voice of Mahmoud, my master, was heard at that very moment. He took his eyes from the people and spinning victoriously around shouted, "Load it on!" and the guards got down to work, and their skill and their knowhow was indeed surprising. One of them who was sitting on the "Charcharkheh" and holding the reins of both horses in his hands, drove the "Charcharkheh," that huge symmetrical framework, gradually backward, bringing the rear of the "Charcharkheh" to a place right in front of the man bound to the rack. He did this in such a way that the horses might not chance to see the dismembered man on the rack. Mahmoud knew very well that if the sideways glance of one of the horses should chance to fall upon one of the blood-smeared arms, if they should chance to see but once a leg of the dismembered man or his metamorphosed face, they would bolt in such an extreme of panic that they would never again be coerced to return to men or the city or the harness of the "Charcharkheh."

The people, standing in curved lines in that vast desert of sun and earth, eyeing me and Mahmoud and the horses and the dismembered man from not too far away, showed by emitting slight sounds that they had the indefatigable desire to be drowned in wonder and awe. The sun was high above – the earth vast – the horses beautiful – the "Charcharkheh" rhythmical – the man bound to the rack luminous and exciting and tragic: What more could they want? They were set on a plane face to face with nature as well as art, with life and the living as well as with death and the dead, with beauty as well as with tragedy. All of the elements of their bedazzled state had a geometric harmony, which even at the height of artificiality had not lost its natural essence and seemed so apropos, so symmetrical, so glorious and exciting that no one could have any doubt of the grandeur of a power that could create such harmony. Not only were the fingerprints of Mahmoud on the arms of the dismembered man, on his severed legs, on his blood-soaked tongue pulled out by the roots, but his shadow was imprinted on the sun and the very air which carried the sunlight to the earth, on the very light of day which caused the grains of sand to glitter like the stars. The fingerprints of Mahmoud were imprinted upon everything everywhere, and they stood in awe of his all-conquering, all-corrupting, beautiful and exalted magnificence.

Having witnessed a ritual which was both primitive and civilized, they were savoring the rich taste of a feeling of holiness, and this feeling of holiness reached its climax when, at the order of Mahmoud and with my help, the tall guards uprooted the two posts on either side of the man bound to the rack from where they had been driven into the ground and several of them who were the strongest lifted the rack with such perfect rhythm, care and power that the dead man on the rack was not joggled even slightly, raising it slowly from several sides onto their shoulders and carrying it slowly and setting it down on the "Charcharkheh." Then arose the voice of the people, and wild screams arose in unison, in harmony changing now into a panther-like chorus. Devoid of meaning, they were something savage, a drawn-out single-toned shriek. It expressed agony, but not agony alone, and it expressed pleasure, but not pleasure alone; it expressed a combination of both. It was a shriek, savage and ominous and fiery, genuine and rich, an instinctive shriek but devoid of meaning.

When they had heard the word "Charcharkheh" from the tongue of Mahmoud, they had plunged into an orgy of universal copulation, but now that the man bound to the rack and the huge figure of his body could be seen looming above them the shrieks they emitted plunged them into utter savagery. They forgot their identities; they forgot their own history; they were forgetting their own culture, the virile erection of a phallus in the pages of history; and the only things that they saw and could see were the blood-dripping mouth, the tightly closed eyes, the severed stumps of arms, the severed stumps of legs which grew larger moment by moment, invading their whole mind and soul, and they, in agony combined with pleasure, were emitting such a brutal and savage shriek that no word in the lexicon of human tongues could suffice to define it. And this shriek reminded me of a shriek I had uttered at one of the stages of the many stages of my metamorphosis in the course of my history, and this shriek should have reminded me of that shriek, for although that shriek had been the shriek of an individual, it had always stood implanted in my mind like a long spear, always erect, a fiery blood-red flame. This spear of shriek I had never forgotten. I had uttered this shriek when metamorphosed from subject into object, and behold now the shriek of my nation, the shriek which they utter in their metamorphosis from subject into object! My nation, my passive nation, penetrated by all actions, subjugated by all the verbs, all the verbs like spears, which, once erected, must penetrate and subjugate. For this very reason, I, whose curls had been trimmed at the hands of Mahmoud,[4] who was a specimen of this great family of mankind, meaning this passive nation of mine, must speak of my remembrances of my own shriek during the

---

4. It is recounted in many Persian works that one night Soltan Mahmoud became drunk and, moved by his favorite slave's beautiful hair, wanted to make love to him right in front of all his guests. An adviser pointed out that the king should be careful not to commit such a sin in public. Mahmoud had Ayyaz' hair cut with a knife, but next day he was full of regret and anger. A poet, sent to pacify him, composed a quatrain, the famous line of which reads: "The cypress to be beautiful must be trimed."

metamorphosis from subject to object in order to explain the meaning behind the shriek of my passive nation. Because what has happened to me as an individual, in bedrooms, on the rocks and on the sands, has happened to my nation collectively. Everything that has happened to me individually, in my body, in my heart, in my brains and in my depths, in the everywhere of my roots and sinews, my skin and flesh and bones and cartilage, yes cartilage, has happened as well to these cartilage people of my nation. My nation, my passive nation, trapped in this cartilage state; in the course of history my people have not become flesh as flesh that they might decay and under the dynamic sway of time and flood and invasion and devastation pass away, nor have they stood erect in correlation to the word "bone," in the form of bone as bone, to fall violently upon the jagged lines of history and smash them to pieces. My nation, my passive nation, from my point of view, as I, I whose curls were trimmed at the hands of Mahmoud, see it, is a shrieking cartilage. I am part and parcel of you, and when you flip through my pages you flip through your own. When Mahmoud trimmed my curls, he laid his hands upon your curls as well. I am a page of history, and every page of history is but a reiteration of the trimming of my curls, for the cypress to be beautiful must be trimmed.

1965–69
Translated by Carter Bryant

Howard Fast

■

THE LARGE ANT

*During a lifelong career of left-wing activism, which
included a youthful stint as a member of the American
Communist Party, Howard Fast found in both the history
of his own country and that of the ancient world examples
of the social ideals he himself fought for. Whether Tom
Paine or Spartacus, the heroes of his novels struggle against
social injustice without any certainty of success; in fact, for
the reader of Fast's fiction, knowledge that his heroes will
not succeed lends a terrible and tragic irony to their efforts.
Fast's novels are a catalogue of liberal social causes: in*
Freedom Road *he attacked racial prejudice, in* Clarkton,
the exploitation of the poor; in Agrippa's Daughter, *he
advocated pacifism. Fast learned of such struggles first-
hand. When Senator Joseph McCarthy initiated his
nationwide militant anti-Communist crusade, Fast
became one of McCarthy's earliest targets: his books were
blacklisted and he was sent to prison although he had
resigned as a member of the Communist Party in 1953.
After McCarthy's fall, Fast turned his hand to a different
kind of fiction. He began writing what he called "Zen*

stories" – fable-like tales that look at our inexplicable human behaviour. But even here the social concerns are never very far off: the hero of "The Large Ant," for instance, is Everyman, for whom violence is the natural response, and whose ancestors are Cain, the world's first murderer, and the soldier responsible for the My Lai massacre, as well as the companions of Columbus and the bureaucrats of Senator McCarthy.

■

THERE HAVE BEEN all kinds of notions and guesses as to how it would end. One held that sooner or later there would be too many people; another that we would do each other in, and the atom bomb made that a very good likelihood. All sorts of notions, except the simple fact that we were what we were. We could find a way to feed any number of people and perhaps even a way to avoid wiping each other out with the bomb; those things we are very good at, but we have never been any good at changing ourselves or the way we behave.

I know. I am not a bad man or a cruel man; quite to the contrary, I am an ordinary, humane person, and I love my wife and my children and I get along with my neighbors. I am like a great many other men, and do the things they would do and just as thoughtlessly. There it is in a nutshell.

I am also a writer, and I told Lieberman, the curator, and Fitzgerald, the government man, that I would like to write down the story. They shrugged their shoulders. "Go ahead," they said, "because it won't make one bit of difference."

"You don't think it would alarm people?"

"How can it alarm anyone when nobody will believe it?"

"If I could have a photograph or two."

"Oh, no," they said then. "No photographs."

"What kind of sense does that make?" I asked them. "You are willing to let me write the story — why not the photographs so that people could believe me?"

"They still won't believe you. They will just say you faked the photographs, but no one will believe you. It will make for more confusion, and if we have a chance of getting out of this, confusion won't help."

"What will help?"

They weren't ready to say that, because they didn't know. So here is what happened to me, in a very straightforward and ordinary manner.

Every summer, some time in August, four good friends of mine and I go for a week's fishing on the St. Regis chain of lakes in the Adirondacks. We rent the same shack each summer; we drift around in canoes and sometimes we catch a few bass. The fishing isn't very good, but we play cards well together, and we cook out and generally relax. This summer past, I had some things to do that couldn't be put off. I arrived three days late, and the weather was so warm and even and beguiling that I decided to stay on by myself for a day or two after the others left. There was a small flat lawn in front of the shack, and I made up my mind to spend at least three or four hours at short putts. That was how I happened to have the putting iron next to my bed.

The first day I was alone, I opened a can of beans and a can of beer for my supper. Then I lay down in my bed with *Life on the Mississippi*, a pack of cigarettes and an eight-ounce chocolate bar. There was nothing I had to do, no telephone, no demands and no newspapers. At that moment, I was about as contented as any man can be in these nervous times.

It was still light outside, and enough light came in through the window above my head for me to read by. I was just reaching for a fresh cigarette, when I looked up and saw it on the foot of my bed. The edge of my hand was touching the golf club, and with a single motion I swept the club over and down, struck it a savage and accurate blow and killed it. That was what I referred to before. Whatever kind of a man I am, I react as a man does. I think that any man, black, white or yellow, in China, Africa or Russia, would have done the same thing.

First I found that I was sweating all over, and then I knew I was going to be sick. I went outside to vomit, recalling that this hadn't happened to me since 1943, on my way to Europe on a tub of a Liberty ship. Then I felt better and was able to go back into the shack and look at it. It was quite dead, but I had already made up my mind that I was not going to sleep alone in this shack.

I couldn't bear to touch it with my bare hands. With a piece of brown paper, I picked it up and dropped it into my fishing creel. That, I put into the trunk of my car, along with what luggage I carried. Then I closed the door of the shack, got into my car and drove back to New York. I stopped once along the road, just before I reached the Thruway, to nap in the car for a little over an hour. It was almost dawn when I reached the city, and I had shaved, had a hot bath and changed my clothes before my wife awoke.

During breakfast, I explained that I was never much of a hand at the solitary business, and since she knew that, and since driving alone all night was by no means an extraordinary procedure for me, she didn't press me with any questions. I had two eggs, coffee and a cigarette. Then I went into my study, lit another cigarette, and contemplated my fishing creel, which sat upon my desk.

My wife looked in, saw the creel, remarked that it had too ripe a smell, and asked me to remove it to the basement.

"I'm going to dress," she said. The kids were still at camp. "I have a date with Ann for lunch – I had no idea you were coming back. Shall I break it?"

"No, please don't. I can find things to do that have to be done."

Then I sat and smoked some more, and finally I called the Museum, and asked who the curator of insects was. They told me his name was Bertram Lieberman, and I asked to talk to him. He had a pleasant voice. I told him that my name was Morgan, and that I was a writer, and he politely indicated that he had seen my name and read something that I had written. That is formal procedure when a writer introduces himself to a thoughtful person.

I asked Lieberman if I could see him, and he said that he had a busy morning ahead of him. Could it be tomorrow?

"I am afraid it has to be now," I said firmly.

"Oh? Some information you require."

"No. I have a specimen for you."

"Oh?" The "oh" was a cultivated, neutral interval. It asked and answered and said nothing. You have to teach at least five semesters at a college to develop that particular "oh."

"Yes. I think you will be interested."

"An insect?" he asked mildly.

"I think so."

"Oh? Large?"

"Quite large," I told him.

"Eleven o'clock? Can you be here then? On the main floor, to the right, as you enter."

"I'll be there," I said.

"One thing – dead?"

"Yes, it's dead."

"Oh?" again. "I'll be happy to see you at eleven o'clock, Mr. Morgan."

My wife was dressed now. She opened the door to my study and said firmly, "Do get rid of that fishing creel. It smells."

"Yes, darling. I'll get rid of it."

"I should think you'd want to take a nap after driving all night."

"Funny, but I'm not sleepy," I said. "I think I'll drop around to the Museum."

My wife said that was what she liked about me, that I never tired of places like museums, police courts and third-rate night clubs.

Anyway, aside from a racetrack, a museum is the most interesting and unexpected place in the world. It was unexpected to have two other men waiting for me, along with Mr. Lieberman, in his office. Lieberman was a skinny, sharp-faced man of about sixty. The government man, Fitzgerald, was small, dark-eyed and wore gold-rimmed glasses. He was very alert, but he never told me what part of the government he represented. He just said "we," and it meant the government. Hopper, the third man, was comfortable-looking, pudgy, and genial. He was a United States senator with an interest in entomology, although before this morning I would have taken better than even money that such a thing not only wasn't, but could not be.

The room was large and square and plainly furnished, with shelves and cupboards on all walls.

We shook hands, and then Lieberman asked me, nodding at the creel, "Is that it?"

"That's it."

"May I?"

"Go ahead," I told him. "It's nothing that I want to stuff for the parlor. I'm making you a gift of it."

"Thank you, Mr. Morgan," he said, and then he opened the creel and looked inside. Then he straightened up, and the two other men looked at him inquiringly.

He nodded. "Yes."

The senator closed his eyes for a long moment. Fitzgerald took off his glasses and wiped them industriously. Lieberman spread a piece of plastic on his desk, and then lifted the thing out of my creel and laid it on the plastic. The two men didn't move. They just sat where they were and looked at it.

"What do you think it is, Mr. Morgan?" Lieberman asked me.

"I thought that was your department."

"Yes, of course. I only wanted your impression."

"An ant. That's my impression. It's the first time I saw an ant fourteen, fifteen inches long. I hope it's the last."

"An understandable wish," Lieberman nodded.

Fitzgerald said to me, "May I ask how you killed it, Mr. Morgan?"

"With an iron. A golf club, I mean. I was doing a little fishing with some friends up at St. Regis in the Adirondacks, and I brought the iron for my short shots. They're the worst part of my game, and when my friends left, I intended to stay on at our shack and do four or five hours of short putts. You see –"

"There's no need to explain," Hopper smiled, a trace of sadness on his face. "Some of our very best golfers have the same trouble."

"I was lying in bed, reading, and I saw it at the foot of my bed. I had the club —"

"I understand," Fitzgerald nodded.

"You avoid looking at it," Hopper said.

"It turns my stomach."

"Yes — yes, I suppose so."

Lieberman said, "Would you mind telling us why you killed it, Mr. Morgan."

"Why?"

"Yes — why?"

"I don't understand you," I said. "I don't know what you're driving at."

"Sit down, please, Mr. Morgan," Hopper nodded. "Try to relax. I'm sure this has been very trying."

"I still haven't slept. I want a chance to dream before I say how trying."

"We are not trying to upset you, Mr. Morgan," Lieberman said. "We do feel, however, that certain aspects of this are very important. That is why I am asking you why you killed it. You must have had a reason. Did it seem about to attack you?"

"No."

"Or make any sudden motion toward you?"

"No. It was just there."

"Then why?"

"This is to no purpose," Fitzgerald put in. "We know why he killed it."

"Do you?" I nodded. "You're clearer on the subject than I am."

"The answer is very simple, Mr. Morgan. You killed it because you are a human being."

"Oh?" I borrowed that from Lieberman.

"Yes. Do you understand?"

"No, I don't."

"Then why did you kill it?" Hopper put in.

"I saw it," I answered slowly, "and somehow I knew that I must kill it. I didn't think or decide. I just grabbed the iron and hit it."

"Precisely," Fitzgerald said.

"You were afraid?" Hopper asked.

"I was scared to death. I still am, to tell the truth."

Lieberman said, "You are an intelligent man, Mr. Morgan. Let me show you something." He then opened the doors to one of the wall cupboards, and there stood eight jars of formaldehyde and in each jar a specimen like mine – and in each case mutilated by the violence of its death. I said nothing. I just stared.

Lieberman closed the cupboard doors. "All in five days," he shrugged.

"A new race of ants," I whispered stupidly.

"No. They're not ants. Come here!" He motioned me to the desk and the other two joined me. Lieberman took a set of dissection instruments out of his drawer, used one to turn the thing over, and then pointed to the underpart of what would be the thorax in an insect.

"That looks like part of him, doesn't it, Mr. Morgan?"

"Yes, it does."

Using two of the tools, he found a fissure and pried the bottom apart. It came open like the belly of a bomber; it was a pocket, a pouch, a receptacle that the thing wore, and in it were four beautiful little tools or instruments or weapons, each about an inch and a half long. They were beautiful the way any object of functional purpose and loving creation is beautiful – the way the creature itself would have been beautiful, had it not been an insect and myself a man. Using tweezers, Lieberman took each instrument out of the brackets that held it, offering each to me. And I took each one, felt it, examined it, and then put it down.

I had to look at the ant now, and I realized that I had not truly looked at it before. We don't look carefully at a thing that is horrible or repugnant to us. You can't look carefully at a thing through a screen of hatred. But now the hatred and the fear were diluted, and as I looked, I realized it was not an ant although like an ant. It was nothing that I had ever seen or dreamed of.

All three men were watching me, and suddenly I was on the defensive. "I didn't know! What do you expect when you see an insect that size?"

Lieberman nodded.

"What in the name of God is it?"

From his desk, Lieberman produced a bottle and four small glasses. He poured it and we drank it neat. I would not have expected him to keep good Scotch in his desk.

"We don't know," Hopper said. "We don't know what it is."

Lieberman pointed to the broken skull, from which a white substance oozed. "Brain material – a great deal of it."

"It could be a very intelligent creature," Hopper nodded.

Lieberman said, "It is an insect in developmental structure. We know very little about intelligence in our insects. It's not the same as what we call intelligence. It's a collective phenomenon — as if you were to think of the component parts of our bodies. Each part is alive, but the intelligence is a result of the whole. If that same pattern were to extend to creatures like this one —"

I broke the silence. They were content to stand there and stare at it.

"Suppose it were?"

"What?"

"The kind of collective intelligence you were talking about."

"Oh? Well, I couldn't say. It would be something beyond our wildest dreams. To us — well, what we are to an ordinary ant."

"I don't believe that," I said shortly, and Fitzgerald, the government man, told me quietly,

"Neither do we. We guess. We comfort ourselves, too."

"If it's that intelligent, why didn't it use one of those weapons on me?"

"Would that be a mark of intelligence?" Hopper asked mildly.

"Perhaps none of these is a weapon," Lieberman said.

"Don't you know? Didn't the others carry instruments?"

"They did," Fitzgerald said shortly.

"Why? What were they?"

"We don't know," Lieberman said.

"But you can find out. We have scientists, engineers — good God, this is an age of fantastic instruments. Have them taken apart!"

"We have."

"Then what have you found out?"

"Nothing."

"Do you mean to tell me," I said, "that you can find out nothing about these instruments – what they are, how they work, what their purpose is?"

"Exactly," Hopper nodded. "Nothing, Mr. Morgan. They are meaningless to the finest engineers and technicians in the United States. You know the old story – suppose you gave a radio to Aristotle? What would he do with it? Where would he find power? And what would he receive with no one to send? It is not that these instruments are complex. They are actually very simple. We simply have no idea of what they can or should do."

"But there must be a weapon of some kind."

"Why?" Lieberman demanded. "Look at yourself, Mr. Morgan – a cultured and intelligent man, yet you cannot conceive of a mentality that does not include weapons as a prime necessity. Yet a weapon is an unusual thing, Mr. Morgan. An instrument of murder. We don't think that way, because the weapon has become the symbol of the world we inhabit. Is that civilized, Mr. Morgan? Or are the weapon and civilization in the ultimate sense incompatible? Can you imagine a mentality to which the concept of murder is impossible – or let me say absent. We see everything through our own subjectivity. Why shouldn't some other – this creature, for example – see the process of mentation out of his subjectivity. So he approaches a creature of our world – and he is slain. Why? What explanation? Tell me, Mr. Morgan, what conceivable explanation could we offer a wholly rational creature for this," pointing to the thing on his desk. "I am asking you the question most seriously. What explanation?"

"An accident?" I muttered.

"And the eight jars in my cupboard? Eight accidents?"

"I think, Dr. Lieberman," Fitzgerald said, "that you can go a little too far in that direction."

"Yes, you would think so. It's a part of your own background. Mine is as a scientist. As a scientist, I try to be rational when I can. The creation of a structure of good and evil, or what we call morality and ethics, is a function of intelligence – and unquestionably the ultimate evil may be the destruction of conscious intelligence. That is why, so long ago, we at least recognized the injunction, 'Thou shalt not kill!' even if we never gave more than lip service to it. But to a collective intelligence, such as that of which this might be a part, the concept of murder would be monstrous beyond the power of thought."

I sat down and lit a cigarette. My hands were trembling. Hopper apologized. "We have been rather rough with you, Mr. Morgan. But over the past days, eight other people have done just what you did. We are caught in the trap of being what we are."

"But tell me – where do these things come from?"

"It almost doesn't matter where they come from," Hopper said hopelessly. "Perhaps from another planet – perhaps from inside this one – or the moon or Mars. That doesn't matter. Fitzgerald thinks they come from a smaller planet, because their movements are apparently slow on earth. But Dr. Lieberman thinks that they move slowly because they have not discovered the need to move quickly. Meanwhile, they have the problem of murder and what to do with it. Heaven knows how many of them have died in other places – Africa, Asia, Europe."

"Then why don't you publicize this? Put a stop to it before it's too late!"

"We've thought of that," Fitzgerald nodded. "What then

– panic, hysteria, charges that this is the result of the atom bomb? We can't change. We are what we are."

"They may go away," I said.

"Yes, they may," Lieberman nodded. "But if they are without the curse of murder, they may also be without the curse of fear. They may be social in the highest sense. What does society do with a murderer?"

"There are societies that put him to death – and there are other societies that recognize his sickness and lock him away, where he can kill no more," Hopper said. "Of course, when a whole world is on trial, that's another matter. We have atom bombs now and other things, and we are reaching out to the stars –"

"I'm inclined to think that they'll run," Fitzgerald put in. "They may just have that curse of fear, Doctor."

"They may," Lieberman admitted. "I hope so."

But the more I think so, the more it seems to me that fear and hatred are the two sides of the same coin. I keep trying to think back, to recreate the moment when I saw it standing at the foot of my bed in the fishing shack. I keep trying to drag out of my memory a clear picture of what it looked like, whether behind that chitinous face and the two gently waving antennae there was any evidence of fear and anger. But the clearer the memory becomes, the more I seem to recall a certain wonderful dignity and repose. Not fear and not anger.

And more and more, as I go about my work, I get the feeling of what Hopper called " a world on trial." I have no sense of anger myself. Like a criminal who can no longer live with himself, I am content to be judged.

1960

E. B. Dongala

■

THE MAN

*For half a century, the Congo (Brazzaville) was a French
colony, part of what was known as French Equatorial
Africa. After becoming independent in 1960, the Republic
of Congo attempted to survive as a democracy between
the interests of its African neighbours and those of the
European powers. Eight years later it became a Marxist
state and was renamed the People's Republic of the Congo.
Coup after coup, the government changed hands from one
general to another, each one maintaining a strict control
over any form of free expression under the one-party
system. The condition of the Congolese people has scarcely
improved over the past decades: though the literacy rate is
high, health conditions are very poor, and infant mortality
is among the world's highest. The Congolese media, long
owned and controlled by the government, have recently
been liberalized. But in spite of his reputation as the major
Congolese writer, E. B. Dongala's short stories are still
banned in his native country.*

■

N O, THIS TIME he won't get away! After forty-
eight hours, he had been tracked down, his
itinerary was known and the village where
he was hiding identified. But how many false leads there had
been! He had been seen everywhere at once, as if he had the
gift of ubiquity: dedicated militants had apparently run him
down in the heart of the country without, however, managing to capture him: a patrol which had been parachuted into
the northern swamps claimed they had badly wounded him,
providing as their only proof traces of blood that disappeared
into a ravine; frontier guards swore they had shot him in a
canoe (which had unfortunately sunk) as he tried to escape
by river: none of these claims survived closer investigation.
The already tight police net was tightened still further, new
brigades of gendarmes were created, and the army was given
carte blanche. Soldiers invaded the working-class quarters of the
city, breaking down the doors of houses, sticking bayonets into
mattresses filled with grass and cotton, slashing open sacks of
foo-foo, beating with their rifle butts anyone who didn't answer
their questions quickly enough, or quite simply cutting down
anyone who dared to protest at the violation of his home. But
all these strong-arm tactics achieved nothing, and the country
was on the verge of panic. Where could he be hiding?

It had been an almost impossible exploit, for the father-
founder of the nation, the enlightened guide and saviour of the
people, the great helmsman, the president-for-life, the com-
mander-in-chief of the armed forces and the beloved father of
the people lived in a vast palace out of bounds to the ordinary

citizen. In any case, the circular security system contrived by an Israeli professor with degrees in war science and counter-terrorism was impregnable. Five hundred yards from the palace perimeter, armed soldiers stood guard at ten-yard intervals, day and night, and this pattern was repeated at a distance of two hundred and then one hundred yards from the perimeter. The palace itself was also surrounded by a water-filled moat of immense depth swarming with African and Indian crocodiles and caymans imported from Central America which most certainly didn't feed solely on small fry, especially during the campaigns of repression that regularly fell upon the country after every genuine or mock *coup d'état*. Behind the moat was a ditch full of black mambas and green mambas whose power-ful venom killed their victims on the spot. The perimeter wall itself – an enormous sixty-foot high structure of brick and stone as imposing as the wall of the Zimbabwe ruins – bristled with watch-towers, searchlights, nails, barbed wire and bro-ken glass; access was by two enormous doors which also served as a drawbridge and were controlled from the inside alone. Finally the palace itself, the holy of holies, where the beloved father of the people lived: one hundred and fifty rooms in which scores of huge mirrors reflected everything and every-one, multiplying and reducing them *ad infinitum*, so that visi-tors always felt uneasy and oppressed, aware that their least gestures were being watched. Every movement, however small, was carried like an echo from room to room, from mir-ror to mirror, until it reached the ultimate mirror of all, the eye of the master himself, watching over that entire universe. No one knew in which room the founder-president slept, not even the well-versed prostitutes he employed for several nights at a stretch for his highly sophisticated pleasures; even less likely to know were the unspoilt, happy little girls he enjoyed deflowering between the promulgation of two decrees from his palace of wonders. But, if the beloved-father-of-the-nation-the-supreme-and-enlightened-guide-the-comman-der-in-chief-of-the-armed-forces-and-beneficent-genius-of-mankind was invisible in the flesh to the majority of his sub-jects, he was, on the other hand, everywhere present: it was a statutory requirement that his portrait should hang in all homes. The news bulletins on the radio always began and ended with one of his stirring thoughts. The television news began, continued and finished in front of his picture, and the solitary local newspaper published in every issue at least four pages of letters in which citizens proclaimed their undying affection. Everywhere present but inaccessible. That was why the exploit was impossible.

And yet he had carried it off: he had succeeded in getting into the palace, bypassing the crocodiles, the mambas and the Praetorian guards; he had succeeded in outwitting the trap of the mirrors and had executed the father of the nation as one kills a common agitator and fomentor of coups. And then he had made the return journey, avoiding the watchtowers, the drawbridge, the green mambas, the black mambas, the croco-diles, and the Praetorian guards. And escaped! Forty-eight hours later he was still free!

. . . And then came the rumour, no one knew where from: he had been tracked down, his itinerary was known, and the village where he was hiding had been identified; he was surrounded. This time he wouldn't get away!

Armoured cars, jeeps, and lorries full of soldiers set off at three in the morning. The tanks didn't trouble to go round the houses in the villages through which they passed, a straight

line being the shortest distance between two points: villages
were left burning behind them, crops were laid waste, corpses
piled up in the furrows made by their caterpillar tracks. Conquerors indeed in a defeated country, they soon reached their
destination. They woke up the villagers with their rifle butts.
They searched everywhere, emptied the granaries, looked in
the trees and inside lofts. They didn't find the man they were
looking for. The officer in command of the soldiers was furious, and his neck seemed to explode under his chinstrap:

"I know he's here, the bastard who dared to murder our
dear beloved founder-president who will live for ever in the
pantheon of our immortal heroes. I know the miserable wretch
has a beard and is blind in one eye. If you don't tell me within
ten minutes where he's hiding, I'll burn all your houses, I'll
take one of you at random and have him tortured and shot!"

The ten minutes passed amid a frightened silence as deep
as the silence that preceded the creation of the world. Then
the officer in command of the soldiers ordered the reprisals to
begin. They manhandled the villagers: some were strung up
by their feet and beaten; others had red pimento rubbed into
their open wounds; yet others were forced to eat fresh cow
dung . . . The villagers didn't denounce the hunted man. So
they burned all the houses in the village, and the harvest as
well, the fruits of a year's labour in a country where people
rarely have enough to eat. The villagers still didn't give them
the information they were seeking. In fact, the reason for
their silence was quite simple: they genuinely did not know
who had carried out the deed.

The man had acted alone. He had spent months making
his preparations, reading, studying, planning; then he had put
on a false beard and covered his left eye with a black band, like

a pirate. He had found how to penetrate the impregnable palace and kill the great dictator; the way he had done it was so simple he had sworn to himself that he would never reveal it, even under torture, for it could be used again. He was nevertheless surprised to see the soldiers in his village. But had they really discovered his identity or were they just bluffing? Clearly, they didn't know who he was, standing there in front of them, among his fellow villagers who were themselves in total ignorance of what he had done. There he stood, clean-shaven and with both his eyes, waiting to see what would happen next.

The officer in charge of the soldiers, a commandant, got angrier still, confronted by his victims' silence:

"I repeat for the last time! If you do not tell me where he is hiding, this bastard one-eyed-son-of-a-whore without balls who has murdered our beloved president-for-life, founder of our party and leader of the nation, I'll take one of you at random and shoot him! I'll give you five minutes!"

He looked feverishly at his quartz watch. Two minutes. One minute. Thirty seconds.

"I assure you, commandant," the village chief pleaded, "we don't know him and we assure you he isn't in our village."

"Too bad for you. I'm going to take a man at random and shoot him in front of you all. That will perhaps help you to understand. You, there!"

The commandant was pointing at him. He wasn't even surprised, as if he had always expected it. Deep down, it was what he wanted, for he doubted that he would be able to go through the rest of his life with an easy conscience if he allowed someone else to die in his place. He was pleased, for he would have the satisfaction of dying with his secret.

"You will be the innocent hostage who has to be sacrificed because of the obstinacy of your chief and your fellow villagers. Tie him to a tree and shoot him!"

They kicked him and beat him with rifle butts, they slashed him with bayonets. He was dragged along the ground and tied to a mango tree. His wife flung herself on him, to be brutally pulled away. Four soldiers took aim.

"One last time, tell us where the murderer is hiding."

"I don't know, commandant!" pleaded the chief.

"Fire!"

His chest jerked forward slightly, then he collapsed without a sound. They would never find him now!

The smoke cleared. The villagers remained plunged in a deep, stunned silence, looking at the body slumped in the coarse liana ropes. The commandant, having carried out his threat, stood before them. He hesitated, not quite sure what to threaten them with now. Overcome by an inner panic, he struggled, at least to preserve the honour of his stripes.

"Well?" he asked.

At last the villagers became aware of him again.

"Well what!" roared the chief angrily. "I told you we didn't know the man you're looking for. You didn't believe us and now you have killed one of us. What more can I say!"

The commandant could find nothing by way of reply. He rocked on his feet, uncertain what to do next, and at last called out an order to his men:

"Attention! Form up! The hunt goes on. The bastard may be hiding in the next village. There's no time to waste. Forward march!"

Then, turning to the villagers, he screamed: "We'll find him, the son of a bastard, we'll flush him out wherever he's hiding, we'll pull off his balls and his ears, we'll pull out his nails and his eyes, we'll hang him naked in public in front of his wife, his mother and his children, and then we'll feed him to the dogs. You have my word on that."

The jeeps and the tanks moved off and went elsewhere in search of "the man".

They are still looking for him. They sense his presence; somewhere he is hiding, but where? Crushed by dictatorship, the people feel their hearts beat faster when there is talk of "the man". Although the country is more police-ridden than ever, although it is crawling with spies, informers and hired killers, and although he has appointed as heads of security men from his own tribe entirely loyal to his cause, the new president, the second beloved father of the nation, entrusted with the task of continuing the sacred work of the father-founder, no longer dares go out. In order to frustrate the spell, he has issued a decree proclaiming himself unkillable and immortal, but still he hides away in the depths of his palace, with its labryinth of passages and corridors, mirrors and reflections, walled up because he doesn't know when "the man" will suddenly appear to strike him down in his turn, so that freedom, too long suppressed, may at last burst forth.

"The man", the hope of a nation and a people that says NO, and watches . . .

1982
Translated by Clive Wake

Antonio Skármeta

■

THE

COMPOSITION

To undermine Salvador Allende's presidency, the first freely elected Marxist government in Latin America, in 1973 the CIA *assisted a bloody coup in 1973 that put Chile into the hands of a military dictator, General Pinochet. In the following decade, thousands of civilians were imprisoned, tortured, "disappeared," and killed, while many more fled into exile. Among the writers who managed to escape were Isabel Allende, who carried with her to Venezuela a handful of Chilean earth, and Antonio Skármeta, who settled first in Buenos Aires and then in West Berlin. In his important novel of 1975,* I Dreamt the Snow Was Burning, *Skármeta brought together his love of soccer and his admiration for the Chilean poet Pablo Neruda in a tale set at the time of the military coup. In 1983 he published* Burning Patience, *later made into the successful film* Il Postino. *Here too Neruda stands for the redeeming and liberating forces of literature in a world overshadowed by violence and fascism.*

■

ON HIS BIRTHDAY, they gave Pedro a soccer ball. Pedro complained, because he wanted one made out of white leather with black patches, just like the ones the professionals use. This yellow one made of plastic seemed too light.

"You try to make a goal with a header, and it just takes off flying like a bird, it's so light."

"So much the better," his father said. "That way you won't scramble your brains."

And then he gestured with his fingers for Pedro to be quiet because he wanted to hear the radio. Over the last month, since the streets of Santiago had been filled with soldiers, Pedro had noticed that every night his dad would sit in his favorite easy chair, raise the antenna of the green appliance, and listen intently to news that came from far away.

Pedro asked his mother: "Why do you always listen to the radio with all that static?"

"Because what it says is interesting."

"What's it say?"

"Things about us, about our country."

"What things?"

"Things that are going on."

"And why is it so hard to hear?"

"Because the voice is coming from far away."

And Pedro sleepily looked out over the mountain range framed by his window, trying to figure out over which peak the radio voice was filtering.

In October, Pedro starred in some great neighborhood

soccer games. He played in a tree-lined street, and running through the shadows in spring was almost as pleasant as swimming in the river during the summer. Pedro imagined that the rustling leaves were the sound of an enormous grandstand in some roofed stadium, applauding him when he received a precision pass from Daniel, the grocer's son, and made his way, like Simonsen, through the big kids on defense, to score a goal.

"Goal!" Pedro would shout, and he would run to hug everyone on his team, and they would pick him up and carry him like a kite or a flag. Though Pedro was already nine years old, he was the smallest kid for blocks around, so they nicknamed him "Shorty."

"Why are you so small?" they would ask him sometimes, to pester him.

"Because my dad is small and my mom is small."

"And for sure your grandpa and grandma too, because you're itty-bitty, teeny-tiny."

"I'm small, but I'm smart and quick. When I get the ball, nobody can stop me. The only quick thing you guys have is your tongue."

One day Pedro tried a quick move along the left flank, where the corner flag would be if that had been a perfect soccer field, and not a dirt street in the neighborhood. When he got to Daniel, the store owner's son, he faked a move forward with his hips, stopped the ball so it rested on his foot, lifted it over Daniel's body, who was face down in the dirt already, and made it roll softly between the stones that marked the goal.

"Goal!" Pedro shouted, and ran toward the center of the playing field, expecting a hug from his team mates. But this time no one moved. They were standing motionless, looking toward the store. A few windows opened and eyes appeared, staring at the corner as if some famous magician or the Circus of Human Eagles with its dancing elephants had just arrived. Other doors, however, had been slammed shut by an unexpected gust of wind. Then Pedro saw that Daniel's father was being dragged away by two men, while a squad of soldiers was aiming machine guns at him. When Daniel tried to approach, one of the men stopped him by putting a hand on his chest.

"Take it easy," the man yelled at him.

The store owner looked at his son.

"Take good care of the store for me."

The jeep took off, and all the mothers ran outside, grabbed their kids and took them back inside. Pedro stood by Daniel in the middle of the dust cloud raised by the departing jeep.

"Why did they take him away?" he asked.

Daniel stuck his hands in his pockets, and at the bottom he squeezed the keys.

"My dad is a leftist," he said.

"What's that mean?"

"That he's antifascist."

Pedro had heard that word before, the nights his dad spent next to the green radio, but he didn't know what it meant, and most of all, it was hard for him to pronounce. The "f" and the "s" rolled around on his tongue, and when he said it, a sound full of air and saliva came out.

"What does anti-fa-fascist mean?" he asked.

His friend looked at the long, empty street and told him, as if in secret:

"That they want our country to be free. For Pinochet to leave Chile."

"And for that they get arrested?"

"I think so."

"What are you going to do?"

"I don't know."

A worker came slowly toward Daniel and ran a hand through his hair, leaving it more mussed than ever.

"I'll help you close up," he said.

Pedro headed home kicking the ball, and since there was no one in the street to play with, he ran toward the next corner to wait for the bus that would bring his father home from work. When he arrived, Pedro hugged him around the waist and his father bent over to give him a kiss:

"Hasn't your mother come home yet?"

"No," the boy said.

"Did you play a lot of soccer?"

"A little."

He felt his father's hand take his head and hug it against his jacket.

"Some soldiers came and took Daniel's dad prisoner."

"Yes, I know," his father said.

"How did you know that?"

"They called me."

"Daniel is in charge of the store now. Maybe now he'll give me candy."

"I don't think so."

"They took him away in a jeep. Like the ones you see in the movies."

His father said nothing. He breathed deeply and stood looking sadly down the street for a long time. In spite its being daylight and springtime, only men returning slowly from work were out in the street.

"Do you think it will be on TV?"

"What?" his father asked.

"Don Daniel."

"No."

That night the three of them sat down to dinner, and although no one told him to be quiet, Pedro didn't say a word, as if infected by the silence with which his parents were eating, looking at the designs on the table cloth as if the embroidered flowers were in some far-off place. Suddenly his mother started to cry, without making a sound.

"Why's Mom crying?"

His dad first looked at Pedro, and then at her, and didn't answer. His mother said:

"I'm not crying."

"Did someone do something to you?" Pedro asked.

"No," she said.

They finished dinner in silence, and Pedro went to put on his pyjamas, which were orange, with a lot of drawings of birds and rabbits. When he came back, his mother and father were sitting on the sofa with their arms around each other, and with their ears very close to the radio, which was giving off strange sounds, made more confusing than ever by the low volume. As if guessing that his father would put his finger to his mouth and gesture for him to be quiet, Pedro quickly asked:

"Dad, are you a leftist?"

The man looked at his son, and then at his wife, and immediately both looked at him. Then he nodded his head slowly up and down, in assent.

"Are they going to take you prisoner, too?"

"No," his father said.

"How do you know?"

"You bring me good luck, Kid," the man said smiling.

Pedro leaned on the doorjamb, pleased that they weren't

sending him directly to bed, like other times. He paid attention to the radio, trying to figure out what it was that drew his parents to it every night. When the voice on the radio said "the fascist junta," Pedro felt that all the things that were rolling around in his head came together, just like when one at a time the pieces of a jigsaw puzzle fit together into the figure of a sailing ship.

"Dad!" he exclaimed then. "Am I antifascist, too?"

His father looked at his wife as if the answer to that question were written in her eyes, and his mother scratched her cheek with an amused look until she said:

"You just can't tell."

"Why not?"

"Children aren't anti-anything. Children are simply children. Children your age have to go to school, study a lot, play hard, and be kind to their parents."

The next day, Pedro ate a couple of French rolls with jelly, got one finger wet in the sink, wiped the sleep out of his eyes, and took off on the fly to school so they wouldn't mark him tardy again. On the way, he found a kite tangled in the branches of a tree, but no matter how much he jumped and jumped, there was no way.

The bell hadn't stopped ringing when the teacher walked in very stiff, accompanied by a man in a military uniform, with a medal as long as a carrot on his chest, a gray moustache, and sun glasses blacker than the dirt on your knee. He didn't take them off, maybe because the sun was coming in the room like it was trying to set it on fire.

The teacher said:

"Stand up, children, and very straight."

The children got up and waited to hear from the officer,

who was smiling with his toothbrush moustache below his dark glasses.

"Good morning, my little friends," he said. "I am Captain Romo, and I have come on behalf of the government, that is to say, on behalf of General Pinochet, to invite all the children from all the classes in this school to write a composition. The one who writes the nicest composition of all will receive personally from General Pinochet a gold medal and a ribbon like this one with the colors of the Chilean flag."

He put his hands behind his back, jumped to spread his legs, and stretched his neck out, raising his chin slightly.

"Attention! Be seated!"

The children obeyed, scratching themselves as if they didn't have enough hands.

"All right," the officer said, "take out your notebooks . . . Notebooks ready? Good! Take out a pencil . . . Pencils ready? Write this down! Title of the composition: 'My home and my family.' Understood? In other words, what you and your parents do from the time you get home from school and work. The friends who come over. What you talk about. Comments when watching TV. Whatever occurs to you with complete freedom. Ready? One, two, three: let's begin!"

"Can we erase, sir?" one boy asked.

"Yes," said the captain.

"Can we write with a Bic pen?"

"Yes, young man, of course!"

"Can we do it on graph paper, sir?"

"Certainly."

"How much are we supposed to write, sir?"

"Two or three pages."

The children raised a chorus of complaint.

"All right, then, one or two. Let's get to work!"

The children stuck their pencils between their teeth and began looking at the ceiling to see if inspiration would descend on them through some hole. Pedro was sucking and sucking on his pencil, but he couldn't get a single word out of it. He picked his nose and stuck a booger that happened to come out on the underside of his desk. Leiva, his deskmate, was chewing off his fingernails one by one.

"Do you eat them?" Pedro asked him.

"What?" his friend said.

"Your fingernails."

"No. I bite them off with my teeth, and then I spit them out. Like this. See?"

The captain approached down the aisle, and Pedro could see his hard, gilded belt buckle from just inches away.

"And aren't you working?"

"Yes, sir," Leiva said, and as fast as he could, he furrowed his brow, stuck his tongue between his teeth and put down a big "A" to start his composition. When the captain went toward the blackboard to talk with the teacher, Pedro peeked at Leiva's paper.

"What are you going to put down?"

"Whatever. And you?"

"I don't know."

"What did your folks do yesterday?"

"The same old thing. They came home, ate, listened to the radio and went to bed."

"That's just what my mom did."

"My mom started to cry all of a sudden."

"Women go around crying all the time, didn't you ever notice?"

"I try not to cry ever. I haven't cried for over a year."

"And if I beat the shit out of you?"

"What for, if I'm your friend?"

"That's true."

The two stuck their pencils in their mouths and stared and stared up at an unlit bulb and the shadows on the walls, and their heads felt as empty as their piggy banks and as dark as a blackboard. Pedro put his mouth close to Leiva's ear and said:

"Listen, Skinny, are you antifascist?"

Leiva kept an eye on the captain. He gestured for Pedro to turn his head, and said, breathing into his ear:

"Of course, you dumb shit!"

Pedro scooted away a little bit and winked at him, just like the cowboys in the movies. Then he leaned toward his friend again, pretending to write on the blank paper:

"But you're just a kid!"

"That doesn't matter!"

"My mom told me that kids . . ."

"That's what they always say . . . They arrested my dad and took him north."

"They did that to Don Daniel, too."

"I don't know him."

"The store owner."

Pedro looked at the blank page, and read his own hand-writing:

"What My Family Does at Night," by Pedro Malbran, Syria School, Third Grade-A.

"Skinny," he said to Leiva, "I'm going to try for the medal."

"Go for it, man!"

"If I win, I'll sell it and buy a professional-size, white, leather soccer ball, with black patches."

"That's if you win."

Pedro wet the end of his pencil with a little spit, sighed deeply, and started writing without interruption.

A week went by, during which one of the trees in the neighborhood fell over just from old age, a kid's bike was stolen, the garbage man didn't come by for five days, and flies blundered into people's faces, and even got into their noses, Gustavo Martínez, from across the street, got married, and they gave big pieces of cake to the neighbors. The jeep came back and carried off Professor Manuel Pedraza under arrest, the priest refused to say Mass on Sunday, Colo Colo won an international match by a huge score, and the school's white wall had a red word spread across it: "Resistance." Daniel got back to playing soccer and made one goal *de chileno* and another *de palomita*, the price of ice cream cones went up, and, on her eighth birthday, Matilde Schepp asked Pedro to kiss her on the mouth.

"You must be nuts!" he responded.

After that week, still another went by, and one day the captain came back with an armful of papers, a bag of candy and a calendar with the picture of a general.

"My dear little friends," he said to the class, "your compositions are very nice and the armed forces have been very pleased with them. On behalf of my colleagues and of General Pinochet I must congratulate you very sincerely. The gold medal didn't come to this class, but to another, somebody else got it. But to reward your nice work, I'm going to give each one of you a piece of candy, your composition with a note on it, and this calendar with a picture of our illustrious leader on it."

Pedro ate his candy on the bus, on the way home. He stood on the corner waiting for his father to get home, and later, he put his composition on the dining room table. At the bottom, the captain had written in green ink: "Bravo! Congratulations!" Stirring at his soup with a spoon in one hand, and scratching his belly with the other, Pedro waited for his father to finish reading it. His father handed the composition to his wife, and looked at her without saying anything. He started on his plate and didn't stop until he had eaten the last noodle, but without taking his eyes off her.

The woman read:

When my dad gits home from work, I go wait for him at the bus stop. Sometimes my mom is in the house and when my dad comes in, she says to him hi, how'd it go today? Okay, my dad says, and how did it go for you? Okay, my mom says back. Then I go out and play soccer, and I like to try to make goals with headers. Daniel likes to play goalie and I get him all worked up because he can't intercept me when I spike one at him. Then my mom comes and says it's time to eat, Pedro, and we sit down to eat, and I always eat everything except the beans, which I can't stand. Afterwards, my dad and mom sit on the sofa in the living room and play chess, and I do my homework. And after that we all go to bed, and I try to tickle their feet. And after that, way after that, I can't tell any more because I fall asleep.

Signed: Pedro Malbran

P.S. If you give me a prize for my composition, I hope it's a soccer ball, but not a plastic one.

"Well," his dad said, "we'll have to buy a chess set, just in case."

1980
Translated by Donald L. Schmidt and Federico Cordover

Ken Saro-Wiwa

∎

VERDICT

In 1990, Ken Saro-Wiwa, a successful forty-nine-year-old writer, became president of the Movement for the Survival of the Ogoni People and began a campaign to bring world attention to their suffering at the hands of Nigeria's military government and the Shell Oil Company. Three years later, he was imprisoned (an ordeal he chronicled in A Month and a Day: A Detention Diary*). In May 1994, after four pro-government Ogoni leaders were killed during a riot, Saro-Wiwa was again arrested, together with eight others, and charged with murder. After a widely condemned trial before a military tribunal, he and his co-defendants were sentenced to death on November 2, 1995. Despite international protests, the executions were carried out eight days later. "He and his colleagues," wrote Salman Rushdie, "did not die because of his literary output, but as a result of their fight for the Ogoni people's survival and against the tyranny of the Abacha regime. That fight must now become the world's fight."*

■

I STOOD IN THE COURT, mouth agape, like a dead goat as I heard everyone say in unison, "As the court pleases." I could not believe my ears. I think I must have stared at the High Court judge, His Lordship Justice Benjamin Arokare, for some time, for I remember that he did not as much as look in my direction, deliberately packing his books and papers, standing up, fixing his gown properly on his shoulders, and moving back to his chambers. He stumbled as he stepped from the dais, but no one noticed, for at that moment the shout "Court!" reverberated through the hall and everyone stood up.

Outside, I could hear the drums throbbing away. But something told me it was not the sound of the Alarape family, my clients. Certainly, the Bolaji family were the ones celebrating. I could decipher the name-call of the drums.

I could not bear to look at Chief Mogaji Alarape, the head of the family. The assurances I had given him, and which had convinced him to bring his drummers and praise-singers to the court, had fallen flat on their face. And I was as bewildered as he was. In my confusion, I disrobed, removed my wig, and made as if I was putting my files and books in order. Of course, I did not have to do that. I had another case in the same court, and it would be heard when Mr. Justice Arokare returned after the short break. I would have to see the judge in his chambers immediately.

I dared not look in the direction of my adversary, the defence counsel, Deinde Braithwaite. I knew the satisfaction that would suffuse his puffy face. The beefy man with stubby fingers and a paunch which rolled over his wide belt and split the lower buttons of his shirt would be savouring a victory he had always wanted, but which he clearly did not deserve.

I know that in the finest traditions of our profession, I should have gone to shake hands with him, to congratulate him. After all, there was nothing personal between us. We were only doing our professional duties – each representing a client and, personally, being well paid for it. Yes. But for me, it was a little more than that. I had inherited the case from my lawyer-father with whom I practised for a few years before his death. He had held the brief for ten years and he had died five years to the day judgment was being delivered. It was an important case, and my reputation depended on it, somewhat. And the memory of my father spurred me on to make sure that I prepared the case thoroughly.

Indeed, my father, the late Mr. Olubusola Pratt, had lectured me thoroughly on the matter before the court. He knew the plaintiffs' family very well, as he did the defendants'. And he was absolutely sure that the piece of land, a hundred-acre piece of marshland, belonged to the Alarape family. His father, my grandfather, had been a close friend of the Alarapes. The problem was that their cousins, the Bolajis, had grown rich and famous and were now imposing on the poorer branch of the family, the Alarapes. They had laid claim to the piece of land, believing that they would browbeat the owners, whom they thought not to be in a position to contest the claim through the courts.

The Alarapes might not have fought back, and might have satisfied themselves agreeing to split the land with their cousins, but for the insistence of my father who saw injustice being done and decided that it should not be. He offered his services free of charge, only saying that if he won the case, he would like to buy an acre of land at a nominal fee. This offer suited the Alarapes fine and appeared to be a godsend. They agreed it with my father.

Fifteen years is a long time for any case to remain in court. But here in Ibadan, land cases do last a long time. It is normally a family affair and rests in the family as an inheritance to the living bequeathed by the dead. Chief Mogaji Alarape had inherited the case from his father, as had Chief Akin Bolaji. I had inherited the brief from my father, as I have said. The only man who had been in it from the first day was Deinde Braithwaite, my father's colleague and, I should add, rival. They were both well known as good barristers and had been adversaries in cases and become quite good friends.

Ever before his death, my father had put me on my guard in respect of the case. "It should not be a hard nut to crack. The facts are clear. But the land is no longer mere marshland in the middle of nowhere. Reclaimed, it is now worth several millions and there are now many people interested in it. However, justice must be done to the Alarapes. They must not be robbed. If you look at the evidence of the defendants, you'll find nothing but a tissue of lies. No judge can examine those lies properly and admit them in law." And years later he had added, when the case came up again for hearing, "It's just as well Mr. Justice Ben Arokare is presiding over the case. He is an upright man, brought up in the old school, not one of these newfangled judges who don't know their right from their left and make a mockery of the law by their ignorance. You can rely on good old Ben. He's good." Thus my father and more.

When eventually the case was called up, I did not have much to do, merely dotting the i's and crossing the t's. Nor did Mr. Deinde Braithwaite do much more than he had done before. I addressed the court as eloquently as I could and received congratulations from my colleagues at the bar. Mr. Braithwaite was also at his best. But he did not seem to me to have a good case. Because he was much older than me, the best I could do was tease him when we met outside of court.

"It's a pity, learned senior, that the Bolajis won't be smiling on the day of judgment."

"Ah, don't be too sure of that. You made an excellent address, and I can tell you, I was impressed. You are a chip off the old block. Your father, were he alive, would have been very proud of you. He might not have done much better. However, we shall see."

I felt happy with myself. Deinde Braithwaite did not often lavish praise on his juniors as he had done that day. I looked forward to the day judgment would be delivered, a month from the day I addressed the court.

Two weeks to the day, I was in my chambers on Ekiti Street when my receptionist indicated to me that Chief Mogaji Alarape and two others were waiting to see me. I was a bit surprised at that. I did not have an appointment with them and I was busy with other clients. "Ask them to come back next week," I told the receptionist.

She came back to let me know that Chief Mogaji refused to accept the appointment. He had indicated that he would have to see me that day as the matter would brook no delay.

"Ask him to wait, then. It may take me a long time to finish what I'm doing. They'll have to be patient."

I did not finish with my client until ten o'clock that night and I was as tired as could be. But Chief Alarape and his men were still waiting for me even at that time. They needed an hour and a half to get back to their homes from my chambers. I asked that they be shown in.

Chief Mogaji Alarape was a gaunt man, five foot eleven inches tall and perpetually swathed in long robes with a matching cap – the one with floppy ears which made the wearer look like a clown. He walked jauntily and, since his clothes were never properly ironed, cut a rather sorry figure. His Adam's apple was big, and when he spoke, it bobbed up and down like a buoy on a rough sea. He and his friends walked slowly into my office and I offered them seats in front of my desk.

"What can I do for you?" I asked.

It took Chief Alarape some time to speak. First he cleared his throat and then he looked about the office as if to assure himself that there was no one else around. When he finally found his voice, he said, "It is about the land case."

"Yes, what about it?" I inquired.

"You know it has been in the court for fifteen years now. That is a long time."

"I know, Chief Alarape. But we are getting to the end now. Judgment will be given in a fortnight."

"I know. That is why we came to see you." Chief Alarape looked at his companions, and they nodded to indicate that they were together in the decision to meet with me.

"I have done all that I ought to do. I am optimistic that we shall win the case."

"Amen," chorused the three men.

"Fifteen years is a long time for one case to stay in court," Chief Mogaji Alarape repeated.

"It wasn't my fault," I said. "I'm sure I speak for my father when I say that we would have been happier if the case had ended in one year."

"That is the point, Barrister," Alarape replied. He would never call me by my name. I was always "Barrister" to him. "Do you know why the case stayed in the court for such a long time?"

"Well, there were always all sorts of problems. The lawyers often sought long adjournments; the courts are full of cases and there are not enough judges; Mr. Justice Arokare spent two years on the Special Tribunal set up to try drug cases. All sorts of things were in the way. But we've finally got to the last bend now. You've been patient all these years. Another two weeks and it will be over."

Chief Alarape put both arms on my desk and craned his neck forward to speak to me in low tones. "Don't be annoyed, Barrister, but I used to tell your father that there were many ways to make the case end the sooner, but he did not believe me."

"You know the way to a faster hearing? So did my late father. He filed many motions for accelerated hearing, as you well know."

"I agree. But did he win the motions?"

"He did. Some. The entire thing was not in his hands alone."

"Exactly. That's why I told him to do what everyone else is doing to get their cases heard quickly."

"What's that?" I asked, the hostility in my voice undisguised.

"I asked him to see the judge privately. But your father would not hear of it."

"My father was dead right."

"So our case remained in court for all those years, whereas other cases were being heard and disposed of quickly."

"Well, that's the way my father learned how to practise his profession. I studied at his feet, so to speak, and that is the only way I know too. We are not into this business of 'seeing judges privately.' In any case, we do not have to worry about a hearing now. Judgment will soon be delivered. Two weeks. That's all. We can wait."

"But suppose the judge does not deliver judgment on that day?"

"He will."

"But he can postpone it for another month or two months. Even three months."

"He won't do so."

"But we know that judges do postpone judgment until they are seen." Alarape looked for confirmation from his companions who nodded.

"Mr. Justice Arokare is different. He doesn't do that. He has built a reputation over these many years. He is soon to retire. He won't ruin his reputation this last minute."

One of the men came over to Chief Alarape and whispered something urgent into his ears. It was obviously something important because I saw Chief Alarape stiffen, or rather, spring to life.

"Barrister," he called to me, his tone now plaintive, "suppose the judgment goes against my family?"

"We will go on appeal."

"But we don't want to lose the case."

"Nor do I. As I told you, all the signs are that we will win."

"Barrister, you are talking as if you do not know Nigeria. You have not been living in Ibadan all your life. We know what happens here, more than you do."

"Tell me what happens here," I said impatiently. I was getting really hungry and the wall clock indicated eleven o'clock. I did not care to be on the dark, dangerous streets late at night.

"You can have a good case, but the judge will spoil it for you. Award the judgment to your opponent."

"Why?"

"Because your opponent has seen the judge while you did not see him. All the lawyers in Ibadan know that."

"Really?"

"Barrister, please don't behave as if you don't know what is happening. Everybody knows it."

I could see that Chief Mogaji Alarape and his friends were terribly worried. I decided to put their minds at rest and to give myself some time to think things over. "Let's meet again, this time next week. That will give me time to sort things out."

"Ah, thank you, Barrister. Thank you."

I could feel relief slithering down Alarape's spine. As far as he was concerned, he had made progress. He and his friends trooped out of my office.

Hastily, I closed the windows, shut the office, walked to my car, and drove off.

As I drove home, several questions yammered in my brain. They came with such rapidity that I could not put them in any order. To shut them out, I turned the dial of the car radio and light music suffused the car, giving me some relief. After I got home, I had a heavy late meal and immediately went to bed and dropped off into deep sleep.

I did not think about Chief Alarape and his problems until the day of his appointment. I knew that there was corruption in the courts, but I had always thought that it was limited to some magistrates, some registrars, and probably one particular judge whose name came up for mention on occasion. I always set the judges above it all. And I never thought of Justice Arokare as ever being involved in it. No, it was impossible. Besides, I blamed clients who I thought were the ones who plied magistrates with bribes, tempting them into crime. I was certainly not going to give way to Chief Alarape's imprecations. Not on my life.

When he and his friends turned up at the appointed time, I noticed that Chief Alarape had a battered brown suitcase in his hand. A man carrying a suitcase is no surprise, I thought, but I was surprised at its size. Alarape appeared to be lugging it along. It must have been heavy.

As usual, the three men greeted me respectfully and, I would have thought, reverentially, on this occasion. Looking at Chief Alarape, I could see that the man was a bundle of worry. He began to speak as soon as he found a place on the seat which I offered him: "Barrister, I think you have considered what we told you last time."

"Yes, indeed," I replied. "I'm not going to meddle in that matter. I've done my work. If you think there is a better way to achieve the results we want, it's all up to you."

"Ah, Barrister, don't be angry. Please, there are many things happening nowadays which did not happen before. You don't know about it because of the way your father brought you up. But everybody's father was not a successful, rich lawyer. Please understand."

I have to confess that that touched me. Made me feel guilty. A moth had been playing about the electric light bulb in the office. I watched it now intently and saw it fly too close to danger and then fall to the carpet, flapping and scrabbling uselessly on the floor. I sighed with some exasperation.

"What do you want me to do?" I demanded of Chief Alarape.

"We have brought this," he said, patting the battered object somewhat fondly, I thought.

"I don't know what it contains," I said, "and do not want to know."

"All right, Barrister."

"Now, what do you want me to do with it?"

"Send it to the judge, Barrister."

Good grief, I muttered under my breath, what have I got myself into? Frankly, I wished my father had never involved himself in the Alarape family land case. I wondered what he would have done, faced with a similar situation. A myriad of thoughts hammered away in my brain. I needed time to think.

"Every judge has a clerk," I reminded Chief Alarape.

"We know that, Barrister. But we have asked questions and received answers. That's why we have come to you. Please trust me. Help us."

"I'll have to ask questions too. Judgment is to be given in a week. You can take away your suitcase. Come and see me the day before the verdict."

And the Alarape family duly trooped out of my chambers. The voice of my education, bought by my father at great cost locally and overseas, spoke to me and said, "Drat the Alarape family." Go forth into the world in peace. Hold fast to that which is good. It was always drummed into me at school. Then the words of my father: "The Alarape family are being cheated by their richer cousins. Such oppression should not be allowed." I needed time to order all this in my mind and to take a decision. I would have to go to the club – Lordes – on Wednesday without fail.

Lordes was a highbrow place. It was virtually a cult. Only the high and mighty in Ibadan got into it. Most people did not know of it, nor where it was situated. My father had got me admitted just before he died. I was not really ripe for membership, but a favour was being done my father, who had done so much in his lifetime to grow the club and widen its influence. It was so private an institution that judges had no hesitation in becoming members, if they would be admitted. I confess that I was going there in the half hope that I would meet Mr. Justice Arokare.

On the Wednesday, I was in luck. Mr. Justice Arokare was playing billiards, his favourite game. We did not have time to talk, but he did mention to me in passing that he had not seen me in his home for some time. Did I care to call on Sunday? As late as possible. He would be working late and he did not mind how late I called. He was a man of the night. I was not sure whether this was a hint or not. The verdict in the *Alarape v Bolaji* case was to be given the following day.

The only person I could confide in was my wife, Kemi. She was a senior magistrate. We had met in the law school and married a year after we graduated. She was not just a wife. She was my friend. A confidant. And I trusted her judgment. When I told her what was going on, she was stunned. "It's not because I don't know what goes on in the courts sometimes. It's a corrupt country, after all, and corruption permeates the whole society. But the people involved in this one give me the creeps. I hope you are not in danger. That a trap is not being set for you. I sincerely hope not."

"So what should I do?" I asked.

"Put it to the Lord in prayer. I'll be in Church all Sunday."

I had guessed that Kemi would say that. She had recently

found God in the way the Pentecostal churches were preaching and selling the Heavenly Father. And this had brought some strain into our otherwise happy marriage. I think it was our childlessness which drove Kemi to it. And nothing I did or said would turn her away from her new-found love. I loved Kemi dearly; I was not going to let this ruin our marriage. But whenever she consigned anything to the Lord, I knew that I could no longer discuss it with her. Besides, the matter I had consulted her on required immediate answers. I was not sure that the Lord would answer Kemi and she in turn advise me in time for me to take the decision I had to take. And there, I'm afraid, I let the matter rest.

I was in my chambers on Sunday evening. I had asked Chief Mogaji Alarape to meet me there at ten o'clock at night. I would be alone. Three members of the family duly turned up with the battered suitcase. After the usual exchange of greetings, I let them sit in front of me for well over an hour, while I flipped through a magazine. In truth, I was not reading the magazine. I was only debating with myself whether I should ask them to go back with the battered suitcase or whether I should do their bidding – deliver the suitcase to Mr. Justice Arokare. I was in torment. And they appeared to be in torment too, for no one spoke a word. When I stole a look at them later, they appeared lost in thought.

At eleven-thirty on the dot, I suddenly stood up and ordered them to follow me. They made to give me the suitcase, but I declined it. I asked them to follow my car, in their car. I drove towards Mr. Justice Arokare's residence. A full moon shone brilliantly, and as I drove I did think of Kemi and her love of a God that made the moon shine so wonderfully with metronomic regularity.

Close to the gate of Mr. Justice Arokare's residence, I stopped my car, kept the engine running, and asked Chief Mogaji Alarape to transfer the suitcase to the empty front seat of my car. "Follow me until I get past the gate of the house, and then you can go," I said.

Chief Mogaji obeyed me. I was apparently expected at Mr. Justice Arokare's and was allowed in by the night watchman dressed in nondescript clothes. I switched off the engine of my car, took up the battered suitcase, noting in the process how very heavy it was, and pressed the front-door bell.

After a while, Mr. Justice Arokare himself answered the door bell and let me in. He must have noted that I was heavily laden because I saw his eyes travel down to my right hand. "You are early," he said dryly.

"It's midnight," I said, looking at my watch.

"I know. I'm still in my study. I'm writing an important judgment." Smudges of insomnia were carved beneath his eyes.

"Maybe I should go away and come back later?" I essayed.

"Oh, no. You're not in the way. Sit here. There are drinks over there in the case. Enjoy yourself. I need your opinion, which is the reason I invited you. When I'm done, I'll call you. If you feel like it, take a snooze." He laughed in his throaty way and returned to his study.

I fixed myself a whisky and soda. The house was absolutely quiet. All the windows were shut. I found the split air-conditioning and switched it on. Then I settled down to read some law reports which I found on a dust-mantled nest of stools in a corner of the lounge. I sipped my whisky and soda and read on.

I had certainly nodded off because when I woke up, Mr. Justice Arokare was at my elbow. I rubbed my eyes and noted that my whisky and soda was unfinished and the law report I had been reading had slipped to the floor.

"Come into my study," Justice Arokare invited me.

I followed him, now wide awake. After we got in, he closed the door, switched on the air-conditioner, and offered me the seat by the desk. He himself drew another chair and sat next to me.

"My boy," he said, "I think I'm going to take you into confidence, this once. Maybe it's the memory of your father. Maybe, my admiration for you. For you are a brilliant lawyer, well groomed, a pride to your father. I congratulate you. The Alarape-Bolaji case has been around a long time. In writing my judgment, I feel like I'm doing an obligation to the law, but also to your late father, my friend from our earliest days. I've written the judgment. Put a final stop to my decision. I can let you see it. If there's anything wrong, I mean from a legal point of view, you can tell me. It's right here before you. It's longish, but take your time and read and digest it. When you're through, we'll talk. OK?"

And that is how I came to know that I had won the case. The argument of the judge was thorough, in my view, and the references were apt and properly researched. My joy knew no bounds. It was not just that my clients had won. But the logic leading to the victory was the elixir.

It had taken me an hour to read it. It would have taken at least six to write, given that all the references were available. And the judge would probably need two hours or two hours and a half to read it in court.

Well, yes, it was not quite right that I should have read the judgment. Anyway, I had not influenced it in any way whatsoever. But would Mr. Justice Benjamin Arokare have given it me to read if the judgment had gone the other way? He probably would have, I reasoned, if what he was looking for was an editor. But was he giving it to me as an editor? Could I have made a difference to it if I had wanted to? These thoughts raced through my mind as I stood up to bid Justice Arokare a very good morning.

"We will meet in the court later," I said as he opened the door to let me out.

"Thanks indeed."

I had left the battered suitcase near the settee on which I had settled in the lounge. I did not make any mention of it, and Justice Arokare did not, either. But I think we both understood what it was all about.

As I started my car and drove out of the compound, I noticed the headlamps of another car behind me. It was already four o'clock and one or two cars in the streets would not have been unusual. All the same, I stepped on the gas. There were just too many armed robbers and car snatchers around. I looked into the rear mirror and noticed that I was not being followed. The car might well have turned into the compound I had just left. I recalled that Justice Arokare's car had not been in the driveway when I arrived.

I let myself into my house and caught three hours' sleep. By eight o'clock, I was up and about. I had a light breakfast and drove to the court premises in good heart.

The Alarape family were out there on the premises. I did not give them any more than the usual attention. And I did not tell them whatever privileged information I had. I did notice, however, that they were so self-assured that they had brought drummers. A sure sign that they expected to win the case.

However, the Bolaji family were also there with their drummers. Which might have bothered me, had I not known what I knew. I walked into court with strong, sturdy steps. Mr. Deinde Braithwaite was there before me, and he extended me a friendly hand. "Today is D-day," he joked. "I hope you're ready for the expensive lunch I'm going to offer you."

"Offer me the lunch, learned senior," I said. "I expect to win the case."

"Don't count your chickens, my boy, before they . . ."

At that point, Justice Arokare came in and we all had to acknowledge his entrance.

Our matter was the first on the cause list. I sat petrified as I heard something entirely different to what I expected. My stomach turned and churned. I wished that the ground would open and swallow me. Had I ruined myself and angered Mr. Justice Benjamin Arokare with that wretched battered suitcase? Heavens, what had I done? And when, finally, judgment was delivered in favour of the defendants, all I felt was as I put it at the beginning of my narration.

I did go to Mr. Justice Arokare's chambers. He sat at his table, speaking to the clerk of court. When I came in, he dismissed the clerk peremptorily.

"Don't ask me what happened, my boy," he said after motioning me to a seat.

"But . . . but . . . I left you at four o'clock this morning and . . ."

"Time enough to do what had to be done, my boy," he said, and drew his chair closer to me and spoke confidentially.

"What I'm going to tell you now is not pleasant. It may give you a certain impression of me. But I can live with it. There are extenuating circumstances, you understand. You see, after you left me this morning, I had another caller. He brought in two battered suitcases. Superior to the single suitcase you left behind. I had to oblige the caller. You understand? I retire next month. After all these years on the higher bench, I do not have a house of my own and my savings are paltry. What does a judge earn? And you must know what inflation is doing to everyone. What's my pension? Won't keep me alive each month. You at the bar are lucky. You earn good money. But judges and magistrates – ah, that's another matter. We have to live, you understand? Businessmen, lawyers, they do pretty well. We scrounge. I needed a good retirement benefit. I think I got it. God's providence. No? Well, anyway, my clerk will deliver your suitcase to your chambers. There's a little extra extracted from the other suitcases for your troubles. Don't refuse it. The system doesn't protect us all equally. The moralists starve, the crooks live it up. It's everyone for himself and God for us all. You must forgive today, forgive an old man protecting his retirement. And don't you worry. You can always go on appeal. I'm sure you'll win at the Appeal Court."

The words formed and dried on my lips. I stumbled out of his chambers, asked a colleague to stand my other case down, and I left pleading sudden ill health. Yes, I was sick.

1994

Reinaldo Arenas

■

TRAITOR

The Cuban Revolution of 1959 offered itself as a uniquely hopeful prospect for the rest of Latin America. Here at last was a revolution that brought the possibility of establishing an independent nation, concerned with the welfare of its citizens and resilient to foreign ambitions. Very soon, the illusion crumbled. Pressured by the United States embargo and seduced by the Soviet offers of help, Cuba became a totalitarian system closed in on itself where, in exchange for better living conditions and guaranteed literacy, individual freedom was curtailed and opposition to government policies deemed treason. Critics of Castro's measures, intellectuals interested in democratic ideas, homosexuals were all branded anti-revolutionaries. Some dissidents were condemned to penal servitude; the fortunate ones managed to go into exile. Abroad, the Cubans who had left set up a parallel culture: among them, the writers Guillermo Cabrera Infante, Severo Sarduy, and Reinaldo Arenas.

■

I AM GOING TO SPEAK FAST, just as it comes. So don't expect much from your little gadget. Don't think you're going to get a lot from what I tell you, and that you are going to patch it up, add this and that, make it into a big opus, or whatever, and become famous on my account . . . Though I don't know, maybe if I speak just out of my head, it might work out better for you. It might go over better. You could exploit it more. Because you are the devil. But since you're already here, and with all that paraphernalia, I'll talk. A little. Not much. Only to show you that without us you are nothing. The ashtray is over there, on top of the sink, use it if you want . . . What a show, impeccable shirt and all – is it silk? Can you get silk now? – but you'll have to stand there, or sit on that chair with the ruined cane seat – yes, I know it could be repaired now – and you can start asking me.

And what do you know about him? What does anyone know? Now that Fidel Castro has been ousted, well, overthrown, or he got tired, everybody is talking, everybody can talk. The system has changed again. Oh, now everybody is a hero. Now, everybody was against him. But then, when on every corner, day and night, there was a Surveillance Committee always watching every door, every window, every gate, every light, and every one of our moves, and every word, and every silence, and what we heard on the radio, and what we did not, and who were our friends, and who were our enemies, and what kind of sex life we had, and what kind of letters, and diseases, and dreams . . . All of these were also being checked. Ah, I see you don't believe me. I'm an old woman.

Think whatever you want to. I am old, and out of my mind. Keep thinking that way. It's better. Now it's possible to think – oh, you don't understand me. Do you not understand that then one could not think? But now you can, right? Yes. And that in itself should make me worry, if there were still something that could make me worry. If you can think out loud, you have nothing left to say. But, listen to me, they are still around. They have poisoned everything, and they are still around. And now anything that is done will be because of them, either for them or against them – not now, though – but because of them . . . I'm sorry, what am I saying? Is it true I can say whatever I please? Is it true? Tell me. At first I couldn't believe it. And I still can't believe it. Times change. I hear talk about freedom again. Screams. That is bad. Shouts of "Freedom" usually mean just the opposite. I know. I saw . . . There must be a reason why you came, looked me up, and you're here now with your little machine.

It works, doesn't it? Remember that I'm not going to repeat anything. There will be plenty of people to spin their tales. Now we'll have the testimonials, of course, everybody has a story to tell, everybody makes a big fuss, everybody screams, and everybody was – isn't that nice? – against the tyranny. And I don't doubt it. Oh, but then! Who didn't have a political badge, awarded, of course, by the regime? Make sure you find out, didn't your father belong to the militia, didn't he do voluntary work? *Voluntary*, that was the word. Even I, when Castro was thrown out of power, almost got executed as a *castrista*. How awful! What saved me were the letters I had written to my sister, who was living in exile. What if I didn't have them anymore? She had to send them back to me fast, or else I would be dead and gone. And that's why I haven't dared go out of the house, because some, a lot, of that still exists. And I don't want to get any closer to it. I . . . so you are asking me to speak, to contribute, to cooperate – I'm sorry, that's not the way you say it now – with whatever I know, because you intend to write a book or something, with one of the victims. A double victim, you will have to say. Or triple. Or better, a victimized victim. Or better still, a victim victimized by the victims. Well, you'll have to fix that. Write whatever you want. You don't need to give it to me for approval. I don't want to see anything. I'm taking advantage, however, of this freedom of "expression" to tell you that you are a vulture. Turkey vultures we called them. Have they all been eliminated? No longer needed? What wonderful birds! They used to feed on carrion, on corpses, and then, they soared into the skies. And what was the reason for their extermination? Didn't they clean up the Island under every regime? And how they gorged themselves . . . Perhaps they got poisoned by eating the bodies of those executed by justice – is that still how you say it? – that is, by you . . . Listen, will you bring that machine closer to me? Quickly, because I'm in a rush, and I'm old and tired. And to tell you the truth, I've been poisoned too. This machine – is it working? – was very popular, though people usually never knew when it was being used . . . Today you tell me what you're going to do and why you have come to see me. We talk. And nobody is watching at the corner, right? And nobody will come and search my house after you're gone, right? Anyway, I have nothing else to hide. And is it true I can say whether I'm for something or against it? Right now I can, if I want to, speak against the government, and nothing would happen? Maybe. Is it so, really? Yes, everything is like that now. Right there on the corner, they were selling beer today. There was a lot of noise. Music, they call it. People don't look so scraggly, or so angry anymore. There are no more slogans on the trees. People are going out, I see it, and you can get genuinely sad, with your own brand of sadness, I mean. People have food, aspirations, dreams (do they have dreams?), and they dress in bright colours. But I still don't believe this, as I already told you. I've been poisoned. I have seen . . . but, oh well, we should go straight to the point, which is what you want. We cannot waste any more time. Now we have to work, right? Before, the main thing was to pretend you were working. Now we have aspirations . . . It's a simple story. Yes; of course. But anyway, you won't understand these things. Practically nobody can anymore. These things can't be understood unless you have experienced them, like almost everything . . . He wrote some books that should be around somewhere. Or maybe not. Maybe they were burned during the early dismantling of the regime. Then, at the very beginning, of course, those things happened. Inherited bad habits. I really know it's been difficult to overcome all these "tendencies" – can you still call them that? All those books, as you know, spoke well of the deposed regime. However, it's all a lie. You had to go to the fields, and he went. Nobody really knew that when he was working like a maniac, he was not doing it out of loyalty to the regime, but out of pure hate. You really had to see the fury with which he broke the lumps of earth, how he sowed the seeds, weeded, dug. Those earned the big bonus points then. Oh, God! there was such hate in him while he was doing everything and contributing to everything. How much he hated the whole thing . . . They made him – he made himself – "a model youth", "a front-line worker", and they awarded him "the pennant". If an extra shift of guard duty was needed, he would volunteer. If one more hand was needed at the sugarcane harvest, there he went. During his military service, was there anything he could say no to, when everything was official, patriotic, revolutionary, that is, inexcusable? And even out of the service, everything was compulsory. But by then it was worse, because he was not a youth anymore. He was a man, and he had to survive; that is, he needed a room, and also, for instance, a pressure cooker; and, for instance, a pair of pants. Would you believe me if I told you that the authorization for buying a shirt, and being able to pick it up, involved political privilege? I see you don't believe me. So be it. But I hope you always can do that . . . Since he hated the system so much, he spoke little; and since he didn't speak much, he didn't contradict himself, while others did, and what they said one day, they had to retract or deny the next – a problem of dialectics, people called it. And then, since he didn't contradict himself, he became a well-trusted man, a respected man. He would never interrupt the weekly meetings. You had to see his attitude of approval while in reality he was dreaming of sailing, travelling, or being somewhere else, in "the land of the enemy" (as it was called), from which he would fly back carrying a bomb; and right there at the meeting – just like so many that he, ominously, had attended and applauded – in a plaza full of slaves, he would drop the bomb . . . And so, for his "exemplary discipline and dutifulness in the Circles of Study" (that was the name given to the compulsory sessions on political indoctrination), he received another diploma. He would be the first one, when the time came, to read from *Granma* – I still remember the name [of the official newspaper] – not because he was really interested, but because his hatred for that publication was such that in order to get it over with quickly (as you would with anything you abhor), he would read it right away. When he raised his hand to donate this or that – we donated everything in public – how he secretly laughed at himself; how, inwardly, he exploded . . . He would always do volunteer work for four or five extra hours – and pity thee if you didn't! He did his compulsory guard duty with a rifle on his shoulder, and the building he was protecting had been built by the former regime – he was protecting his own hell. How many times had he thought of blowing his head off while shouting "Down with Castro," or something like that . . .

But life is something else. People change. Do you know what fear is? Do you know what hatred is? Do you know what hope is? Do you know what total helplessness is? . . . Take care of yourself, and do not take anything for granted, don't trust anything. Not even now. Even less now. Now that everything seems trustworthy, this is precisely the time to mistrust. Later it will be too late. Then you will have to obey orders. You are young, you don't know anything. But your father, no doubt, was in the militia. Your father, no doubt, . . . Don't take part in anything. Leave! – can one leave the country now? It's incredible. To leave . . . "If I could leave," he would tell me, he would whisper in my ear after coming home from one of those everlasting events, after three hours of beating his palms. "If I could leave, if I could escape by swimming away, since any other way is impossible now, or soar above this hell and get away from it all . . ." And I: *Calm down, calm down, you know very well that is impossible, fragments of fingernails is what the fishermen are bringing back. Out there, they have orders to shoot pointblank, even if you surrender. Look at those searchlights . . .* And he himself at times had to take care of those same searchlights, and clean and shine the guns, that is, to watch over the tools of his own subjugation. And how disciplined he was, how much passion he put into it, you might say he was trying to create a cover-up through his actions, so that they would not reveal his authentic being. And he would come home exhausted, dirty, full of slaps on his back, and badges of honour. "Oh, if I had a bomb," he would then tell me, or rather whisper into my ear, "I would have blown myself up with it all. A bomb so powerful that there would be nothing left. Nothing. Not even me." And I: *Calm down, for goodness sake, wait, don't say anything else, they can hear you, don't spoil everything with your rage* . . . Disciplined, polite, hard-working, discreet, unpretentious, normal, easy-going, extremely easy-going, well adapted to the system precisely for being its complete opposite – how could they not make him a member of the Party?

Was there any job he didn't do? And he was fast. What criticism didn't he accept with humility? . . . And that immense hatred inside, that feeling of being humiliated, annihilated, buried, unable to say anything and having to submit in silence. And how silently!, how enthusiastically!, in order not to be even more humiliated, more annihilated, totally wiped out. So that, someday perhaps, he could be himself, take revenge: speak out, take action, live . . . Ah, how often he wept at night, very quietly in his room, in there, the next one on this side. He wept out of rage and hatred. I shall never be able to recount – it would take more than a lifetime – all the vituperations he used to rattle out against the system. "I can't go on, I can't go on," he would tell me. And it was true. Embracing me, embracing me – remember that I was also young, we were both young, just like you; though I don't know, maybe you're not so young: now everybody is so well fed . . . Embracing me, he would say: "I can't take it any longer, I can't take it any longer. I'm going to cry out all my hatred. I'm going to cry out the truth," he whispered, choking. And me?, what did I do? I used to calm him down. I would tell him: *Are you insane?* — and I would rearrange his badges. *If you do it, they are going to shoot you. Keep on pretending, like everybody else. Pretend even more than the others, make fun of him that way. Calm down, don't talk nonsense.* He never stopped performing his tasks dutifully, only being himself for a while at night, when he came to me to unburden his soul. Never, not even now when there is official approval, and even encouragement, did I ever hear anybody reject the regime so strongly. Since he was in the inner circle, he knew the whole operation, its most minute atrocities. Come morning, he would return, enraged but silenced, to his post, to the meeting, to the fields, to the raising of hands to volunteer. He accumulated a lot of "merits". It was then that the Party "oriented" him — and you don't know what that word meant then — to write a series of biographies of high officials. "Do it," I would say to him, "or you will lose all you have accomplished until now. It would be the end." And so he became famous — they made him famous. He moved away and was assigned a large house. He married the woman they oriented him to . . . I had a sister in exile. She used to come, though, and visit me. Very cautiously, she would bring his books under her arm. And she told me the truth: they were all monsters . . . Were they? Or were we? What do you think? Have you found out anything about your father? Have you learned anything else? Why did you choose precisely this tainted character for your job? Who are you? Why are you looking at me that way? Who was your father? Your father . . . "At the first opportunity, I'll leave," he used to tell me, "I know there is strict surveillance, that it's practically impossible to defect, that there are many spies, many criminals on the loose; and that even if I manage to, someone shall murder me in exile. But before that I shall speak out. Before that, I will say what I feel, I will speak the truth . . ." *Calm down, don't talk*, I would tell him – and we were not that young anymore – *don't do anything crazy*. And he: "Do you think that I can spend my whole life pretending? Don't you realize that going so much against myself I won't be me anymore? Don't you see that I'm already but a shadow, a marionette, an actor who is never off the stage, where he only plays a shady character?" And I: Wait, wait. And I, understanding, weeping with him, and harbouring as much, or even more, hatred in me – after all, I am, or was, a woman – pretending just like everybody else, conspiring secretly in my thoughts, in my soul, and begging him to wait, to wait. And he managed to wait. Until the moment came.

It happened when the regime was overthrown. He was tried and sentenced as an agent of the Castro dictatorship (all the proofs were against him) and condemned to the maximum punishment, death by shooting. Then, standing in front of the liberating firing squad, he shouted: "Down with Castro! Down with tyranny! Long live Freedom!" Until the full discharge silenced him, he kept on shouting. Shouts that the press and the world defined as "cowardly cynicism". But that I – and please write this down, just in case your machine is not working – I can assure you that this was the only authentic thing your father had ever said out loud in his whole life.

1981
Translated by Dolores M. Koch

Rachid Mimouni

■

THE

ESCAPEE

From 1954 to 1962, the Algerians fought a bloody war of independence against their French colonial masters. Having secured their freedom, they proceeded to nationalize their country's resources and industries. A coup in 1965 and a new constitution in 1976 destabilized Algeria's frail political structure. At first, the government refused to acknowledge the swelling religious movement; by the time it had acquired strength and political momentum, it was too late to satisfy its leaders by democratic means. Algeria began to suffer ferocious guerrilla attacks from the excluded fundamentalists, who targeted Westerners and liberal Algerians. Gradually the fundamentalists began imposing their rules on education, the status of women, cultural industries, and many of the nominal government's policies, leaving Algeria in a state of near civil war. Rachid Mimouni, one of Algeria's foremost writers, argues that the country's present state is due not merely to unkept promises in its past but to a lack of political perspective. "A people's memory," he writes, "is only worth recovering if it includes the future."

■

IN HIS INFINITE SOLITUDE, for his birthday, the Supreme Leader, beloved of the people and awesome forger of History, has decreed this Wednesday a legal holiday, public and generously paid, for the personnel of all administrations and enterprises, including those remunerated by the hour or by the day; a school holiday for pupils, students and scholars, to whom will be distributed free of charge a meal accompanied by little flags with his effigy which should, when the time comes, be waved frenetically and ceaselessly before the cyclopean eye of cameras released on to the streets of the capital, more exuberant than crazed young calves longtime quarantined. To the lower steps of his sheltered residence, the peasants will come to deposit their most beautiful verses, and the most beautiful girls to howl their adulation. The shops in the town have received an imperious order from the administration not to lower their shutters until past midnight despite their impoverished windows which will have to remain illuminated through the night; just like the cafés which throughout the day have, on orders from on high, taken delivery of cargoes of multicoloured lemonades and a variety of juices; like the restaurants with starved menus which, for the occasion, will be able to offer their fortunate guests not only meat, red and white, and ten varieties of fish but even, for dessert, exotic fruit so long missing from the traders' stalls that our children are unaware of their existence; and the bars, always watched over like dens of intellectuals, will be licensed by a permit from the Prefecture to serve male bacchantes until dawn with beer that froths and all sorts of liqueurs imported with hard currency, whose bottles of a thousand shapes have ended up adorning shelves more naked than the languid pose of a mistress with eyes for the lover whose desire is appeased, and the sight of which brings tears of nostalgia to the eyes of the old drunkards who recall times more distant than joy. This evening they will shamelessly over-indulge in those drinks of yesteryear miraculously reappeared.

For the great day, they have repainted all the buildings in uniform blue and white, dusted down the sickly and scrofulous trees, given lights to the blinded lamps, flushed down the arteries of the town to the detriment of the inhabitants who know they must pay for this liquid prodigality with several days of sterile taps. They have stopped the drains from emptying into the streets, the beggars and tramps from showing themselves, restricted to their homes the few intellectuals still at liberty, erased the cases of suicide and hysteria from the statistics, remembered to wind up the public clocks which forgetfulness has made arthritic, decorated with multicoloured bulbs and sky-blue slogans the façades of buildings, cloaked with integrity all the officials of the Great Party of the People, proceeded to rewrite all the books of History, expelled the foreign journalists, called on the sky to obliterate its clouds, stifled in his hotel room the last political opponent whom they had earlier decided provisionally to reprieve in order that he might serve as a scapegoat for future popular disturbances, embellished the *curricula vitae* of the high dignitaries of the regime with great exploits and subtly trimmed down those of their wives, ordered all the bigots to shave their heads and peopled the streets with a profusion of banners required simply to flutter in spite of the ardent breeze.

Motorists will be able to hoot their horns to their hearts' content and park where they want. Foreign embassies have been authorized to accept every visa request, but for the one glorious day only and on condition that they immediately hand over to the police the names of the applicants for travel. Common convicts will be able to watch on television the scenes of public rejoicing.

Adolescent boys know that the girls will come out, priggish or provocative, but they will only dare approach them under cover of the shadows or, more easily still, the throngs of pseudopodia who will enliven the great public places around orchestras equipped with infernal sound systems imported by the planeload from countries that worship music.

The newspapers have announced that a generous amnesty, decided by the Supreme Leader, beloved of the people and awesome forger of History, has liberated a thousand prisoners. Released: the bakers, starvers of the masses, who speculated on the weight and price of a loaf; the unscrupulous grocers who trafficked in the powdered milk of sucklings by mixing it with plaster; the pharmacists, peddlars of out-of-date medicines; the distracted printer who gave blue eyes to the portrait of the Supreme Leader, beloved of the people and awesome forger of History; the young hooligans who plundered the flowers of the few public gardens by way of protest against the slow death planned for them; and, finally, the solitary demonstrator whose death from a heart attack the press had announced one month previously.

Towards the middle of the afternoon, the people invade the streets *en masse*. The populous areas spew out the contents of their entrails into the great boulevards. The cinemas can no longer lure in customers to dream, the *pâtisseries* are besieged by ravenous young girls who jostle each other, each buttock tenderized by precious silk chaffing against the coarse cotton of jeans. The illicit street vendors of coloured stones see their prices and products take off.

The crowd flows with more and more difficulty and thickens in the squares where stands for the orchestras have been erected.

It was at dusk of the great day, as the festivities were beginning, that the Chief of State Security received the news. This night-bird who handled such dark secrets that he'd had all the windows of his office walled up, more inaccessible than the path to paradise, had bit by bit transformed himself into a chthonic monster, deformed and vicious, of which only the eyes glowed with a day-blind beauty. He lived for his dossiers more cherished than his four children, to fabricate or dismantle the wiliest of plots with the joyful ferocity of a muraena attacking its prey. He had undertaken to assassinate all the Comrades whose past might cast a shadow over the Supreme Leader, beloved of the people and awesome forger of History; to kidnap and torture to death all political opponents, even those who'd taken refuge abroad; to compromise in scandalous affairs all potential rivals who found themselves condemned to perpetual solitary confinement, and in their prison died one by one of an epidemic of heart failure; to exile to the most forgotten of embassies any would-be dauphins who dared to believe in their future; to recommend the immediate resignation of competent ministers; to infiltrate all the workers' unions however strictly obedient, just as he had planted his own agents into the universities and the ministerial cabinets, the enterprises and the mosques, the dark corners of the town and the queues in front of the supermarkets. His disquieting tentacles spread throughout the country and the mention of his name sowed terror.

There was only one man whom he had managed neither to corrupt nor intimidate nor diminish. Thus he'd had him locked up in the most terrible of prisons.

"He has escaped!"

The Chief of State Security immediately convened the gaoler of the prison, the chiefs-of-staff of the three armies and a mysterious stranger with a beard.

As though gripped by nausea, the barracks surrounding the capital began vomiting up their soldiers, their police, their parachutists, their élite units, their rapid-intervention groups, their special guards, their shock commandos, their anti-riot brigades, their anti-terrorist sections, their man-hunting experts all armed with pistols, shotguns, grenades, machine-guns and all sorts of apparatus of detection, of location, of listening, of jamming, of tracking, of clearing. Motorbikes, police cars marked and unmarked, trucks, half-tracks, jeeps, armoured cars on wheels, on tracks, amphibian, overland, poured out at full speed into the streets, while the sky was enlivened by a saraband of helicopters, of hunting planes and of bombers.

He had been shut away for so long that he had forgotten the face of his mother, lost his childhood memories, no longer knew the colour of the sky. He did not know what the babbling of an infant was like and no longer felt nostalgia for an old refrain casually hummed. For centuries, he had lived only the nocturnal hours whose darkness reinforced the anguish, amid the thud of boots, the clank of loaded firearms, the passwords murmured behind his back. He dreaded above all the intrusion of those occult and icy emissaries who never lost either their temper or their heart. They obstinately returned to the charge, asking the same question for the thousandth time, receiving with candour the same response that was noted with the same application. They never wavered from their cold restraint except, from time to time, to venture some false confidence by way of a menace. These polite and respectable men seemed to know nothing about the torturers who followed on their departure and who did not leave until the pale dawn light. And the prisoner came to realize that he feared the first more than the second.

His past had been more closely examined than the life of the Prophet, and the least of his acts and gestures gave rise to long exegeses.

Against a single word, they had promised him everything: radiant mornings for the last of men; for the most nostalgic, return to the past; public admission by the leaders of all errors committed, of their denials of justice and abuses of power; the end of potato shortages and a kilo of meat less dear than the smile of my last-born; for every citizen the right to denounce the meanness of their bosses, and once every decade the assurance of making them eat their words; for him a salary higher than the highest mountain in the country, not counting the various perks and the possibility of converting every year the equivalent of his monthly pay into hard currency, the granting of an armoured car directly imported from Japan which would bid him welcome the moment the door opened, a tri-coloured card which would allow him access without having to queue at the most prestigious of shops reserved for the buying of all the cheeses of the world, not to mention butter which melts in the sun like my heart under the caresses of my wife, the assurance of having his children educated in Switzerland, transported by private aeroplane, morning and night, together with those of high dignitaries; the abolition of surtax on whisky; the possibility for the citizen to go abroad without fuss or hard currency and for the most desperate, the right to say "shit".

Against a single word, they promised him everything.

He told them "shit".

He set off at a run across town, instinctively taking the most obscure paths, the narrowest streets, the least used, the least usable, in the hope of emerging in the quarter of his birth, the only possible refuge. But they were not to be found – the street of his childhood, the street of the butchers with bloody stalls, of the tanners with their sickening pits of steeping skins, the dyers with skeins of multicoloured wool dripping in the sun, the braziers barely visible in their dark hovels, the street of illicit vendors of merchandise pilfered from smart shops, itinerant secondhand dealers offering their own clothes for sale, the street of pickpockets whose strict professional code of ethics prohibits them from robbing an inhabitant of the quarter, the street of brothels of the poorest quality, alone in surreptitiously accepting minors on condition that the latter relieve themselves in less than one minute, which hardly presents them with a problem, the street of all contraband, of vagrants and beggars of all sorts, of layabouts, drunkards, unemployed, orphans, the hungry, the infirm . . .

But everything had changed in the town, once comely and inviting, smiling in her sunlit mornings, coquettishly allowing herself to be photographed by tourists, today turned in on herself like a porcupine under attack, fearful and menacing, hostile to strangers, with her new boulevards at angles too acute, her avenues leading nowhere, her quarters cut off, her imperious hoardings, her neurasthenic colours, her nights forsaken. More serious still, the town had repudiated the sea which lapped at her feet and had mislaid the populous quarters which the fugitive sought. From alley to alley, the escapee collided against the impassibility of carriage gateways, always rejected and out of breath, resumed his disorderly course of a blind bumblebee towards other doorways just as indifferent, and the same inhospitable pavements.

Suddenly he emerges into a semi-circular square, illuminated to profusion by one thousand pitiless searchlights. He falls to his knees, panting. He blinks his eyes. Blinded, the bird of night. Too late to turn back. Already some passers-by are surrounding him. The man gets up painfully. He is immense, as though mounted on stilts. Equilibrium ill-assured, he sways on his long legs, torso bending, ventures some hasty steps to regain his stability, and the strollers recoil, frightened, making a space which isolates him. His bulging eyes, staring, are crazed, a false smile making ape-like his face which sweats with fear. The large red cloak in which he is covered turns him into an entertainer of revellers who gather round in a semi-circle.

He is cornered, can no longer flee.

He recoils, backwards, to trust his back to the wall. He tries to catch his breath, swallows, mouth open. Grotesque efforts.

He advances once more, awkwardly.

"Brothers, help me," he croaks with an effort from the depths of his being.

His glance sweeps over the spectators, more rapid than a kaleidoscope. The deep lines which furrow his cheeks accentuate the singularity of his tormented face. The oldest, attentive to the constrained smile, believe they detect in it an air of familiarity. It was long ago, so long ago, generations before, when the nights of the town were still animated, the bars properly stocked with liquor, political opponents alive and at liberty to express themselves, magazines and newspapers open to writers, prisons transformed into museums not yet reconverted into prisons, when books packed the shelves in bookshops, when the universities were forbidden to the police, when the Great Party of the People tolerated opposition, when girls dressed as they wanted without dread of being assaulted, when dignitaries dared to go shopping without fear of being lynched, when one could still sing in the street, even in the rain, without the risk of being hauled up before the Court of State Security, when they knew how to make the country work without the help of the crutch of petroleum, when the maritime pines stood tall and proud, heads held high towards the sky, and my violinist friend took pride in the tribulations of his art, when a *baguette* was four times cheaper, when all my friends were unemployed but not yet drunkards, when the American embassy, ransacked on a day of popular rage, was still in ruins, the cinemas usable, the books of History uncensored, and the sea still there playing with the petticoats of the town. In those times immemorial, the face of this man brightened the front page of newspapers, illuminated the screen of televisions. He was seen everywhere, a familiar profile immediately recognized and celebrated, in meetings and popular demonstrations, processions and days of voluntary service, come to support dockers on strike, with peasants from the hinterland, at the pillage of the American embassy today rebuilt, or simply in the street strolling about at nightfall.

And then abruptly the man had disappeared, seized by the snare of nothingness. The old newspapers in which his name and photograph appeared had to be pulped, certain images had to be expurgated from the documentary films of the period, the chair which he had occupied in workers' assemblies and congresses had to be emptied, all his confidants and friends locked up, the place of his birth put under strict surveillance, before deciding to relocate it, the citation of his name forbidden and all namesakes obliged to change theirs, the house in which he had lived razed in order to lay out a public garden, all the books in his library burned after having been leafed through in search of secret or compromising documents, several pages ripped from the books of History, his face erased from the memories of the common people.

"Since the leaders of this country cannot be moved to pity, help me corrupt them. Pour out before me mountains of money, your wives' gold and jewellery, what you've received in inheritance, what you've been able to steal from the coffers of banks or the purses of housewives, by cheating the State with the complicity of foreign companies or, on the contrary, what you've been able to save patiently, each day weighed down by labour, each night of bad wakefulness. For the lowest in the hierarchy, it will take a fortune of which the wildest imagination cannot conceive, so much have they grown used to luxury and muddle, to bathrooms with taps of solid gold electronically controlled from their innumerable bedrooms which oblige them to get up throughout the night to enjoy all their beds, their wives bedecked in jewellery more heavy than the branches of the pomegranate tree at the end of autumn, the whims of their children more demanding than the film star of my dreams, their offices as tellingly decorated as an up-market brothel with their obsession with the wives of others, to their hunger for foreign gadgets to the accumulation of products complacently offered by companies of State."

He pulled himself up, more protracted than a day of absence of a loved one.

"You and I know that power has made them more over-bearing than the monarchs of Divine Right, more arrogant than victorious generals on the eve of battle, more ferocious than the lions of our legends, more contemptuous towards us than towards their wives whom they humiliate unfailingly morning and night, the more so towards all other fallen women, more hypocritical than a famished crocodile, more nauseating than the garbage cans of the residential quarters which the hurried collectors forget to empty, more crafty than the chameleon lying in wait for its prey, ready to take on all colours and qualities, prepared to hold all discourses, cheerfully cursing that which they adored yesterday to adore today that which they have damned, more corrupt than assistants in the state-run shops, but also more anxious than peasants hoping for the first rains, than mothers keeping an eye on the fever of their child, than an unemployed person in his apprehension of tomorrow, than a fiancée awaiting the return from exile of the beloved in order to melt against him in a passionate embrace but whose conscience, initial desire assuaged, will be titillated by suspicions of infidelity, the more unfair since she knows nothing of the bitterness of exile and its atrocious nights of solitude, the torments of the lonely darkness that hugs the sides of the streets searching for an untraceable kindred spirit. Yes, they are even more anxious, and if you want, this evening, shoulder to shoulder, we can march towards the area where, in the shade of the large trees, their residences shamefully hide. We will go via the streets of people who at first invitation will agree to follow us. On the way, we will slash the huge hoardings which display their deceitful smiles, we will set fire to the special cooperatives where they supply themselves shamelessly with pure imported produce. Our rage will make the walls of their air-conditioned offices quake. And, if you feel like it, we will go and ransack the beauty salons where their wives go to patch up their appearance. In passing, we will not forget to pillage the premises of the radio which bores us to death with syrupy talks and to pull to pieces all the gleaming state cars along the way. It will be easy for us to overrun the barricades and the lines of spikes which they are bound to erect to contain us, to turn against them the rifles of the guards whom they pay at the price of gold but who have always hated them. And when fear has jammed their automatic machine-guns treacherously ensconced at the corners of the streets, rendered mute their alarm sirens relayed direct to all the barracks of the country, demobilized the delicate mechanisms of the locks of their armoured doors, entombed the secret tunnels at the exit of which helicopters ready for take-off await, then we will discover them stripped bare, faces decomposed by terror."

A child's smile has just illuminated his face.

"We will make them admit everything. They must tell us why their mothers refused to sing over their cradles, why their wives found their way to suicide or to asylum, why their children are repulsed by their smile, why the air shudders when they appear, the animals flee, the young girl in love stops singing, the sky rumbles in anger, the flowers wither, the springs dry up, the babies cry, God trembles in fear. They must tell us at the cost of how many assassinations they took power, at the cost of how many others they have held on to it, by what miracle they were able in so short a time to squander the riches of the country, for what reason they entrusted everything from our subsoil to the air we breathe to foreigners: factories to be constructed, hotels to be run, roads and railways to be laid, their illnesses to be treated, mosques to be built, sanctuaries to be erected, hospitals to be equipped, their children to be educated, subways to be excavated, their wives to be clothed, statues of national heroes to be sculpted, the secrets of our finances to be scrutinized. They must tell us how to distinguish the true from the false plots which they have announced, how this spy condemned for delivering to wicked foreigners that which no longer remains our State secret and executed for high treason, how he was able to become a high dignitary once more. They must explain to us why they traffic in information, in History, in ballot boxes, in GMT, in meteorology, in the figures of national book-keeping."

The semi-circle continues to thicken.

"After having stripped their archives and their recording tapes, we will put them on public trial. We will expose all their depravity, their infamy, their shady dealings, their ignoble hagglings, their black manoeuvrings, and all their villainy. We will publish all useful documents and hold them accountable for their crimes before a serene assembly. We do not seek vengeance but fair punishment. We will scrupulously see to it that they enjoy all the rights granted them by the texts which thousands upon thousands of times they have flouted but which they themselves had conceived strictly for their own convenience."

He falls silent, and the murmurs of the crowd approve his speech.

"Then we will have to choose the wisest among us and ask them to prescribe for us regulations and laws which mistrust all powers. In spite of that, we will remain vigilant."

The crowd is ready to follow him.

Slowly, the mysterious stranger with the beard breaks through the semi-circle and advances on the square gleaming with light, pistol in hand. The orator, who has just recognized him, recoils, back to the wall. The man points his weapon at the temple of the escapee and presses the trigger once. Then he turns and calmly walks away.

Nobody has moved.

1990
Translated by Shirley Eber

Guillermo Martínez

■

VAST

HELL

*The military dictatorship that ruled Argentina from 1976
to 1982 was responsible for the torture and murder of thousands of civilians. The army targeted not only the guerrilla
groups but anyone who for whatever reason might have
been suspected of anti-government opinions, or even of
sympathy with those who held such opinions. The dictatorship developed an entire vocabulary to name the atrocities
it was committing under seemingly innocuous guises.
"A terrorist," said General Jorge Videla, one of the
regime's leaders, in 1978, "is not just someone with a gun
or a bomb, but also someone who spreads ideas contrary to
Western and Christian civilization." The most common
method to rid the government of "undesirables" was to
make them "disappear." The person (man, woman, or
child) would be captured by anonymous members of the
security forces and held in secret prisons, tortured and killed,
and then buried in an unmarked mass grave. Officially, all
knowledge of such persons would be denied, so that friends
and relatives would have their grief at the disappearance*

compounded by uncertainty. This reign of terror was called by the military "the Process," to lend it a sense of civilizing progress. In 1984, two years after democratic rule was reinstated in Argentina, the National Commission on Disappeared People, led by the novelist Ernesto Sábato, having waded through 50,000 pages of testimony and documentation, published its report under the title Nunca Más: *"Never again."*

■

> *"A small town is a vast hell."*
> – *Argentinian proverb*

O FTEN, WHEN the grocery store is empty and all you can hear is the buzzing flies, I think of that young man whose name we never knew and whom no one in town ever mentioned again.

For some reason I can't explain, I always imagine him as we saw him that first time: the dusty clothes, the bristling beard, and especially the long dishevelled hair that almost covered his eyes. It was the beginning of spring, which is why when he came into the store I took him for a camper headed south. He bought a few tins and some *maté* (coffee); as I added up his bill, he looked at his reflection in the window, brushed his hair off his forehead, and asked me if there was a barber in town.

In those days, there were two barbers in Puente Viejo. Now I realize that if he'd gone to Old Melchor's he might never have met the French Woman, and no one would have gossiped. But Melchor's place was at the other end of town, and in any case, I don't think that what happened could have been avoided.

The fact is that I sent him to Cerviño's place, and it seems that while Cerviño was giving him a haircut, the French Woman appeared. And the French Woman looked at the boy the way she looked at all the men. And that was when the bloody business started, because the boy stayed on in town and we all thought the same thing: that he'd stayed on because of her.

It hadn't been a year since Cerviño and his wife had settled in Puente Viejo, and what we knew about them was very little. They weren't sociable with anyone, as the whole town used to point out angrily. If the truth be told, in poor Cerviño's case it was little more than shyness, but maybe the French Woman was, in fact, quite stuck up. They'd come from the big city; they had arrived the previous summer, at the beginning of the season, and when Cerviño opened his barbershop, I remember thinking that he'd soon bring Old Melchor under, because Cerviño had a hairdresser's diploma and had won a prize in a crewcutting competition, and he owned a pair of electric clippers, a hair dryer, and a swivelling chair, and he would sprinkle vegetable extracts onto your scalp and would even spray some lotion on you if you didn't stop him in time. Also, in Cerviño's shop there was always the latest sports magazine in the rack. And, above all, there was the French Woman.

I never quite knew why they called her the French Woman, and I never tried to find out: I'd have been disappointed to discover that, for instance, the French Woman had been born in Bahía Blanca or, even worse, in a little town like this one. Whatever the truth, the fact is that I'd never before met a woman quite like her. Maybe it was simply that she didn't wear a bra: even in winter one could see that she wasn't wearing a thing under her sweater. Maybe it was her habit of appearing barely dressed in the barbershop and putting on her makeup in the mirror, right there in front of everyone. But that wasn't it: there was in the French Woman something even more disturbing than her body, which always seemed uneasy in its clothes, even more unsettling than the low plunge of her neckline. She would stare into your eyes, steadily, until you had to look down, and her eyes were full of incitement, full of promise, but also with a mocking glimmer, as if the French Woman were testing us, knowing in advance that no one would take up her challenge, as if she had already made up her mind that no one in town measured up to her wild standards. So she'd provoke us with her eyes, and scornfully, also with her eyes, she'd draw away. All this in front of Cerviño, who seemed to notice nothing, bent in silence over the backs of our necks, clicking his scissors in the air from time to time.

Oh yes, the French Woman was at first Cerviño's best publicity, and in the early months his barbershop was very busy. But I had been mistaken about Melchor. The old man was no fool, and he gradually started to lure his clients back: he somehow managed to get some porno magazines, which the military in those days had forbidden, and later, during the World Cup, he gathered all his savings and bought a colour TV, the first one to appear in town. Then he started saying, to whoever would listen, that in Puente Viejo there was one and only one barbershop for men; Cerviño's was a hairdresser's for poofs.

However, I believe that if many returned to Melchor's barbershop, it was, once again, because of the French Woman; there aren't many men who will bear for very long a woman who humiliates or makes fun of them.

As I was saying, the young man stayed on. He set up his tent on the outskirts of town, behind the dunes, not far from the house of Espinosa's widow. He rarely came to the grocery store; whenever he did, he'd buy groceries for a long haul, for a fortnight or a month, but every single day he'd visit the barber's. And since it was hard to believe that he went there with no other purpose than to read the sports pages, people started feeling pity for Cerviño. Because that is what happened: in the beginning, everyone felt sorry for Cerviño. The truth is that it wasn't difficult to feel sorry for him: he had the innocent air of a cherub and an easy smile, as shy people often seem to have. He was a man of very few words, and at times he appeared to sink into a tortuous and distant world; his eyes would wander into space and he'd stand for a long while, sharpening his razor blade or interminably clicking his scissors, so that you had to cough to bring him back to reality. Once or twice I surprised him in the mirror, staring at the French Woman with dumb, concentrated passion, as if he himself weren't able to believe that such a woman was his wife. And we were filled with pity by his devoted gaze, which held not the shadow of a doubt.

On the other hand, it was equally easy to condemn the French Woman, above all for the town's married women and for the spinsters in search of husbands who, from the very start, had made common cause against her fearful necklines. But many men also felt resentful against the French Woman:

in the first place, those who had a reputation as the lady-killers of Puente Viejo, such as Nielsen the Jew – men who weren't accustomed to being slighted and even less to being scorned by a woman.

And either because the World Cup was over and there was nothing left to talk about, or because there was a dearth of scandals in town, all conversations ended up discussing the goings-on of the French Woman and her young man. From behind the counter, I'd hear over and over the same comments: what Nielsen had seen one night on the beach – it had been a cold night and yet they both stripped naked and they must have been on drugs because they had done something which Nielsen would not describe, even alone among the men; what Espinosa's widow had said – that from her window she could always hear laughter and moaning coming from the boy's tent, the unmistakable sound of two bodies rolling around together; what the eldest of the Vidals had told us – that right in the barbershop, right there in front of him and of Cerviño . . . Who knows how much of all that gossip was true.

One day we realized that the boy and the French Woman had both disappeared. I mean, the boy didn't seem to be around any more, and no one had seen the French Woman, either in the barbershop or on the pathway down by the beach where she liked to go for walks. The first thing we all thought was that they'd run away together, and, maybe because running away always has a romantic ring, or maybe because the dangerous temptress was now out of reach, the women seemed willing to forgive the French Woman. It was obvious that there was something wrong in that marriage, they'd say;

Cerviño was too old for her, and also the boy was very handsome . . . And with secretive giggles they'd confess that maybe
they would have done the same.

One afternoon, when the matter was being discussed once
again and Espinosa's widow was in the grocery store, the
widow said in a mysterious voice that in her opinion something far worse had taken place; the boy, as we all knew, had
set up his tent near her house, and even though she, like all of
us, hadn't seen him since, the tent was still there and it seemed
to her very strange – she repeated the words, *very strange* – that
they would not have taken the tent with them. Someone said
that maybe the police should be told, and then the widow
muttered that it might also be convenient to keep an eye
on Cerviño. I remember becoming angry and yet not knowing what to answer: my rule is never to enter into an argument with a client. I began by weakly saying that no one
should be accused without proof, that in my opinion it was
impossible that Cerviño, that someone like Cerviño . . . But
the widow cut in: it was a well-known fact that shy people,
introverted people, can be extremely dangerous when pushed
too far.

We were still going round in circles when Cerviño appeared
at the door. There was a deep silence; he must have realized
that we were talking about him, because everyone tried looking in other directions. I saw him blush and, more than ever,
he seemed to me like a helpless child who had never attempted
to grow up. When he gave me his order I noticed that he had
asked for only a few groceries and that he hadn't bought any
yogourt. While he was paying, the widow abruptly asked him
about the French Woman. Cerviño blushed once more, but
gently now, as if feeling honoured by so much solicitude. He

said that his wife had travelled up to the city to look after her father, who was very sick, but that she would soon be back, maybe in a week's time. When he finished speaking, a curious expression, which at first I found hard to define, had crept over all the faces: disappointment. And as soon as Cerviño was gone, the widow renewed her attack. She, said the widow, had not been taken in by that humbug: we'd never see the poor woman again. And in a low voice she insisted that there was a murderer on the loose in Puente Viejo, and that any one of us might be the next victim.

A week went by, a whole month went by, and the French Woman hadn't returned. Nor had the boy been seen again. The kids from town started using the tent to play at cowboys and Indians, and Puente Viejo divided itself into two camps: those who were convinced that Cerviño was a criminal and those of us who believed that the French Woman would come back – and we were becoming fewer and fewer. One could hear people say that Cerviño had slit the boy's throat with a razor while cutting his hair, and mothers would forbid their children to play on the street outside the barbershop and would beg their husbands to go back to Melchor's. However, and this may seem strange, Cerviño wasn't left bereft of clients: the boys in town would dare one another to go sit in the doomed barber's chair and ask for a razor haircut, and it became a sign of virility to wear one's hair brushed upwards and sprayed.

When we'd ask for news of the French Woman, Cerviño would repeat the story about the sick father-in-law, which no longer sounded believable. People stopped greeting him, and we heard that Espinosa's widow had told the police inspector that he should be arrested. But the inspector had answered that until the bodies were found, nothing could be done.

The town started making conjectures about the bodies: some said that Cerviño had buried them in his patio; others, that he'd cut them into strips and thrown them into the sea. And gradually, in the town's imagination, Cerviño grew into an increasingly monstrous being.

In the grocery store, listening constantly to the same talk over and over again, I began to feel a superstitious fear, the presentiment that in these endless discussions something awful was being hatched. In the meantime, Espinosa's widow seemed to have gone out of her mind. She went about digging holes everywhere, armed with a ridiculous children's spade, hollering at the top of her voice that she wouldn't rest until she'd found the bodies.

And one day she found them.

It was an afternoon at the beginning of November. The widow came into the store and asked me if I had any shovels, and then, in a loud voice so that everyone would hear, she said that the inspector had sent her in search of shovels and of volunteers to dig in the dunes behind the bridge. Next, slowly dropping the words one by one, she said it was there that she had seen, with her very own eyes, a dog devouring a human hand. A shiver ran down my back; suddenly, it had all become true, and while I was looking for the shovels and while I locked up the store, I kept on hearing, without quite believing it yet, the horrible conversation: "dog," "hand," "*human* hand."

Proudly, the widow led the march. I trailed behind, in the rear, carrying the shovels. I looked at the others and saw the usual faces, the people who came to the store to buy pasta and tea. I looked around me and nothing had changed, no sudden gust of wind, no unexpected silence. It was an afternoon like all others, at that useless hour at which one wakes up from one's nap. Below us, the houses stood in an ever-decreasing line, and the sea itself, in the distance, seemed provincial, unthreatening. For an instant I thought I understood my own feelings of incredulity. Because something like this couldn't be happening here, not in Puente Viejo.

When we reached the dunes, the inspector had not yet found anything. He was digging bare-chested, and his shovel rose and fell unhampered. Vaguely he pointed around, and I handed out the shovels and sunk mine in the spot that looked safest. For a while, all that was heard was the dry thuds of the metal hitting the sand. I was losing my fear of the shovel and was thinking that maybe the widow had made a mistake, that maybe what she had told us wasn't true, when we heard a furious barking. It was the dog the widow had seen earlier, a poor anemic creature running desperately in circles around us. The inspector tried to shoo it away by throwing bricks at it, but the dog came back again and again, and at a certain point seemed almost to jump up at the inspector's throat. And then we realized that this was indeed the place. The inspector started to dig once again, faster and faster; his frenzy was contagious, the shovels dug in all together, and suddenly the inspector shouted that he'd hit something. He dug a little deeper and the first body appeared.

The others barely threw a glance at it and went back to their shovels, almost enthusiastically, searching for the French Woman, but I went up to the body and forced myself to look at it closely. It had a black hole in the forehead and sand in the eyes. It wasn't the boy.

I turned around, to warn the inspector, and it was like stepping into a nightmare: they were all digging up bodies. It was as if the bodies were sprouting from the earth: every time a shovel dug in, a head would roll out or a mutilated torso would appear. Wherever you looked there were dead bodies and more dead bodies, and heads, and more heads.

The horror made me wander from one place to another; I wasn't able to think, I wasn't able to understand, until I saw a back riddled with bullets and further away a blindfolded head. Then I realized what it was. I looked at the inspector and he too had understood, and he ordered us to stay where we were, not to move, and went back into town to ask for instructions.

Of the time that went by until he came back, I remember only the incessant barking of the dog, the smell of death, and the figure of the widow prodding with her children's spade among the corpses, shouting at us to carry on, that the French Woman had not yet been found. When the inspector returned, he was walking straight-backed and solemn, like someone ready to give orders. He stood in front of us and told us to bury the bodies again, just as we had found them. We all went back to our shovels, no one daring to say a word. While the sand covered the bodies, I asked myself whether the boy might not be here as well. The dog was barking and jumping up and down, as if crazy. Then we saw the inspector, one knee on the ground and his gun in his hand. He fired a single shot. The dog fell down dead. Then he took two steps still holding the gun and kicked the dog's body away, for us to bury it as well.

Before going back, he ordered us not to speak to anyone about this, and jotted down, one by one, the names of all of us who'd been there.

The French Woman returned a few days later: her father had completely recovered. We never mentioned the boy again. The tent was stolen as soon as the holiday season started.

1985
Translated by Alberto Manguel

Gabriel García Márquez

■

BON VOYAGE, MR. PRESIDENT

Before becoming a novelist, when he was still a young man, Gabriel García Márquez worked for many years as a reporter for the Colombian newspaper El Espectador, *establishing, with colleagues in other Latin American countries, a new style of journalism that made use of the devices of fiction to report on the fiction-like reality of their beleaguered countries. In books such as* Clandestine in Chile, *in which he reported on the underground adventures of a political exile returned to Pinochet's Chile, and in* News of a Kidnapping, *concerning the abduction of a group of Colombian journalists by the Colombian drug lord Pablo Escobar, García Márquez made use of that innovative style. The fantastically ferocious political reality, on the other hand, informed much of his fiction: the novels* The Autumn of the Patriarch *and* The General in His Labyrinth *and stories such as "Bon Voyage, Mr. President" make use of his journalistic experience.*

"There are aspects of our reality," he once said, "that can only be reported as fiction. Told in a newspaper article, for instance, they become contaminated with improbability."

∎

H E SAT ON A wooden bench under the yellow leaves in the deserted park, contemplating the dusty swans with both his hands resting on the silver handle of his cane, and thinking about death. On his first visit to Geneva the lake had been calm and clear, and there were tame gulls that would eat out of one's hand, and women for hire who seemed like six-in-the-afternoon phantoms with organdy ruffles and silk parasols. Now the only possible woman he could see was a flower vendor on the deserted pier. It was difficult for him to believe that time could cause so much ruin not only in his life but in the world.

He was one more incognito in the city of illustrious incognitos. He wore the dark blue pin-striped suit, brocade vest, and stiff hat of a retired magistrate. He had the arrogant mustache of a musketeer, abundant blue-black hair with romantic waves, a harpist's hands with the widower's wedding band on his left ring finger, and joyful eyes. Only the weariness of his skin betrayed the state of his health. Even so, at the age of seventy-three, his elegance was still notable. That morning, however, he felt beyond the reach of all vanity. The years of glory and power had been left behind forever, and now only the years of his death remained.

He had returned to Geneva after two world wars, in search of a definitive answer to a pain that the doctors in Martinique could not identify. He had planned on staying no more than two weeks but had spent almost six in exhausting examinations and inconclusive results, and the end was not yet in sight. They looked for the pain in his liver, his kidneys, his pancreas, his prostate, wherever it was not. Until that bitter Thursday, when he had made an appointment for nine in the morning at the neurology department with the least well-known of the many physicians who had seen him.

The office resembled a monk's cell, and the doctor was small and solemn and wore a cast on the broken thumb of his right hand. When the light was turned off, the illuminated X-ray of a spinal column appeared on a screen, but he did not recognize it as his own until the doctor used a pointer to indicate the juncture of two vertebrae below his waist.

"Your pain is here," he said.

For him it was not so simple. His pain was improbable and devious, and sometimes seemed to be in his ribs on the right side and sometimes in his lower abdomen, and often it caught him off guard with a sudden stab in the groin. The doctor listened to him without moving, the pointer motionless on the screen. "That is why it eluded us for so long," he said. "But now we know it is here." Then he placed his forefinger on his own temple and stated with precision:

"Although in strictest terms, Mr. President, all pain is here."

His clinical style was so dramatic that the final verdict seemed merciful: the President had to submit to a dangerous and inescapable operation. He asked about the margin of risk, and the old physician enveloped him in an indeterminate light.

"We could not say with certainty," he answered.

Until a short while before, he explained, the risk of fatal accidents was great, and even more so the danger of different kinds of paralysis of varying degrees. But with the medical advances made during the two wars, such fears were things of the past.

"Don't worry," the doctor concluded. "Put your affairs in order and then get in touch with us. But don't forget, the sooner the better."

It was not a good morning for digesting that piece of bad news, least of all outdoors. He had left the hotel very early, without an overcoat because he saw a brilliant sun through the window, and had walked with measured steps from the Chemin de Beau-Soleil, where the hospital was located, to that refuge for furtive lovers, the Jardin Anglais. He had been there for more than an hour, thinking of nothing but death, when autumn began. The lake became as rough as an angry sea, and an outlaw wind frightened the gulls and made away with the last leaves. The President stood up and, instead of buying a daisy from the flower vendor, he picked one from the public plantings and put it in his buttonhole. She caught him in the act.

"Those flowers don't belong to God, Monsieur," she said in vexation. "They're city property."

He ignored her and walked away with rapid strides, grasping his cane by the middle of the shaft and twirling it from time to time with a rather libertine air. On the Pont du Mont-Blanc the flags of the Confederation, maddened by the sudden gust of wind, were being lowered with as much speed as possible, and the graceful fountain crowned with foam had been turned off earlier than usual. The President did not recognize his usual café on the pier because they had taken down the green awning over the entrance, and the flower-filled terraces of summer had just been closed. Inside the lights burned in the middle of the day, and the string quartet was playing a piece by Mozart full of foreboding. At the counter the President picked up a newspaper from the pile reserved for customers, hung his hat and cane on the rack, put on his gold-rimmed glasses to read at the most isolated table, and only then became aware that autumn had arrived. He began to read the international page, where from time to time he found a rare news item from the Americas, and he continued reading from back to front until the waitress brought him his daily bottle of Evian water. Following his doctors' orders, he had given up the habit of coffee more than thirty years before, but had said, "If I ever knew for certain that I was going to die, I would drink it again." Perhaps the time had come.

"Bring me a coffee too," he ordered in perfect French. And specified without noticing the double meaning, "Italian-style, strong enough to wake the dead."

He drank it without sugar, in slow sips, and then turned the cup upside down on the saucer so that the coffee grounds, after so many years, would have time to write out his destiny. The recaptured taste rescued him for an instant from his gloomy thoughts. A moment later, as if it were part of the same sorcery, he sensed someone looking at him. He turned the page with a casual gesture, then glanced over the top of his glasses and saw the pale, unshaven man in a sports cap and a jacket lined with sheepskin, who looked away at once so their eyes would not meet.

His face was familiar. They had passed each other several times in the hospital lobby, he had seen him on occasion riding a motor scooter on the Promenade du Lac while he was contemplating the swans, but he never felt that he had been recognized. He did not, however, discount the idea that this was one of the many persecution fantasies of exile.

He finished the paper at his leisure, floating on the sumptuous cellos of Brahms, until the pain was stronger than the analgesic of the music. Then he looked at the small gold watch and chain that he carried in his vest pocket and took his two midday tranquilizers with the last swallow of Evian water. Before removing his glasses he deciphered his destiny in the coffee grounds and felt an icy shudder: he saw uncertainty there. At last he paid the bill, left a miser's tip, collected his cane and hat from the rack, and walked out to the street without looking at the man who was looking at him. He moved away with his festive walk, stepping around the beds of flowers devastated by the wind, and thought he was free of the spell. But then he heard steps behind him and came to a halt when he rounded the corner, making a partial turn. The man following him had to stop short to avoid a collision, and his startled eyes looked at him from just a few inches away.

"Señor Presidente," he murmured.

"Tell the people who pay you not to get their hopes up," said the President, without losing his smile or the charm of his voice. "My health is perfect."

"Nobody knows that better than me," said the man, crushed by the weight of dignity that had fallen upon him. "I work at the hospital."

His diction and cadence, and even his timidity, were raw Caribbean.

"Don't tell me you're a doctor," said the President.

"I wish I could, Señor. I'm an ambulance driver."

"I'm sorry," said the President, convinced of his error. "That's a hard job."

"Not as hard as yours, Señor."

He looked straight at him, leaned on his cane with both hands, and asked with real interest:

"Where are you from?"

"The Caribbean."

"I already knew that," said the President. "But which country?"

"The same as you, Señor," the man said, and offered his hand. "My name is Homero Rey."

The President interrupted him in astonishment, not letting go of his hand.

"Damn," he said. "What a fine name!"

Homero relaxed.

"It gets better," he said. "Homero Rey de la Casa – I'm Homer King of His House."

A wintry knife-thrust caught them unprotected in the middle of the street. The President shivered down to his bones and knew that without an overcoat he could not walk the two blocks to the cheap restaurant where he usually ate.

"Have you had lunch?" he asked.

"I never have lunch," said Homero. "I eat one meal at night in my house."

"Make an exception for today," he said, using all his charm. "Let me take you to lunch."

He led him by the arm to the restaurant across the street, its name in gilt on the awning: Le Boeuf Couronné. The interior was narrow and warm, and there seemed to be no empty tables. Homero Rey, surprised that no one recognized the President, walked to the back to request assistance.

"Is he an acting president?" the owner asked.

"No," said Homero. "Overthrown." The owner smiled in approval.

"For them," he said, "I always have a special table."

He led them to an isolated table in the rear of the room,

where they could talk as much as they liked. The President thanked him.

"Not everyone recognizes as you do the dignity of exile," he said.

The specialty of the house was charcoal-broiled ribs of beef. The President and his guest glanced around and saw the great roasted slabs edged in tender fat on the other tables. "It's magnificent meat," murmured the President. "But I'm not allowed to eat it." He looked at Homero with a roguish eye and changed his tone.

"In fact, I'm not allowed to eat anything."

"You're not allowed to have coffee either," said Homero, "but you drink it anyway."

"You found that out?" said the President. "But today was just an exception on an exceptional day."

Coffee was not the only exception he made that day. He also ordered charcoal-broiled ribs of beef and a fresh vegetable salad with a simple splash of olive oil for dressing. His guest ordered the same, and half a carafe of red wine.

While they were waiting for the meat, Homero took a wallet with no money and many papers out of his jacket pocket, and showed a faded photograph to the President, who recognized himself in shirtsleeves, a few pounds lighter and with intense black hair and mustache, surrounded by a crowd of young men standing on tiptoe to be seen. In a single glance he recognized the place, he recognized the emblems of an abominable election campaign, he recognized the wretched date. "It's shocking!" he murmured. "I've always said one ages faster in photographs than in real life." And he returned the picture with a gesture of finality.

"I remember it very well," he said. "It was thousands of

years ago, in the cock pit at San Cristóbal de las Casas."

"That's my town," said Homero, and he pointed to himself in the group. "This is me."

The President recognized him.

"You were a baby!"

"Almost," said Homero. "I was with you for the whole southern campaign as a leader of the university brigades."

The President anticipated his reproach.

"I, of course, did not even notice you," he said.

"Not at all, you were very nice," said Homero. "But there were so many of us there's no way you could remember."

"And afterward?"

"You know that better than anybody," said Homero. "After the military coup, the miracle is that we're both here, ready to eat half a cow. Not many were as lucky."

Just then their food was brought to the table. The President tied his napkin around his neck, like an infant's bib, and was aware of his guest's silent surprise. "If I didn't do this I'd ruin a tie at every meal," he said. Before he began, he tasted the meat for seasoning, approved with a satisfied gesture, and returned to his subject.

"What I can't understand," he said, "is why you didn't approach me earlier, instead of tracking me like a bloodhound."

Homero said that he had recognized him from the time he saw him go into the hospital through a door reserved for very special cases. It was in the middle of summer, and he was wearing a three-piece linen suit from the Antilles, with black-and-white shoes, a daisy in his lapel, and his beautiful hair blowing in the wind. Homero learned that he was alone in Geneva, with no one to help him, for the President knew by heart the city where he had completed his law studies. The hospital administration, at his request, took the internal measures necessary to guarantee his absolute incognito. That very night Homero and his wife agreed to communicate with him. And yet for five weeks he had followed him, waiting for a propitious moment, and perhaps would not have been capable of speaking if the President had not confronted him.

"I'm glad I did, although the truth is, it doesn't bother me at all to be alone."

"It's not right."

"Why?" asked the President with sincerity. "The greatest victory of my life has been having everyone forget me."

"We remember you more than you imagine," said Homero, not hiding his emotion. "It's a joy to see you like this, young and healthy."

"And yet," he said without melodrama, "everything indicates that I'll die very soon."

"Your chances of recovery are very good," said Homero.

The President gave a start of surprise but did not lose his sense of humor.

"Damn!" he exclaimed. "Has medical confidentiality been abolished in beautiful Switzerland?"

"There are no secrets for an ambulance driver in any hospital anywhere in the world," said Homero.

"Well, what I know I found out just two hours ago from the lips of the only man who could have known it."

"In any case, you will not have died in vain," said Homero. "Someone will restore you to your rightful place as a great example of honor."

The President feigned a comic astonishment.

"Thank you for warning me," he said.

He ate as he did everything: without haste and with great care. As he did so he looked Homero straight in the eye, and the younger man had the impression he could see what the older man was thinking. After a long conversation filled with nostalgic evocations, the President's smile turned mischievous.

"I had decided not to worry about my corpse," he said, "but now I see that I must take precautions worthy of a detective novel to keep it hidden."

"It won't do any good," Homero joked in turn. "In the hospital no mystery lasts longer than an hour."

When they had finished their coffee, the President read the bottom of his cup, and again he shuddered: the message was the same. Still, his expression did not change. He paid the bill in cash but first checked the total several times, counted his money several times with excessive care, and left a tip that merited no more than a grunt from the waiter.

"It has been a pleasure," he concluded as he took his leave of Homero. "I haven't set a date yet for the surgery, and I haven't even decided if I'm going to have it done or not. But if all goes well, we'll see each other again."

"And why not before?" said Homero, "Lázara, my wife, does cooking for rich people. Nobody makes shrimp and rice better than she does, and we'd like to invite you to our house some night soon."

"I'm not allowed to have shellfish, but I'll be happy to eat it," he said. "Just tell me when."

"Thursday is my day off," said Homero.

"Perfect," said the President. "Thursday at seven I'll be at your house. It will be a pleasure."

"I'll come by for you," said Homero. "Hôtellerie Dames, Fourteen Rue de l'Industrie. Behind the station. Is that right?"

"That's right," said the President, and he stood up, more charming than ever. "It appears you even know my shoe size."

"Of course, Señor," said Homero with amusement. "Size forty-one."

What Homero Rey did not tell the President, but did tell for years afterward to anyone willing to listen, was that his original intention was not so innocent. Like other ambulance drivers, he had made certain arrangements with funeral parlors and insurance companies to sell their services inside the hospital, above all to foreign patients of limited means. The profits were small and had to be shared with other employees who passed around the confidential files of patients with serious illnesses. But it was some consolation for an exile with no future who just managed to support his wife and two children on a ridiculous salary.

Lázara Davis, his wife, was more realistic. A slender mulatta from San Juan, Puerto Rico, she was small and solid, the color of cooked caramel, and had the eyes of a vixen, which matched her temperament very well. They had met in the charity ward of the hospital, where she worked as a general aide after a financier from her country, who had brought her to Geneva as a nursemaid, left her adrift in the city. She and Homero had been married in a Catholic ceremony, although she was a Yoruban princess, and they lived in a two-bedroom apartment on the eighth floor of a building that had no elevator and was occupied by African émigrés. Their daughter, Bárbara, was nine years old, and their son, Lázaro, who was seven, showed signs of slight mental retardation.

Lázara Davis was intelligent and evil-tempered, but she had a tender heart. She considered herself a pure Taurus and believed with blind faith in her astral portents. Yet she had never been able to realize her dream of earning a living as an astrologer to millionaires. On the other hand, she made occasional and sometimes significant contributions to the family's finances by preparing dinners for wealthy matrons who impressed their guests by making them believe they had cooked the exciting Antillean dishes themselves. Homero's timidity was painful, and he had no ambitions beyond the little he earned, but Lázara could not conceive of life without him because of the innocence of his heart and the caliber of his member. Things had gone well for them, but each year was more difficult and the children were growing. At the time of the President's arrival they had begun dipping into their savings of five years. And so when Homero Rey discovered him among the incognito patients in the hospital, their hopes were raised.

They did not know with precision what they were going to ask for, or with what right. At first they planned to sell him the complete funeral, including embalming and repatriation. But little by little they realized that his death did not seem quite as imminent as it had at the beginning. On the day of the lunch they were confused by doubts.

The truth is that Homero had not been a leader of the university brigades or of anything else, and the only part he ever played in the election campaign was to be included in the photograph that they managed to find as if by miracle under a pile of papers in the closet. But his fervor was true. It was also true that he had been obliged to flee the country because of his participation in street protests against the military coup, although his only reason for still living in Geneva after so many years was his poverty of spirit. And so one lie more or less should not have been an obstacle to gaining the President's favor.

The first surprise for both of them was that the illustrious exile lived in a fourth-class hotel in the sad district of Les Grottes, among Asian émigrés and ladies of the night, and ate alone in cheap restaurants, when Geneva was filled with suitable residences for politicians in disgrace. Day after day, Homero had seen him repeat that day's actions. He had accompanied him with his eyes, sometimes at a less than prudent distance, in his nocturnal strolls among the mournful walls and tattered yellow bell-flowers of the old city. He had seen him lost in thought for hours in front of the statue of Calvin. Breathless with the ardent perfume of the jasmines, he had followed him step by step up the stone staircase to contemplate the slow summer twilights from the top of the Bourg-de-Four. One night he saw him in the first rain of the season, without an overcoat or an umbrella, standing in line with the students for a Rubinstein concert. "I don't know why he didn't catch pneumonia," Homero said afterward to his wife. On the previous Saturday, when the weather began to change, he had seen him buy an autumn coat with a fake mink collar, not in the glittering shops along the Rue du Rhône, where fugitive emirs made their purchases, but in the flea market.

"Then there's nothing we can do!" exclaimed Lázara when Homero told her about it. "He's a damn miser who'll give himself a charity funeral and be buried in a pauper's grave. We'll never get anything out of him."

"Maybe he's really poor," said Homero, "after so many years out of work."

"Oh, baby, it's one thing to be a Pisces with an ascendant Pisces, and another thing to be a damn fool," said Lázara. "Everybody knows he made off with the country's gold and is the richest exile in Martinique."

Homero, who was ten years her senior, had grown up influenced by news articles to the effect that the President had studied in Geneva and supported himself by working as a construction laborer. Lázara, on the other hand, had been raised among the scandals in the opposition press, which were magnified in the opposition household where she had been a nursemaid from the time she was a girl. As a consequence, on the night Homero came home breathless with jubilation because he had eaten lunch with the President, she was not convinced by the argument that he had taken him to an expensive restaurant. It annoyed her that Homero had not asked for any of the countless things they had dreamed of, from scholarships for the children to a better job at the hospital. The President's decision to leave his body for the vultures instead of spending his francs on a suitable burial and a glorious repatriation seemed to confirm her suspicions. But the final straw was the news Homero saved for last, that he had invited the President for a meal of shrimp and rice on Thursday night.

"That's just what we needed," shouted Lázara, "to have him die here, poisoned by canned shrimp, and have to use the children's savings to bury him."

In the end, what determined her behavior was the weight of her conjugal loyalty. She had to borrow three silver place settings and a crystal salad bowl from one neighbor, an electric coffeepot from another, and an embroidered tablecloth and a china coffee service from a third. She took down the old curtains and put up the new ones, used only on holidays, and removed the covers from the furniture. She spent an entire day scrubbing the floors, shaking out dust, shifting things around, until she achieved just the opposite of what would have benefited them most, which was to move their guest with the respectability of their poverty.

On Thursday night, when he had caught his breath after climbing to the eighth floor, the President appeared at the door with his new old coat and melon-shaped hat from another time, and a single rose for Lázara. She was impressed by his virile good looks and his manners worthy of a prince, but beyond all that she saw what she had expected to see: a false and rapacious man. She thought him impertinent, because she had cooked with the windows open to keep the smell of shrimp from filling the house, and the first thing he did when he entered was to take a deep breath, as if in sudden ecstasy, and exclaim with eyes closed and arms spread wide, "Ah, the smell of our ocean!" She thought him stingier than ever for bringing her just one rose, stolen no doubt from the public gardens. She thought him insolent for the disdain with which he looked at the newspaper clippings of his presidential glories, and the pennants and flags of the campaign, which Homero had pinned with so much candor to the living room wall. She thought him hard hearted, because he did not even greet Bárbara and Lázaro, who had made a gift for him, and in the course of the dinner he referred to two things he could not abide: dogs and children. She hated him. Nevertheless, her Caribbean sense of hospitality overcame her prejudices. She had put on the African gown she wore on special occasions, and her *santería* beads and bracelets, and during the meal she did not make any unnecessary gestures or say a single superfluous word. She was more than irreproachable: she was perfect.

The truth was that shrimp and rice was not one of the accomplishments of her kitchen, but she prepared it with the best will, and it turned out very well. The President took two helpings and showed no restraint in his praise, and he was delighted by the slices of fried ripe plantain and the avocado salad, although he did not share in their nostalgia. Lázara resigned herself to just listening until dessert, when for no apparent reason Homero became trapped in the dead-end street of the existence of God.

"I do believe God exists," said the President, "but has nothing to do with human beings. He's involved in much bigger things."

"I only believe in the stars," said Lázara, and she scrutinized the President's reaction. "What day were you born?"

"The eleventh of March."

"I knew it," said Lázara with a triumphant little start, and asked in a pleasant voice, "Don't you think two Pisces at the same table are too many?"

The men were still discussing God when she went to the kitchen to prepare coffee. She had cleared the table, and longed with all her heart for the evening to end well. On her way back to the living room with the coffee, she was met with a passing remark of the President's, which astounded her.

"Have no doubt, my dear friend: it would be the worst thing that could happen to our poor country if I were president."

Homero saw Lázara in the doorway with the borrowed china cups and coffeepot and thought she was going to faint. The President also took notice. "Don't look at me like that, Señora," he said in an amiable tone. "I'm speaking from the heart." And then, turning to Homero, he concluded:

"It's just as well I'm paying a high price for my foolishness."

Lázara served the coffee and turned off the light above the table because its harsh illumination was not conducive to conversation, and the room was left in intimate shadow. For the first time she became interested in the guest, whose wit could not hide his sadness. Lázara's curiosity increased when he finished his coffee and turned the cup upside down in the saucer so the grounds could settle.

The President told them he had chosen the island of Martinique for his exile because of his friendship with the poet Aimé Césaire, who at that time had just published his *Cahier d'un retour au pays natal*, and had helped him begin a new life. With what remained of his wife's inheritance, the President bought a house made of noble wood in the hills of Fort-de-France, with screens at the windows and a terrace overlooking the sea and filled with primitive flowers, where it was a pleasure to sleep with the sound of crickets and the molasses-and-rum breeze from the sugar mills. There he stayed with his wife, fourteen years older than he and an invalid since the birth of their only child, fortified against fate by his habitual rereading of the Latin classics, in Latin, and by the conviction that this was the final act of his life. For years he had to resist the temptation of all kinds of adventures proposed to him by his defeated partisans.

"But I never opened another letter again," he said. "Never, once I discovered that even the most urgent were less urgent after a week, and that in two months one forgot about them and the person who wrote them."

He looked at Lázara in the semi-darkness when she lit a cigarette, and took it from her with an avid movement of his fingers. After a long drag, he held the smoke in his throat. Startled, Lázara picked up the pack and the box of matches to light another, but he returned the burning cigarette to her. "You smoke with so much pleasure I could not resist," he said. Then he had to release the smoke because he began to cough.

"I gave up the habit many years ago, but it never gave me up altogether," he said. "On occasion it has defeated me. Like now."

The cough jolted him two more times. The pain returned. The President checked his small pocket watch and took his two evening pills. Then he peered into the bottom of his cup: nothing had changed, but this time he did not shudder.

"Some of my old supporters have been presidents after me," he said.

"Sáyago," said Homero.

"Sáyago and others," he said. "All of us usurping an honor we did not deserve with an office we did not know how to fill. Some pursue only power, but most are looking for even less: a job."

Lázara became angry.

"Do you know what they say about you?" she asked.

Homero intervened in alarm:

"They're lies."

"They're lies and they're not lies," said the President with celestial calm. "When it has to do with a president, the worst ignominies may be both true and false at the same time."

He had lived in Martinique all the days of his exile, his only contact with the outside world the few news items in the official paper. He had supported himself teaching classes in Spanish and Latin at an official *lycée*, and with the translations that Aimé Césaire commissioned from time to time. The heat in August was unbearable, and he would stay in the hammock until noon, reading to the hum of the fan in his bedroom. Even at the hottest times of the day his wife tended to the birds she raised in freedom outdoors, protecting herself from the sun with a broad-brimmed straw hat adorned with artificial fruit and organdy flowers. But when the temperature fell, it was good to sit in the cool air on the terrace, he with his eyes fixed on the ocean until it grew dark, and she in her wicker rocking chair, wearing the torn hat, and rings with bright stones on every finger, watching the ships of the world pass by. "That one's bound for Puerto Santo," she would say. "That one almost can't move, it's so loaded down with bananas from Puerto Santo," she would say. For it did not seem possible to her that any ship could pass by that was not from their country. He pretended not to hear, although in the long run she managed to forget better than he because she lost her memory. They would sit this way until the clamorous twilights came to an end and they had to take refuge in the house, defeated by the mosquitoes. During one of those many Augusts, as he was reading the paper on the terrace, the President gave a start of surprise.

"I'll be damned," he said. "I've died in Estoril!"

His wife, adrift in her drowsiness, was horrified by the news. The article consisted of six lines on the fifth page of the newspaper printed just around the corner, in which his occasional translations were published and whose manager came to visit him from time to time. And now it said that he had died in Estoril de Lisboa, the resort and refuge of European decadence, where he had never been and which was, perhaps, the only place in the world where he would not have wanted to die. His wife did die, in fact, a year later, tormented by the last memory left to her: the recollection of her only child, who had taken part in the overthrow of his father and was later shot by his own accomplices.

The President sighed. "That's how we are, and nothing can save us," he said. "A continent conceived by the scum of the earth without a moment of love: the children of abductions, rapes, violations, infamous dealings, deceptions, the union of enemies with enemies." He faced Lázara's African eyes, which scrutinized him without pity, and tried to win her over with the eloquence of an old master.

"Mixing the races means mixing tears with spilled blood. What can one expect from such a potion?"

Lázara fixed him to his place with the silence of death. But she gained control of herself a little before midnight and said good-bye to him with a formal kiss. The President refused to allow Homero to accompany him to the hotel, although he could not stop him from helping him find a taxi. When Homero came back, his wife was raging with fury.

"That's one president in the world who really deserved to be overthrown," she said. "What a son of a bitch."

Despite Homero's efforts to calm her, they spent a terrible, sleepless night. Lázara admitted that he was one of the best-looking men she had ever seen, with a devastating seductive power and a stud's virility. "Just as he is now, old and fucked up, he must still be a tiger in bed," she said. But she thought he had squandered these gifts of God in the service of pretense. She could not bear his boasts that he had been his country's worst president. Or his ascetic airs, when, she was convinced, he owned half the sugar plantations in Martinique. Or the hypocrisy of his contempt for power, when it was obvious he would give anything to return to the presidency long enough to make his enemies bite the dust.

"And all of that," she concluded, "just to have us worshipping at his feet."

"What good would that do him?" asked Homero.

"None at all," she said. "But the fact is that being seductive is an addiction that can never be satisfied."

Her rage was so great that Homero could not bear to be with her in bed, and he spent the rest of the night wrapped in a blanket on the sofa in the living room. Lázara also got up in the middle of the night, naked from head to toe – her habitual state when she slept or was at home – and talked to herself in a monologue on only one theme. In a single stroke she erased from human memory all traces of the hateful supper. At daybreak she returned what she had borrowed, replaced the new curtains with the old, and put the furniture back where it belonged so that the house was as poor and decent as it had been until the night before. Then she tore down the press clippings, the portraits, the banners and flags from the abominable campaign, and threw them all in the trash with a final shout.

"You can go to hell!"

A week after the dinner, Homero found the President waiting for him as he left the hospital, with the request that he accompany him to his hotel. They climbed three flights of steep stairs to a garret that had a single skylight looking out on an ashen sky; clothes were drying on a line stretched across the room. There was also a double bed that took up half the space, a hard chair, a washstand and a portable bidet, and a poor man's armoire with a clouded mirror. The President noted Homero's reaction.

"This is the burrow I lived in when I was a student," he said as if in apology. "I made the reservation from Fort-de-France."

From a velvet bag he removed and displayed on the bed the last remnants of his wealth: several gold bracelets adorned with a variety of precious stones, a three-strand pearl necklace, and two others of gold and precious stones; three gold chains with saints' medals; a pair of gold and emerald earrings, another of gold and diamonds, and a third of gold and rubies; two reliquaries and a locket; eleven rings with all kinds of precious settings; and a diamond tiara worthy of a queen. From a case he took out three pairs of silver cuff links and two of gold, all with matching tie clips, and a pocket watch plated in white gold. Then he removed his six decorations from a shoe box: two of gold, one of silver, and the rest of no value.

"It's all I have left in life," he said.

He had no alternative but to sell it all to meet his medical expenses, and he asked Homero to please do that for him with the greatest discretion. But Homero did not feel he could oblige if he did not have the proper receipts.

The President explained that they were his wife's jewels, a legacy from a grandmother who had lived in colonial times and had inherited a packet of shares in Colombian gold mines. The watch, the cuff links and tie clips were his. The decorations, of course, had not belonged to anyone before him.

"I don't believe anybody has receipts for these kinds of things," he said.

Homero was adamant.

"In that case," the President reflected, "there's nothing I can do but take care of it myself."

He began to gather up the jewelry with calculated calm. "I beg you to forgive me, my dear Homero, but there is no poverty worse than that of an impoverished president," he said. "Even surviving seems contemptible." At that moment

Homero saw him with his heart and laid down his weapons.

Lázara came home late that night. From the door she saw the jewels glittering on the table under the mercurial light, and it was as if she had seen a scorpion in her bed.

"Don't be an idiot, baby," she said, frightened. "Why are those things here?"

Homero's explanation disturbed her even more. She sat down to examine the pieces, one by one, with all the care of a goldsmith. At a certain point she sighed and said, "They must be worth a fortune." At last she sat looking at Homero and could find no way out of her dilemma.

"Damn it," she said. "How can we know if everything that man says is true?"

"Why shouldn't it be?" said Homero. "I've just seen that he washes his own clothes and dries them on a line in his room, just like we do."

"Because he's cheap," said Lázara.

"Or poor," said Homero.

Lázara examined the jewels again, but now with less attention because she too had been conquered. And so the next morning she put on her best clothes, adorned herself with the pieces that seemed most expensive, wore as many rings as she could on every finger, even her thumb, and all the bracelets that would fit on each arm, and went out to sell them. "Let's see if anyone asks Lázara Davis for receipts," she said as she left, strutting with laughter. She chose just the right jewelry store, one with more pretensions than prestige, where she knew they bought and sold without asking too many questions, and she walked in terrified but with a firm step.

A thin, pale salesman in evening dress made a theatrical bow as he kissed her hand and asked how he could help her.

Because of the mirrors and intense lights the interior was brighter than the day, and the entire shop seemed made of diamonds. Lázara, almost without looking at the clerk for fear he would see through the farce, followed him to the rear of the store.

He invited her to sit at one of three Louis xv escritoires that served as individual counters, and over it he spread an immaculate cloth. Then he sat across from Lázara and waited.

"How may I help you?"

She removed the rings, the bracelets, the necklaces, the earrings, everything that she was wearing in plain view, and began to place them on the escritoire in a chessboard pattern. All she wanted, she said, was to know their true value.

The jeweler put a glass up to his left eye and began to examine the pieces in clinical silence. After a long while, without interrupting his examination, he asked:

"Where are you from?"

Lázara had not anticipated that question.

"Ay, Señor," she sighed, "very far away."

"I can imagine," he said.

He was silent again, while Lázara's terrible golden eyes scrutinized him without mercy. The jeweler devoted special attention to the diamond tiara and set it apart from the other jewelry. Lázara sighed.

"You are a perfect Virgo," she said.

The jeweler did not interrupt his examination.

"How do you know?"

"From the way you behave," said Lázara.

He made no comment until he had finished, and he addressed her with the same circumspection he had used at the beginning.

"Where does all this come from?"

"It's a legacy from my grandmother," said Lázara in a tense voice. "She died last year in Paramaribo, at the age of ninety-seven."

The jeweler looked into her eyes. "I'm very sorry," he said. "But their only value is the weight of the gold." He picked up the tiara with his fingertips and made it sparkle under the dazzling light.

"Except for this," he said. "It is very old, Egyptian perhaps, and would be priceless if it were not for the poor condition of the diamonds. In any case it has a certain historical value."

But the stones in the other treasures, the amethysts, emeralds, rubies, opals – all of them, without exception – were fake. "No doubt the originals were good," said the jeweler as he gathered up the pieces to return them to her. "But they have passed so often from one generation to another that the legitimate stones have been lost along the way and been replaced by bottle glass." Lázara felt a green nausea, took a deep breath, and controlled her panic. The salesman consoled her:

"It often happens, Madame."

"I know," said Lázara, relieved. "That's why I want to get rid of them."

She felt then that she was beyond the farce, and became herself again. With no further delay she took the cuff links, the pocket watch, the tie clips, the decorations of gold and silver, and the rest of the President's personal trinkets out of her handbag and placed them all on the table.

"This too?" asked the jeweler.

"All of it," said Lázara.

She was paid in Swiss francs that were so new she was afraid her fingers would be stained with fresh ink. She accepted the bills without counting them, and the jeweler's leave-taking at the door was as ceremonious as his greeting. As he held the glass door open for her, he stopped her for a moment.

"And one final thing, Madame," he said. "I'm an Aquarius."

Early that evening Homero and Lázara took the money to the hotel. After further calculations, they found that a little more money was still needed. And so the President began removing and placing on the bed his wedding ring, his watch and chain, and the cuff links and tie clip he was wearing.

Lázara handed back the ring.

"Not this," she said. "A keepsake like this can't be sold."

The President acknowledged what she said and put the ring back on his finger. Lázara also returned the watch and chain. "Not this either," she said. The President did not agree, but she put him in his place.

"Who'd even try to sell a watch in Switzerland?"

"We already did," said the President.

"Yes, but not the watch. We sold the gold."

"This is gold too," said the President.

"Yes," said Lázara. "You may get by without surgery, but you have to know what time it is."

She would not take his gold-rimmed eyeglasses either, although he had another pair with tortoiseshell frames. She hefted the pieces in her hand, and put an end to all his doubts.

"Besides," she said, "this will be enough."

Before she left she took down his damp clothes, without consulting him, to dry and iron them at home. They rode on the motor scooter, Homero driving and Lázara sitting behind him, her arms around his waist. The street-lights had just turned on in the mauve twilight. The wind had blown away the last leaves, and the trees looked like plucked fossils. A tow truck drove along the Rhone, its radio playing at full volume and leaving a stream of music along the streets. Georges Brassens was singing: *Mon amour tiens bien la barre, le temps va passer par là, et le temps est un barbare dans le genre d'Atilla; par là où son cheval passe l'amour ne repousse pas.* Homero and Lázara rode in silence, intoxicated by the song and the remembered scent of hyacinth. After a while, she seemed to awaken from a long sleep.

"Damn it," she said.

"What?"

"The poor old man," said Lázara. "What a shitty life!"

On the following Friday, the seventh of October, the President underwent five hours of surgery that, for the moment, left matters as obscure as they had been before. In the strictest sense, the only consolation was knowing he was alive. After ten days he was moved to a room with other patients, and Homero and Lázara could visit him. He was another man: disoriented and emaciated, his sparse hair fell out at a touch of the pillow. All that was left of his former presence was the fluid grace of his hands. His first attempt at walking with two orthopedic canes was heartbreaking. Lázara stayed and slept at his bedside to save him the expense of a private nurse. One of the other patients in the room spent the first night screaming with his terror of dying. Those endless nights did away with Lázara's last reservations.

Four months after his arrival in Geneva, he was discharged from the hospital. Homero, a meticulous administrator of the President's scant funds, paid the hospital bill and took him home in his ambulance with other employees who helped carry him to the eighth floor. They put him in the bedroom of the children he never really acknowledged, and little by little he returned to reality. He devoted himself to his rehabilitative exercises with military rigor, and walked again with just his cane. But even in his good clothes from the old days, he was far from being the same man in either appearance or behavior. Fearing the winter that promised to be very severe, and which in fact turned out to be the harshest of the century, he decided, against the advice of his doctors, who wanted to keep him under observation for a while longer, to return home on a ship leaving Marseilles on December 13. At the last minute he did not have enough money for his passage, and without telling her husband Lázara tried to make up the difference with one more scraping from her children's savings, but there too she found less than she expected. Then Homero confessed that without telling her he had used it to finish paying the hospital bill.

"Well," Lázara said in resignation. "Let's say he's our oldest son."

On December 11 they put him on the train to Marseilles in a heavy snowstorm, and it was not until they came home that they found a farewell letter on the children's night table, where he also left his wedding ring for Bárbara, along with his dead wife's wedding band, which he had never tried to sell, and the watch and chain for Lázaro. Since it was a Sunday, some Caribbean neighbors who had learned the secret came to the Cornavin Station with a harp band from Veracruz. The President was gasping for breath in his raffish overcoat and a long multicolored scarf that had belonged to Lázara, but even so he stood in the open area of the last car and waved goodbye with his hat in the lashing wind. The train was beginning to accelerate when Homero realized he still had his cane. He ran to the end of the platform and threw it hard enough for the President to catch, but it fell under the wheels and was destroyed. It was a moment of horror. The last thing Lázara saw was the President's trembling hand stretching to grasp the cane and never reaching it, and the conductor who managed to grab the snow-covered old man by his scarf and save him in midair. Lázara ran in utter terror to her husband, trying to laugh behind her tears.

"My God," she shouted, "nothing can kill that man."

He arrived home safe and sound, according to his long telegram of thanks. Nothing more was heard from him for over a year. At last they received a six-page hand-written letter in which it was impossible to recognize him. The pain had returned, as intense and punctual as before, but he had resolved to ignore it and live life as it came. The poet Aimé Césaire had given him another cane, with mother-of-pearl inlay, but he had decided not to use it. For six months he had been eating meat and all kinds of shellfish, and could drink up to twenty cups a day of the bitterest coffee. But he had stopped reading the bottom of the cup, because the predictions never came true. On the day he turned seventy-five, he drank a few glasses of exquisite Martinique rum, which agreed with him, and began to smoke again. He did not feel better, of course, but neither did he feel worse. Nevertheless, the real reason for the letter was to tell them that he felt tempted to return to his country as the leader of a reform movement – a just cause for the honor of the nation – even if he gained only the poor glory of not dying of old age in his bed. In that sense, the letter ended, his trip to Geneva had been providential.

1979
Translated by Edith Grossman

■

NOTES ON
CONTRIBUTORS

The dates given below are of the first publication in the *original* language; to facilitate understanding, the titles have been translated into English, whether they have been published in English or not.

Reinaldo Arenas (Cuba, 1943-90): His novels include *Singing from the Well* (1967), *The Ill-Fated Peregrinations of Fray Servando* (1969), *The Palace of the White Skunks* (1975 in French, 1980 in Spanish), *Old Rosa* (1980), *Graveyard of the Angels* (1987), *The Doorman* (1989), and *The Assault* (1991). Arenas also published poetry, short stories, and essays. His autobiography was published posthumously under the title *Before Night Falls* (1992).

Isaac Babel (Russia, 1894-1941): After an encounter with the great Maxim Gorki, Babel began publishing the stories that made him famous, collected under the titles *Red Cavalry* (1926) and *Odessa Stories* (1931). He also wrote several screenplays, including *Wandering Stars* (1926) and *Korol: The King* (1926). A number of his unpublished stories were collected and edited by his daughter, Nathalie Babel.

Reza Baraheni (Iran, 1935): Baraheni, who now teaches at the University of Toronto and York University (Toronto), has published about fifty books of fiction, poetry, literary criticism, and translation. His works have been translated into many languages, including English, French, German, and Spanish. Among his English books: *The Crowned Cannibals* (1977) and *God's Shadow* (1976).

Paulé Bartón (Haiti, 1916-74): A goatherd by profession, Bartón was imprisoned under Papa Doc, left Haiti, and lived in several Caribbean countries, including Jamaica and Trinidad, before settling in Costa Rica. His only book is a collection of short stories, posthumously collected and translated by Howard A. Norman, *The Woe Shirt: Caribbean Folk Tales* (1980).

E.B. Dongala (Congo, 1941): One of Africa's leading satirists, Dongala studied chemistry in the United States and France before becoming a writer. He teaches literature at a university near Chicago. Dongala is the author of three novels, *A Gun in My Hand, a Poem in My Pocket* (1973), *Original Fire* (1987), and *Little Boys Are Also Born from Stars* (1998), and a collection of short stories, *Jazz and Palm Wine* (1982).

Howard Fast (United States, 1914): American novelist of historical fiction. His books range from novels about the early history of the United States, such as *Two Valleys* (1933), to epics of ancient Rome, such as *Spartacus* (1952). Among his best-known books are *The Last Frontier* (1941), *The Unvanquished* (1942), *Citizen Tom Paine* (1943), *My Glorious Brothers* (1948), *The Naked God* (1957), *Moses, Prince of Egypt* (1958), and *Agrippa's Daughter* (1964).

Gabriel García Márquez (Colombia, 1928): After working as a journalist for many years, he began publishing short stories; his first published novella was *Leaf Storm* (1955). He achieved international fame with *A Hundred Years of Solitude* (1967) and later with

The Autumn of the Patriarch (1975) and *Love in the Time of Cholera* (1985). In 1982 he was awarded the Nobel Prize for Literature.

Natalia Ginzburg (Italy, 1916-91): Her many books include *The Road to the City* (1942), *Voices in the Evening* (1961), *The Little Virtues* (1962), *Five Short Novels* (1964), and her autobiographical *Family Sayings* (1963).

Nedim Gürsel (Turkey, 1951): Gürsel's work – with the exception of a few stories – has not been translated into English. His collections of short stories are *The Commander's Rabbits* (1985) and *The Last Streetcar* (1988). His novels include *A Long Summer in Istanbul* (1975), *The First Woman* (1983), and *The Book of the Conqueror* (1996). Gürsel has also published critical essays and travel writings, including *Return to the Balkans* (1995).

Bessie Head (South Africa, 1937-86): Two collections of short stories – *The Collector of Treasures and Other Botswana Village Tales* (1977) and *Tales of Tenderness and Power* (1989) – and several novels including *When Rain Clouds Gather* (1969) established Bessie Head as one of South Africa's finest voices. Her autobiographical writings were collected after her death in *A Woman Alone* (1990).

Guillermo Martínez (Argentina, 1962): He has published a collection of short stories, *Vast Hell* (1988), which was awarded the Fondo Nacional de las Artes prize, and two novels, *Regarding Roderer* (1992) and *The Woman of the Master* (1998).

Rachid Mimouni (Algeria, 1945-95): He is the author of a collection of short stories – *The Ogre's Embrace* (1990) – and of several novels: *Spring Will Be Even More Beautiful* (1978), *A Liveable Peace* (1983), *The Diverted River* (1982), *Tombéza* (1984), *The Honour of the Tribe* (1989), and *Pain of Living* (1991). *Of Barbarism in General and Fundamentalism in Particular* (1992) is a fierce denunciation of religious fanaticism in Algeria.

Vladimir Nabokov (Russia/United States, 1899-1977): Novelist, poet, and critic. His books include *King, Queen, Knave* (1928), *The Defence* (1930), *Laughter in the Dark* (1932), *The Real Life of Sebastian Knight* (1941), *Lolita* (1955), *Pale Fire* (1962), and *Transparent Things* (1972).

Seán O'Faoláin (Ireland, 1900-91): Seán O'Faoláin's stories were collected in 1980 in one volume. Individual volumes include *Midsummer Night Madness* (1932), *Teresa* (1947), *The Talking Trees* (1970), and *Foreign Affairs* (1976). His autobiography is *Vive Moi!* (1964).

Ken Saro-Wiwa (Nigeria, 1941-95): Though he published his first book in 1983, he is best known for his satirical *Sozaboy: A Novel in Rotten English* (1985). *A Month and a Day: A Detention Diary* was published the year of his death.

Anna Seghers, pseudonym of Netty Radvanyi (Germany, 1900-83): Among her many books are *The Revolt of the Fishermen* (1928), *The Seventh Cross* (1942), *Transit: A Novel* (1944), *The Dead Girls' Outing and Other Stories* (1946), *The Dead Stay Young* (1949), *Bread and Salt* (1958), and *Benito's Blue* (1967).

Antonio Skármeta (Chile, 1940): Novelist, playwright, and scriptwriter, Skármeta has also translated Herman Melville, F. Scott Fitzgerald, and William Golding for Chilean readers. He won the Casa de las Americas Prize for his stories in 1969. In addition to the novels *I Dreamt the Snow Was Burning* (1975) and *Burning Patience* (1985), his books include *Chileno!* (1980), *The Insurrection* (1982), *Match Ball* (1989), and the short-story collection *Watch Where the Wolf Is Going* (1991).

Edmundo Valadés (Mexico, 1915): A leading journalist, Valadés has chronicled the peasants' struggles in two books of short stories: *Permission for Death Is Granted* (1955) and *Sinister Dualities* (1966).

Vercors, pseudonym of Jean Bruller (France, 1902–91): Illustrator, novelist, and publisher, during the German occupation of Paris he founded Les Éditions de Minuit. Of his several novels and novellas, *The Silence of the Sea* (1942; in Britain, *Put Out the Light*), *Guiding Star* (1943), and *You Shall Know Them* (1952; in Britain, *Borderline*) are the most famous.

Wang Meng (China, 1934): His story "The Young Newcomer in the Organization Department" brought Wang into prominence in 1956, and a year later he was exiled to the Xinjiang autonomous region. After his rehabilitation, he published numerous stories and novels. Several have been translated into English, including *Bolshevik Salute* (1979), *The Butterfly* (1980), and *The Movable Parts* (1982). "The Stubborn Porridge" first appeared in China in 1989.

■

SOURCES

Every reasonable effort has been made to locate and acknowledge the owners of copyrighted material in this volume. The publishers would welcome any information regarding errors or omissions.

Bartón, Paulé, "Emilie Plead Choose One Egg," from *The Woe Shirt*, translated by Howard Norman. Copyright © 1979 by Howard Norman. Permission granted by Melanie Jackson Agency.

Dongala, E.B., "The Man": "L'Homme," in Dongala, *Jazz et vin de palme*, collection Monde Noir Poche, © 1982 Hatier Paris. Translated by Clive Wake in Chinua Achebe and C.L. Innes, eds., *The Heinemann Book of Contemporary African Short Stories*, 1982.

Fast, Howard, "The Large Ant," from *The Howard Fast Reader*. Reprinted by permission of Sterling Lord Literistic, Inc. Copyright 1960 by Howard Fast.

García Márquez, Gabriel, "Bon Voyage, Mr. President," from *Strange Pilgrims* by Gabriel García Márquez, translated by Edith Grossman. Copyright © 1993 by Gabriel García Márquez. Reprinted by permission of Alfred A. Knopf Inc. and Jonathan Cape.

Ginzburg, Natalia, "Winter in the Abruzzi," from *Little Virtues* by Natalia Ginzburg, translated by Dick Davis (1985). Reprinted by permission of Carcanet Press Limited.

Gürsel, Nedim, "The Graveyard of Unwritten Books." Reprinted by permission of the author. Translation © 1999 by Alberto Manguel.

Head, Bessie, "The Prisoner Who Wore Glasses," from *Tales of Tenderness and Power* published by Heinemann International in the African Writers Series. Copyright © The Estate of Bessie Head 1989.

Martínez, Guillermo, "Vast Hell," © Guillermo Martínez, 1989. Translation © 1999 by Alberto Manguel.

Mimouni, Rachid, "The Escapee," from *The Ogre's Embrace*, translated by Shirley Eber. © Editions Seghers, Paris, 1990.

Nabokov, Vladimir, "Tyrants Destroyed," from *The Stories of Vladimir Nabokov* by Vladimir Nabokov. Copyright © 1995 by Dmitri Nabokov. Reprinted by permission of Alfred A. Knopf Inc.

O'Faoláin, Seán, "The Death of Stevey Long," from *Midsummer Night Madness*. Reprinted by permission of Constable Publishers. Copyright © 1983 by Seán O'Faoláin. From *The Collected Stories of Seán O'Faoláin* published by Atlantic-Little Brown. Reprinted by permission of Curtis Brown, Ltd.

Saro-Wiwa, Ken, "Verdict," © 1994. Printed by permission of Ken Wiwa and Westwood Creative Artists Ltd.

Seghers, Anna, "The Dead Girls' Outing": "Der Ausflug der Toten Mädchen" from *Erzählungen* by Anna Seghers (Netty Radvanyi). © Aufbau-Verlag GmbH, Berlin 1948. Translation © 1999 by Alberto Manguel.

Skármeta, Antonio, "The Composition," translated from the original Spanish by Donald L. Schmidt and Federico Cordover, from Skármeta, *Watch Where the Wolf Is Going*, English translation copyright Readers International 1991.

Valadés, Edmundo, "Permission for Death Is Granted," from *Dark Arrows*, edited by Alberto Manguel. Translation © 1999 by Alberto Manguel.

Vercors, "The Silence of the Sea," © 1942 Vercors (Jean Bruller), reprinted by permission of Rita Vercors. English translation © 1944 Cyril Connolly, reproduced by permission of the Estate of Cyril Connolly, c/o Rogers, Coleridge & White Ltd., 20 Powis Mews, London W11 1JN.

Wang Meng, "The Stubborn Porridge," from *The Stubborn Porridge and Other Stories*, translated by Zhu Hong. Reprinted by permission of Van der Leun & Associates.

■

*The text of this book is set in Bembo.
Based on an early sixteenth-century
typeface by the Venetian punchcutter
Francesco Griffo, this version of
Bembo was designed in 1929 by
Stanley Morison. It has since proven
to be one of the most popular types
for the composition of books.*

*Book design by
Gordon Robertson*